Tropic of Stupid

ALSO BY TIM DORSEY

Florida Roadkill

Hammerhead Ranch Motel

Orange Crush

Triggerfish Twist

The Stingray Shuffle

Cadillac Beach

Torpedo Juice

The Big Bamboo

Hurricane Punch

Atomic Lobster

Nuclear Jellyfish

Gator A-Go-Go

Electric Barracuda

When Elves Attack

Pineapple Grenade

The Riptide Ultra-Glide

Tiger Shrimp Tango

Shark Skin Suite

Coconut Cowboy

Clownfish Blues

The Pope of Palm Beach

No Sunscreen for the Dead

Naked Came the Florida Man

Tropic of Stupid

Tim Dorsey

HARPER LARGE PRINT
An Imprint of HarperCollins*Publishers*

This book is a work of fiction. References to real people, events, establishments, organizations, or locales are intended only to provide a sense of authenticity, and are used fictitiously. All other characters, and all incidents and dialogue, are drawn from the author's imagination and are not to be construed as real.

HarperCollins books may be purchased for educational, business, or sales promotional use. For information, please e-mail the Special Markets Department at SPsales@harpercollins.com.

FIRST HARPER LARGE PRINT EDITION

ISBN: 978-0-06-306192-7

Library of Congress Cataloging-in-Publication Data is available upon request.

21 22 23 24 25 LSC 10 9 8 7 6 5 4 3 2 1

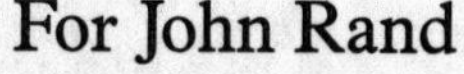
For John Rand

Tropic of Stupid

Prologue

One Month Ago

The rain had just stopped when the convenience store clerk asked the customer not to heat up his urine in the microwave.

The customer explained that the urine he was heating wasn't his.

Which meant it was Florida.

At the other end of the store stood two Abbott-and-Costello-shaped customers.

"Serge, what are you looking for?" asked the plump one.

"Coleman, I told you at the last store," said the thin one. "Baseball cards and kites."

"What are those guys up there arguing about?" asked Coleman.

"Urine heating," said Serge. "Sunshine State Tip Number 327: Never use convenience store microwaves because there's now an epidemic of addicts borrowing someone else's peepee for drug tests, but many were getting caught since the samples were too cold, so the drug culture had some kind of meeting to resolve it, and now I can't melt the cheese on my Cuban sandwiches."

At the cash register, an argument broke out with another clerk over a cardboard box on the counter. "No, you can't trade your pet snake for beer. Just money . . ."

Coleman idly pulled a gift card for international cell minutes to El Salvador off a pegboard hook. "Why are you in such a bad mood?"

"The golden age of convenience stores is officially dead." Serge's eyes scanned the shelves. "The priority of convenience stores used to be the children. They were magical places where your allowance money set you free. It was total empowerment, the first time you alone could make purchase decisions without your parents around, and the mini-marts had everything you could dream of: yo-yos, wax lips, slingshots, bags of green army men, plastic handcuffs, suction-cup dart guns where the suction cups were easily removed for further empowerment. But baseball cards and kites stood at the top of the mountain. The cards were obviously popular because they were the currency of the schoolyard, but kites took it to a whole 'nother level."

Coleman put the gift card for Central America back on the hook. "Kites?"

Serge continued scrutinizing shelves in vain. "Even more empowerment. Kites allowed six-year-olds to send something up into FAA airspace. Most important, you had to assemble them from flimsy sticks and even flimsier paper, then the tail, and learn how to deal with the wind. You had to *earn* your empowerment. Today, kids just pull a drone out of a box." Serge turned around in sadness to face a locked display case. "It's all gone now. Instead of wax lips, we have glass hash pipes, roach clips and bongs."

Coleman reached into his pocket. "I think I have some allowance money."

"Don't reward them for stealing childhoods." Serge picked up a box and headed for the register. One person was ahead of them.

"Fine! I'll take my urine elsewhere!"

It was Serge's turn. He placed the box on the counter.

The clerk rang it up and made change. "Will there be anything else today?"

"Just the drone," said Serge. "Please think of the children."

As they headed out of the store, there was a rumbling

sound overhead. Then a muted scream. The ceiling tiles busted open and a naked woman fell into the potato chips.

Coleman nodded. "Drugs."

Serge pushed the door open. "I don't even notice anymore."

Miami

An oversize brown corkboard hung from a wall in a bright office. It was an open floor plan with a grid of gray government-purchased desks. On another wall hung a law enforcement seal.

The corkboard was covered with photographs and notecards, names and dates, witnesses and victims, locations of bodies. It was all tacked up with different-colored pushpins, and connected with crisscrossing strands of yarn. All arranged roughly in the shape of a pyramid. In the middle, a final notecard, blank except for a question mark.

In another part of Florida hung another corkboard. Quite similar, in fact. Photos, cards, pins and yarn. But the room was not bright. Actually, it was quite dark. Some of the photos had been taken while the victims were still alive. There was no card in the middle with a question mark.

Chapter 1

A Week Before Christmas

Down on the southernmost tip of England lies a quaint fishing village in the county of Cornwall. Simply called Looe.

During the seventeenth and eighteenth centuries, the British constructed six ships named after the town, including the HMS *Looe*, a forty-four-gun frigate commissioned in 1740.

The ship saw military action during something called the War of Jenkins' Ear, because someone got his ear cut off and, naturally, war. The conflict was primarily fought in the Caribbean and off the coasts of Georgia and Florida. In 1744, the *Looe* captured a Spanish merchant ship and towed it along the coast about twenty-five miles from Key West. Just after midnight on the fifth of February, it ran aground on an unnamed sandbar in the Gulf Stream.

In the centuries since, the sandbar has washed away, as well as much of the doomed vessel. But the ship left something else behind, her name, and today the place where she went down is called Looe Key.

Looe isn't an actual key, as it rests entirely underwater, consisting of a patch reef with parallel rows of coral fingers. What makes it so distinct is that it lies seven miles offshore south of Ramrod Key, rising up out of the deep surrounding ocean to unexpectedly shallow depths. It has become known for some of the finest diving, both scuba and snorkeling, in all the Keys. In 1981, it was named part of a national marine sanctuary.

Sometime in the 1950s, a modest concrete-block motel went up on Ramrod, housing twenty rooms on its two floors. It was the opposite of fancy, just this plain rectangular box, providing a cheap roadside layover for weary motorists. Then someone had a brainstorm.

There was a canal behind the motel, leading out to the sea. And that fabulous finger reef. The owners bought a boat and air compressors, and converted half of the motel office into a dive shop, and, in 1978, the Looe Key Reef Resort was born.

"There it is!" Serge pointed through the windshield

at a red sign with a diagonal white stripe. "My home away from home!"

Coleman popped a magic mushroom in his mouth and chased it with a Jäger Bomb. "Doesn't look like a resort."

"Can you not splash that stuff all over the car? The guy I borrowed the last one from won't talk to me because of an upholstery beef."

"Mostly on my shirt, but it's worth it." Coleman upended the cocktail to chase the toadstool. "Just drop a shot glass of 'meister into a bigger glass of Red Bull."

"And what can possibly go wrong?" Serge pulled into a gravel parking space just shy of mile marker 27. "The 'resort' part of the nomenclature is a misnomer, sort of."

Coleman did a line of coke off the back of his hand and unwrapped a Twinkie.

"Man, you're in overdrive," said Serge. "But it's the Keys, so there's blame to go around."

"Resort?" Coleman wiped frosting and white dust from his upper lip. "Explain."

"People say 'resort' and you think of gilded luxury and wallet-busting prices, which are equally negative," said Serge. "I don't want amenities, I want authenticity, and this is as real as it comes down here, a bargain with bells!"

"Groovy."

"But wait! There's more! You walk out the back door of your room, and you're on the dock, and a few more steps, you're on the *Kokomo Cat II*, a spacious pontoon dive boat—mere seconds from bed to on-board! Plus there's a convenience store next door, and not just next door but right up against the building. That's *my* definition of resort. And the tiki bar!"

Coleman bolted upright in battle-station mode. "Tiki bar?"

"I know what you're thinking: tiki bar, a little shack with bottom-shelf rum. But not here! It's a huge open-sided lounge with live music most nights under a vaulted, thirty-foot-high thatched roof, with a full seafood menu including my required smoked-fish dip. After showering off brine, the divers congregate here in their endorphin glows to compare notes and tips and underwater video like an aquatic Algonquin Round Table. Once, I set up at the counter with my briefcase and busted out my latest Internet find, a January 1906 edition of *National Geographic* with an article on the Keys before there were any bridges, and everyone was all over me like yellowtails on puke."

"Wow, that really is a resort."

"But I'm not done!" Serge got out and walked

around the back of the car. "A quick stroll up the road is the Five Brothers Grocery Two, spun off from the original in Key West on Southard Street, a delightfully crammed corner store with an espresso machine and pressed cheese toast. One of my favorite routines at this resort is to get up way before dawn and stroll up the road in total darkness for the grocery, then stand outside with all the construction workers and their pickups, waiting for the clock to strike six, and then we all rush inside for nirvana: a Cuban *breakfast* sandwich. When I first saw it on the menu board, I was like, 'Heart be still! You mean someone has figured out how to genetically splice the ecstasy of an Egg McMuffin and a Cuban sandwich? I don't think I can handle that much morning goodness.' . . . And of course there's a Dion's just over the bridge on Summerland Key." He popped the trunk.

"Mmmmm! Mmmmm! . . ."

Coleman's head jerked. "They have a Dion's near here?"

"I know, I know. It's just finger-licking rapture." Serge grabbed a tire iron. "Now normally any food that's deep-fried in a vat at a gas station should set off civil defense sirens to don biological warfare suits. But not Dion's! Some of the best fried chicken you'll ever taste!" He swung the tire iron until the trunk's passenger became quiet. "And the mashed potatoes! The gravy! You won't find a lot of tourists in Dion's because, well, it's a gas station. But all the locals know and love it, and at noon every day the residents form long lines for their Styrofoam boxes of to-go joy. Ask anyone. It's a Keys thing."

He closed the trunk and led Coleman through the office door.

"Serge!" "You're back!" "We got your regular room!"

Serge smiled at Coleman. "They kind of know me here." He pointed along the front of the counter at a row of homemade Christmas stockings with names: "'Will,' 'Wanda,' 'Christian,' 'Robert,' 'Tony,' 'Kim,' 'Phil,' 'Mark,' 'Tim (aka Boss Man!),' 'McMoosie,' 'Divemaster Diane' to differentiate from the other 'Diane,' 'Capt. James,' and 'Twins plus Kelly.'

"For quick reference, that's the staff," said Serge. "You've just got to love a place that hangs Christmas stockings for the whole crew. It's family around here, not like those big cattle-boat diving outfits that talk shit behind your back." He bellied up to the counter with his wallet. "Since I've auditioned all your rental gear on my previous excursions, I'm ready to buy! Holiday presents for myself!"

"What do you want?" asked Christian.

Serge pointed to the right side of the office, which displayed every manner of diving equipment. "The works! Snorkeling is my life! One of everything! Especially those super-long, steel-reinforced open-ocean fins! I really zip in those things. And booties and a wrist strap for my new GoPro camera!" After loading all the top-of-the-line snorkel gear in a giant custom mesh backpack, Serge hoisted the padded straps over his shoulders. "And book two for the afternoon trip."

The manager looked at the office clock. "It leaves in a half hour."

"More than enough time." He headed for the door. "To the reef!"

They walked around the corner, past rows of palms and natural limestone boulders, arriving at the last unit on the west end.

"Room number one! My favorite!" Serge kissed the door and opened it.

Then he was back in the car.

"Don't we have a boat to catch?" asked Coleman.

"Yes, but this is mandatory." Serge navigated isolated roads up through scrub on the north side of the island. "You have to see Ramrod Beach to properly focus your third eye for a dive trip."

"I like beaches," said Coleman. "You get to drink beer, even if you have to sneak."

"And they do drink at this one, but it's not like the others." Serge looked out the window at a swath of hurricane-downed palms. "Only the locals know about it."

A blue-and-white Cobra approached the end of the island, far from all the homes and everything else, including decent pavement. Palmettos and buttonwoods. Then the tires were on dirt where scrub plants dropped to knee-high. Serge parked in marl amid the quiet of a cool breeze off the back country. "Here we are."

Coleman got out, confused. "Where's the beach?"

"This is it. We have it all to ourselves right now because it's a weekday."

"I'm still not seeing it."

"That's because beaches are different here due to geology." Serge took a panoramic video of the pine-green shrubs, pale-orange dirt, gray plateaus of rock, and bright mint-green water. "The upper Keys run parallel to the highway and are composed of ancient marine life that created beds of what's called Key Largo Limestone. But down here after the Seven Mile Bridge, the islands lie perpendicular to the road, and the bedrock becomes a less porous type of limestone called Miami Oolite."

"Where's the sand?"

"There isn't any," said Serge. "The beach is these large slabs of limestone with tidal fissures. Isn't it great?"

"No beer or big bikini boobs?"

"Walk this way." Serge led him over to a remote spot where, in the middle of nothing, stood what was barely a twig of a bleached, leafless tree about four feet high. Someone had draped the pitiful thing with Christmas ornaments, solar-powered lights, and a frosty star on top.

"That's freaking weird," said Coleman. Then a giggle. "Know what it reminds me of? Charlie Brown's poor tree in those TV specials."

"That's exactly what it is," said Serge. "More importantly, this tells you everything you need to know about the species of people around here." He looked at his dive watch.

Then a breakneck race back to the motel room. Serge immediately unbuckled and dropped his cargo shorts. "Coleman, I know this violates the theory of relativity, but you're going to have to be fast. Get your swim trunks on." He pointed out the back window at a perfect view down the main canal bisecting the southern half of Ramrod Key. Other motel guests were almost finished boarding the forty-eight-foot pontoon boat. "Our ride's here!"

Moments later, they exited the back door of room 1, took a few steps and climbed aboard.

"Man, that was convenient," said Coleman. "Less chance for problems with the ground."

A voice from behind the center-console steering wheel. "Well, if it isn't Mr. First-In-Last-Out."

Serge stood at attention and saluted. "Aye-aye, Captain Katie."

"Serge," said Coleman, "why did she call you that?"

"Because I'm always the first in and last out at the dive sites. I like to milk my snorkeling dollar."

The captain set out the tip jar. "I'm surprised you almost missed the boat. You're usually jumping up and down by the cleats before the crew even arrives."

"Had to show my friend Ramrod Beach."

"Why am I not stunned?" said Katie. "You're the only non-local who knows more local spots than the locals."

"Due diligence," said Serge. "I showed him the Charlie Brown Christmas tree."

"It's a Keys thing."

The last divers boarded and they secured the gate

chains. The captain got the attention of the dozen passengers for safety instructions and locations of life preservers. ". . . And the weather service is calling for three-foot swells, so it might get a little rough out there today. If you feel like you're going to get sick, lean over the side. Not in the boat, please."

Coleman bent over the starboard railing and began heaving.

"We haven't even left the dock," said Katie. "That's a first."

"Not for Coleman."

Serge reached for a pump bottle and smeared his face. Then he took a seat directly in front of the console as Coleman came back wiping his mouth. "You look weird. Your face is all white, like one of those Japanese dancers."

"Because I care," said Serge, smearing his arms. "This is coral-friendly sunscreen. I'm trying to get the word out. Most stuff for sale in stores contains chemicals that wreak havoc on reef ecosystems."

Coleman took a seat next to him and looked around. "Everyone else seems to be putting it on and not looking all white. They're staring at you."

"The key to life is always to risk social awkwardness for the good of the planet."

The *Kokomo Cat* pushed off and idled down the

canal. Near the end, the captain: "Everyone, hold on. We're about to pick up speed."

The craft turned the corner toward open water and aligned the bow with a narrow cut marked by orange and green channel markers. The throttle went up, and the boat took off at surprising velocity for pontoons.

Coleman gazed over the side. "It's only a few inches deep. And it looks like solid stone."

"Because you're looking outside the channel," said Serge. "We're in the cut that was hewn through the ancient rock. Some tourist clowns come down here and rent boats, then ignore the channel markers and snap propellers so fast they have to duck."

The boat cleared the channel and planed across Newfound Harbor. In the middle, they passed the tiny sandbar called Picnic Island, with sparse brush, a couple of lawn chairs, and an anchored houseboat flying a pirate flag. Passengers got out cameras as a pair of dolphins leaped playfully in the vessel's wake. The *Kokomo* skirted west around the Little Palm Island resort, still torn up from the last storm.

Then ocean.

The bow slammed across the swells for another five miles, sliding stuff around the deck and spraying salt water.

The captain leaned over the console to Serge. "Revised forecast: It's going to get even rougher than I thought today."

"Damn the torpedoes!"

Miami

Harsh sunlight streamed through the blinds, creating a striped pattern on the commercial-grade tile floor.

A thin man with a thin black tie entered the room carrying a box with a cellophane window on the lid.

"Doughnuts!"

A stampede.

Someone named Archibald brought up the rear. "Dammit, you all take the jellies first."

Someone named Dudley spoke with his mouth full. "It's Darwinian. If you can't get here fast enough, you don't need jellies . . . Hey, Heather! Want one?"

"When have I ever?" She resumed sipping a protein shake at her desk.

On the wall sat an institutional white clock with black hands that were always five minutes late. Above it hung a circular seal depicting the shape of Florida over a golden starburst with some letters.

FDLE.

The Florida Department of Law Enforcement is like the state's FBI. Exactly like. Headquartered in Tallahassee, with seven regional operation centers and thirteen field offices. The doughnuts were being swarmed in the satellite location in Miami, sandwiched between Florida International University and the Dolphin Mall, which now had a Bass Pro Shop.

Someone named Drago held up a glazed cruller. "Heather? One left?"

No response.

In the last thirty-six hours, a bank robbery had been solved, a hostage rescued, and a shipment of counterfeit basketball shoes intercepted at the port. Now, nothing. That was the pattern. Periods of franticness followed by dead time. But they were still expected to keep working.

"Heather, what are you working on?" asked another agent, named Snooki.

"If you were working, too, you'd know." She opened an evidence box. "Cold case."

"Which one?" asked Archibald.

"That serial killer who started twenty years ago." She removed a sealed plastic bag containing a medical vial. "May have gone dormant a decade back."

"May have?"

"The more recent cases haven't been definitely linked yet because of a profile shift."

"What kind of shift?"

"They're getting weirder."

"What's in the test tube?" asked Dudley.

"Medical examiner said there was enough DNA from the Hialeah case that he could spare some. He prepared a sample."

"What are you going to do with it that he can't?"

Heather logged on to a website. "You know that genealogy company, Ancestors R Us?"

"Yeah?"

"I'm sending it to them."

"I don't think they track serial killers," said Drago. "Just great-great-grandparents from Albania."

"I'm not telling them it's a serial killer." Heather swabbed the inside of the test tube with a Q-tip. "I'm pretending it's me researching my family tree. See what hits."

"I doubt the serial killer has sent his DNA to the company."

Heather sighed. "Familial hits."

"What's that?"

"If we're lucky, you'll find out."

"But you can't use your own name."

"Duh."

"I got it," said Snooki. "How about Lykes Redrum?"

"Very clever," said Heather. "Backwards for 'Murder' from *The Shining*."

"So you really like it?"

She resumed typing on her keyboard. "I'm busy."

Two weeks later.

Another box with a cellophane window, and another pastry scrum.

"Heather?" said Dudley. "They're good."

"Shhhhhh!" She leaned toward her screen.

"What is it?"

"Just got the results back from Ancestors R Us."

"And?"

"We caught a break." She leaned back in her chair and pointed at the digital spreadsheet. "A second cousin, a third cousin, and a fourth cousin once removed."

"I thought you said it was a break." Archibald continued chewing. "What can we possibly do with that?"

She gave him a momentary blank stare. "How long have you been doing this?"

A napkin wiped crumbs. "A while."

She gestured at an empty corkboard on the wall. "We build a family tree."

"I'm still not following."

"I'll explain it as simply as I can," said Heather.

"There's no way in the present that we can find all the living relatives with this wide range in relationships. So we need to go back"—she stopped to analyze the spreadsheet again—"about five generations to find the one common ancestor of these three hits. Once we identify that person, we reverse the process, and flow back down until we have a list of all his current descendants. Then we check 'em out."

"How many is that?"

"Probably hundreds."

"Is what you're doing even legal?" asked Snooki.

Heather got up and headed for the corkboard. "Sometimes it's better to ask forgiveness than permission."

The corkboard soon overflowed.

There were photos, notecards, colored pushpins and strands of crisscrossing yarn.

Doughnuts notwithstanding, the rest of the team pitched in like eager beavers, scouring birth certificates, newspaper obituaries, passports and driver's licenses.

Dudley tacked up another notecard on the cluttered board and stood back, pleased, with hands on hips. "This plan of yours is really coming together."

"Don't get too excited yet," said Heather, snipping a

piece of yarn. "Computerized records are only good for a couple of generations. And I miscalculated. It's now looking like we need six or seven generations. From here on out, it's going to slow down exponentially."

"What's that mean?"

"We'll need to put in for travel expenses," said Heather. "Visit a lot of old courthouses and cemeteries, small-town libraries, even knock on some doors to see family albums."

"Ewww, family albums . . ."

Heather ran her whole plan up the chain of command, and they took a liking to the project. Agents from other field offices were reassigned to pick up the slack while the cold case team was out of town.

A fleet of Crown Vics with blackwall tires dispersed in various directions across the state.

Heather was partnered with Archibald. "Call me Archie." After a barren drive along the west coast, they trotted up some steps in the town of Mayo, Florida.

"Look at the size of this big honking building in the middle of all this emptiness," said Archie.

"The Lafayette County Courthouse, built 1908, one of the oldest in the state," said Heather. "Neoclassical from Indiana limestone, with a clock tower and everything."

"Must have cost a fortune."

"Forty-seven thousand back then."

"Where'd you get all these facts?"

"I'm a fan of historic Florida architecture. You should see my library at home."

"I didn't know that about you."

"Why would you?"

Chapter 2

Looe Key

Pontoons crashed across ocean swells.

The *Kokomo Cat II* cut a straight bearing toward something in the distance: a single triangular orange marker amid whitecaps over the shallows. A handful of other boats were already scattered above the reef, attached to mooring buoys installed by the preservation authorities to prevent anchor damage.

Conversation among the divers quieted, a counterpoint to the boat's hull loudly smashing up and down on the waves, shooting water over the railings. Many of the passengers—especially first-time visitors—watched over the side as the sea went by, getting naturally stoned on the Keys phenomenon of the rapidly changing palette of vibrant colors, from emerald green to turquoise, aqua and ultramarine blue.

The orange triangle grew larger as the *Kokomo* began to slow. Starboard passengers pointed at a giant shell of a loggerhead turtle bobbing remotely atop the depths. Others leaned over the port side to view silhouettes of stingrays a couple of feet under the surface.

"Coleman, listen up and learn something." Serge turned around toward the captain's console. "Katie, you'll dig this. You know how Looe Key got its name?"

"Of course. The British ship."

"Yeah, but I dug deeper because history is the shit! The name all started when some dude got his ear chopped off!"

"What?"

"I swear it's all true!" said Serge. "In 1731, the Spanish boarded the *Rebecca*, a big-rigged English sailing ship, right off the coast of Florida. Then they cut off the captain's ear because I guess that was supposed to be funny back then. But the British weren't laughing, and the drums of war began beating, and there's even a story that the severed ear was actually held up in Parliament to rally the base. I think that's the natural progression of where Washington is heading today, so don't be surprised when C-SPAN gets bloody. Anyhow, it started a conflict that raged around the coasts of Florida and

Georgia, and one of the dispatched ships was the HMS *Looe*, commanded by Captain Ashby Utting. In 1744, it captured a Spanish ship and was towing it along the Keys, but both vessels ran aground because who would expect it to be so shallow this far from shore? Then it really does get funny . . ." Serge's eyelids began fluttering like he was possessed.

"Are you okay?" asked the captain.

"Just throwing my imagination's engine room into warp speed." He began slapping his cheeks with both hands. "I'm overlaying eighteenth-century images on today's vista up ahead. See all those dive boats moored at the buoys? Now imagine a wacky scene where they're all chasing each other around like Keystone Cops."

"Are you making this up?" said Katie.

"If I'm lying I'm dying," said Serge. "After the boats grounded, there were other Spanish ships in the area, and the British were sitting ducks. So they dropped the frigate's three smaller patrol boats in the water, but they didn't have nearly the capacity for the whole crew. And of course the Spanish are freaking out in the towed vessel, and one of the patrol boats spots a sloop called *Betty*—no insight there—and starts chasing it around, and other Spanish boats are coming in to join the swirling bumper-car madness. The sloop is captured, and the British offload onto it and set their ship on fire, and everyone scatters like roaches when the lights come on, with the various vessels ending up in South Carolina, the Bahamas and Cuba. Can you dig it? Can you see it?"

Katie just smiled in amusement as she throttled all the way down, and the first mate grabbed a long pole with a hook to snag one of the buoys.

"Hey, I got an idea!" said Serge. "Let's chase the other dive boats! It'll be fun!"

"Serge . . ."

"No, seriously! Look at them out there all relaxed, not expecting military conflict. We'll come barreling down on them screaming about an ear! Imagine their delight at the extra-value entertainment from their trip as we disperse them in panic-circles!"

"Serge . . ."

"I'll bet nobody's thought of it before. It'll become your signature feature, distinguishing you from the boring dive services that just dive. Next time we can even drag a shitty old boat to set on fire! You'll make the news!"

"That's what I'm afraid of."

"You're probably right about fire," said Serge. "But please consider scheduling a reenactment."

"On another subject," said Katie, "I know you're good to go in the water, but do you think your friend needs a safety vest? He can always inflate it by blowing in that little tube if he gets in trouble."

"In that case we'd better inflate it now."

Serge fitted the yellow vest over Coleman's head and blew it up. "Okay, buddy, this is it. They're about to unhook the chain and the captain will say 'The pool's open,' and you just follow me in."

Serge zipped up his booties and strapped on the fins and mask. Then he sat coiled like he was about to parachute out the back of a troop transport plane.

The chain unsnapped.

"The pool's—"

Serge plunged over the side.

"—open." A laugh. "Mr. First-In-Last-Out lives up to his name."

Serge popped back to the surface. "Coleman, what are you waiting for? The water's great!"

"How do I get in?"

"Just step off the side and let gravity do the rest."

"Here goes." Coleman meant to drop straight in, but instead managed to pinwheel off the boat and belly flop. "Ow."

Serge helped his buddy turn his mask back around. "You know what a grouper is?"

"A fish sandwich?"

"There are a couple of famous goliath groupers out

here," said Serge. "Huge suckers, five hundred pounds. They like the shade under the boat."

"Cool."

"I'm telling you this to prepare you," said Serge. "I want you to enjoy the experience and not have a heart attack. There's one under the *Kokomo* right now."

Coleman turned around. "Shit!"

"Exactly."

"No, shit, like, for real." Coleman reached behind to feel the seat of his swim trunks. "Whew, false alarm."

"Don't be embarrassing me. I've got to see these people again." And then Serge took off, flattening out on the surface and furiously pumping the giant fins, making a series of impressively fleet laps around the boat.

Coleman bobbed like a puffy yellow cork, keeping an eye on the grouper. He felt something on his shoulder and screamed.

"Pipe down. It's just me," said Serge, aiming his GoPro camera below. "Want to see something really cool?"

"Sure."

Serge pointed into the sea. "Stick your mask in the water and look that way."

Coleman did. And immediately came halfway out of the ocean. "Ahhhh! Shark! Shark!"

"Just a reef shark," said Serge. "Won't bother nobody."

Coleman splashed wildly toward the swim ladder. He started up the steps, but Serge grabbed the safety vest's straps from behind and pulled him back into the sea.

"What did you do that for?"

"You're not going back on the boat."

"But I really want to."

"This time you do have a load in your britches," said Serge. "I'm taking a wild stab, but I think they appreciate that on the deck less than spit-up."

Coleman began whimpering. "But I don't like it in here."

Serge dragged Coleman by the vest around the bow. "Deal with it."

"Then can I get back on the boat?"

"Then I *want* you back on the boat."

Coleman eventually climbed up the ladder and headed straight for the cooler where the crew sold beer.

"Excuse me," said Captain Katie. "We're only at the beginning of the first stop. You can't drink until you're done diving for the day."

"Oh, I'm done all right." He popped the tab on a cold one and chugged.

At the end of the initial hour, Serge waited in the water behind the final scuba diver and climbed aboard.

"Last out," said Katie.

"Wouldn't have it any other way."

"Your friend sure can drink."

Serge covered his eyes. "Where is he?"

"Resting."

Serge walked toward the stern and kicked Coleman's legs.

"Ow!"

"You can't lie on the deck."

"Why not?"

"You just can't. I asked you not to embarrass me."

The *Kokomo* motored over to the second dive site, where Serge again squeezed every second from the hour. The boat headed back to port with the buddies sitting in front of the captain.

"How was it out there today?" asked Katie.

"Ultra-outrageous!" Serge flapped a laminated marine identification card. "I saw three sharks, a whole school of barracuda, that monster grouper of course, a queen angel, a French angel, a buttload of yellowtail, rainbow parrotfish, two spotted rays and a turtle . . ."

Coleman was slumped over when they arrived back at the dock. Serge shook him. "Wake up."

Still out.

Another shake. "Come on! It's time for the tiki bar."

That was like smelling salts. Coleman charged

through the group departing the boat, ran around the corner of the dock toward the freshwater cleaning tanks and disappeared.

"See you in the tiki?" asked Katie.

Serge strapped on his mesh backpack. "For the record, I just met him."

Traffic blew by on the Overseas Highway as the sun set in a blaze. A stout ocean breeze whipped palm fronds, both the live ones on the motel's trees and the others on the tiki's roof. The evening's five-piece live band launched into Bob Seger.

". . . Ramblin' gamblin' man! . . ."

Coleman quickly made himself a fixture on his stool, simultaneously working on a poor man's boilermaker and directing the bartender's attention to different bottles of booze.

Serge finished station-keeping in the fabulous Room One and headed out to the blue-and-white Cobra to stow his diving backpack. He popped the trunk.

"Mmmm! Mmmm! Mmmm!"

"Oh, sorry," said Serge. "Forgot you were in there. The gear will have to go in the back seat because I wouldn't want to cramp your style. Need new duct tape?"

"Mmmm! Mmmm! Mmmm!"

"No? Great!" *Slam.*

Serge entered the bar. He was the only customer pulling a hard-shell suitcase.

"*. . . Even the losers get lucky . . .*"

He commandeered an empty table and threw the lime-green luggage on top. Coleman ambled over with a glass in each hand and another clutched to his chest. "You're back! Man, this is the greatest place!"

Serge reached for a tiny key on a chain around his neck. "I must be getting old. Or maybe too excited about where we are."

Coleman upended one of the drinks. "Why do you say that?"

"I completely forgot about the guy in the trunk."

"Don't feel bad." Guzzle. "I forgot about him, too."

"But it's your job to forget stuff." He stuck the key in the suitcase. "I'm losing a step."

"Aren't you worried about him making noise and getting us discovered?"

"Normally I would have conked him on the head," said Serge. "But the band's volume is effectively taking care of that."

"*. . . You are a shooting star! . . .*"

Coleman waved the glass in his left hand, sloshing

Maker's Mark bourbon. "This is like freakin' heaven!" He spun his face toward the rafters. "The monster of all tiki bars!"

"Always has been." Serge scribbled. "But the roof used to be lower, not much above our heads."

Coleman's right hand sloshed Bombay. "Why did they change it?"

"They didn't. Hurricane Irma did," said Serge. "It was the cataclysmic storm of 2017, projected to churn straight up the west coast through all the metropolitan areas. And it did, in a way, wrecking large parts of Naples, Fort Myers and the suburbs east of Sarasota and Tampa."

"Stop! Back up to the part about this bar! What happened?"

"The place was supposed to be evacuated, but for some insane reason two guys stayed behind in one of the rooms, and when Hurricane Irma came ashore, it was daylight. They watched the storm spin off one of its many tornadoes, which danced across the parking lot before lifting the entire original tiki bar straight up into the sky like Dorothy's farmhouse."

"Freaky."

"Please watch your beverages. I have archives here . . ."

A tradition: Some of the staff noticed Serge's new

piece of luggage, and they slowly congealed, pulling up chairs around the table. *"What now?" "Funky artifacts?" "Gravestone rubbings?" "View-Masters?" "That was a great magazine you showed us last time." "Wasn't that 1906?"*

"Gets even better this time. Gather 'round." Serge flipped the lid on his cushioned hard-shell, revealing four brown leather slipcases. Each held six to eight periodicals, and all the cases sported the gold embossed seal of the National Geographic Society.

"Here's your 1906," said Serge. "And I raise you with a 1921 and a '22, both of fishes off Florida, then a 1927 of the first published underwater color photos, taken in the Tortugas, and another from '47, which, if you compare it to the 1927 issue, you'll notice they're short one island, which was erased by the Labor Day Hurricane of 1935 . . ."

The evening ended early so everyone could go diving again in the morning. Coleman was the last one out on the dance floor, gyrating bare-chested with stomach flab rolls, twirling his shirt over his head. "*Woooo!*"

Serge gently packed up his suitcase. His pal staggered over and crashed into the table.

"Will you watch it?" said Serge.

"What do you want to do now?"

"I don't know about you," said Serge. "But the band

just quit for the night, so I need to go back to our car's trunk and deal with noise control. Same old, same old."

Coleman plopped down in a chair. "You said we're on Ramrod Key?"

"Used to be called Roberts Island."

"What's a ramrod?"

"The plunger for a Revolutionary War–era muzzle-load rifle."

"How'd they get the new name?"

"Another shipwreck." Serge grabbed the suitcase's handle. "Nobody knew how to sail back then."

Chapter 3

Palm Beach

The television's remote control was so complicated that it had its own screen. A finger pressed a button.

A TV flashed to life. Not just any TV, but the latest curved 110-inch ultra-high-definition that almost nobody could afford.

Here's what came on:

Seagulls gliding above a sunrise over the Atlantic. Children playing Little League. A church letting out. A grandmother knitting. Students graduating high school. A bride throwing a bouquet over her shoulder. A father teaching his daughter to ride a bicycle. A cocker spaniel licking a laughing baby's face. A flowing

American flag. And then, almost as an afterthought, three handsome men in tailored suits walking slow-motion up the courthouse steps in downtown West Palm Beach.

Finally, the trio froze as a company name shimmered across the screen.

REINHOLD, NASH & SPARROW, ATTORNEYS-AT-LAW. PERSONAL INJURY.

A finger pressed the remote again, pausing the commercial. A roar of applause from the audience. In its midst, three men smiled and accepted pats on the shoulders.

Then back to live action. White-gloved caterers circulated with silver trays of champagne flutes and hors d'oeuvres that involved bacon, water chestnuts and sprigs of green. Outside at the curb, boys in white shorts snatched keys off a portable valet stand and ran to fetch six-figure cars.

Chatter at the cocktail party was high on the decibel needle, partly due to alcohol, partly because there were nearly two hundred people.

Sounds like a lot, but it wasn't remotely a tight fit in the twelve-thousand-square-foot house, an all-white post-modern assemblage of blocks and glass. Lots of glass. For the view. It sat on the western shore of the island of Palm Beach, and the twinkling nightscape over Lake Worth was dizzying. It's what had drawn a number of guests out back onto a lawn that looked like it had been tweezered by the grounds crew from Augusta National. Evenly spaced royal palms. A fountain with a statue of the Greek god Poseidon, trident and all.

The evening wore on.

Chatter and laughs became looser. The steadiest people were the catering staff, militantly poised as they arrived with more trays. The help was under a firm edict: Do not speak unless asked a question. But they couldn't help listening: whining about taxes, complaining about domestic servants, tips on offshore banking, upcoming tennis engagements, what to name a new yacht, griping about how poor people were screwing them. Oh, and they loved the new security team with the metal detection wands that screened all the caterers each time they entered or left the house.

Thank *Mother Jones* magazine. It was just a few miles away in the same county, back in 2012, that presidential candidate Mitt Romney spoke at a $50,000-a-plate Boca Raton fundraiser. Allegedly he had been rude to a bartender on the staff, who proceeded to secretly film some comments about people of lesser means, and the video found its way onto the magazine's website, causing quite the row. So now most staffs had to sign draconian non-disclosure agreements. And in a few cases, like with the service company running the show tonight, the employees also had to submit to the airport-style security wands in case someone tried to sneak in a banned cell phone. It helped put the guests at ease. They also enjoyed the indignity of the process.

In the wee hours, a tipsy socialite crawled atop the grand piano and reclined like Lauren Bacall.

That was the signal for the law partner named Nash to take a seat and show off his skills tinkling the ivories. And not too bad, but the voice was a few notes off Sinatra.

". . . I did it my way! . . ."

Then a call for an encore of the TV ad. It began playing on a perpetual loop. More drinking, which did what drinking does. Two guests were going at it on the granite sink top of one of the nine bathrooms, and a pair of caterers were doing the same in the next. The party was such a success that it required reinforcement. A handful of employees were dispatched on an emergency run for more supplies. They arrived back at the front door, out of breath, with fresh cases of liquor and finger food.

"Hold it," said a security guard.

"Seriously?" said a caterer, using a knee to shift the weight of a box of booze. "We were just here."

"And you left." The guard ran his detecting wand over each of them. "Okay, you're good to go in."

"Unbelievable."

"I heard that!" the guard yelled as they disappeared into the kitchen. Then he glanced around surreptitiously, and pulled out his own phone . . .

One of the guests staggered up to Nash. "But the commercial doesn't say anything."

"It's not supposed to." The lawyer smiled. "That's how it works."

"He's right," said another guest. "I talked to some ad guys, and they say it's pure genius. People project onto it what they want, and it's all positive . . . What is this? The twentieth ad?"

"Twenty-sixth," said Nash.

A whistle. "Must cost a fortune."

"Two fortunes," said Nash. "The best production values money can buy."

The guest was right. The ads had made the attorneys local celebrities, and now strangers were stopping them on the street to have pictures taken with them. TV is magical that way. Everyone loved the commercials.

Almost everyone.

"I hate those fucking commercials," said a guest double-fisting champagne glasses on the back lawn.

"Shhhh!" said his friend. "They might hear you."

"I couldn't care less. I hate the whole law firm."

"Then why do you come to these parties?"

"Because I have to do business with these assholes." He drained one of the glasses, then the other. "It's just not fair. Those ads are starting to taint the jury pools. As soon as those jerks walk in the courtroom, it's like movie stars have arrived on the red carpet."

"TV has that odd effect," said the friend. "See someone on the tube enough times, and then meet them in person and it's belly up. Go figure the human psyche."

"They can blow me."

"You really should keep your voice down. I hear they're actually skilled litigators."

"The best. That's why it's so unfair." One of his glasses fell to the ground, and he grabbed a new one from a passing caterer. "Our insurance company has some of the most experienced number-crunchers in the business, and they head off ninety-nine percent of trials with the smallest cash settlements. But all that goes out the window with these guys. They get at least double the normal offers, just so we can avoid those awestruck looks in the jurors' eyes . . ."

His friend reached out for the glass in his other hand. "I don't think you really need that drink."

The caterers packed up, and the valets loaded their key-ring stand into the back of a panel truck. Just the three law partners were left, sitting out back by the water with cigars and cognac.

"It doesn't get any better," said Nash.

"We finally have everything we always wanted," said Reinhold.

Sparrow puffed his stogie. "I want more."

Chapter 4

South Florida

A blue-and-white 1970 Ford Torino Cobra approached the SunPass transponder lanes at one of the southernmost tollbooths in the country. Twin royal-blue sport stripes ran over the muscle car's roof and down the turbo hood scoop to the front bumper.

"Hot damn!" Serge slapped the steering wheel with the hand that wasn't taking photos out the window. "I love these trademark curved canopies over the toll lanes here. I become like Pavlov's dog and start drooling. Figuratively, not like what you're doing."

"Why?" Coleman wiped his mouth and cracked another Schlitz between his legs.

"Because those canopies tell me the Rickenbacker Causeway is coming up. I *love* the Rickenbacker! I always get tingles when I head out the bottom of Miami and across the bay, first to tiny Virginia Key, which still holds sway with that now-vintage gold geodesic dome over the dolphin tank at the Miami Seaquarium. I still can't get my head around the fact it's now almost seventy years old."

"That's more than a century." Coleman burped.

"And on the left . . ." Serge made the sign of the cross. "Former site of Jimbo's, the ramshackle eclectic smoked fish and bocce court compound, which was filmed as an eerie Everglades outpost in the inaugural season of *Miami Vice.* R.I.P."

"I remember that place." Coleman scratched an armpit. "I fell off the dock."

"And in the middle of a big magazine model shoot no less." Serge crested the bridge. "That's what made Jimbo's authentic. Its milieu was so crusty that it crossed the axis into glamour. I will never understand the fashion industry."

The Cobra eased off the gas, touching down on an island and racing through a corridor of coconut palms and sea grapes. Camera still out the window.

"Crandon Park!" *Click, click, click.* "It's what makes

Key Biscayne so special, dangling down out here in the Atlantic, the north and south ends totally nature-protected parks, and in between a tiny community. But what a community! . . .” Serge cut the wheel hard and wound his way west on Harbor Drive to a tiny side street.

“Why are you slowing down?” asked Coleman.

Tires pulled to the curb. “There it is! There it is!”

“What? Big houses?”

“It looks different now, but the ghosts still haunt.” Serge swept an arm out the window. “At 490 Bay Lane, Nixon bagman and confidant Bebe Rebozo held court, and the president became enamored with the island and purchased his so-called Southern White House at 500 Bay Lane—”

Bam, bam, bam!

Coleman turned around in his seat and looked toward the trunk. “It’s that guy again.”

Serge’s head sagged. “I can’t tell you how tiresome that gets. You can only turn up the radio so loud.” He reached under his seat for a tire iron. “Wait here. I won’t be long.”

Coleman watched as Serge exited the car and popped the trunk. *Wham, wham, wham.* The trunk closed. Serge got back in. “Where were we?”

“The president.”

“Right!” The Cobra pulled away from the curb.

"Between these houses you can catch a glimpse of what's affectionately been dubbed Nixon Beach."

"I'm seeing a lot of boats near shore."

"It's a Saturday. Just wait . . ." He drove at barely above idle speed.

They began hearing music drifting in off the water on a breeze, louder and louder.

". . . I . . . want to rock and roll all night! . . ."

"Holy shit!" said Coleman. "There's now a million boats! Look at all the bikinis! All the booze! Someone just fell overboard! It's off the hook!"

"It's the infamous Nixon Beach sandbar," said Serge. "Who would have thought that Tricky Dick's lasting legacy would be wild weekend flotillas so bacchanalian that they're chronicled on YouTube?"

"Can we go?" asked Coleman. "Please?"

"We're going someplace even better."

"Count me in!"

A few minutes later, a few miles south, the Cobra rolled toward a guard booth in the middle of the road.

"Coleman, open the glove compartment and hand me the book."

"This thing? What is it?"

"Only my new bible." Serge set it in his lap as they neared the shack. "It's changed my life. And I owe it all to the state's foremost keepers of the flame."

"Who's that?"

"Why, our Florida park rangers, of course!" Serge held up the book. "A few years back they launched an over-the-top program and began selling these spiral-bound faux-leather green albums."

"Looks small."

"But it packs a wallop." Serge thumbed pages. "This is their passport book, where you can collect official stamps for the state's more than one hundred and seventy parks. I've already visited most of them, but that was before the book, which requires me to come back. The sly devils."

A smiling ranger came to the window as the Cobra eased to a stop. "Good afternoon, fellas."

"And a glorious afternoon back at you!" He displayed a card from his wallet. "This is my annual pass, so no fee coming from this car. That's the way it goes when you foolishly offer a volume discount to someone of my personality composition. I feel like I'm actually making money! . . . And this, as I'm sure you're well aware, is your passport book, you wily fiends! I mean that affectionately. It promotes such a bonding human transaction: I hand over the treasured book from my sweaty, eager palms, and you in turn get to pull out your little ink pad and super-authority stamper. Don't you see? It empowers us both. I only have one quibble. Check out these two opposing pages. The Skyway Fishing Pier in Tampa Bay is a state park, but look at this ridiculousness. The guy stamped the wrong page, the one for Egmont Key. *And* he stamped it upside down. I said, 'You just fucked up my whole book!' He shrugged and said sorry. But you know why this happened? Because that park is the only one where a real ranger doesn't stamp your book, but instead some dude behind the fishing counter selling bait is issued the sacred ink pad. I mean, they don't let just anyone be notary publics. Actually they do, but you understand what I'm getting at. Then I ask him where's his stamp for Egmont Key, which they also have because it takes a ferry to get to the island in the mouth of the bay where there's no office. And he pulls it out—upside down again—but luckily I was on high alert and threw my hand over the page just in time, and he stamped the back of my hand, and I said, 'Whoa! Give me that thing before you hurt yourself.' And he just shrugs again and passes it over, which I know is a major security breach that you'll now be required to report for investigation, but citizens can only be pushed so far. Right? Staying with me? . . ."

"Uh, cars are beginning to stack up behind you."

"Then stamp away and we'll be off!"

Ink hit the page and tires squealed. *"Wooo-hooo!"*

"That was weird." Coleman looked around. "So where's this place that's better than chicks and booze?"

"We're in it," said Serge, sticking his freshly stamped page an inch from Coleman's face. "Bill Baggs State Park, hanging off the bottom of Key Biscayne at Cape Florida."

"Doesn't sound better."

"Just wait and see . . ."

Serge cupped hands around his mouth and yelled straight down a hundred feet. "Coleman, what are you doing down there?"

"I'm tired."

"But you're missing everything!" He clutched the antique railing below a huge ring of glass. "It's the nineteenth-century Cape Florida Lighthouse, arguably the most prominent in all the state! Don Johnson was up here when he had amnesia and thought he was a drug dealer."

Coleman remained flat on his back. "I gave it my best."

"You only made it ten steps up the spiral staircase."

"Like I said."

"But—" Serge waved an arm over the southern tip of the island. "You can see Stiltsville—the authentic old Florida—sticking out of the water in a channel a mile offshore. Who knows how long before a hurricane wipes out the last half-dozen wooden pioneer homes? In the mid-1900s, it had mushroomed into a swinging scene the likes of which Florida may never see again, a virtually lawless rebel enclave with places like the Calvert Club, Crawfish Eddie's, the Bikini Club and the Quarterdeck, which was featured in *Life* magazine and later raided over gambling rumors."

"Stilts." Coleman sarcastically twirled a finger in the air. "Wooo."

Serge shook his head and climbed back down.

Coleman followed him to their car. "I don't know why you're so sore."

"Because these moments are more fun if you can share them. Destiny, for better or worse, has stuck me with you as my soul mate. Who decides this shit?" He opened the driver's door and pulled something out of the back seat.

"A kite?" asked Coleman.

"I'm having a personal kite rebirth. Kites are back! And they're also perfect for the beach." They began trekking across the sand, Coleman with his flask and Serge wearing a backpack. "People grow up and forget the childhood joy of kites. It was my first taste of the empowerment theme I've been annoyingly beating to death, able to send something aloft beyond the surly bounds of earth. But I never realized how much technology had evolved since those early days of flimsy paper and sticks . . ."

A half hour later, a huge dragon-shaped kite swooped through the clear sky.

Coleman chugged his furtive flask of Jim Beam. "Why did we walk way the hell over to this end?"

"Because all the other people are back on the popular part of the beach," said Serge. "Don't get me wrong: I love people, but I'm a big believer in absence making the heart grow fonder."

Coleman looked around. "We're totally alone over here."

"To enjoy our thoughts and camaraderie."

Another chug, followed by a nod. "Have to admit that's a pretty righteous kite."

"One of the latest state-of-the-art models." Serge deftly maneuvered it against the onshore wind. "I started with a small one and practiced like mad. Then I saw all these insane kites on the Internet and ordered this baby."

"I've never seen a kite like that," said Coleman. "You're controlling it with plastic handles in each fist."

Serge independently rotated his hands, maneuvering the kite in a soaring, twisting display like something from a Blue Angels air show.

"Wow," said Coleman. "You're damn good at this."

"As they say, how do you get to Carnegie Hall?"

"Subway?"

"Confession time." The kite tilted at the top of its arc. "This is my second new kite. I destroyed the first one while perfecting my signature dive-bombing run. Couldn't pull up in time. Luckily no pilot was aboard."

Coleman shielded his eyes as he watched the kite plummet earthward. "Another dive bomber?"

"Carnegie Hall. Practice. Freakin' hours. But when I lock in on something . . ." The kite increased to ferocious velocity. "Three feet from the ground, max."

"Serge," said Coleman. "You better pull up. It's going to crash."

"Not yet . . . Ready, ready . . . Now!" He stepped back quickly, arching his back and jerking his arms in, spinning both handles the same direction. The kite swooped low over the beach at the last second, then peeled off in a horizontal curl with astounding centrifugal force. "Like I said, three feet max."

"More like two." Coleman took another snort from the flask. "That was trippy . . . But why does that kite look like one I've never seen before?"

"Because it's from India." Serge twirled the handles again, executing a series of loop-de-loops. "Over here, kites are whimsical wisps of joy, but in India it gets downright vicious."

"How so?"

"They have kite-flying competitions that are every bit as intense and harrowing as NASCAR." Serge worked his hands for another wicked swoop toward the ground, then a skyward zoom. "The contests are utterly savage, with many people using glass-coated string called 'Chinese manja' that is razor sharp and used to slice up the other guys' kites in aerial dogfights. But the wind is the unpredictable variable, and it can get hairy on the ground."

"That's bullshit."

"Look it up. My smartphone's in my left pocket. Google 'kite manja decapitation.'"

"Yeah, right . . ." Coleman pressed buttons. "Whoa, you're not kidding. I got a whole bunch of hits . . . Ooh, gross."

Serge kept his eyes skyward. "Some people always ruin a good thing. And yet I hear they're nice to cows."

Serenity settled over the pair as they stared upward at their majestic flying dragon. Coleman's eyes returned to land. "Hey, something's rustling in those bushes."

"Almost forgot," said Serge, attention still upward. "The guy from our trunk. I let him rest there until the tranquilizer I injected him with wore off."

"It's wearing off. He's up." Coleman took a strong pull on his flask. "What did he do again?"

"Another asshole ripping off seniors in retirement parks with bogus appliance schemes."

"But I thought that ended when we left those old people back at Boca Shores."

Serge worked his controls. "In Florida, it never ends."

"What's the bonus round?"

"He's allowed to run."

"He's running."

Serge bit his lower lip in concentration. Wrists twisted left and right.

"Your dragon kite's swooping down again in another dive-bomb run," said Coleman.

Serge quickly arched his back again. "And here comes the pull-up for the hard horizontal curl."

Coleman pointed with the flask. "It's going after the guy!"

"I'll bet he's never even *seen* Carnegie Hall."

"It's wrapping around his neck—" Coleman jolted backward. "Jesus! I didn't see that coming! Blood's spurting everywhere."

"That would be the jugular."

"But how? . . ."

"I also sort of ordered a spool of Chinese manja."

"He's grabbing his throat, trying to make it stop."

"Good luck."

"Now he's trudging out into the water. He fell down." Coleman whistled. "Man is that blood spreading."

"Definitely not applying enough pressure."

Coleman jolted again. "Where'd that shark come from?"

"All statistics will tell you the majority of attacks occur in just a few feet of water." Serge began reeling his dragon in. "Not one of his better days."

Coleman finished off his flask as Serge finally got hold of the kite and handed it to him. Then Serge took off his backpack and pulled something out.

"When did you get that?" asked Coleman.

"Coleman, you were with me. Another toy of empowerment." They headed back to the car.

"Sorry for doubting you . . ." Coleman pointed back over his shoulder. "When you said this would be better than Nixon Beach . . ."

"Then you're really going to love our next stop."

Coleman looked back a final time. "I still can't believe kite string could do all that."

"It's simply irresponsible," said Serge, flying a drone in front of them. "Someone needs to ban that stuff."

Chapter 5

Fifty Years Ago

A concrete block propped up one end of a piece of plywood. The other end lay on the sidewalk.

Thump-*thump*. Thump-*thump*.

A screen door opened on the west side of a duplex. "Where is that child?"

Thump-*thump*. Thump-*thump*.

The sound continued rhythmically.

A woman walked down the driveway of the home and looked in the direction of the noise.

Thump-*thump*. Thump-*thump*.

"Bobby!" she shouted. "What do you think you're doing?"

Thump-*thump*. Thump-*thump*.

A small boy pedaled his bicycle up the makeshift plywood ramp, catching some air and flying maybe three feet before hitting the sidewalk. Then another boy, and another. A half-dozen in all, jumping the ramp and circling back in the street to line up on the sidewalk for another go at it, over and over with unlimited energy. The priceless essence of childhood.

The woman walked sternly and raised her voice. "Bobby! Did you hear me?"

"I'm jumping a ramp!" He flew and landed. "I'm going to be the next Evel Knievel."

"In your good clothes! You're going to be late for Sunday school!"

The bike screeched to a stop. "Mom! We just went to church!"

"And now you go to Sunday school! You know that!"

"But, Mom! Football's coming on TV. I want to watch the Dolphins—"

"You give me this argument every week. Now get going!"

Bobby hung his head, then peeled off from the formation of bikes with one of his friends and pedaled down the street.

The other boy was named Ricky, and they rode side by side in the dusty street.

"I hate Sunday school!" said Bobby.

"Me too," said Ricky. "The only way I can get through regular school all week is to look forward to these two days off, and one of them gets ruined."

"If church isn't enough, we have to go to catechism."

"What does catechism mean, anyway?"

"It means that since our folks can't afford private Catholic school, we're not getting enough religion, so we have to go to this. It's like a church rule or something."

"I'll tell you what it really means," said Ricky. "We don't get to watch the Dolphins."

"And they're playing the Jets today. That means Joe Namath."

"Don't remind me . . ."

The boys didn't know that the word *Allapattah* is Seminole for "alligator," but that was the name of their neighborhood. They swerved their bikes around potholes on the south side. It wasn't necessarily a bad neighborhood, but you definitely couldn't say it was good. Their area was seriously working-class. And hard work. There was some heavy industry, textiles and dry docks down on the Miami River. Housing prices had hit the skids when they built Interstate 95 through the middle of it all like the march of General Sherman, and many of the homes only had weeds for lawns. Bobby and Ricky didn't know they were poor, because it was all they knew.

Another reason they didn't think they were poor was they had these great bikes. Not expensive, but they had saved up allowance for creative modifications. They were originally the old banana bikes popular throughout the elementary schools, and the two boys had received theirs on the same Christmas morning. Soon, socket wrenches twisted nuts, removing the banana seats and raising extension bars. New seats were installed, along with thicker, more rugged tires. The boys didn't know it, but they had beaten the market by almost fifteen years, creating motocross prototypes. Their tickets to freedom, roaming far and wide, discovering their world and getting exercise and sun in a lifestyle of youth forgotten since the dawn of the digital age.

They continued pedaling their amped-up machines toward the church. Then childhood exuberance resumed as the boys began aimlessly slaloming back and forth across the street and popping wheelies.

"We should get new grips for the handlebars," said Bobby.

"And bigger pedals . . ."

A distant noise brought them back to earth.

"Damn," said Bobby. "Why did that have to remind us?"

It was a faint roar. Miami International was nearby

and the noise of the planes was so common that it didn't even register with the residents. This roar was different. A large crowd.

Ricky looked in the direction of an expressway. "They just kicked off at the Orange Bowl."

Crestfallen. "And we're going to Sunday school."

"Hey, you know what we should do?" said Ricky. "We should go to the game."

"We don't have tickets," said Bobby. "We don't have *money*."

"Doesn't matter. And we've only ever seen them on TV. This is our chance." Ricky told him what he had in mind.

Their bikes stayed still in the middle of the road, all feet on the ground.

"I don't know," said Bobby. "We'll get in so much trouble."

"How will our parents ever find out?"

They stared at each other, then broke into smiles. They put it in high gear, whipping the bikes around the corner . . .

The Orange Bowl, opened in 1937, was as Florida as it got, and purists still mourn its demolition in 2008. But as the two childhood pals pedaled their bikes on the hot Sunday afternoon, the stadium was still going strong. As they grew near, they saw a particular feature of the bowl that made it instantly recognizable in any telecast. It featured a double-deck horseshoe design, leaving one end zone wide open. Behind it stood a grove of vibrant palm trees, the backdrop of many a touchdown.

The boys dismounted their bikes and walked them toward the trees until they reached a fence. They clenched the barrier with their small fingers and peeked inside. Mesmerized.

The New York Jets, in their bright white away uniforms, were driving the ball toward them. They had followed football on TV with a religious fervor that their parents only wished they had for the church. But now, in person, clutching the outside of the fence, they were stunned at how fast the players were, how violent—and loud—the collisions.

"There's Namath," said Ricky, watching the quarterback drop back in the pocket.

Shoulder pads crashed. Painful grunts of exertion. Then Namath released. It was a perfect fade route that hit Don Maynard in the deep corner of the end zone right in front of them.

The boys exchanged openmouthed looks . . .

They could talk of nothing else on their bike rides home.

"I can't believe we got that close!"

"We could see their faces through the masks."

They reached Bobby's house first. His mother was standing in the middle of the front yard with firmly folded arms.

"Uh-oh," said Ricky. "See you later . . ."

Bobby hopped off his bike. "Uh, hi, Mom."

"Did you go to Sunday school?"

"What? Sure, of course."

"No you didn't!" said his mother. "I called."

"You called?"

"I call every week."

"I didn't know that." Bobby recognized the shoe box at her feet. "What are you doing with my football cards?"

"This is what!" She went to the garbage can at the curb and removed the lid.

"Mom!"

"Don't you 'Mom' me! I didn't raise a liar, and you're not going to start now! Plus you missed catechism, which is another sin. Confession starts at four. Turn that bike around and get going!"

"But I'll miss the second football game on TV."

"As well you should!" She stomped back into the house and slammed the screen door.

Bobby began pedaling again. How could such a great day turn so crappy?

He arrived at the church and went inside the cavernous quietness. There was only one person waiting in line outside the confessional. Ricky turned around. "You too?"

"She threw out my football cards."

"Damn. I'm getting off easy."

After Ricky emerged with a lengthy assignment of Hail Marys, it was Bobby's turn. He knelt in the dark booth. Soon, a wooden panel slid, revealing a cloth curtain and an ominous silhouette. Why did it have to be so creepy?

"Father, I have sinned . . ." Bobby laid out the whole day, and received his own penance.

A few more straggling parishioners arrived to clear their slates. Then it was idleness for a good fifteen minutes. The priest opened his door and peeked outside. Nothing but the flickering of votive candles for the souls in purgatory. He closed up shop and headed out the front door of the church.

He stopped when he saw a young boy sitting on the steps, grumbling and punching the air with his right fist.

"Son, is everything okay?"

"I want to kill someone!" Another punch in the air.

"Didn't you just go to confession?"

"I thought you weren't supposed to know it was me in there," said Bobby. "That curtain."

The priest took a seat on the steps next to Bobby. "I'm Father Al. Why don't you tell me what's wrong?"

"Somebody stole my bike while I was in there!" Two punches this time. "If I catch them, I'm going to beat them up."

The priest smiled to himself. "What are you, Cassius Clay?"

"Who's that?"

"Muhammad Ali."

"Who?"

"The champion boxer," said Father Al. "That's how he got his start."

"By stealing bikes?"

"No, somebody stole *his.* And he was fit to be tied. A police officer took him under his wing and suggested the boy channel his anger into something positive, and took him to a gym."

"I don't want to box." More punches in the air.

Father Al smiled again. He had been here many times. Exactly here. Sitting on the steps of the church with someone. And not always kids. He was the consummate flock tender. "Mind if I ask you some questions?"

"Why not?"

"How old are you?"

"Nine."

"Tell me about your family. Your father?"

The boy shook his head. "Never knew him."

"Where is he?"

"I don't know. Mom won't talk about it."

"And what about your mother?"

"She's the best. Really strict, but only to help me."

"What does she do?"

"Cleans other people's houses," said Bobby.

"Where do you live?"

"In a duplex with another family."

"Well, that's how duplexes work," said the priest.

"No, I mean another family lives in our side of the duplex with us."

"That bicycle was pretty important to you, wasn't it?"

"The best," said Bobby. "I don't know how I can get around without it. It's a long walk home and my mom's expecting me."

"Besides the bike, do you have anything else that's important to you?"

Bobby stared at the ground. "I *used* to have some football cards."

"Do me a favor and wait here."

Bobby was puzzled as he leaned forward on the steps and watched the priest disappear around the corner in the direction of the rectory. A good ten minutes passed, and Bobby was beginning to think that Father Al had forgotten about him. But just then he reappeared.

Bobby's face pinched up. "That is one ugly bicycle. You actually let people see you riding that thing?"

"I'll loan it to you until you can get another," said the priest. "You need to be starting home."

"Thank you."

"You can pay me back by meeting me here tomorrow after school."

"Why?"

"You like baseball?"

"I like football better."

"But you *do* play baseball?"

"Of course. Everyone does."

The priest pointed at the private Catholic school across the parking lot from the church. "You know the baseball field on the other side? Three o'clock."

"You play baseball, too?" asked Bobby.

"Priests can play baseball."

"I didn't know that."

"Bring your glove."

"I don't have a glove."

"Then I'll bring two. Now get home. And mind your mother."

Chapter 6

The Present

Click, click, click.

Coleman stared up at a vintage yellow-and-pink neon sign.

Click, click, click. Serge lowered his camera. "You know what's been bugging me? The expression 'Don't make any false moves.' How can a move be false? It's still a move. It may not be an *appreciated* move . . ." He began pirouetting on the sidewalk, frantically flapping his arms and shooting birds at passing traffic. He stopped and nodded. "See? Now that's what I call 'unappreciated moves.' I'm going to get the expression started. I think it has legs."

Coleman looked down from the sign. "Where are we now?"

"The Upper East Side. Not Manhattan. Miami."

"My feet hurt."

"You're just going to have to suck it up." Serge resumed a brisk stroll. "Dusk is the perfect time to photograph old neon. I've already got the Shalimar, the South Pacific, the Sinbad Motel, but there's so much more: the Saturn, the Biscayne Inn, the Vagabond, not to mention the gigantic landmark Coppertone girl sign, which has been lovingly restored and reinstalled on Seventy-Third Street after the heartbreak of Hurricane Andrew whacked her good on the side of the old Parkleigh Building."

Coleman's head swiveled. "I just see a bunch of old dumpy roadside motels."

"Bite your tongue!" *Click, click, click.* "You're in the midst of the spectacular MiMo district, a contraction of 'Miami Modern,' running up Biscayne Boulevard from roughly Fiftieth Street to Seventy-Sixth. Some of the finest examples of midcentury architecture to be found anywhere . . . True, true, the area scraped bottom for a time, and the vice cops couldn't keep up. But that was a good thing."

"Doesn't sound good."

"The neighborhood was so undesirable that nobody bulldozed these hidden gems to put up condos and IKEAs. And now it's undergoing a renaissance! Young entrepreneurs with vision are pouring in venture cash to restore the area to its former glory. It's still in transition, and you'll get the occasional hooker with a broken leg on the corner, trying to flag your car down with one of her crutches, but how are you ever going to stop that?"

"There's one waving at us now."

Serge stowed his camera. "Time to check into our motel and establish the base camp . . ."

A blue-and-white Ford Cobra pulled into a parking lot off Sixty-Fifth Street and stopped in front of the curved 1950s facade of a motel office. Above, more retro signage:

NEW YORKER. POOL. AIR CONDITIONING. VACANCY.

Serge spread his arms and his smile. "I absolutely love the New Yorker!"

Coleman squinted. "Just another old roadside place."

"Ahhhh, have I got a surprise for you," said Serge. "It's one of the payoffs of my trademark brand of Florida research, getting out on foot and investing shoe leather, peeking in forbidden alcoves, interrogating the bus stop people and taking soil samples. Follow me!"

"Did I mention my feet hurt?"

"I have just the cure."

They rounded the corner of the building and entered a wide alley. Coleman stopped. "What the hell?"

At the end of the corridor stood a large painted sign of a Rita Hayworth–style pinup girl reclining with a martini glass.

PATIO BAR.

And a motto: WE PREFER TO SHAKE IT. An arrow pointed behind the building under a small brick archway.

They entered.

Coleman froze again. "Holy crap! Look at this bar!"

"More like a fantastically spacious outdoor lounge plastered with abstract murals and a painting of the hotel's flamingo logo."

They made respective beelines for the bar and the free coffee, before settling into turquoise-cushioned wicker at a table with a tower of Jenga blocks.

"Have to give you credit," said Coleman. "From the street you wouldn't have the slightest clue that all this is back here. You wouldn't expect this behind *any* old motel."

"The benefits of boots-on-the-ground research." Serge chugged his coffee and turned to a gathering of Europeans smoking clove cigarettes in nearby furniture. "Excuse me! I'd like your honest feedback: 'False move' or 'unappreciated move'?"

"What?"

Serge jumped up, flapping his arms again and shooting birds. Coleman pulled a Jenga piece and the tower collapsed, scattering wooden blocks across the brick patio.

The Europeans quickly left the lounge.

Serge nodded to himself. "Definitely unappreciated . . . Coleman, time to unpack!"

They entered room 110.

Coleman upended his flask. "This place just keeps getting cooler and cooler!"

More turquoise, this time the color of the walls. There was a spleen-shaped mirror and another with spindles holding a constellation of tinier mirrors. Terrazzo floor.

Coleman pointed at another wall and a massive framed black-and-white photo of four people playing pool. "Who are those guys?"

"Can't you read?"

"I'm on vacation."

"Just the whole Rat Pack, Sinatra and all. They used to stay here."

"You're shitting me."

"Hold that thought." Serge tactically performed his mandatory tests before unpacking in any Florida motel room. He checked the air-conditioning—ice cold—and the TV—perfect picture. He sat at the foot of the bed with a coffee refill and a remote control, surfing channels. "Ready for our new mission?"

Coleman peered through the bathroom blinds at the patio bar. "Hit me."

"Discover the Meaning of Life."

"Sounds like a lot of work."

"Not really." Serge hit buttons and sipped from a Styrofoam cup. "First you have to start with the premise that we'll *never* know the meaning of life. Nearly fourteen billion years ago, the universe exploded from a tiny packet of energy, then matter and antimatter smashed together, hydrogen atoms, nebulae, supernovas creating the rest of the elements, amino acids, single-celled organisms, the first fish crawl onto land, and, finally, Beyoncé. Who can figure that out?"

"Don't look here."

"All that unfathomable complexity and design tells me two things: First, there definitely is a God. And second, anyone who claims they can quote him in order to boss you around is a douche-cadet."

"But if we'll never know, then why are you looking?"

"Because if the human brain is inadequate to perceive the Big Picture, that requires us to invent our own meaning of life. And that starts with not coveting your *own* life. We're just here for a blink, part of an endless cycle of rejuvenation." A big chug of coffee. "Coleman, do you realize that in the time you've been alive, most of the cells in your body have replaced themselves countless times? Hell, since you got up this morning you've generated thousands of new cells."

"I do feel kind of shiny today."

"So if our own existence is fleeting and irrelevant, I think religion has the answer. Or at least the founding theology before it became an excellent idea for war. And since the meaning of life isn't about us, it must be how we treat others. I've been zeroing in on Jesus's message from the Sermon on the Mount."

"Which is?"

"Make as many motherfuckers as happy as possible, as often as possible."

"Jesus said that?"

"I just kind of skimmed the Gospels, but I think so."

"Wow. That's deep."

Serge flipped open a notepad. "There's much preparation to do. We need to make lists of good deeds and worthy recipients. But we have to think outside the box because most of the charities have all the obvious good deeds covered." He tapped his chin in thought, then began scribbling. "Nobody's done that deed before, and that either, and they'll never be expecting that . . ."

A few minutes later, he tossed the pad aside. "More on the topic later." Another chug from Styrofoam. He changed the channel.

A commercial came on. A child blowing out birthday candles. A mother holding a newborn in the hospital. Kittens playing with string. A Thanksgiving dinner. A high school prom.

Coleman took a seat on the end of the bed next to Serge and pointed at the TV. "What's this ad for?"

"Personal injury attorneys."

The commercial ended and another began. A child blowing out birthday candles. A mother holding a newborn in the hospital. Kittens playing with string. A Thanksgiving dinner. A high school prom.

Coleman gestured at the screen again. "More personal injury lawyers?"

"No, this ad's for one of those DNA services, called Ancestors R Us." Serge suddenly jumped up. "I've got a great idea! I should send in my own DNA! It is loosely related to our mission."

Serge got out his laptop and logged on to the Internet.

"Can I send mine in, too?" asked Coleman.

"Absolutely."

"Great. I've been meaning to jerk off, but it's just been one thing after another."

"Coleman, you do realize they take saliva? Epithelial skin cells?"

"I like my way better."

"Then the people in their mail room are in for a treat."

Coleman stood up. "Wait here."

"I'll fight the urge to follow."

"But you walked in on me that one time."

Serge rolled his eyes. "Because I thought you were in distress."

"Those were just my regular noises."

"Dammit! Can you stop!" Serge tapped the keyboard. "I'm still scarred."

"I'll be right back."

Serge yelled after him. "No noises!"

"I'll try."

Chapter 7

Fifty Years Ago

The priest was waiting, and Bobby was right on time, despite taking an unaccustomed route so nobody he knew would see him on the loaner bike.

Father Al tossed him a glove. "We'll start by warming up."

They spread out on the first base line and began playing catch. Bobby never had a father to play catch with before, clergy or biological.

"Now go in the outfield and I'll hit you some flies."

Bobby took up position in center field, and the priest tossed a ball in the air and smacked it with a bat. Bobby watched it sail high over his head.

"Oops, sorry," said Father Al.

"You hit it out of the park!" said the impressed youth. "You hit a home run!"

"Didn't mean to."

"How'd you do that?"

"Used to play a little at Jesuit."

Bobby knew all about Jesuit, always fielding a highly ranked team that annually vied for the state championship. Bobby also knew something else about the place. There were regular Catholic high schools, and then there were the elite preps like Jesuit. Father Al had attended back in the day when it was affordable and still building a reputation, decades before tuition went north of twenty grand.

The boy's reverence deepened. "You played baseball for Jesuit?"

"A little." Father Al readied the bat on his shoulder. "Look alert. Here comes another one. I'll try to keep it in the park . . ."

And so began a long series of afternoons at a field that was otherwise empty because it was still football season.

"You want to impress your friends?" asked the priest. "Let me show you how to throw a knuckleball."

"Cool."

They talked some more about grades and bullies and saving up money for another bicycle.

A couple of days later, Bobby arrived at the field and got off a girl's bike.

Father Al smiled and wheeled something out of the dugout.

"My bike!" Bobby sprinted over. "And it has new handle grips! But how?"

"I've gotten to know a number of boys like you over the years. I put the word out."

"You got someone to snitch?"

"No, it was just left on the front steps of the rectory with an apology note."

"Thanks!" Bobby ran down the first base line and raised his glove. "Ready when you are . . ."

It went that way for the next few weeks. But then, one Friday while they were warming up playing catch: "Bobby, listen, you can always come to me if you have any problems or just want to talk."

The boy threw the baseball. "I know that."

The priest caught the ball, but didn't throw it back. "What I'm trying to say is that we won't be able to keep playing baseball like this. Maybe once in a while, but the season's about to start and you can get on your own team."

"I don't understand," said Bobby. "I thought you liked me. Did I do something wrong?"

"Oh, no, no, no. You're fine." Father Al finally threw

the ball. "I wanted to let you know you're special. That someone cares. But this is a large parish, and there are a lot of other people I need to try to help."

"I understand. So this is our last day?"

"For a while."

The next afternoon, Father Al was sitting at a desk in his room at the rectory. It was a tight fit. A single bed and a small bookcase, with one shelf devoted to cans of soup. And the desk was barely that, just a small wooden table against the wall under a crucifix. A hot plate on the corner. There was a stack of stationery and envelopes, next to a stack of letters he had just completed to members of his congregation, young and old, with adversity and reasons for joy. All of them were signed *Shalom*. Father Al opened his Bible to the Gospel of Matthew. The room was painted dark green, which made it seem even smaller. A knock at the door.

"Come in."

Another priest opened. "Someone's here to see you."

"Who is it?"

"Don't recognize him."

Father Al marked his place in the Bible and went to the front door of the rectory.

"Bobby, what are you doing here?"

"My mom wants you to come to dinner."

"She does?"

"She's really Catholic."

He thought about his soup cans. "Well, I always enjoy a good home-cooked meal . . ."

The priest arrived at the mildewed front door of a duplex to meet a grateful mom. She ignored his outstretched hand and instead hugged him tight. "I can't thank you enough for the interest you've taken in Bobby. He never knew his father."

"He told me."

"And he doesn't like church. Or Sunday school."

"Most boys his age don't. But he's a great kid."

"The school he goes to is a little rough, a lot of bad influences. I try my best, but usually get home late."

"He also mentioned how hard you work and how much you love him."

"You can sit at the head of the table as the guest of honor."

He entered the home and remained poker-faced at the sparse surroundings. He hadn't realized they were *this* poor. Bobby was an only child, but a total of nine people squeezed up to the dinner table, thanks to the other family helping with the rent. His mother placed a hot meal in front of the priest.

Father Al looked down and smiled at a bowl of soup.

"I usually say grace," said the mother. "But you're, well . . ."

"A professional? I'd be happy to." They all bowed their heads . . .

The next day, Bobby threw a baseball to Father Al. "My mother sure can talk, can't she?"

No kidding, thought the priest. She must have thanked him a million times. After that, how could he cut off their afternoons at the ball field? But eventually the time came again.

"Bobby, I really have to spread myself around. There are some things I need to do."

"Like what?"

"Not fun stuff like baseball."

"Can I come along?" asked Bobby.

"Seriously, you aren't going to enjoy it. If you think you hate Sunday school—"

"I want to come."

The next evening, Bobby stood next to the priest behind a long table. They both had serving utensils, filling plates at the homeless shelter.

Bobby spooned out a mixture of peas and carrots. "How often do you do this?"

"Try to get by at least once a week, but sometimes things come up."

"Like me?"

"You make it worthwhile. Did you have a chance to read the Gospel passages I suggested? The Sermon on the Mount?"

"Oh yeah, that stuff made sense." Bobby nodded. "I can get with that."

"Then find your way," said Father Al. "Follow your heart."

"It sounds simple."

"It's far from simple," said the priest. "Most people have the ability to know what the right things are to do in given circumstances, but they choose not to listen to their inner voice. They just want what they want. Because doing the right thing isn't always easy or fun, and sometimes it's downright sacrifice. You have to become the kind of person who wants to do the right thing more than what you personally desire."

"I'll get the Bible back to you tomorrow."

"Keep it," said the priest. "It's the one thing we have plenty of at the parish."

A few days later, Father Al sat at a stark counter talking on the telephone. The person on the other end of the line sat a few feet away on the opposite side of thick glass in the prison visiting room.

"Who's the little guy?" asked the inmate.

"Bobby," said the priest.

"Reminds me of me at that age," said the prisoner. "I'm so sorry I let you down after all the time you gave me."

"You just hang in there," said the priest, ignoring the young man's black eye and busted lip. "You'll get through this and go on to do great things."

A guard arrived and stood behind the young convict.

"Father, I have to go. Thanks for coming by again."

Bobby had a lot of questions as they left the prison.

"I knew him since he was your age," said the priest. "Know his father, too. Serving life up in Union County."

The next week, Bobby tagged along again as they arrived in front of a modest ranch house. The priest had explained the situation. "Are you sure you want to come in with me? It's going to be a little rough."

"I'm sure," said Bobby.

"You're still pretty young. You can't let them see you react."

"I'm good."

They were greeted at the door and went inside. The entire home had been converted for intensive long-term care. So had the family. The hospital bed and medical equipment were too big for any of the bedrooms, so it all sat in the middle of the living room.

Father Al had known the girl growing up, all-county

volleyball player and track star at the parish school. Glowing picture of health before the brain aneurism. The priest walked up to the bed with metal railings on the sides. He held a hand that was unable to hold his back. He stroked her hair and smiled.

"How are you doing today, Sarah?"

Eyes widened. Her mouth tried to smile but made an unintended shape. Then non-verbal noises communicated delight at seeing Father Al. That was the hardest part. Her brain was still going strong. Someone was still in there.

Bobby looked around at the living room's walls. They were covered with glossy photos. All autographed. All sports celebrities. The Miami Dolphins, the Miami Hurricanes, Wimbledon, the Olympics. It was Sarah's hobby, what got her through, looking forward to the next surprise in the mail.

Father Al smiled bigger and held up a large envelope. "You got another one! Let's see who it is."

He pulled out a basketball photo from the Miami Floridians of the ABA. Louder non-verbal noises of glee.

After they left the house, Bobby was full of questions again. "How did she get all those autographed photos? There must be a hundred."

"Letters to the players."

"How can she write letters?"

"She doesn't. I do."

"You wrote all those letters?"

"The family has their hands full." Then the priest turned. "Bobby, I don't know if you're trying to change the subject or not. That was pretty hard in there for someone your age. Are you sure you're okay?"

Bobby nodded. "I will never complain about a bicycle again."

Bobby was surprising Father Al in a lot of ways, but today was something new. The pair sat at a table in the main communal room of the church rectory.

"Here's my report card, like you asked."

"Not bad," said Father Al. "A nice number of A's."

"But too many B's for my mother's liking. She says I can do better."

"She's probably right. There's a B here in science. That's your favorite subject."

Bobby hung his head back in exasperation. "I'm just so bored! My classes are huge, and we're out in those hot portable buildings because of overcrowding. And we're always changing teachers, and then they go back over stuff I already know, and we never get to the end of the textbooks where the good stuff is."

"You'll just have to bear down."

"Okay, can we talk about something else?"

"Like what?"

"Religion."

The priest's eyebrows went up. "You want to talk about religion?"

"Religion seems to be a big part of your life."

"What tipped you off? The clothes?"

"I want to be just like you."

Father Al's head pulled back. "You want to be a priest?"

"No, I mean like you as a person. You're the coolest guy I know."

"Well, I don't know about *cool*."

"Definitely." Bobby nodded with emphasis. "But I don't get it."

"Don't get what?"

"My mom forces me to go to mass and Sunday school, and it's not for me. It doesn't make sense, just a lot of weird rules and rituals for old people." The boy sat back. "But if you're down with all of that, I must be missing something."

The priest thought hard to choose words. "Faith is a complicated thing. An individual thing. It's what each person makes of it. You can't just adopt beliefs that someone orders you to. It has to grow from inside your heart. Some of the finest people in this parish don't agree with a lot of the edicts."

"But you do?"

"Yes."

"Now I'm even more confused."

"Tell you what . . ." Father Al reached for a Bible on the table. "I want to give you something."

"You already gave me a Bible."

"Not that," said the priest. "I was going to write down some new passages to read that might help you understand. If you want to read more, that's up to you."

"Okay, I'll give it a shot."

A month later, just after dark, a priest arrived at a homeless shelter.

"Hey, Father Al," said one of the volunteers.

"Hi, Jerry." He removed a light jacket. "Sorry I haven't been around for a while. Got busy."

The volunteer just stopped and laughed. "That kid's quite a character."

"Who?"

Jerry pointed at the dinner line. Bobby waved at him with a serving spoon.

Now it was Father Al's turn to chuckle. "He likes to tag along with me. Guess he heard I was coming to-night."

"No," said Jerry. "He's been here two or three times a week since you last came."

"He has? . . ."

A few days later, Father Al pulled a chair toward a glass partition and picked up a prison phone. An inmate on the other side picked up his own phone.

"Great to see you again, Father Al."

"You too."

"And thanks for sending your friend to visit."

"I didn't send anyone."

"Yes, you did. That kid Bobby."

"Bobby's been here?"

"A few times."

"But how—? A little kid can't get in a prison. And where'd he get a ride way out to this place?"

"Told me there are a few families in his neighborhood who come on visiting days, and he catches a ride and slips through security with them . . ."

The priest was talking to himself as he left the prison. "Wonders never cease."

He was correct.

The next evening he entered a living room and held a hand. "Hi, Sarah." Then he noticed something, and turned to the parents. "Where did those new autographed photos come from? I didn't write them letters."

"No, Bobby did," said the mother. "He came by a couple of times to drop them off."

Chapter 8

The Present

A 1970 Ford Cobra sat at a gas pump on U.S. 1 in Miami. Serge squeezed the handle in his hand. A look of terminal exasperation.

Coleman stood next to him openly chugging a can of Pabst. "What's the matter?"

"This is totally unnecessary!" snapped Serge. "Another thing that pisses me off: Gas pump handles that don't have that little metal thing to latch it, forcing you to stand here with the fucking thing in your hand. Other pumps have latches, so there *is* the technology. You can just leave the pump in your car and get on with life by reorganizing your trunk or buying Skittles in the store. But no, at pumps like this, these bastards are plucking precious golden droplets of time from my existence that I'll never get back. And it's always the slowest pumps. Everyone knows this is happening and yet nobody ever mentions it. We need to caucus about this."

"But it's just a few minutes," said Coleman.

"*Life* is just a few minutes!" Serge stared at the digital numbers gradually counting gallons, and he hit himself in the forehead. "This pump is slower than snail shit! But I'll tell you what's worse. New Jersey."

"Oh, yeah, Jersey," said Coleman. "I've heard the rumors."

"No, the state's great. The people are great," said Serge. "But I found myself in Jersey once. Don't ask me why. I was just in Jersey. And they have this weird state law that you're not allowed to pump your own gas. I didn't know this. So I get out of my car and grab the gas pump, and this dude comes out of the station and tries to take the handle away from me, and I say, 'Get the hell off me,' and he says, 'You can't pump your own gas,' and I say, 'Of course I can. I've done it a million times.' And then he does manage to grab the handle, and there's a wild struggle until another car pulls up and the driver sees my Florida plate and tells me about the law."

Coleman crumpled an empty can. "Why do they have such a law?"

"Probably how all laws start," said Serge. "There must have been some huge statewide crisis, residents unable to master the procedure, gasoline spilling everywhere, flash fires and explosions. Or more likely, the people up there *did* caucus over this: 'Hey, where's the goddamn metal thing to latch the pump!' Then general ugliness, gas stations getting trashed, employees beaten with garbage cans. That's how Jersey rolls."

"Where are you going?"

"Inside the store. Have to use the bathroom."

Coleman sat in the passenger seat of the parked Cobra. He looked at his fingernails and tasted them. "When did I get mustard in there?" He checked his pockets and found a piece of jerky and ate it. Then for ten minutes, he stared out at the sidewalk and the wide variety of people-shapes, and this is what was going on inside his head: crickets.

Serge climbed back in the driver's seat.

"What took you so long?" asked Coleman. "And why is your face all red?"

Serge began repeatedly punching the ceiling. "Motherfuckers!"

"What happened?"

"These corporations won't spring for a cheap latch for you to comfortably pump gas. Yet they'll install expensive motion detectors in the restrooms so you won't waste a tenth of a cent of electricity. I'm sitting in one of the stalls doing my business, and nobody had come in for a while, so the motion detector turns off the lights! I'm in pitch darkness! So I try desperately waving my arms, but I'm behind the closed stall door blocking the motion sensor. I'll spare you the details, but I was at the stage of the game where I needed to see what I was doing. What's with these sudden bursts of terror in life?"

The Cobra drove away.

"Where to now?" asked Coleman.

"A little neighborhood called Keystone Islands." The Cobra pulled back onto the highway. "You know another subconscious facet of human behavior that nobody has meetings about? Really slow cars."

"I hate them."

"But I'm fascinated by the universal reaction of all the other drivers," said Serge. "We don't even realize we're doing it, but whenever we see a really slow car and have to pull around to pass, we also slow down ourselves as we go by. We just *have* to look. Because we've judged ahead of time: 'I can't resist seeing what kind of dysfunction is in that car' . . ."

"Here's one now."

"Let's pull around." Serge got in the passing lane

and let off the gas. Their heads turned. "Yep, some loser on the phone *and* eating a sandwich."

"There's another one a couple blocks ahead," said Coleman.

"Let's speed up so we can slow down."

They pulled alongside another car and looked.

"Dang, that woman must have fifty stuffed animals on the dashboard," said Coleman. "How can she see out the windshield?"

"And why that glazed look on her face like she's on Thorazine? It's as if the car's driving itself."

They sped up.

"So what's with this Keystone place we're heading to?"

Serge tapped the map in his lap. "An elusive item on my bucket list. The Florida home of the gangster Hyman Roth from the second *Godfather* movie."

"Roth?"

"Modeled after Meyer Lansky, who lived just south of here." Serge turned onto a side street, holding a thumb and index finger an inch apart. "I was this close to finding the place once."

"What happened?"

"Hollywood trickery." The Cobra made another turn. "This is Hibiscus Drive, a figure-eight street with a canal all the way around, only one way in and out. Last time I was here, I had just studied the movie scene frame by frame. Al Pacino comes from the city and makes a left turn up the road to the house. So, logically, I did the same thing, but I couldn't find the place for the life of me. But upon further film analysis, I discovered that Pacino turns the corner from the direction of the water, not land, which makes no sense."

"What do you think happened?"

"Obviously Pacino got lost and later gave Roth a bunch of shit about lousy directions, but those parts hit the editing room floor because the movie was long enough already." The Cobra stopped at a curb. A camera went out the window. *Click, click, click.* "Just like I remember it from the movie, except without the cool metal palm tree on the screen door. I can't get enough of those screen doors! But at least I finally found the house."

"Strike it from the list."

"Damn straight."

The Cobra patched out.

A short while north in Hallandale Beach, Serge pulled up to another home.

"What movie was this in?" asked Coleman.

"No movie." Serge got out of the car. "This is the first stop discovering my roots. I just got the results back from Ancestors R Us."

He rang the doorbell. An old bald man answered the door with stains on his T-shirt. "Yeah?"

"Are you Raúl Dixon?"

"Who's asking?"

Serge's face lit up as he shot out his right hand. "Cuz!"

The resident just looked at it. "What are you selling?"

"Selling?" He glanced at Coleman. "Nothing. I finally took the big leap and sent my saliva in to Ancestors R Us. Coleman sent in his . . . well, let's not go there. But guess what? Your name popped up! You're like my fourth cousin once removed. Name's Serge Storms."

"Never heard of you."

"You would have if you sent in your saliva after I did." Serge pulled a Q-tip from his pocket and brushed lint off the end. "Can I take a swab inside your cheek for my souvenir box?"

"Not really."

"Then I guess you definitely wouldn't be up for Coleman's idea. We'll circle back to that later." He stowed the Q-tip and rubbed his palms together. "So tell me all about my kin! And don't leave out the black sheep! Who's estranged and who's not? Got some family albums lying around? How were the holiday dinners?

Did everyone sing carols or was there wrestling? Any freaky genetics I should know about, like all that hair growing out of your ears?"

The man started closing the door, but Serge blocked it with his foot.

A sigh from inside. "What do you want from me?"

"Why, to make you happy!" said Serge.

"What?"

"It's a dual road trip. First, my roots. Second, I've been skimming the Bible and want to make as many cats as happy as possible. And you're lucky number one!" Serge looked around the yard. "Your lawn's gone to hell. I can plant some grass plugs, or maybe get my razor from the car and trim your ears. Your choice."

"What?"

"Plus I've already turned over some icon leaves on another genealogical site that doesn't require fluid, just data," said Serge. "The crap I'm finding out is incredible! Did you know we share a great-grand-uncle who was pivotal in history? You and me, cuz! I'll bet you're just dying to hear the details!"

Dixon tried closing the door again, but Serge was adamant.

"Move your foot, asshole!"

"Wait! Wait!" said Serge. "I know you're overcome

with astonishment and not thinking straight. You just have to hear about our uncle! The place? Miami! The year? 1933! It was a chilly night at Bayfront Park, near the current basketball arena. A huge crowd had assembled to hear a speech. You know who was giving it?"

"Who cares?" said Dixon.

"Franklin Delano Roosevelt! Only a few days into his first term! He was delivering the speech from the back of an open car, a tactic he used to conceal that he couldn't walk from polio."

"Like I said—"

"Shhhhh! There's more! Our uncle came from a hitherto unknown Italian branch of the family. And this is the best part: He was an anarchist! Today that's just soccer hooligans, but back then it was the real deal. Guido was always yelling 'Anarchists unite,' which would defeat the whole point, and he had trouble getting a room together. And on that night so long ago, he went down to the edge of the water with his pals to heckle, as they relentlessly did, which is why anarchists are a real test as dinner companions. And Guido suddenly sees another guy he knows . . ."

Serge began slowly moving his arms, serpentine, in front of his chest and staring up at the sky.

Dixon sipped the cheap beer in his hand. "What in the fuck are you doing?"

"A fade-out," said Serge. "It seems like it was only yesterday . . ."

A small Italian man in suspenders and a derby arrived at the foot of Flagler Street near Biscayne Bay. Went by Guido Nomellini. Guido worked his way through the adoring mob, fidgeting to catch a glimpse of the new commander in chief.

Closer to the front of the roadside crowd, hearty applause and shouts: "Hoover sucks!"

The diminutive Guido spotted someone he knew. "Hey, Giuseppe, I called a meeting. Where were you?"

"Shut up. I'm busy."

Then Guido noticed that Giuseppe was standing on a folding chair in the crowd, because he was also quite short, and this woman in front of him was wearing a ridiculously big hat that blocked his view.

Guido couldn't see, either. "Got another chair?"

"Right over there," said Giuseppe. "Now will you leave me alone?"

"Why are you so cranky tonight?" Guido set up his own chair and stood a couple of people over from his political colleague. "I'm serious about these meetings," Guido yelled over the din of the audience. "We can't just whip together an overthrow . . . Are you listening?"

Giuseppe wasn't. His head moved left and right, trying to see around the woman's hat for a view of the open-roofed car.

"Gee, you really are in a cruddy mood tonight. Excuse me for caring about the movement." Then he happened to look down by Giuseppe's side. "Whoa, what are you doing with that gun?"

"For the movement!"

"Are you out of your mind?" said Guido. "Fuck the movement! I was just in it to get laid!"

Giuseppe raised his arm.

Guido lunged. "Somebody stop him!"

The first shot rang out.

The woman with the big hat heard the bang next to her head. She turned and seized his arm. Four more shots fired before Guido and other bystanders gang-tackled the gunman and disarmed him. Mayhem in the street. The president's car sped off, and police dragged Giuseppe away.

Guido reached down to help a woman up. "Thank God you have fast reflexes. I can't believe how quickly you grabbed his arm." He retrieved something from the ground and handed it to her. "Here's your hat. What's your name?"

"Lillian. Lillian Cross."

"So Lillian," said Guido. "You got any plans tonight after this? . . ."

Serge dropped his arms and blinked a few times.

"Wow, that was exciting," said Coleman. "Was the president killed?"

"No, you idiot. He was elected a total of four times," said Serge. "But while FDR was unscathed, one of the errant bullets struck Chicago mayor Anton Cermak, who later died."

"What about the assassin?" asked Coleman.

"Giuseppe Zangara got the death penalty and went to the electric chair at Raiford ten days later. They really kept the line moving back then, like they were selling lottery tickets." Serge whistled. "The way history randomly pinballs around always amazes me. Can you imagine the hairpin turn in the fate of the entire world if it weren't for a woman from Miami? That hat just might have stopped Hitler."

Dixon was trying to kick Serge's foot clear so he could close the door.

"Ouch," said Serge. "What are you doing?"

"I'd like you to leave now."

"But I haven't made you happy yet."

"Leaving would make me very happy."

"It would?"

"Most definitely."

"Gee, if that's all it takes, then you must have life totally figured out." He glanced at Coleman again and back at the resident. "Then leave we will!"

The door slammed behind them as the pair headed back to their car.

"Man, he sure was easy to please," said Coleman.

"I wonder if they're all going to go this smoothly."

Chapter 9

A Couple of Decades Ago

Right out of school, Nathan Sparrow landed a job with one of Palm Beach County's largest law firms.

Nathan had told the partner who interviewed him that they wouldn't be sorry if they hired him. But that turned out very much not to be the case.

At first it was golden. Nathan was a fast study and soon bringing in more revenue than attorneys who had been there for years. His compensation rocketed at a record pace for the firm, and the partners counted their blessings that he had come to their door first.

"This is for you," one of the partners told him at a Christmas party.

Nathan looked at the check in the envelope. "Is this number a mistake?"

"No mistake," said the partner. "Now put it away and don't tell the others."

Nathan quickly gained case experience, surprising opposing attorneys by showing up with unexpected arsenals of evidence. Medical documents and actuarial projections sympathetic to his client. And damning details on their own clients that they never would have guessed, thanks to his firm's private investigators.

But Nathan Sparrow was learning more than just how to leverage juicy pre-trial settlements. He was learning the model of a successful personal injury firm. And he studied the other lawyers. Two young attorneys, in particular, caught his eye. They also had received Christmas party envelopes on the hush-hush. The lawyers began meeting privately after work in a series of dive bars where they wouldn't be noticed.

"I'm in," said Reinhold.

"Me too," said Nash.

"But we have to get all our ducks in a row first," said Sparrow. "And we need to persuade some of the doctors to play ball. I know at least four whose referrals we can strip away from the firm to get us started."

"What about the no-compete contracts they made us sign?"

"Did some research," said Sparrow. "A circuit decision last year put even the most ironclad contracts on shaky ground, and the crap they had us sign is a joke. If they try to pull anything, we'll threaten to countersue. In fact, I hope they do try something, because we'll win."

Reinhold whistled. "The shit's going to hit the fan."

"Bring your umbrellas," said Sparrow.

The three young attorneys decided on the nuclear option. They went in after midnight to pack up all their belongings and copy hard drives, leaving only a few worthless items on the desks to create the appearance nothing was up. Then they came in the next day and called together all the firm's partners for an announcement that everyone was expecting to be some kind of cause for celebration.

Instead, the screaming could be heard through the walls. "*After all we've done for you!*" "*You were like our sons!*" "*We'll take you to court!*" "*Get the fuck out!*"

The trio was escorted from the building by security.

"That went just about like I expected," said Reinhold.

"Screw 'em," said Nash.

"We have an office lease to sign," said Sparrow.

The lease was for space in a strip mall next to a Hungry Howie's pizzeria, but everyone starts somewhere, and the new law firm of Reinhold, Nash &

Sparrow was, as they say, off to the races. They were three young Turks who had stamina for insane hours. They distilled the business model of their previous employer, and recruited more doctors for referrals. Money poured in over the transom. They got out of their lease and the pizza smell in their clothes, and moved into a prestigious office tower address. Then Nathan Sparrow added a touch of genius.

"We take every case to trial."

"You mean every case where the offer is too low."

"No, every case," said Nathan. "Even when the offer's fair. *Every single case.*"

"But that makes no business sense," said Nash. "We might earn more on a particular judgment, but it will eat up time to settle ten others out of court. It'll kill our volume."

"Can you trust me on this?"

What could the others say? Sparrow had started it all, and he did bring in a ton of clients with his social connections.

"Sure."

"I'm with you."

It significantly choked their revenue stream in the short run, then crippled it.

"How long are we going to do this?" asked Reinhold.

"Just wait," said Nathan. Then he took it to another

level, stretching out trials with costly discovery depositions and motions and ancillary witnesses nobody had any reason to call.

A judge banged a gavel, and a flock of defense attorneys stormed out of the courtroom with prickliness. Nathan was content.

Reinhold latched his briefcase next to him. "I'm not doubting you, but this seems to be going nowhere. We're making a fraction of what we did last year and yet you're smiling?"

"We're in for the long game, like a new fast-food chain that sells hamburgers for ninety-nine cents."

"Hamburgers?"

"Hamburgers, law—it's the same meat grinder."

"If you say so."

The trials continued, and so did the extension tactics that featured giant poster photos on easels, videos of distant relatives, and accident-scene dioramas with tiny toy vehicles that Nathan had loved as a child.

"Your Honor," said a defense attorney. "Matchbox cars? Seriously?"

"They have the right to put on their case," said the judge, turning to Nathan. "Is that a Fleetwood? . . ."

Outside the courthouse, Reinhold turned around on the steps: "This makes even less sense now. The other lawyers are looking at us like we're loons."

"Perfect," said Nathan. "That means the plan's working."

"I don't see any plan at all," said Nash.

"Give it another month."

That was more than enough time.

"What's wrong with you guys?" asked a defense lawyer. "We crunch the same numbers. You know this offer is more than adequate!"

Nathan cracked his knuckles with a mischievous smirk. "I just like courtrooms."

The young lawyers were working their way up in the world, unmarried, no real obligations, able to take a fiduciary beating. The insurance companies, on the other hand, were stammering to explain the losses to their shareholders. Not only were they paying at least as much as if they had settled out of court, but it was costing them weeks of litigation fees in what had become no less than wars of economic attrition. What started with a table of two lowly paid defense attorneys became whole teams of six-hundred-dollar-an-hour suits just to finish it off.

"You win," said one of the top liability defense lawyers in the state. "What will it take to stop this?"

"A jury verdict."

"You're not acting logical!" said the other counsel. "No, you're mad!"

"Crazier than a shit-house rat."

The upstart firm began getting a reputation, and word quickly spread: Prepare your opening statements accordingly, because it ain't going to be happening out in the hall.

A month later, Nathan led his two partners outside a courtroom. The in-house legal team from another insurance giant was waiting.

"You wanted to talk to us?" asked Sparrow.

"I don't know why I'm wasting my breath, but I have to report back to the company that I at least went through the motions." The defense attorney handed Nathan a piece of paper with a dollar sign and a number. "That's the highest we'd ever pay for a case like this. Our final offer to settle."

Nathan smiled and handed it back. "Sounds fair to me."

"Wait, what?"

"Sure," said Sparrow. "We're reasonable. We'll take it."

"But—"

"Draw up the paperwork and send a courier to our office." Sparrow and his partners walked away, leaving a team of slack-jawed lawyers wondering if the world had just tilted on its axis.

Reinhold turned as they trotted down the front

steps. "Why did you do that? I thought we were taking every case to trial."

"The strategy has accomplished its goal."

"Which was?"

"To set our price point."

Word again swept the hallowed halls of justice, and everyone came ready to settle for top dollar. The firm's income went through the proverbial roof. Case volume spiked because of the time savings from avoiding the lengthy trials.

The founding partners began handing the cases over to their junior associates. Because of the firm's rep, the out-of-court offers remained premium, big numbers for rookies who'd just passed the bar. All was good in the kingdom.

A few weeks later, however, one particular set of lawyers got cocky because it's in their DNA. They saw the fresh young faces and scoffed. They'd be damned if they were going to just roll over and give these kids the keys to the treasure chest. They lowballed them.

"Excuse me," said one of the younger lawyers, pulling out his cell phone. "I have to make a call . . ."

In less than twenty minutes, the defense lawyers had their backs straight up against a marble wall, swallowing hard, facing Nathan and his partners.

The lead attorney, by the name of Pickering, cleared his throat and handed over another sheet of paper. "Here's our new offer."

Nathan showed his partners the number, and they nodded. "Seems fair to us."

"Great. And sorry about making you drive over here." The attorney grabbed the handle of the briefcase standing on the ground next to his legs. "Can't blame us for trying."

"No, we can't," said Nathan. "You were dealing with inexperienced attorneys and saw an opening. I would have done the same."

"Then we have a deal."

"Not even close."

"What? But you said it was a fair offer."

"More than fair," said Nathan. "If only you had given our associates that number to begin with."

"What do you want?"

"To go to trial."

The opposing attorney clicked a pen open. "We'll increase the offer. How much?"

"They haven't invented that number yet."

"Why are you doing this?"

"Because you made us drive over here," said Nathan. "We're going to fuck you."

"You're an asshole!"

"Hold that impression till the verdict. You might want to amend it upward."

It was their lengthiest trial yet, with lots of photos and diagrams and charts, all blown up on the regular glossy poster boards and easels. A misty-eyed jury came back with a judgment $5 million higher than the best offer. The defense slammed their briefcases shut and stormed out. They knew they had just lost their biggest client, and probably a number of others still to come. The legal community is small and people talk.

Reinhold closed his own briefcase and marveled at the verdict. "Now *that* was worth going to trial for."

"It was worth more than the money," said Nathan. "It was worth the cautionary tale. Before those clowns know it, they'll be back doing wills and bankruptcies."

He was right. And he wasn't done. "Time to rub it in. Press conference!"

The local stations assembled on the courthouse steps and set up their microphones. Three attorneys waited for the lights to come on. "Good evening. My name is Nathan Sparrow of Reinhold, Nash and Sparrow, and today I'm here to announce that our justice system works for all of us . . ."

Nearby, in a swank martini lounge on Clematis Street, the news came on the TV over the bar, and the screen filled with three prevailing attorneys taking turns at the mikes. On one of the bar stools, a dashing man in a black suit and yellow tie hung his head in defeat. He pulled out his wallet, then folded a twenty in half lengthwise and held it suavely between two fingers toward the bartender. “Change the channel.”

The bartender nodded and took the Andrew Jackson. He picked up the remote and clicked the TV over to entertainment news and something about Tom Hanks’s biggest regret. The bartender returned and looked at a nearly empty martini glass. “Another Belvedere, Mr. Pickering?”

The customer placed a palm over the top of his glass. “Two’s the limit. Got a case in the morning.”

“Yes sir, Mr. Pickering. If you need anything else . . .” The bartender wasn’t a particularly polite or attentive person, but the tips at this place could change your worldview. The bartender zeroed in on another lawyer holding a folded twenty and rushed off.

Because of its proximity to the courthouse, the bar was well known for its attorney clientele. And because of that, it was known for something else. A scientifically improbable concentration of drop-dead-gorgeous women. It was the rare kind of bar where the females dangled the pickup lines. And it was usually this: “What firm are you with?” Some checked for wedding bands; others didn't care. Neither did the men. Marriages came and went in this place. The women attorneys who practiced at the courthouse were uniformly disgusted by the whole scene and never set foot inside.

"You look like you could use a friend," said a voice behind a stool. ". . . Hello? . . . Anybody home?"

"What?" Pickering turned around. "Oh, sorry. Just distracted." Then he looked again. A dark-haired dream in a long black dress right out of the Hollies song. "Can I buy you a drink?"

She took the stool next to him. "What are you having?"

"Belvedere vodka martini." He went to signal the bartender, but she beat him to it and held up a pair of fingers. "Two Belvederes."

"No," said Pickering, hand over his glass again. "I'm just about to leave."

"Oh, come on. Have some fun." Then a sultry smile that caught the lawyer in headlights. "I know your type. Too responsible. That's a good thing, but so is lightening up once in a while. Something's on your mind . . ."

"This stupid case today. I hate that firm. You know, the one with the ads . . ."

The bartender arrived and silently awaited his decision.

Pickering pushed the empty glass forward. "Sure, why not."

A commercial came on.

The lawyer grimaced. "What's with the kittens and string?" He pointed at the set, and the bartender swung into action, switching over to a singing competition with snarky judges.

The drinks arrived, and the woman raised hers. "Cheers." Glasses clinked. "So tell me why so glum? . . ."

Two hours later, they were laughing and touching in incidental ways that weren't incidental. The kind of woman who made men break rules. Pickering was on the business end of his fifth Belvedere when she whispered something in his ear. Another wilting smile. "I just have to go powder my nose . . ."

He watched intently as she sashayed toward the restrooms. "Damn, that'll turn a bad day around."

Pickering sipped his last drink of the evening. Eventually he glanced toward the back of the lounge and checked his watch. "What's taking her so long?"

Finally, Pickering stood up from his stool and placed a final tip on the bar. "Knew it was too good to be true." He got in his black Lexus and turned onto Clematis.

Immediately, his rearview lit up with flashing red and blue lights. "Of all the bad luck!"

It wasn't luck. The patrol car had been waiting at the curb, thanks to the anonymous tip: "I tried to stop him, but he's leaving the bar anyway. I'd feel terrible if someone got hurt. . . . Yes, a black Lexus." *Click.*

A block away, in the dim back booth of another lounge, Nathan Sparrow held out a folded stack of hundreds. A woman in a black dress reached for it, and he yanked it back. "You need to sign this first."

"What is it?"

"Non-disclosure agreement. It's standard."

She took his pen and began writing. "Are you seeing anybody? . . ."

The next day, a pheasant lunch in the conference room of a law office. The DUI was all over the news and the talk of the courthouse, thanks to Pickering's stature in the community.

Reinhold chewed an expensive bite. "Man, if he thought he was going to lose clients because of that verdict . . ."

Nash pointed with a salad fork. "You had something to do with this, didn't you?"

Sparrow pointed at his chest. "Me?"

"Don't answer," said Reinhold. "But I heard the whispers at the courthouse this morning. Everyone suspects."

Nathan stabbed his own bite. "Good."

"Good? It could be trouble."

"How?" said Nathan. "What statutory line was crossed? Hypothetically somebody paid a woman to flirt with a guy. Nobody forced him to drink, forced him to drive off in his car."

The other partners stared off in thought. Legal permutations flickered in their eyes. Nash nodded. "You're right. But why? You already crushed him in the courtroom."

Sparrow dabbed his mouth with a napkin. "That's the problem with people today. No work ethic. When you knock someone down, make sure they can't get up."

The courthouse talk continued, and it became a source of admiration and lore. In these circles, ruthlessness was the coin of the realm. Mercy was a bounced check. From then on, everyone either wanted to be their best friends or stayed clear. Money gushed in too fast to spend, and the sky was the limit.

Reinhold actually said it. "The sky's the limit."

"I want to go into orbit," said Nathan.

Chapter 10

The Present

Coleman opened a glass door and pulled a twelve-pack from a shelf in the beer cooler. "Serge? You seem distracted."

"I am." Serge held an energy drink in his hand, as if to read the ingredients, but he was surreptitiously looking to the side. "Here's a travel tip for those at home planning to visit Florida. If you're in a convenience store paying a cashier, always check your surroundings before pulling out your wallet, and then grip it tight against your stomach and hunch your shoulders to shield it with your body."

"Why?

"The first time I noticed the phenomenon was in

Daytona. I was walking up to the store and the door suddenly flew open and this girl comes flying out like Usain Bolt, really booking it and not stopping for five blocks. I went inside, and the customer at the counter was staring weird at his upturned hands like it was the first time he'd ever seen them."

"What happened?"

"That's what I asked, and the guy said he was about to buy a sandwich and the girl just grabbed his wallet and took off. Another time I was in Miami at one of those stores where the cashier is behind bulletproof glass and you slide your money underneath through a curved metal slot—which is a red flag that you should take your tourist dollars elsewhere—and this guy is buying a single beer with a large bill, and as soon as the cashier places the change in the slot, the customer gets seriously hip-checked out of the way by this younger cat who grabs eighteen bucks from the slot and it's a sprint again."

"How often is this happening?" asked Coleman.

"I talked to some cashiers, and they said all the time since meth and heroin took hold. And only getting worse because of credit cards."

"I don't follow."

"You used to be able to swipe a credit card, but now most have security chips, which ironically decreases security. Customers have to stick it in a slot and wait for the machine to do its magic while they have that final-*Jeopardy!*-answer countdown music playing in their heads. And then they're shocked when their card is yanked out of the slot by another track star."

"Why don't they just call and cancel the card?"

"Most do, but not in time because the number to call about a lost or stolen card is on the *back* of the card, and you have to go home to look up paperwork. A design flaw if you ask me. The problem is so rampant that our state had to pass a special law called 'sudden snatching,' to fill the gap between simple theft and strong-arm robbery. Which pisses me off on another level. '*Sudden* snatching.' How do you have confidence in a government that can't even master the basic language? Is there slow-motion snatching?"

"The distraction?" asked Coleman.

"Oh, right. I got distracted." Serge glanced to the side again. "A few months ago, some surveillance camera footage from Florida went viral. Turns out this one customer was ninety years old and looked every bit as frail. In the video, he's got his wallet out, slowly counting his money like it's going to take him another ninety years, and meanwhile this muscular young guy is pacing back and forth behind him. Finally, the thief didn't even have to snatch. He just gently lifted the wallet from the guy's hands and walked out of the store. But the saddest part was the old man's delayed reaction, looking down puzzled like a dog that eats a last bit of food and then is surprised to see an empty bowl and thinks, 'What the fuck just happened?' The Internet post of the video got a thousand comments from Floridians that were all variations on 'Kill this piece of shit,' which made me swell with local pride."

"And that's why you're looking over at that old geezer standing by the machine that turns the hot dogs?"

"Yep," said Serge. "Going through his wallet without a care."

"Some young guy's walking behind, checking him out."

"Already on my radar," said Serge. "And the old man has one of those military-veteran baseball caps. That should be a nationwide hands-off symbol. What's wrong with people?"

"I think it's about to happen," said Coleman.

"This shouldn't take long," said Serge. "Keep the old guy company while I'm gone."

The wallet was lifted, and the thief sprinted out of the store, followed quickly by Serge.

Coleman ambled up to the confused vet. "So, how's your day going? . . ."

Ten minutes later, Serge returned with a smile and a billfold. "I think you dropped this. Thank you for your service." He placed it back in the man's hands, triggering a second round of confusion.

Serge walked up to the cashier with his energy drink. He stuck a pre-paid credit card in a slot, then leaned over the machine and wrapped his arms around it.

"What are you doing?" asked the cashier.

"Fighting crime. Tell me when the payment clears . . ."

A 1970 Ford Cobra sped north on U.S. 1.

"That was fast," said Coleman. "How'd you get the guy's wallet back?"

"I have the gift of persuasion." Serge pulled a stun gun from his pocket and stowed it under his seat.

"Oh, I get it," said Coleman. Then he heard a noise and turned around.

Bam, bam, bam.

Coleman pointed at the trunk. "Bonus round?"

"Afraid so. Look for a motel."

The Cobra continued north as the occupants in the front seat swayed and sang.

"Ohhhhhhh! The bonus round! The bonus round! Shits and giggles sure to abound! . . ."

Bam, bam, bam.

It was noon, and the budget motel room was dark.

Someone vainly tried to yell from a mouth covered with duct tape.

Suddenly, a slit of light where Coleman was peeking out through the blinds toward the beach.

A head slowly rose from the water. Serge removed his mask and snorkel and slapped ashore with big swim fins.

Coleman stepped aside as his buddy entered the back door with the fins under his arm. "Hand me a towel."

Coleman complied. "How was it?"

"Fantastic!" He rubbed his hair dry. "I've just rededicated my entire life to snorkeling and all things snorkel-like! I usually go offshore by boat in the Keys, but this is possibly the best spot accessible right from the beach."

"Where are we?"

"Lauderdale-by-the-Sea." He waved an arm in the direction of waves. "I dove the Datura Avenue Shipwreck Snorkel Trail, just south of the pier at Commercial Boulevard."

"They actually have a trail for snorkeling?"

"It's the rage now, like the new one at Phil Foster Park in Riviera Beach." Serge opened the blinds and pointed. "Great visibility in shallow water that goes out a couple hundred feet to a reef and a so-called shipwreck, which is actually replica cannons and anchors that the townspeople kindly planted like Easter eggs." He began enthusiastically counting off on his fingers.

"I saw tarpon and lobster and rays and nurse sharks, a turtle, a moray eel—"

"Mmmm! Mmmm!"

"What?" Serge asked their guest. "You don't like snorkeling?"

"He doesn't like being tied up," said Coleman. "And duct-taped."

"Probably the chair. It lacks that ergonomic look." Serge walked over and began tapping the hostage on the head with his snorkel. "Is it the chair?"

"Mmmm! Mmmm!"

Serge turned around to Coleman and nodded. "It's the chair."

"Mmmm! Mmmm!"

"Sorry, it's the only one in the room," Serge told the guest. "Should have figured that into your plans today when you strayed from the decency herd."

Coleman sat at the foot of a bed and clicked the TV on. A local broadcast began. "Hey, Serge, isn't that the place we were at earlier?"

"Shhhhh!"

". . . We lead off tonight's news with the story everyone's talking about. A convenience store surveillance camera captured this footage . . ."

Coleman gestured with a beer. "There's the guy grabbing the wallet. And there you go."

"Watch the suds!"

". . . The theft is trending heavily on the web with comments we cannot repeat on the air. Fortunately, we're able to report the story has a happy ending as this anonymous Good Samaritan was somehow able to retrieve the wallet and return it to its rightful owner . . ."

"And there you are coming back in the store!"

Serge just glared at Coleman and toweled Schlitz off his arm.

"Mmmm! Mmmm!"

"Hold tight a sec," Serge told the hostage, before draining an entire cup of 7-Eleven coffee. "Ahhhh, that's better. Now relax, because you're in the best hands possible. I know it doesn't intuitively seem that way with all your rope and tape, but we've done this a hundred times, and I'm all about safety. If you're staying in a budget Florida motel, you can never be too careful. First, strictly obey the sign inside your motel room, saying not to open the door for people unknown to you. Of course, I always open up because I'm a professional. I *have* to open up. Call it curiosity: What is the nutty backstory of the person knocking? One time I was in this bargain-basement motel and opened the door and it was this woman with a duffel bag asking if I had any detergent because the laundry vending machine was out. I said sure, but I require payment. She said she only had enough change for the wash, and I said, 'Not money, I want backstory.' So I walked with her to the laundry, and she starts pulling socks and T-shirts out of the duffel bag and brushing off all these twigs and leaves before dumping them into the washer, and she tells me how grateful she was to be staying at the motel. I asked where she was staying before. She says, and I quote, 'Sleeping in the woods sucks!' I asked how she suddenly became upwardly mobile, and she tells me she went down to the employment office and got a waver. I'm thinking she meant 'waiver,' like for unemployment money or something, and she says, 'No, I got a job waving a sign on the sidewalk outside a strip mall. Today was my first day, and they pay at the end of the shift, and I was able to get a room here tonight.' Then she reaches in the duffel and pulls out this costume for the washer, and I said, 'Holy crap, you're one of the Statue of Liberty sign wavers?' She says it was that or the gorilla. And now every time I'm driving and see someone waving a sign in a Statue of Liberty costume, I think, damn, that's all that's standing between sleeping in the woods. So now I always carry extra little boxes of detergent to accelerate the process. Other times I get bored in a motel room because nobody knocks, so *I* knock. And when someone answers I say, 'You shouldn't have opened up. Please observe the warning on the back of the door. Luckily, it's just me. Backstory, please.' And the stories! Hoo-wee! One guy said he was there because his wife was hurling a series of heavy objects again and he got tired of ducking. Another had blood all over his T-shirt and said it was from shaving and could he borrow my ID. But enough about me! Let's see how you're trending, shall we?" Serge grabbed his smartphone and looked up the Internet post of the wallet snatching. He kept glancing dubiously at the hostage as he scrolled down through the profane comment thread. He whistled and turned the phone off. "Trust me, seeing that will only complicate your digestive tract. But suffice it to say there's a massive lynch mob out there looking for you right now. I guess you're just lucky to be in here with us."

"Mmmm! Mmmm!"

"Coleman, I think he wants to see my new toys." Serge picked something up off the bed. "First, the mask is key to snorkeling, like speakers to a stereo. If you can't see shit, what's the point? Second, a self-purging top-of-the-line snorkel. Next, my booties, which allow me to wear these super-long open-ocean fins that cost a fortune. Then this—"

"Mmmm! Mmmm!"

"What? It's just a speargun," said Serge. "You think

I'm going to use it on you? Please! Give me more credit for imagination."

Finally, Serge picked up a small pole that the prisoner didn't recognize and Serge didn't explain. He reached into his backpack for a hacksaw and began cutting the end off the stick. "There. That about does it."

"Time for the bonus round?" asked Coleman.

Chapter 11

Twenty-Five Years Ago

Long black eyelashes flickered in the soft dawn sunlight drifting into the second floor, through fronds of royal palms and gossamer linen curtains.

"Good morning, sunshine!"

A young girl raised her head off a pillow and yawned.

Someday she would be famous.

But for right now it was just roller skating and getting those darn training wheels off her bike.

"Are you sure you're ready?"

She nodded, strapping on a tiny helmet covered with daisies. Her knee and elbow pads were already in place. She checked out all the equipment like an astronaut. In a way, it *was* a space race. Three boys on the block her age were getting close to losing their own training wheels, and she couldn't let them beat her to it.

"Do you need help?"

She shook her head. Then clicked a socket wrench to the counterclockwise setting and grunted as a nut became unstuck and began to turn.

"How'd you learn to do that?"

"Figured it out." She cast one of the wheel struts aside with scorn like someone finally able to throw away crutches. She went to work on the other one.

Her mother watched with concern. And curious pride. The socket wrench was no surprise. She remembered the time a couple years earlier, after her daughter's fourth birthday, when the youngster received an artistic easel for crayon drawings. The mother wanted to nurture her creative side. That afternoon she had checked in on her daughter's bedroom and found her coloring away at her desk. The drawing was a happy scene of a house with two equally happy people looking out the windows. The daughter had to imagine the chimney with smoke, because they didn't have a fireplace in Florida. A dog they didn't have ran across the front lawn. The mother smiled, and made a mental note to get a puppy, and closed the door.

A half hour later, the mom heard a sound she couldn't

fathom. She opened the door. "Dear Lord, what are you doing?"

The child looked up from the floor, where she had sawed the legs off the easel. "Building a go-cart."

"Where'd you get the wheels?"

"Lawnmower."

"We don't have a lawnmower."

"Mr. Holcomb next door does. He also has a saw."

The mother covered her eyes briefly, then collected the contraband and walked the child next door for a teachable moment.

"We're so sorry, Mr. Holcomb." She looked down at her daughter. "Say you're sorry."

"Sorry."

The mom looked back up. "It won't happen again. Here are your wheels and saw."

The neighbor was more impressed than angry. "How on earth did she . . . ?"

Of course, there were conceptual flaws with Operation Go-Cart, but the Wright Brothers also had their false starts. Today, however, with the training wheels properly removed, it was all systems go.

The girl straddled her pink bike with feet on the sidewalk and assessed the task at hand. What an idyllic time and place to be a child with all of life lying ahead! The smell of the grass on a Saturday morning, laughter from nearby yards where kids played tag. A warm sun, and other parents loading up a car of gleeful children for a five-minute trip to the beach. More tots giggled and splashed in an inflatable pool.

A different mood on the pink bicycle. A fierce glare of determination that bordered on predatory.

"Are you sure you're ready for this?" her mom asked again.

The child answered by placing her right foot on a pedal and pushing off. And promptly toppling over into the grass.

"Are you okay?"

"I'm fine." The child righted the bike and started again and fell over again on the lawn. Another five attempts with the same results. She had traveled only twenty feet on the sidewalk. Then another ten failed tries with no sign of discouragement. The next attempt resulted in a particularly nasty spill on the pavement that pulled down a safety pad and scraped a knee bloody.

"Oh, dear." The mother bent down to provide aid.

"Don't touch me!"

That surprised her mom. It was the first such firm utterance from her daughter. But it wasn't disrespectful; it was independence. Her mother had worried about that for a while. She'd read all the magazine articles about the effects of single-parent households, especially on an only child—how some children stray into bad influences and a general life trajectory of that is the antithesis of purpose. Other children, however, compensated for the domestic void with an almost clinical obsession to reject failure.

It began to grow dark. Her mother watched the streetlights come on. How many hours could she keep this up?

On her next attempt, she actually made it ten yards before the spill. That was the watershed. She took stock of what she had done right, and she was off: fifty yards, a hundred, two hundred, turning into the street and making circle after circle like she'd been born on a bike.

She raced back to their driveway and skidded to a stop.

Her mother hugged her hard. "I'm so proud of you, Heather!"

Heather removed her headgear and looked at the daisies. "You think I can get a new helmet?"

Two decades later, Heather took another ugly spill.

She had just been clubbed good with the end of a pugilistic stick.

Heather got up from the ground with a shirt caked in mud and sweat. She took off again, grabbing a rope and vaulting a wooden barricade. The obstacle course subconsciously reminded her of training wheels. She reached the finish line and grabbed her knees and panted.

A man with a crew cut clicked a stopwatch. "Not good enough! Can't you cut it?!"

Heather just took a deep breath and trotted back to the start, beyond the envelope of exhaustion. She again entered the gauntlet of padded clubs, then a ramp and a leap over a water hazard that came up short. More mud, this time on her face.

A stopwatch clicked again at the finish line. "Still no good." The man looked at the darkening sky. "We'll pick it up again tomorrow."

"No!" said Heather. "One more time!"

All the others in attendance just exchanged glances. They got ready with their padded sticks and clubbed her the hardest yet. She vaulted the barrier and hit the ramp. She didn't clear the water hazard again, because it was designed so nobody could, but this time kept her footing, which was the edge she needed. She hit the finish line. The stopwatch clicked.

Heather wiped dirt from her face and looked up. "Well?"

No answer. The instructor shot her a derisive glare before walking away. Heather walked the other way with a smile.

The police academy was particularly brutal on Heather. Whatever they dished out to the men, Heather got a second helping. No encouragement or camaraderie, just vicious, profane insults designed to crush her spirit.

It was purely because she was a woman, and all the extra abuse wasn't fair. But it was because everyone at the academy cared about her. Because the street wasn't fair. Ask anyone in law enforcement, particularly correctional guards. Criminals are masters of exploiting perceived weakness, and they particularly zero in on women. Heather was being prepared.

With brains and grit, Heather rose through the ranks. Not meteoric, but steady. Then came the landmark case. Some boys were playing in a stormwater ditch, trying to hit frogs with rocks, as they are known to do.

An hour later, crime tape, sticks with little flags, detectives in gloves. The bones were photographed where they were found, then bagged and tagged, including a skull with two bullet holes. At first they thought it would be easy, because most of the teeth were intact. Then it wasn't easy. If bones are relatively fresh, forensics is pretty good at pinpointing how long they've been in the ground. But the further back you go, the bigger the margin of error, and without a timeline to look up dental records, it's close to hopeless.

Despite help from the media and pleas to the public, the remains remained anonymous. After six months, Jane Doe went in a box in evidence storage.

It wasn't Heather's case, and she stayed respectfully in her lane. But when it was finally appropriate, she knocked on a lieutenant's door. She had an idea how to solve the case and laid it out. The lieutenant had no idea what she was talking about, and he also had nothing to lose.

The lieutenant was even more shocked when Heather came back with a rough date of birth, 1966, maybe '67. From there it was a simple matter of collecting missing persons reports in that age range, then correlating the home addresses with the geographical location of the grave and moving outward in concentric circles. They got their ID, and arrested the victim's former husband in a retirement park.

"But where on earth did you get such an idea?" asked the lieutenant.

"I like science," said Heather. "I knew we had a crack at it. A long shot, but still a shot. And a bit of luck. We were just fortunate that the victim was alive between 1945 and 1980."

"I'm still confused."

"Mass spectrometry," said Heather. "Before the superpowers knew any better, Cold War atomic testing took place above ground until the ban on atmospheric blasts. Tiny amounts of radioactive fallout circled the entire globe, and anyone alive in that era ended up with varying amounts of isotope in their teeth that, given recent advancements in instrumentation, are highly effective at determining a D.O.B."

Chapter 12

The Present

The budget motel room at Lauderdale-by-the-Sea was still dark. But exciting.

"Mmmm! Mmmm!"

Serge hopped up and down with a big smile. "Be right back . . ." He ran out to the car and returned in a jiff, placing two new items on the bed. He picked up his snorkel and hit the hostage in the head again. "In case you're just tuning in, this is a contest. Some call it a reeducation camp. In either case, the stakes couldn't be higher. Which brings us to the bonus round. Play it right, and you're free to go. Ready?"

"Mmmm! Mmmm!"

"Great! Let's get to it!" He reached for the bed and

held up the two items he'd just brought inside. "This is the first half of the bonus round. Your choice. Which will it be?"

"Mmmm! Mmmm!"

"Good selection!" He cast the kite aside. "This one it is! I wasn't sure which you were going to pick, so I just have a little more tinkering to do."

He reached into the backpack again and unfolded a leather travel tool kit. He grabbed a wrench and some pliers . . .

An hour later, Serge folded the kit back up. "Ding! Ding! Ding! That's the opening bell! Let the contest begin!"

He helped the hostage out of the chair, and Serge put a gun to the back of his head. "I'm going to untie you and remove the tape from your mouth, but no screaming or unappreciated moves or it's no bonus round for you. Do we have a deal?"

A head urgently nodded.

"Okay." Serge ripped the tape and sliced the bindings. "Here's your bonus round. I deduced from that little messiness at the store earlier today that you're big on sprinting. So I'm going to open the back door of this motel, and you can sprint down the beach. If you get away, then you're free."

"So you're going to chase me?"

Serge shrugged. "In my own way. Now git!"

The man didn't need to be told twice. He hightailed it away across the sand. Something flew out the door behind him.

"And there goes your drone!" said Coleman.

Serge stepped onto the back porch and worked a joystick on a fancy remote control. "I've been practicing."

"Like the kite?"

"This takes more finesse . . ."

The drone swooped and soared. The released captive finally heard the buzz and noticed it, repeatedly looking back over his shoulder as it chased him down the beach.

"He's not watching where he's going," said Coleman. "He's trampling sandcastles and blankets and just knocked over that umbrella."

"Such inconsideration." The joystick toggled.

"Now people are yelling," said Coleman. "Isn't this kind of public for one of your contests? Aren't you afraid of getting caught?"

"Why? We're hidden back here on this patio." Serge worked the joystick the other way. "The only thing that's public is the drone, and anyone on the beach could be operating it. Plus, the general public itself is an essential ingredient of my project."

More screaming and shouting as the man ran in frantic circles beneath the unshakable drone.

"Why'd you buy that thing anyway?"

"Aerial reconnaissance of historic sites to look for alien instructions."

"And the speargun?"

"An impulse purchase. I didn't think it through."

"How's that?" asked Coleman.

"When you're snorkeling six miles out, you see sharks all the time and it's no bother. But after you spear your first fish, there's blood in the water and competition for a meal. Some of the sharks get a little too belligerent for my taste."

"How do you deal with it?"

"One solution is a bang stick."

"What's that?"

"A short stick with a spring-loaded chamber on the end containing a twelve-gauge shotgun shell. Sharks will start by nudging you to see what they're up against, so you punch them on the snout. Some don't want the hassle and take off, but others like to start shit. So after the second nudge, it's game on, and during the third pass, you poke it with the end of the bang stick and no more shark. So I bought a bang stick."

"Cool!"

"Not cool!" said Serge. "I was figuring out how to use it and then smacked myself in the forehead. 'What am I doing? I've peacefully coexisted in the ocean with sharks for years, and they've provided me the awesome majesty of their presence in their own element. Now, if I have to go around killing them to pursue a hobby, forget it."

The screaming grew louder.

"Something's happening in the crowd," said Coleman.

"Hey! I know that guy! . . ."

"It's the one from TV! . . ."

"He stole that old man's wallet! . . ."

"Get him! . . ."

"I think he's been recognized," said Coleman. "Now there's another chase besides the drone."

Serge worked his lever back and forth. A propeller toy tilted and banked. "Darn it. I thought I'd practiced enough, but the wind is taking it."

"The people are catching up." Coleman was so engrossed he barely had time to chug. "They've got him surrounded."

"You son of a bitch! . . ."

"You piece of shit! . . ."

"Pick on someone your own age! . . ."

"The general public has come into play. Good development, because this is harder to maneuver than a kite, and he was moving around too much." Serge deftly worked the controls, hovering the drone over the vigilante mob. "There we go. You know the hardest part of flying a drone?"

"Not really."

"The landing. Without a soft enough touch you can break the struts off." Another wiggle of the joystick. The drone descended. "Here we go."

"The crowd's closing in," said Coleman. "Some people now have him by the arms. He's crying and saying he's sorry."

"Too little too late." Serge pulled a lever back. "And he's starting to bore me. Let's wrap this up and go snorkeling."

"Me too?"

"Sure," said Serge. "I'll share my stuff."

"Can I use the speargun?"

"Now I have a mental image of one or both of us with a spear sticking out, so the answer's no."

"What about the bang stick?"

"I told you: That thing is cruel."

"Then I guess you wasted your money on it."

"Not exactly. Remember me getting out the hacksaw back in the motel room?"

"Yeah?"

"I cut the spring-loaded chamber off the end of the

bang stick. Then I used a pair of L-shaped mending brackets from Home Depot to attach it to the landing gear."

"You mean the drone?"

Serge nodded and worked the lever.

"Cool." Chug.

The crowd had a good hold of the thief now, pulling him in opposite directions like a wishbone.

"Ow! You're hurting me! . . ."

"Good! . . ."

"Pull him harder! . . ."

"Punch him in the dick! . . ."

Serge had the drone on final approach. He switched the lever all the way back, and the flying contraption dropped quickly toward the top of the thief's head.

Bang.

"Jesus!" Coleman jumped back. "All those people scattered and fell over like bowling pins. They've got blood everywhere on them."

"So much for the bonus round." Serge turned back to the room. "I'm ready for some real excitement. Let's go look at sponges."

Chapter 13

Ten Years Ago

Nathan Sparrow, attorney-at-law, wanted more.

"But how?" asked Reinhold.

"We've already maxed out on medical bills," said Nash. "And pain and suffering."

"We're still low on projected lost wages," said Sparrow. "Most of our clients are the kind of people who take the bus to work."

"Maybe that's because we advertise on bus benches?"

"We need to expand our marketing budget," said Nathan.

"What does that mean?"

"TV."

Everyone has to start somewhere, and the firm

started at the bottom. They hired a local production company, the kind that specialized in making bad commercials. Intentionally bad. So bad that they were good. People saw the ads over and over. And after the viewers forgot the stupidness, all that was left etched into their memories was the name of a used car dealership or a place to buy engagement rings.

On a Tuesday afternoon, a single camera sat on a stand in front of the courthouse. The producer was actually sitting in one of those tall director's chairs. He had given the lawyers their scripts and props. He raised a big cardboard cone, making a fist with the other hand. "And . . . action!"

They filmed the commercial in a single take.

"That's a wrap!" The producer folded his chair.

The lawyers stood bewildered in their spots marked with tape on the sidewalk.

"That's it?" said Sparrow. "No more filming?"

"Why try to improve perfection?"

"I have a question," said Reinhold. "Why were we all swinging gavels like axes?"

"To bang justice into the system."

"Why were we waving a pom-pom in the other hand?" asked Nash.

"To cheer for the underdog."

"Why did we all have to jump in unison at the end?" asked Reinhold.

"That's your signature move. Everyone needs a signature move," said the producer. "I know you're new at this. Trust me."

The trio of attorneys removed medieval knight helmets and handed them to the prop assistant. "When is this supposed to air?"

"Tonight." The producer began packing up a van that featured gray primer paint on rust patches. "I purchased several prime time blocks on local cable between two and four A.M."

"The middle of the night?" said Nathan. "That doesn't sound very prime."

"It's the most prime of all," said the producer. "Everyone in the business knows that. It's when a key demographic is watching."

"Who's that?"

"Drunk people inclined to pick up the phone for an emergency order of easy-listening hits from the eighties. And in your case, the most likely to get injured."

The next morning, in the conference room of a high-rise office building, lawyers had arrived extra early. A flat-screen was on. Waves of shuddering buyers' remorse. The partners finished watching an overnight recording of the commercial for the third time, and Reinhold hit the remote control for a fourth viewing.

"Stop it!" said Nathan. "I can't look at it anymore!"

"We come off as buffoons!" said Nash.

"What's with the fucking helmets?"

"Thank God it's only aired on the graveyard shift so far."

"Can we pull it from the stations?"

"Do you even have to ask?" said Nathan. "I'm calling as soon as their business offices open at nine."

"What time is it now?"

"Eight fifty-nine."

They went out into the lobby. At precisely nine o'clock, the law firm's automated answering service switched over to their live receptionists.

The phone rang. A secretary answered. "Reinhold, Nash and Sparrow . . ."

Then another ring. "Reinhold, Nash and Sparrow . . ."

Another, and another. "Hold, please . . ." "Hold, please . . ." "Please hold . . ."

The partners exchanged looks.

It went on like that the rest of the morning and into the afternoon. All the lawyers' dance cards were full for the next month.

Back to the conference room:

"Never saw it coming," said Nash. "If that's what a *bad* commercial does, imagine a good one."

"But we don't have the capacity," said Reinhold. "Everyone's calendar is now blocked solid."

"Get out all the résumés on file of people we turned down," said Sparrow. "And I'll call the landlord to see about leasing a bigger office."

Thus entered the age of opulence.

If the partners thought they had trouble spending all their money before, this was the stuff of ancient Rome.

They moved into a coveted downtown office address, and bought waterfront homes on Palm Beach. Side by side in the parking garage: a Rolls, a Bentley, a Ferrari.

They got trophy wives with pre-nups, and divorces with restraining orders. They had full domestic staffs, including nannies for unexpected children they never saw. Steinway pianos and Swiss watches, vases from the Ming dynasty and paintings from Sotheby's auctions.

It became like that montage from the movie *Scarface,* when Tony Montana finally hits it big in the cocaine business, with people carrying duffel bags of cash into the bank. No extravagance was too over-the-top for the law firm, except for the movie's live Bengal tiger in Montana's backyard.

The parties started, every weekend bigger and more outrageous, quickly becoming the fodder for local legend. One soiree featured a real oil-pumping derrick in the foyer, spewing champagne. The next saw contortionists and fire-breathers. Then they rented a Bengal tiger.

It continued unfettered for almost a decade, right up until the aftermath of a most recent shindig, which found the three partners sitting alone out back overlooking the water, puffing hundred-dollar cigars.

"It doesn't get any better," said Nash.

"We finally have everything we always wanted," said Reinhold.

Sparrow puffed his stogie. "I want more."

There were no complaints from his law partners. But again: "How?"

"Easy," said Sparrow. "We just increase our contingency fees."

"Contingency" meant that if the law firm wasn't able to collect any damages, then the client didn't owe them any legal fees. But if the attorneys did win, the partners received a third of the total. It was standard.

Since the projected settlements were quite large,

especially considering how poor many of the clients were, and since it was a no-risk deal for injured parties, they all happily jumped at the arranged split. It was standard . . .

The towering office building had the look of a luxury condominium. It rose thirty-five stories over Flagler and Clematis in the heart of downtown West Palm, a monument to raging modern architecture and gaudy gold-mirrored glass windows. The law firm of Reinhold, Nash & Sparrow was the sole occupant of the top floor on a long-term lease. They had negotiated a sweetheart deal for the prime space. Thank TV. The presence of the law firm and their local celebrity in the building helped attract other occupants and drive up rent.

The trio of lawyers sat in a conference room overlooking Lake Worth, the tony island of Palm Beach and the endlessness of the Atlantic Ocean. The door opened and they uniformly shut up. Assistants brought in a catered lunch from a gourmet restaurant so popular that nobody could get in. The plates featured shrimp-stuffed lobster. The day before, it had been lobster-stuffed shrimp. They required variety. The assistants left. The door closed.

"Now then . . ." Phineas Reinhold dipped a bite in

a tiny metal bowl of melted butter. "What were you thinking our new contingency fee should be?"

Sparrow stuck his own fork in a bowl. "Thirty-nine percent."

"How'd you come up with that number?"

Nathan bit off the end of an imported bread stick. "Sounds better than forty."

"I don't know." Shelton Nash sipped a glass of sparkling water from a natural spring at the foot of the Matterhorn. "It could look bad. Remember when the *Miami Herald* ran an article on that firm that charged a mentally challenged client *ninety* percent? All hell broke loose. They got threats."

They remembered the case. Everyone did. Because it was too true to be fiction.

"That was just wrong," said Sparrow. He didn't mean immoral. He meant tactically short-sighted.

"You do realize that we're already receiving six percent above the declared contingency," said Reinhold. "Through other fees hidden in the fine print."

"Even better."

"What if this gets out?" asked Nash. "I'm still worried about the PR."

"I considered that," said Sparrow. "So now we make all of our clients sign non-disclosure agreements, binding them not to reveal the terms of our contracts, including the existence of non-disclosure agreements."

"But why would people agree to our extra terms?" asked Reinhold.

"Because our customers are different from the customers of almost any other business."

"How's that?"

"They're very desperate."

"Looks like you've got it all covered."

Sparrow nodded and took a leafy bite of arugula, and they finished their lunch in silence.

The next week, the trio was already seated in the conference room. A woman pushed a wheelchair inside. No telling how long her son would need it, maybe forever, thanks to a texting driver. She had to quit her waitress job to provide home care.

"It's a tragedy," said Sparrow. "And there's no way anything we say can alleviate the sadness in your heart. But if it's any solace at all, you'll never have to worry about money again."

"How can you be so sure?" asked the woman.

"We have commercials," said Nash.

Reinhold placed a hand on her shoulder. "You haven't signed anything yet? Not with the insurance company or any other attorneys?"

She shook her head.

A contract was placed before her. "Then sign this." Sparrow handed her a pen.

She leaned over the signature line. She stopped. "This is a pretty thick contract. Shouldn't I read it first?"

"No, it's standard."

She leaned again. And stopped again. "Wait, what's this?"

"What?" said Nash.

"Thirty-nine percent? I've got an uncle who knows an attorney, and he told me before I came here that the standard fee is one-third."

"That's right," said Reinhold. "This isn't standard."

"But why should I agree to more?"

"To pay for commercials," said Sparrow.

"It's a bargain," said Reinhold.

"And if you could initial each page," said Nash.

The woman reluctantly put pen to paper.

Four months later, the mother sat rigid in the front row of the courtroom, her son's wheelchair parked nearby. The jurors were already seated in their box. Everyone waiting for the judge to emerge from chambers.

The insurance company's lawyers arranged documents at their table. But none of the jurors were looking at them. They were all gazing agog at three attorneys seated behind the other table. Because they had been on TV.

The team of Reinhold, Nash & Sparrow looked in unison toward their opponents' table. Blank expressions. The insurance attorneys returned the countenance. It became a staring contest. The defendant's lawyers blinked first. One of them made a motion with his thumb: *Let's meet out in the hall.*

Minutes later, the judge dismissed the confused jurors and thanked them for their service. The mother hugged Nathan Sparrow so tightly around the neck that he thought *he* might need an injury attorney.

"Oh, thank you! Thank you! Thank you!" She began to weep. "You've been a godsend!"

A pre-trial settlement of fifteen million will do that to people.

Sparrow gently pulled her wrists away. "No need to thank us. It's what we do. Just take care of your son."

That evening, a family celebration at the woman's house. All the kin were there, hugging and crying. The TV was on, and the local news began.

Three attorneys stood behind a bank of microphones on the courthouse steps, basking in the announcement of the massive settlement. This was even better than commercials. It was free.

An uncle watched the television in the family's living room. He turned around. "Ellen, how much did you say you got?"

She told him.

"That can't be right." He got a pen and some paper and did the math. "I was right. That's way more than a third."

"I know," said Ellen. "But it was well worth it. They were great."

"They were bullshit artists," said the uncle. "They took advantage of you."

"No, they didn't," said Ellen. "I'm happy."

"You were desperate."

The next day, a phone rang on the top floor of an office building in downtown West Palm Beach. The incoming phone call was so loud that the secretary had to hold the receiver away from her head. "I'll call the newspapers! You won't get away with this!" the uncle shouted before he hung up.

That afternoon, the firm's most junior attorney drew the short straw. He sat in a living room with a mother and her son in a wheelchair. An uncle stood fuming with his arms crossed. He wanted to scream and punch someone, but abided by his solemn promise to remain mute.

The young lawyer fidgeted uncomfortably as he

laid it out. The family's share of the settlement had just dropped by a hundred thousand. And the penalty schedule for subsequent violations of the non-disclosure clause only staggered upward. The uncle was welcome to blab to journalists, if they felt it was worth it.

"But I was bragging about you to him!" said the mother. "I was overcome with joy!"

"Doesn't matter," said the young attorney, standing up with his briefcase. "The law is the law."

Chapter 14

The Present

Sunlight glistened off a majestic dome and a ring of twenty-three stained-glass windows. Just as it had since 1943.

Serge pointed up. "That's what gave me the final clue!"

"What?" said Coleman. "It's just a church."

"Not *just* a church," admonished Serge. "It's Saint Nicholas Greek Orthodox Cathedral, the crown jewel of Tarpon Springs. I've been searching forever!"

Coleman scratched his head. "How hard was it to find such a big building?"

"Not the building." Serge snapped photos. "*Sea Hunt*!"

"I remember that TV show," said Coleman. "It was cool."

"More than cool. The legendary Lloyd Bridges, father of Jeff and Beau, played former navy frogman Mike Nelson, who roams the country, inexplicably getting into a series of dramas that can only be solved with a scuba tank."

"It rocked."

Click, click, click. "But here's the best part: Many of the episodes were shot right here in our fine home state. Silver Springs, Cypress Gardens and, last but not least, the very spot where we're standing today."

Coleman looked around his feet. "But there's no water."

"I know." Serge pulled out a switchblade and began cleaning under his fingernails. "During the first season back in 1958, an unknown actor named Larry Hagman made three guest appearances as the dangerous diver Johnny Greco! That was pre–*I Dream of Jeannie*, and way before 'Who shot J.R.?' from the height of *Dallas.* This discovery makes my whole week!"

"Still drawing a blank."

"Okay, here's how TV used to work." Serge handed Coleman the knife. "Two characters meet for the first time and have a huge fight, which automatically makes them best friends. The formula continued right up through the pilot of *Miami Vice*, when Crockett and Tubbs punch each other on the sailboat. That was the golden era of television."

"And today?"

"The simmering nastiness of *The Bachelor*," said Serge. "I started watching it once, and I thought, 'This is great! They're all going to be best pals!' But it just led to worse shit. Times have changed."

"What am I supposed to do with this knife?"

"Point it at me."

"But I don't want to. You're my friend."

"And after you point it at me, we'll be better friends." Serge hopped on the balls of his feet. "Go ahead."

"If you say so." Coleman weakly held out the knife.

Serge quickly disarmed him, making a spinning wrestling move and pinning Coleman to the sidewalk.

Coleman's eyes looked up from where his face was pressed to the pavement. "When does the friend part get better?"

"It just has." Serge helped him up. "This is the precise location where, in episode eighteen of the first season, called 'The Sponge Divers,' Hagman pulls a knife on Bridges. I know because they were standing in front of this ornate old stone wall in front of the house." He slapped it. "And the wall is still standing to this very day! When I initially saw the episode, I said to myself,

'I recognize that wall. This should be an easy find.' So I came over ten years ago and realized a whole bunch of houses around here have walls like this, a needle in a haystack, so it was back to the DVD player for more analysis, but no landmark clues. I toiled for years with a soul-wrenching emptiness that increased carb intake."

"Then how'd you find it?"

"Dumb luck," said Serge. "When I knew we were coming back over here, I watched the episode again, but I accidentally watched it at regular speed instead of my usual super-slow-mo archaeological method, and right at the end as I'm about to turn it off, Bridges arrives back at the house to say goodbye before his next underwater jam. Except he approached the house from the opposite direction of the knife fight, and there it was behind him, big as day, Saint Nicholas Cathedral diagonally across the road, and that's how I nailed it, the first house on Orange Street off Pinellas Avenue. Let's bow our heads in memory of Hagman and Bridges . . . That's enough." He ran back to the car.

The blue-and-white Cobra wound its way slowly down tight Dodecanese Boulevard, past family-owned pastry and souvenir shops. "I can't get enough of Tarpon Springs! The historic Greek enclave of sponge divers! The sponge market dried up when they started making cheap synthetics, but the people remained, tending the flame of their old ways with traditional restaurants and museums for the tourists. But fortunately the Goldilocks phenomenon is in effect: just the *right* amount of tourists so the heritage isn't drowned out by some fucking sponge roller coaster."

"I hate that," said Coleman.

"Damn straight." Serge turned onto an empty side street and passed the shuttered Zorba's belly-dancing lounge. "But my favorite parts of town are the little places where the locals shop, like that one on your right."

"It's just a little bakery."

"Yet Greek Americans go in and out all day just to get a loaf of Greek bread. It's so simple it's outrageous! . . ."

Ten minutes later, the Cobra sat parked at a curb three blocks away. Serge knocked on the door of a modest bungalow.

An old voice inside: "Just a minute."

It was more than a minute. A white-haired woman with a walker opened up. "Hello?"

"Mrs. Diamandis?"

"Yes?"

"Cuz!"

"What?"

"We're family! I was sent by Ancestors R Us! You're one of the hits from my saliva!" He took a bite from a loaf of bread sticking out of a long brown bag. "I stopped at one of your kickin' bakeries. Ridiculous! I'm also on a mission to make you happy." He extended the loaf. "Want a bite?"

"Not right now."

"I also stopped for some of your local coffee. It comes in these teeny cups, but I'm here to tell you—shazam!—that stuff is radioactive!"

"And you are . . . ?"

"Serge Storms! Like I said, we're related! I want to know all about my folks. Can we come in?"

"Okay, I don't get much company."

She took a seat in a lounger and put her feet up. Serge and Coleman plopped down on an old couch that farted dust.

"Serge," whispered Coleman, "I thought your family came to Florida from Cuba."

"They did," said Serge. "But they were allowed to marry other people who had their own family trees."

The old woman stretched back in her chair. "So how can I help you?"

"I'm here to get my Greek on!" Serge pointed out the front window. "Cool stone wall out front. I have a portable DVD player and the complete *Sea Hunt* collection in the car if you want. Do you know a guy named Dixon on the other coast? He's related, too, and has life figured out. Tell me all about my kinfolk!"

"But I've never heard of you."

"We're third cousins. That's how it works now. You pay money on the Internet and show up on people's porches. I'm sure you've seen the ads. Birthday parties, relatives hugging, a moose attacking a car . . . Wait, that's Farmers Insurance."

The woman smiled. "Funny thing. I said I didn't get much company, but you're the second person this week who showed up asking about my family."

"Really?" Serge sat up in excitement. "Another lost relative and link in the chain?"

"I don't think so."

Serge fell back on the sofa. "Shucks."

"Nice young woman. She had a badge. I think her name was Heather." The woman paused and nodded. "Yes, I'm sure it was Heather."

"What did she want?"

"Just some family information for an investigation. But she said it wasn't important."

"That means she's looking for a serial killer."

"What?"

"That's also how it works now. Or so I'm guessing, because if I was trying to track down the Zodiac or something, that's what I'd do: Get familial hits from the DNA companies and construct a family tree." He turned to Coleman. "This is great news! Not only am

I tracing my roots, but now we're also on the trail of a serial killer!"

"Oh my," said the woman. "Am I in any danger?"

"Naw." Serge flicked his wrist. "The nearest serial killer is probably a million miles away. Got any family albums?"

"Top shelf in that closet."

Serge ran across the room. "Hope you have some pics with those big diving helmets! . . ."

An hour later, various photo albums lay open on the coffee table. The woman had a tray in her lap. "I don't get out much with my legs now." She took a bite of rice and grape leaves. "Can't tell you how good it is to eat the old food. Reminds me of when my husband was still here."

"Glad you like it," said Serge.

"You didn't have to go to the trouble of running out and getting this for me."

"Nonsense," said Serge. "I asked you what I could do to make you happy. And a confession: I'll go all the way to the Parthenon for authentic tzatziki sauce!"

The woman pointed at the TV with a piece of baklava. "Hey, I know that house. I used to walk by there all the time when I was a little girl."

Serge nodded as he dipped a piece of lamb. "Isn't *Sea Hunt* the best?"

Chapter 15

Forty-Five Years Ago

Father Al sat back on the sidelines, enjoyably watching Bobby's life unfold. They were still in contact, but Bobby now had a good grip on things, and the best choice was to give him space to bloom.

That Bobby did. Plus there was a massive growth spurt, which nobody saw coming. He was as tall and strong as anyone in high school, and he was still in the eighth grade. And quite the ballplayer. The priest didn't make his presence known as he stood behind the bleachers for one of Bobby's baseball games. "Holy cow! . . ." He made it a mission to attend every one.

Near the end of the season, the priest sat in a well-appointed office. Two other people smiled back.

"Great to see you, Father Al!" said the principal.

"What brings you around? Reliving glory days on the diamond?" asked a coach. "Heard you were a vacuum cleaner at shortstop."

"A lot has changed since I was here." The priest gazed out the window. "That's a pretty outrageous baseball stadium you've got."

It was. Massive red-brick and granite facade, box seats, oversize scoreboard. Far nicer than most professional minor league parks.

The coach shrugged. "Some of our alumni have done quite well. They like to win state championships."

The principal grinned. "So what does bring you by?"

"I've never asked this before, but there's this kid," said the priest. "His family barely has anything."

The principal maintained cheer. "Of course you realize what our waiting list is, and that's for paying students. But I'd be more than happy to put him through our scholarship process. Except you know the long odds there, too."

"He can hit a baseball a country mile," said the priest. "And he has a knuckleball that'll make you get your eyes tested."

"I know every high school in the district," said the coach. "If he's such a phenom, why haven't I heard about him?"

"Because he's still in eighth grade."

"What? Eighth-graders can't throw knucklers."

"I know it's hard to believe, but if you don't come out to one of his games and see for yourself, you'll be cursing the day you were born when you have to play *against* him next year."

There were zero expectations, but there was also the loyalty of history with Father Al. "Okay, I'll be happy to take a look," said the coach. "When does he play next? . . ."

They sat together in the visiting stands. During the fifth inning, the pair craned their necks back to watch a ball clear the outfield lights. In the bottom of the seventh, they watched a young knuckleballer put the finishing touches on a no-hitter by striking out the side. After the game, the coach simply looked at Father Al without speaking, and hurried to his car.

The next evening the priest was back at Bobby's duplex, and it wasn't dinnertime.

His mother sat on the couch and looked puzzled at the priest. "So what's this big surprise you mentioned on the phone?"

"I've been following Bobby's progress through school, and he's kept up his grades," said the priest. "To a degree."

She turned toward her son. "I keep telling you there's no reason for those B's."

"I think there *is* a reason," said Father Al. "He's bored."

"He's not working hard enough?" She turned to her son again. "Bobby, is this true?"

"If I may," said the priest. "I've had many talks with Bobby over the years, about the Bible, his subjects at the elementary, other stuff. He's extremely inquisitive."

"Always asking questions, that child."

"Don't get me wrong, he goes to a good school," said Father Al. "But the curriculum is broad because the student body is so large. Kids with minds like Bobby's don't thrive unless they're challenged."

"Then I'll challenge him plenty." Another stern glance at the boy.

"I've given this some thought," said the priest. "You know Jesuit? The school?"

"Yeah, the Catholic one. The *expensive* one. They wear suits to class."

"How would you like Bobby to go there next year?" asked Father Al.

"I'd love it, but it ain't going to happen," she said. "We don't have the money for a regular private school. We don't have any money."

"I can take care of that," said Father Al. "Actually, I already have."

"What are you talking about? Priests don't have any money, either."

"No, but the Jesuit alumni do."

"I don't understand."

"Bobby has become quite the ballplayer."

"Thanks to you," said his mom. "But I still don't understand."

"The alumni love their baseball team and championship banners," said the priest. "They've set up a number of scholarships to lure star players from public schools. I talked to the principal and the coach today after Bobby's game last night, and one of the scholarships is now sitting on the table for your son. He'll go for free. All you have to do is agree."

Instead she jumped up and hugged Father Al harder than ever, and cried.

"I'll take that as a yes," said the priest.

A knock on the door of a private room in the rectory. "Father Al, that kid Bobby is here again."

"Coming."

They met outside on the front steps and took a seat together, just like that first day when a bicycle went missing.

"You made my mom crazy happy last night. She was dancing and singing like she was drunk, but she doesn't drink."

"I'm happy, too."

"You probably have a free dinner waiting at our house every night for the rest of your life."

"Your mother is a good woman."

"I have a question," said Bobby. "You've written me letters from time to time. I know a few friends who've also gotten letters encouraging them. I really appreciate it."

"I appreciate the opportunity. You're all children of God. So what's your question?"

"Why do you sign all the letters *Shalom*?"

"It's about peace."

"Isn't that Jewish?"

"Yes, but there are also more than a dozen references in the New Testament, according to academics, except many have been translated. It's just something I feel."

"I get it. Following your heart. Can I ask you something else?"

"Fire away."

"I'm appreciative and all, but I need some advice about Jesuit," said Bobby. "Most of the students there grew up differently."

"Their families have a lot of money, and you're wondering if you'll fit in?"

"Pretty much," said Bobby. "And everyone wears a coat and tie to class."

"I'm guessing you don't have a coat."

"Mom started a jar last night called 'coat.' There's some pocket change at the bottom."

"Wait here."

When Father Al returned, Bobby saw something worse than a girl's bike.

"What kind of coat is that?"

"Corduroy."

"It's brown."

"It's what I wore when I went to Jesuit."

"What about your other coats?"

"Just this," said the priest. "Jesuit wasn't the fancy place it is today, but just as good academically . . . I don't know why I saved it all these years. Sentimentality, I guess. I want you to have it."

A weak "Thanks."

"You're worried about the other students having nicer coats. Don't," said the priest. "You'll be on the baseball team. You'll do fine."

The priest was more than right. Straight out of the gate his freshman year, Bobby started in right field and did some relief pitching, and it only got better. His sophomore year, he anchored the starting rotation and batted fifth, behind the cleanup spot. The next year, he *was* cleanup. The corduroy coat never came up.

Father Al fell out of the picture by his own design. There was a whole new crop of at-risk children. But for the next four years, he dutifully read the newspaper's sports section and checked for Bobby's name in prep box scores. It was always an occasion to smile.

His senior year, Bobby's school went deep into the playoffs, only to lose the title game. But he was named first-team all-state, and had his choice of scholarships. He picked the University of Florida in Gainesville, where he resumed tearing it up on the diamond.

"You know," said the coach. "We can arrange for some clothes in a way that won't affect eligibility."

"I'm fine." And soon everyone on campus knew the guy in the corduroy jacket. Before he realized it, graduation was upon him and so was the major league draft.

He sat in a dean's office.

The dean stared back. "I'm a little surprised to see you here."

"Why?"

"Because the Mets drafted you, and not a bad signing bonus I hear. Everyone was expecting you to be reporting to camp."

"Drafted in the twenty-second round," said Bobby.

"That means probably a year in rookie league, and if I'm lucky a jump to double-A, and then it's a crapshoot."

"I just assumed it was your dream."

"Continuing my education at your school is my dream."

"Well then, if what we offer eclipses pro baseball, I'm sure we can work something out . . ."

Bobby stayed in Gainesville for his graduate work, which to nobody's surprise he completed a year early. He went for his first job interview.

The potential employer was also a graduate of Florida and a staunch alum. "Saw you pitch a few times, and hit the cover off the ball. Heard you were drafted by the Mets."

"Twenty-second round."

"Most of the guys here would give their eyeteeth to be drafted at all."

"This is my calling," said Bobby. "If you give me a chance, I'll give it my all. You won't be sorry."

"Tell you a secret," said the interviewer. "You were hired before you walked in the door. I know the demands a big-time university sports program places on a student, but you also excelled academically and went on to grad work. Your reputation speaks for itself."

"Thank you."

"Just two things."

"Name it."

"Lose the corduroy."

"Done. What's the second?"

"The name Bobby."

"Yeah, everyone's always called me that since I was a kid."

The interviewer held up a résumé. "From your middle name, Robert."

Bobby nodded.

"What's wrong with your first name?"

Bobby shrugged.

"For our clients, your first name would be a much better fit. Do you think you could live with that?"

"Why not?"

The lawyer stood and shook his hand. "Then welcome to the firm."

"Thank you," said Nathan Sparrow.

Chapter 16

The Present

A blue-and-white Ford Cobra pulled through an official state entrance in the upper Florida Keys.

Serge ran inside a building and slapped a small green book open on the counter. “Hit me!”

A park ranger happily stamped the page. Serge pulled out a magnifying glass to inspect the seal: Windley Key Fossil Reef Geological State Park.

“Have you been here before?” asked the ranger.

“Many times, but that was before the temptation of the passport book, you devious bastards!” Serge flipped pages. “Can you also hit me for the offshore Indian and Lignumvitae Keys parks? If you need an affidavit that I’ve been there . . .”

Stamp. Stamp.

"Excellent work," said Serge. "You should see what the guy selling bait did to my book at the Skyway Pier. Actually, I will show you. Check out this nonsense. Is the process really that complicated? . . . We're off!"

Serge led the way to a trailhead that descended down an incline of dirt and big roots. He pulled out his cell phone and hit buttons. Then waited and listened awhile before hanging up. "Damn!"

"What's the matter?" asked Coleman.

"The third distant cousin from my Ancestors R Us report," said Serge. "I've been calling and calling for days but no answer."

"Why don't you just drive to his house?"

"Because it's in Vermont."

"Where's that?"

"Somewhere near the Arctic Circle," said Serge. "Let's hike . . ."

And they did, down the trail, around trees, past interpretive signs. Coleman stopped on the path. "A little dizzy. Let me catch my breath." He reached toward a tree for balance, and Serge seized him around the waist. They both went tumbling, rolling over and over down the steep trail and ending up against a wall.

Coleman got to his knees. "Why'd you do that?"

"Because you were just about to grab a poisonwood

tree. The sap on its peeling orange bark will give you a rash to beat the band."

"I thought you said this was a nature park."

"It is." Serge hopped up and unsnapped a water bottle from his waist. "One of the best. Also one of the most overlooked because everyone's racing by for the Duval Street bar crawl in Key West!"

"Then why is there a huge wall here in the middle of nature?"

"That's the park's unique feature!" A long chug. "Over a century ago, when Henry Flagler was building his Overseas Railroad, he stopped on this island to quarry tons of limestone for construction material. But now after all these years, nature has reclaimed it with tree growth strangling the former signs of man, and our state had the wisdom to preserve it. It's one of the few parks that you climb *down* into, taking winding trails through trees and brush until you come to an eight-foot-high, geometrically precise wall and have to turn at a right angle. And other trails here take you along the tops of the walls. Where else can you get that?"

"This wall looks weird."

"Isn't it great?" Serge's fingertips explored the texture. "The crews were just looking to quarry limestone, which was left over from the ancient coral reefs that gave rise to this archipelago. In the process, they inadvertently created a magnificent record of the Keys' geological history. It emphatically underscores how high the sea used to be and how solid the bedrock is. That's why Ernest Hemingway got mad at one of his four wives."

"Going tangent?"

"He came home to Key West from some kind of macho trip and found she had given him a present of a new swimming pool. At first he was thrilled. Then he learned the cost of chiseling and blasting through solid rock, instead of just scooping out dirt for a pool." Serge's hands continued along the wall. "Check out the cross-sections of these fossilized corals and sea fans."

Coleman pointed the other way. "What are those rusty things?"

"Some of the digging machines they left behind. And over there are a bunch of the multi-ton blocks that I guess were extras, now sitting here like some mystery from Easter Island." Serge made a military-style pivot at a corner of the wall and headed west. "This is one of those tranquil places where I like to review my philosophy on the human condition."

"Such as?"

"You've heard that we are now in the post-fact era?"

"No."

"It's been in the news but nobody believes it." Serge

climbed over another root. “Anyway, I figured it out. The problem is that the human brain has evolved faster than its ability to cope with the consequences of what it perceives. That’s why denial is so big these days: ‘I can’t believe my car just ran out of gas. Who did this to me? I need to vote against some group that looks different.’”

“Denial?”

“Think about it,” said Serge. “Humans are the only creatures on earth with the capacity for denial. With the possible exception of cats: ‘Not my hairball. Ask the other cat.’”

“I had a hairball once.”

“Understanding denial is all part of my mission to make other people happy.” Serge pushed away some vines that swung back and smacked Coleman.

“Ow! I’m not happy.”

“Here’s the Whole Deal of Existence,” said Serge. “When you’re born, life presents you with a precious basket of golden droplets, and each drop is a fleeting second on earth to be happy. It makes no sense to just scatter them in the street because you’re typing another twenty angry posts in a Twitter diss-war.” Serge pulled out his state park passport book, flipping to an element-worn page.

“Why do you keep looking at those upside-down stamps if they make you angry?”

"I'm conditioning myself not to waste the golden droplets," said Serge. "When I'm able to look at these fucked-up stamps with acceptance and unconditional love for the bait industry, I'm ready to move on to the Sermon on the Mount."

"How's it working out?"

He stowed the book. "I don't want to talk about it. Let's get out of here . . ."

They ended up in another economy motel, this one at Everglades City.

A red pushpin stuck a notecard to a corkboard. Serge tied a purple strand of yarn to it, and stretched it down to another pushpin.

Coleman regained consciousness on the floor. "What are you doing?"

Serge stood back and inspected his work. "Running out of corkboard."

"Just buy another one."

Serge turned around. "I see you missed the beds again."

"It's too tricky."

Another notecard went up. "You know, I've been revisiting my thoughts on the Statue of Liberty," said Serge. "I think I need one of those costumes."

"What for?"

"It dovetails with the Sermon on the Mount,"

said Serge. "There's a plaque in New York Harbor at the base of the statue that bears repeating: 'Give me your tired, your poor, your huddled masses yearning to breathe free, the wretched refuse of your teeming shore. Send these, the homeless, tempest-tost, to me.'"

"I can dig it."

"But judging from the current mood of the nation, apparently that plaque has become caked over with mud," said Serge.

"What mood?"

"Haven't you been paying attention?" said Serge. "The whole nation's constantly pissed off. And over what? Sure, there are always improvements to be made, but fundamentally it's a fantastic country full of loving people and neighborhoods with unlimited potential if we just come together as a family, from sea to shining sea, in the only country that cites the pursuit of happiness in its founding creed."

"What's changed?"

"The heartbreak of squandered golden droplets. Large groups of enraged people chanting God knows what," said Serge. "The funny thing is that they really seem to be enjoying themselves. Who would have ever guessed this is where the 'pursuit' would lead? Millions of Americans aren't happy unless they're unhappy."

"What a bummer."

"Someone needs to jump-start those words at the bottom of the statue," said Serge. "That's why I want one of those green costumes. I'm thinking of making a sign." He approached the corkboard and wrote something on another notecard.

Coleman sat up and yawned. "How's it coming?"

"Not bad." He snipped an orange piece of yarn. "I never knew what an interesting family I had, how it spanned the Florida experience. There's that Greek sponge diver from the family album we saw, a cowhand who drove cattle through Yeehaw Junction, a bellhop from old Miami Beach when the Marx Brothers filmed *The Cocoanuts*, a tender of the Canaveral lighthouse, an Ybor reader—"

"What's that?"

"Back in the late nineteenth century, Tampa had all these cigar factories in the Cuban section of town, called Ybor City. A few hundred people would sit at long tables in a massive open room rolling cigars all day." Another notecard was tacked up. "Of course, it got tedious, and the radio hadn't been invented, so one person would sit at the front of the room on a tall stool and read the day's newspapers."

"You got all those notecards from your saliva?"

"No, I told you, I only got three distant familial hits." He turned on his laptop and logged into a website with sepia-tone photos. "But there are other genealogical services that don't use spit. You take what few facts you have—last name, birthday, city, whatever—and plug them in, and sometimes you'll get lucky, and it coughs up more family data, and you plug that stuff in, and so on."

"You're really getting into it."

"And how," said Serge. "Tracking a serial killer makes the family-tree hobby a much happier experience. The services should be adding that as a bonus feature." He stared with his nose a few inches from the cards. "Which ancestor will be the one who cracks the case?"

Coleman got up and pointed with a freshly popped beer. "One of the cards is blank."

"The third familial hit that I've been trying to reach. Remember me calling and calling from the state park?" He flipped open a notebook. "I only got an address in Craftsbury, Vermont, so I paid five bucks for an online directory service and got the phone number I've been trying to call, except it's looking like a dry hole."

"Vermont," said Coleman. "Fuck."

"But I don't know the word 'failure.'"

"I do," said Coleman.

"Shut up, I'm dialing again." He listened. "It's ringing. At least that's something . . ." Suddenly, surprise:

"Oh, uh, hello? Is Mr. Lee there? . . . Who's calling? A long-lost relative that's dying to catch up. . . . He's not there? When will he be back? . . . What do you mean, possibly May? . . . He's in *Florida*? What's he doing down here? . . . Yes, I know it's winter. . . . No, I don't know how freezing Vermont gets. Who would live in such conditions? Why are *you* there? . . . Oh, the caretaker. . . . Listen, actually I'm down in Florida myself, so this is a huge break in tracing my kin and tracking the serial—uh, serial numbers, antique pocket watches, yeah, that's it, a hobby. Any possibility that I can contact him? . . . He likes to stay off the radar? No cell phone or even a clock? Darn! . . . What? An address? Yes, I have a pen . . ." Serge wrote in the palm of his left hand. "Thanks, you've been a great help. And really give the Vermont thing some more thought. Later."

"What happened?" said Coleman.

"Road trip!"

Chapter 17

Palm Beach

Lights twinkled over the water. Champagne glasses clinked. Young men in white shorts sprinted down the driveway with exotic key fobs.

Inside on a flat-screen TV, brilliant red-white-and-blue bursts in the night sky on a Fourth of July. The commercial ended.

Congratulatory slaps on Nathan Sparrow's back.

"I don't know how you do it . . ."

"This one's the best yet . . ."

"You can never go wrong with kittens and string . . ."

Laughter and liquor-loosened chitchat filled the mansion.

"He's late," someone told Sparrow.

"The food's ready," said someone else.

Nathan paused and took a deep breath for a decision. "Okay, let's just get started . . . Everyone! Can I have your attention?"

The hubbub died down. The agenda was slightly different from all the other cocktail parties. A series of elongated dinner tables had been trucked in and now filled the more-than-ample open floor plan of the party room overlooking the water. People took seats, and the white-gloved catering staff began serving the $75,000-a-plate guests.

Goat cheese and walnut salad. Quail. Truffles. Foie gras, created by torturing ducks to enlarge their livers for the enjoyment of the political-donor class.

Six police motorcycles with flashing blue lights came up the street and scattered valets onto lawns.

A limo.

Someone saw the lights through the front windows. "He's here."

The candidate entered with a million-watt smile. Food got cold as guests rose from the table for handshakes and well wishes for the rising star and current darling of half the population. A long, upward career: city council, mayor, congressman, and now the front-runner for bigger things. The candidate wormed his way through the crowd, waving at pretend friends.

The catering staff stood back respectfully, hands clasped in front of them as rehearsed. They'd seen their share of these cynical fetes, but many actually came to like some of the politicians. Most of the candidates were savvy enough to carve out time and visit the kitchen to individually thank the help. But good luck tonight.

After everyone was full and signaling for cocktail refills, Nathan Sparrow tapped a water glass with a spoon.

"Good evening, and thank you all for coming. Oh, and for your money . . ."

Ripples of laughter.

". . . But we're all in agreement that it's for an excellent cause. Good government can't be taken for granted, as unfortunately many do nowadays . . ."

Nodding around the tables. Everyone knew who he was talking about.

". . . Enough of my yapping," said Sparrow. "I'm humbled to introduce the person you've all come to see, the next senator from the great state of Florida, Jack Grayson!"

Grayson patted Sparrow's arm as he took his place at the front of the main table. "Thank you, Nathan, for all your years of support. We go back how far? The council?"

"Actually, school board," said Nathan.

"That's right. Time flies." He faced his audience

again for boilerplate platitudes and stale jokes that produced staler laughs.

". . . Anyway, I'm glad you're all here, because our nation faces serious problems . . ."

He meant the taxes they were all paying, and how the money was all being spent. The remarks were tailored for the private audience. And they went over big, as only divisive remarks can go over. The uglier it got, the happier they got.

So happy, in fact, that nobody noticed the security guard standing along the back wall, holding his cell phone in an unobtrusive manner to conceal the red "record" button.

". . . Thank you! Thank you!" said Grayson, pushing down with his hands. "Please, hold your applause for victory night! . . . In conclusion—"

Shouting suddenly cut him off.

"Stop! What's that?"

"Get your hands off me!"

A scuffle broke out. The candidate strained to see. All heads turned toward a pair of security guards pinning a third guard against a doorway.

Sparrow raced over. "What's the meaning of this outrage! You interrupted our guest of honor!"

"Sir," said one of the guards, "we caught him filming with his phone."

The guard handed the confiscated device to Sparrow, who looked like he had just been given a wet turd. "This is unheard of! Get him out of here! And I'll be calling your company tomorrow!"

The candidate's handlers arrived. Sparrow explained the problem, but said they had nothing to worry about. He had quashed it in time and seized the contraband phone.

"But you swore to us you had procedures in place!" said one of the handlers. "Remember what happened to Romney in Boca?"

"That's right," said Sparrow. "That's why I hired security to check all the caterers. They even use metal detectors."

"But it was one of the security guards who was recording!"

"That's why I have other security guards. The procedures worked." Then he turned with a large smile toward the rest of the silent, curious room. "Everything's fine. Just a little hiccup, but it's all over now." Another turn of his eyes. ". . . Senator—I mean our *next* senator, please continue."

The guests knew that everything definitely was not fine, but they took their host's cue and adopted the fiction that all was dandy. Polite, aside comments.

After an understandably fumbling start, the candidate regained his poise to wrap it up. Finally, a huge two-armed wave. "Thank you all so much for coming!"

There was the usual perfunctory post-event glad-handing. Grayson was still smiling as he whispered out the corner of his mouth to an assistant. The assistant whispered back. The candidate remained cheerful as he shook the last of the hands. Then he stormed down a hallway into one of the many bedrooms, the master, and summoned Sparrow.

A door slammed shut behind them, and Grayson spun toward the lawyer. "Of all the goddamn stupid fucking things! I trusted you, you worthless moron! . . ."

Sparrow held his counsel. He had dealt with enough politicians in his day, which meant enough childishness. How these people could run anything, much less govern, was beyond him. He thought: *Grayson just needs time to vent a little.*

A minute went by. Then two, and three.

"This could blow up in my face, you ignorant cocksucker! . . ."

Okay, this was past venting. Nobody had talked to Sparrow like this in almost thirty years. And in his own house. His own *bedroom.*

The candidate's handlers squirmed as they waited just outside the closed door. At moments like these, it was unspoken that they were not to enter under any circumstances. But the shouting was getting too loud. So much so that departing guests were craning their necks to see down the hall.

The loudest profanity yet reverberated from the door. "Recording me? Jesus Christ! How am I supposed to tell these assholes what they want to hear and still get elected? Fuck me! No, better yet, fuck you! . . ."

The chief of staff outside the door: "Screw it!" He burst into the room. "Sir! You've *got* to lower your voice! People can hear! *Everyone* can hear!"

The candidate gritted his teeth and paused to barely regain control. Finally he stuck a finger in Sparrow's face that actually brushed the tip of his nose. "I'm not done with you!" He stormed back out of the room.

"Sorry about that," a handler told the attorney. "He'll be fine." The chief of staff followed the candidate to the street, and an array of flashing blue lights led the whole ugliness away.

Chapter 18

Pine Island

Just north of Fort Myers, the 1970 Cobra crossed a small bridge with a sign: ISLAND TIME STARTS HERE.

"Hey, I remember this place." Coleman cupped a joint below window level. "It's that hippie-dippy little town with all the psychedelic buildings."

"More like Jamaican buildings." Serge drove extra slow to avoid all the pedestrians hugging the shoulders of the narrow road. "It's the hidden small-town jewel of Matlacha. Arts and crafts galleries and waterfront seafood dining to die for."

The Cobra left the town behind and, a few miles later, crossed another bridge into one of those laid-back communities with no stoplights.

"A cop! He's waving at us!" Coleman swallowed the still-lit joint.

Serge turned slowly. "You have seen a traffic cop before, haven't you?"

"No hard questions right now." Drool down his shirt. "There's something wrong with my tongue."

The cop waved the Cobra onto Stringfellow Road near the Pine Island Public Library. Serge looked at the writing in his left palm. "I wonder where this address is."

Several miles north, past all the palm tree farms, he would have his answer. The Cobra slowly wound through the snaking turns on Pineland Road until they came to the water. "I remember now. This is one of the places to catch a ferry to Cabbage Key." He slowed even more, checking house numbers against his palm. After several mini-mansions of fresh construction, he stopped at a different style of home across from the Tarpon Lodge. Weathered wooden vernacular construction with a screened porch wrapping all the way around. A tiny widow's walk stuck out of the attic. And all of it sitting atop an ancient Indian shell mound. The house number matched Serge's hand.

"How do I know this place?" Serge opened the driver's door. "Oh, well, it'll come to me."

The pair climbed the mound and Serge knocked hard on a wooden screen door that rattled like the hinges were about to give up. "Mr. Lee? Are you in there? . . . *Mr. Lee!*"

Coleman got on his tiptoes to peek in a window. "Maybe he's not home."

Serge pursed his lips. "I don't know. There's an old Buick with a Vermont plate parked over there in the dirt . . . Let's take a look around the property . . . *Mr. Lee!* . . ."

They rounded the corner of the house, where a second Indian mound rose from the other side of the backyard. In the middle of the lawn stood a tall, thin man with a head of wild white hair shooting out from under a cap. The man didn't notice Serge and Coleman because he was concentrating. He had a baseball in one hand. The other hand gripped the bat on his shoulder. He tossed the ball, and smashed it with the Louisville Slugger, sending the ball straight up high into the blue yonder. Then he dropped the bat and picked up a glove on the ground at his feet. He circled around under the falling ball, and just before it got to him, he quickly swung the glove for a perfect behind-the-back basket catch.

That's when he finally saw his two visitors. "Can I help you?"

"Hope so," said Serge. "And that was a nifty trick."

The man shrugged. "Something I've done since

I was a kid, when I want to play baseball but there's nobody to play with . . . So are you friends of Randy?"

"Randy who?"

"White, the writer. This used to be his home. Actually, he still owns it, but now he lives on Sanibel and lets me stay here in the winter."

Serge snapped his fingers. "That's how I know this place. I've seen photos of White's house online."

The man got down on his knees and began pulling weeds from a small garden of Thai basil. "So if you're not friends of Randy, why are you here?"

"Are you Mr. Lee?"

"Yes."

"William Francis Lee?"

"You got him."

"We're related. Distant cousins. If you need proof, the corkboard is in the car. I'm on an ancestry jag, and you popped up in the results from a DNA service." He extended a hand downward to shake. "Name's Storms. Serge Storms."

"Nice to meet you," said the man. "Not sure about the relative thing, but I'm fascinated by history and research like that."

"Don't even get me started on history. The stories I could tell you . . ." Serge's words slowly dribbled off. He looked at the man's Red Sox cap as a growing wave of recognition washed over him. "Wait . . . just . . . a . . . second! . . . The 'William Francis' from the ancestry people threw me off . . . You wouldn't happen to be Bill Lee? Bill *Spaceman* Lee?"

A grin. "That's what they've been calling me for a while now."

Serge was actually jumping without realizing. "Coleman, do you have any idea who we've just stumbled across?"

Coleman was jumping, too. "I know! I know! I can't believe I'm meeting him!"

Serge stopped jumping. "Coleman, sometimes you surprise me. You actually know about the Spaceman?"

"Absolutely!" said Coleman.

"I didn't know you were a baseball fan."

"What are you talking about?" said Coleman. "He was on the cover of *High Times*!"

"Coleman, this is the famous Major League Baseball pitcher: all-star game, World Series, you name it."

"Who cares if he played baseball?" said Coleman. "He was in *High Times.* That's bigger."

"No, it's not," said Serge. "He won a mind-numbing fifty-one games over a three-year span and was renowned for his three-dimensional-chess-like ability to outwit opposing batters with a ridiculous assortment of pitches including his trademark Spaceball or

Leephus—which is a contraction of Lee and Eephus, the famous old 1940s high-arcing surprise pitch. A sportscaster once remarked, 'He's thrown everything up there but the rosin bag!' In 1979, the *Sporting News* even named him left-hander of the year."

Coleman shook his head. "*High Times.*"

Serge turned. "Bill, help me here."

"I was in *High Times.*" A big laugh. "Baseball Commissioner Bowie Kuhn fined me for saying I smoked marijuana. I told him I never said that. He said, then what did you say? I told him I sprinkled it on my pancakes because it made me impervious to automobile exhaust when I jogged through downtown Boston. Still fined me."

"Mr. Lee . . ." Serge pointed at Coleman rolling a joint. "You realize you're only encouraging him."

"I somehow get the feeling he doesn't need encouraging," said Lee.

"You are indeed wise." Serge pointed at the baseball on the ground. "I know we just met, but could I possibly ask you a favor?"

"Sure," said Bill. "I'd be more than happy to autograph it for you."

"No, I don't want you to sign it," said Serge. "I want you to *throw* it."

"You what?"

"I want to play catch."

They scrounged up a spare glove for Serge and paced off the regulation pitcher's mound distance of sixty feet, six inches.

After warming up, Serge held out his glove for a real pitch. "Okay, don't burn me out."

"I won't." Bill demonstrated his grip on the ball. "Two-seam curve, low and away."

The ball did exactly as described, and Serge didn't need to catch it as much as just hold the glove, and the pitch buried itself deep in the webbing.

"My turn," said Serge. "Remember your teammate Luis Tiant? What an insane windup! He'd turn his back completely on the batter with a leg kick toward the outfield, then after a series of gyrations, he'd whip the ball home. Here's my impression of Luis Tiant!"

Serge spun through a menu of spasms before twirling and releasing the pitch with all his might.

Bill looked high in the sky as the ball sailed over the Indian mound and crashed unseen into trees on the other side. "I'll get another ball."

Lee displayed his grip again. "Slider. Watch the laces corkscrew toward you."

The ball spun on an unexpected axis and lodged tight in Serge's glove. "All right. I know what I did wrong. Luis Tiant again! . . ."

The ball flew over the Indian mound.

"I'll get another ball," said Bill. "Actually I'd better get a few."

Fifteen minutes later. "I hope you take requests," said Serge. "I'll die a happy man if you could throw me the ol' 'Leephus' pitch."

Bill grinned. "Been a while, but okay, here it comes."

The windup looked normal, but the ball was released in a high, slow arc that would cross the strike zone at a steep downward angle, leaving batters cross-eyed and stupid.

Serge snatched it with his glove. "That was outrageous!" He hocked in his throwing hand. "And now here's my Gaylord Perry illegal spitball . . ."

They watched his throw fly deep into the trees.

"We are now officially out of baseballs," said Lee, taking off the cap and wiping his forehead. "Want to come on the porch and have a beer?"

"Yes!" Coleman took off running for the screen door.

They sat in the warm sunlight of the rustic wooden screened porch overlooking Pine Island Sound.

"So," said Serge. "What's the Spaceman been up to down here? It must be something radical!"

"Living off the grid and in the moment."

"How do you do that?"

"Gardening."

"That doesn't sound radical."

"But it is," said Lee. "You saw me weeding the basil, plus I've got potatoes, collard greens, avocados, black-eyed peas, mangoes, Key lime. It's like meditation. Growing your own food somehow plugs you into the spiritual current of life."

Coleman fired up a fatty and exhaled a big hit. "Far out."

"Coleman!" snapped Serge. "One of the rules of being a proper houseguest is to not immediately start doing crimes. It might even be the top rule."

"You do it all the time. And leave blood all over stuff."

Serge chuckled at the ballplayer. "He's just jabbering."

Coleman held another toke and offered the joint to the player. "I'd be honored. *High Times.*"

Lee waved it off. "Despite my rep, those were younger days, back in the mist."

Serge opened a notebook and clicked a pen. "Do you mind? Just a few questions?"

"Fire away."

"I'm tracing my family tree and got that hit on you I mentioned earlier. Tell me about your family. Or rather *our* family."

"Well, it's a baseball family," said Lee. "My grandfather played semi-pro in the Pacific Coast League, but the real athletes in my family were the women."

Serge scribbled furiously. "You don't say."

"Remember the movie *A League of Their Own* with Tom Hanks and Madonna? In real life, that was the team my aunt Annabelle played for, throwing the league's first-ever perfect game in 1944 and a no-hitter the following year. She had a wicked knuckleball. She's the one who taught me how to pitch."

"No shit?"

"My grandmother also played, and at age forty-seven broke her leg sliding into second base," said Lee. "If you were in my family, you played baseball until you couldn't."

"What about heirlooms?" said Serge. "Anything I can touch to get a cosmic vibe about my kin."

"Hmmm, there is one thing. It's in my trunk. Don't know how much help it will be."

Serge followed him down the driveway. Lee popped the lid and dug around the bottom of the trunk before pulling out an ancient baseball glove. "I take this with me everywhere. My dad gave it to me when I started playing."

He handed it to Serge, who noticed ink on the various leather fingers. "What's with all this writing?"

"My dad's advice to me as a boy."

Serge looked back down and read the inscriptions:

"*Be smooth,*" "*Keep the ball down,*" "*Don't alibi,*" "*Hustle.*"

"Definitely getting a vibe." Serge handed the glove back. "Which reminds me. Any relatives you think might be a serial killer?"

"What?"

"Oh, this is the coolest part!" Serge smiled wide and clapped his hands. "Besides learning all kinds of mind-blowing stuff about my heritage, I'm also on the trail of a deranged psychopath. Didn't know it when I started, but this third cousin in Tarpon Springs told me she was visited by state agents who got a DNA hit on her and were trying to construct a family tree. What else could it be?"

"A lot of things," said Lee.

Serge vigorously shook his head. "I know how cops think because, well, I have to. It's an off-the-grid thing with me, too."

Lee shrugged. "So where are you from, anyway?"

"Riviera Beach."

Lee's eyes popped. "You've got to be kidding!"

"Why?"

"I *love* Riviera Beach!" said Lee. "After the Red Sox traded me to the Expos in 1979, spring training was in West Palm Beach, and I would ride my bike and jog all over the place. Used to take the Blue Heron Bridge out to Singer Island and fish from the jetty by the pump house because all kinds of outrageous fish come through that inlet from the Atlantic. These Vietnamese guys were always there, giving me tips. And I used to eat at this soul food place on Tamarind Avenue with Andre Dawson. But best of all, there was this famous barbecue joint where I'd order before games and pick it up afterward because the lines were sometimes hours long. Not fancy at all, just a little shack on Dixie Highway, but the food! The cornbread! Except for the life of me I can't remember the name. What was it?"

"You must be talking about Tom's Place," said Serge. "Always long waits, and celebrities like Aretha Franklin and Burt Reynolds a common sight."

Lee snapped his fingers. "That's right! Tom's Place." He whistled. "Heard it closed down decades ago. A shame. But great while it lasted."

"Then you might need to hold on to your hat," said Serge.

"Why?"

"Tom's was such a beloved local institution in the seventies and eighties that people kept talking about the memories long after it boarded up," said Serge. "The accolades continued, with residents stopping to thank the former owners in public, until it reached such critical mass that they decided to resume the tradition. It just reopened a couple years ago in Boynton Beach."

"Don't be messing with me," said Lee.

"This can mean only one thing." Serge grinned mischievously. "An off-the-grid road trip."

The ballplayer hopped to his feet. "Let's roll!"

"Like right now? So fast?"

"I live in the moment," said Lee.

The 1970 Cobra pulled out of the driveway and turned south, just as a Crown Vic with blackwall tires passed them going the opposite way.

The other car pulled up the driveway, and two state agents got out. Heather knocked on the wooden screen door and waited. No answer. She double-checked the address against her spreadsheet. Yep, right place. She peeked inside and turned to her partner, Archibald. "I don't think he's home." Then she looked down at his hands. "Why'd you bring a baseball and pen with you?"

"For an autograph."

"Arch, we're working," said Heather. "That's so far from professional."

He blushed. "But it's the Spaceman."

Chapter 19

West Palm Beach

It began as any other day at the courthouse. A group of attorneys clustered in the hall.

Sparrow shook his head at the opposing counsel. "We strongly believe our client would be better served taking it to the jury."

"Okay, okay," said one of the attorneys for an insurance company. "Our final offer not to go to trial: seventeen million."

Sparrow smiled. "That's more like it." They shook hands and parted.

A cell phone rang. Sparrow fished it out of his pocket. "Hello?"

There was no opening politeness. Nathan quickly

pulled the phone away from his head as a string of shouted profanities made others in the hall turn around.

"Mr. Grayson, please calm down."

"I told you I wasn't finished with you, you fuck-stick," said the Senate candidate. "You think you can let me be secretly filmed at your house, and there won't be repercussions?"

"Mr. Grayson, you really need to take it easy."

"It's about to start raining shit," said Grayson. "I know where your daughter works! I have friends!"

"What's that supposed to mean?" asked Sparrow.

"You'll soon find out!"

Click.

The attorney stared oddly at the phone before returning it to his pocket.

An hour later, another catered lunch in a conference room on the top floor of a gleaming office tower in downtown West Palm. This time, pan-seared pompano.

"Seventeen million," said Reinhold, shaking his head as he took a bite. "We must have really rattled them."

"I've already set up the press conference," said Nash. "We'll need to eat a little faster than usual because I've timed it to lead into the evening news—"

A cell phone rang. The trio all began checking the pockets of their jackets hanging over the backs of their chairs, because they all had the same ring tone, the catchy jingle from their TV commercials.

"That's me," said Sparrow, looking at the display but not recognizing the number. He put it to his ear. "Hello?"

"Dad, it's your daughter."

Sparrow wasn't expecting that. He didn't know whether they were estranged or not because he never tried to make contact. "Uh, hi, Boo-Boo, how are you doing?"

"Dad, nobody's called me that since you and Mom split up."

"You'll always be my little girl."

"Don't act like everything's normal," said the daughter. "After waiting and waiting to hear from you while I was growing up, I finally swore I'd never speak to you again. But this is an emergency."

"What do you mean?"

"I just had a very strange meeting," said the daughter. "I don't know what to make of this. It's my job."

Sparrow immediately un-reclined. "What about your job?"

"They won't tell me. Just that I'm on paid leave. And they said not to tell anyone it's a *paid* leave. Then my supervisor apologized."

"Did he tell you anything else?"

"Yeah, that he wasn't allowed to tell me anything else. But he said if I had any more questions, I might want to call my father . . . Dad, what's going on?"

"Do you mind if I get back to you? I need to make a few calls and look into this."

"Whatever."

The call ended and the partners were staring.

"What was that about?" Reinhold asked with a full mouth.

"Unbelievable!" said Sparrow. "Grayson just won't let this go."

"Grayson's a twit." Nash forked another bite. "He couldn't find his own dick without his staff."

"At least he gets our legislation passed," said Reinhold.

Sparrow stared at the silent phone he had placed on the conference table. "Guys, would you mind if I had the room? I need to make some calls."

"No problem," said Nash.

"Family's everything." Reinhold stood and grabbed the jacket off the back of his chair. "Take care of whatever this is with your daughter."

They left and closed the door, and Sparrow grabbed his phone. Truth is, he wasn't as concerned about his daughter as much as Grayson's affront to his own pride. A half hour and several calls later, the attorney wrapped up another fruitless conversation. "Okay, well thank you for your time anyway."

Sparrow hadn't expected this, either. Over the years, he'd built up a vast network of friends and contacts, the kind who trade favors. So it was no small surprise that his currency wasn't accepted this time around. He stared up at the ceiling. He realized he'd never really studied the track lighting before. His eyes returned to table level, and he dialed again.

"Boo-Boo, it's me."

"Stop it!"

"Listen, for your own good I can't really tell you what's going on."

"It's politics, isn't it?"

"Yes," said Sparrow. "They told me it's only a temporary arrangement. And they promised you'll keep drawing salary. This will blow over before you know it. Just cash your checks and enjoy the free time. You deserve it."

"Dad, it isn't about the money. You wouldn't know how much my work means to me because you don't know anything about me."

"Can you do me a favor and hold tight and ride this out?"

Click.

Sparrow had that wind-knocked-out-of-him feeling

in his gut. From Grayson, no less. What an oaf. The attorneys had always written the campaign checks with a smile, then secretly wondered how such idiotic clowns could fool the public. And now Sparrow wondered even more how one of them was getting the best of him.

The conference room door opened. "Sorry to intrude," said Nash. "But we have to get going if we want to make it."

The bank of microphones was waiting on the courthouse steps.

"Nathan, are you all right?" asked Reinhold. "You seem a bit lost."

"I'm fine."

"You can always sit this one out," said Nash.

"Let's just get it over with."

A cell phone rang. Three men checked pockets.

"That's mine," said Sparrow. Another number he didn't recognize in the display. "Hello?"

"Is this Mr. Sparrow? Nathan Sparrow?"

"Yes, who's this?"

"The Nathan Sparrow who graduated from Miami Jesuit?"

"Yes, I told you! Now, who is *this*?"

"Mr. Sparrow, I'm one of the school's trustees."

"Oh, you're from Jesuit," said Sparrow. "Sorry for

my tone, but it's been one of those days. What can I do for you?"

"I'm sure you remember Father Al."

"This is about Father Al?" The attorney's mood lifted. "How is he?"

"Mr. Sparrow, I'm afraid I don't have good news . . ."

Moments later, the TV lights came on. "Guys," said Sparrow, "I have to go."

And he ran down the courthouse steps.

Chapter 20

Fort Myers

Serge sped through the city, facing the passenger in the back seat. "Hey, Spaceman, I got an idea. Know what we should do?"

"Watch the road?"

"Naw, I know what I'm doing. Anyway, smile!"

"What?"

Click. "I just had to get a photo of the special day I got to meet the Spaceman," said Serge. "Now if you lean forward, I can take a selfie of the two of us."

"Watch out for that truck!"

"Would that make you happy? I'll turn around." Serge settled back normally into the driver's seat. "There, another good deed from the Sermon on the

Mount. I'll even grip the wheel at the approved ten and two o'clock positions. See? Because that's my recent epiphany on the meaning of life: I'm here to make you as happy as freaking possible. And that's how I got this great idea of what we should do before we head across the state to that rib joint. You know what today is?"

"Thursday?"

"The first day of spring training! Florida's Grapefruit League!" Serge slapped the dashboard. "Technically it's still winter, but that's another story, like what the hell is going on in Vermont? The only bigger tragedy of a state is Arizona, which stole a bunch of our spring training teams to play in their silly Cactus League, where fans get to watch their favorite players while having all the moisture sucked out of their eyeballs. But not the Grapefruit League! Humidity is our brand!"

"The road?"

"I saw that bus. Missed it with inches to spare. Anyway, I'm sure you're well aware that the Red Sox play spring training in Fort Myers at a special field that is a mini replica of Fenway Park in Boston, Green Monster left field wall and all, except no Citgo sign. We just have to go!"

"Actually, that is a good idea," said Lee. "I'd like that."

Serge slapped the dashboard again. "Here to make

you happy!" They drove past an economy motel, and Serge did a double take as they went by. Then glanced up in the rearview. "Mr. Lee, can you help me with something?"

"As long as you keep your eyes on the road."

"Deal." Serge focused ahead like a laser, chugging a jumbo travel mug of coffee. "Can you get the word out to the Sox Nation, and the whole baseball world for that matter?"

"What are you talking about?"

Serge hung his head. "It's the Curse of Spring Training."

"Curse?" said Lee. "Like the Sox and the Bambino, or the Cubs and the billy goat?"

"No, not the game," said Serge. "Fan safety. It's about our motels."

"What about them?"

"*Wellllllll*, here's the problem: Many fine fans of the game come down here for a couple weeks to enjoy these hallowed rites of spring-ish winter. And through no fault of their own, they have limited funds and stay at a budget motel."

"Is there a point you're going toward?" asked Lee.

"There's a precise science to budget motels, and I hold an endowed chair. I'm a professor of dive accommodations," said Serge. "And I pity the tourist who comes down here and not only isn't a student of budget motels, but doesn't even know the science exists."

"Uh, okay."

"The problem is that in Florida we suffer from an embarrassment of riches." Serge swerved to miss a dump truck. "Up north, it's painfully obvious what cheap joints not to stay in: 'Yep, that's a place where I'll be robbed with a bowie knife in the middle of the night by the prison escapees staying in the next room.' But down here in Florida, spring training fans arrive and all they see is sun and palm trees, and think a motel is paradise without noticing the prison escapees hiding behind the azaleas."

"I'll pass that along," said Lee.

"And by 'Curse of Spring Training,' I don't mean to put a pox on Florida's magnificent role in the national pastime. I just coined the phrase as a convenient catch-all, but it's the whole tourism industry. Whether it's baseball or theme parks or beaches, wherever you find a high concentration of visitors trying to stretch their vacation dollar, there's a whole cast of bad actors conducting surveillance. Sometimes they don't even wait for visitors to return to their rooms. At one theme park—and I won't mention it by name, but you'd recognize it—two miscreants climbed the fence and robbed a couple at gunpoint at a souvenir kiosk. The park reacted by topping the fences with spools of razor wire, but local officials made them take it down because they said it projected the wrong image."

"That's really true?"

"I'm dead serious, with the emphasis on *dead*," said Serge. "One baseball fan came down a few years ago and picked the wrong place and got targeted by crack addicts who befriended him, and . . . it didn't end well. A number of tourists have flown down here in coach, and flown back in a box in the belly of the plane."

"Jesus," said Lee. "It's that bad?"

Serge nodded hard. "I can handle it because of my trademark tactics of packing a special safety set of bum clothes: the rattiest, stained, torn stuff you can find to make you the least tempting person to rob. In my case, that's a redundant layer of safety because I'm already the least likely to get robbed, for factors that I'm not at liberty to reveal. Sorry . . . But tourists, hoo-wee! There's a whole industry of criminals waiting by airport exits to follow rental cars, or they specifically look for baseball team pennants hanging in budget motel windows near spring training parks."

"I thought we were on the way to the game," said Lee.

"We are."

"Then why are you circling the block around this motel?"

"Just feel like it." Serge grew more distracted as he observed a Red Sox flag in a window. "Always looking for a future bargain . . . Anyway, that's why I need you to go back to Vermont or whatever ridiculousness and tell the people."

"Tell them what precisely?"

"Because of our deceptive splendor, they must be extra discerning when selecting their temporary abodes in the sun. There are safe budget places and unsafe ones. And even the safe ones are unsafe, so they have to employ strategy. Like after dumping luggage in the room, move your car to the closest spot in view of the all-night front desk so it won't be broken into." Serge chugged the travel mug dry. "I was at one of the safest motels I knew and went out to move my car and ended up on the TV show *Cops.* Totally true. Walked out the door with my keys and saw all these cats at the corner of the building in black helmets and Kevlar vests, German shepherds and assault rifles. As soon as I cleared the sidewalk, the SWAT team went flying by! Half of them took up a semi-circular armed perimeter with guns drawn toward the door of this one room, using guests' parked vehicles as shields—and by the way, I don't think they asked permission—and suddenly this super-bright light comes on right behind me and some guy's yelling, 'Get out of the way! Get the hell out of the way!' . . . Guess who? Right, the film crew from *Cops.* I've always been in awe of how the camera guy carrying all that heavy equipment can run so fast and keep up with the chase, and this guy was now sprinting straight for me like a linebacker, not stopping for anything, and I'm about to get creamed, so luckily I was able to high-step it backward just in time and he goes flying by, too. But here's the best part! They were knocking down the motel door with the battering ram just when I blocked the shot, so they couldn't edit me out, and I made the show! Always wanted to be on an episode but for the right reasons. If you're ever watching it and hear the camera guy yelling, and see some joker in a tropical shirt flailing to get out of the way, that's my fifteen seconds of fame." Serge turned around and grinned big.

Lee pointed. "The road."

"Right. Ten and two o'clock."

Coleman belched. "What happened?"

"To what?" said Serge.

"The show *Cops.*"

"I just told you."

"No," said Coleman, "what the police were doing."

"Oh, after knocking down the door, they dragged out two handcuffed dudes not wearing shirts." Serge nodded. "That's a rule on that show: The guilty guys are the ones not wearing shirts. So I'm standing in the parking lot watching the patrol cars come pouring in with lights flashing, and they load the guys into the back seat, and all that excitement made me famished, and I decided to celebrate my new stardom by going to the Waffle House next door, which is like a zoning law down here that there has to be one within a certain radius of an economy motel. This particular joint was up on a little hill, positioned for a perfect view of all the action. And I'm trudging up the grass for the door, and I noticed that the place is packed, except nobody is sitting and eating. And I swear this part is also true: All the customers were lined up at the front windows, swaying back and forth in unison, singing 'Bad boys, bad boys.' That's the beauty of our state! In Florida, Waffle Houses are like luxury sky boxes for the show *Cops.* Eat a sausage link, watch a live episode. And as soon as I went inside a few people said, 'Hey, you just came from one of the rooms over there. What happened?' And I said, 'They grabbed the guys without the shirts.' And they said, 'Naturally.'"

"Uh, Serge," said Lee. "We're still circling the same block."

"Sorry, derailed train of thought." Serge slowed and pretended not to be inspecting the motel again. "Let's get to that game!"

Traffic thickened as they neared the park, and streams of faithful fans wearing red poured in from all directions. Serge pulled up to the curb near the ticket office, and turned around in his seat. "Listen, a last-minute business thing just came up, and I regretfully can't make the game."

"We drove all the way here, and we're not going inside?" said Lee.

"Oh no, you and Coleman go on and enjoy yourselves," said Serge. "I need to run an errand, and I'll meet you right here after the ninth inning."

The pair got out, and Lee stared dubiously as Serge drove off . . .

Chapter 21

Miami

A statue of Jesus with his arms spread stood in one corner. The Virgin Mary stood in another. Nathan Sparrow sat in a chair.

"The funeral is tomorrow," said a solemn prep school trustee. "Sorry for the short notice, but we had a large number of people we needed to locate. I'll tell my secretary to provide you with the details."

"How—how did . . . ?"

The trustee held up a hand. "In his sleep. Very peaceful."

Nathan nodded with his head down.

The trustee formed a sympathetic smile and opened a desk drawer. "I didn't realize how close you two were until we went through his effects in the chaplain's office."

"What do you mean?" asked the lawyer.

"We found an envelope with your name on the front. There was a note attached. In the event of his passing, we were supposed to give it to you." He handed it across the desk. "It hasn't been opened."

Sparrow tucked it inside his jacket. "Thank you."

"Sorry for your loss."

Nathan just nodded again and left.

Nathan Sparrow's walk-in closet was larger than most bedrooms. Rows of suits and blazers and pants and dress shirts for all occasions. Racks of silk ties, and shelves of Italian shoes.

His funeral attire was in the back. He stopped and held the envelope in his hand. Still unopened. He set it on one of the shelves. He slid the hangers of several black suits before making his choice.

Sparrow held out the suit and considered it for a moment. He decided to put it back. Then he went to the far end of the closet and pulled aside everything that had concealed something for decades. A well-worn brown corduroy jacket.

He tried it on. Sleeves a little short, but it would do. He slid the letter in a pocket.

The next day, the church was packed. Sparrow sat in the back row. When communion time came, the lawyer stayed seated. He didn't think he should because he hadn't been to confession since the last time with Father Al.

The cemetery was also crowded. Father Al had touched a lot of lives. The graveside service began, and it wasn't like the movies. No gloomy overcast sky threatening rain, and no bare trees with brown leaves on the cold ground. Instead, a hot sun shining down on coconut palms. Sparrow stood at a distance from the rest of the mourners. Didn't know if he could hold it together.

Eventually, it was quietly over, and the others left, dabbing eyes with handkerchiefs. Only cemetery workers. Sparrow had his privacy as he approached the recently dug hole. He pulled out an envelope and took a steadying breath before tearing it open.

He began to read. He began to cry. He needed to sit on the ground in order to finish it. He returned it to a pocket in the corduroy jacket and cried some more. When the sobs subsided, he pulled out his cell phone. Not to make a call, but to check social media. He found the page he was looking for, and as he scrolled down, he found a photo of a child's birthday party, just like in his law firm's slick ads. The photo was one he'd never seen before, Boo-Boo blowing out three candles on a cake. Now Nathan began to cry again and smile at the same time . . .

It was well after dark when he arrived home in Palm Beach. First he just walked around the outside of the house, slowly shifting his gaze across baby spotlights illuminating various tropical plants. He stared eternally into the deep end of the swimming pool before going inside. Sparrow didn't realize his mouth was slightly parted in a daze, looking at the most expensive kitchen appliances, which much of the populace didn't know existed. It went on like that, room after room, until finally he sat gently on the end of a bed. He pulled out the letter and read it again.

Then Nathan got out his cell phone.

The news broke hard and fast.

All networks all the time. And not just Florida, but the national cable outfits as well.

People gathered around TVs as a transcript scrolled up the screen and a shaky video recording played.

The control of the U.S. Senate might hang in the balance, and everyone with a stake was on the phone. Some screamed that they wanted their money back; others in damage control.

It was all about the night of a big fundraising dinner

in Palm Beach. News anchors kept referencing the Mitt Romney story from 2012, but that was a love-fest compared to this.

The Senate campaign scrambled in disarray. How on earth could the recording have been leaked? That's what Jack Grayson was yelling as he stomped back and forth in his Orlando headquarters. He stopped to berate staffers one by one. "It was your fault! . . . Your fault! . . . You're a loser! . . . You're fired! . . . Is everyone incompetent but me?" Until the campaign director arrived and hustled him into an office.

Then it got worse. Grayson started drinking. He seized the director by the lapels. "How could you let this happen?"

The director swatted his hands away. "Don't you ever, ever touch me like that again!"

"Okay, okay . . ." Grayson started pacing again and grabbed the blue-label bottle of Johnnie Walker. "I just can't figure it out."

"Neither can I."

Grayson chugged a swig. "The security guard?"

The director shook his head. "We stopped him and confiscated his phone."

"Who confiscated it?"

"Sparrow—" The director cut himself off as recognition simultaneously hit them both.

Grayson punched the air. "I'll destroy Nate and his whole family! By the time I'm through with him, he'll wish—"

"Sir, that's the kind of thinking that started all this," said the director. "You just couldn't help going after his daughter, and now we have this steaming pile. What we need to do now is forget about Sparrow and concentrate on getting out ahead of it . . ."

Salvaging the campaign still seemed possible. That's what various pundits were saying on TV. Grayson watched a flat-screen as his director surfed channels with a remote. "See? It's not *that* bad. I'll call some sympathetic commentators and start turning this around."

Optimism resumed. Until the next news cycle.

As they say, revenge is a dish best served cold. And Nathan Sparrow still had another plate to deliver.

The night of the big fundraising dinner, something had happened that was unbeknownst to everyone, including Sparrow. The other security guards had grabbed the phone and given it to the attorney, who'd dropped it in his pocket. Sparrow didn't remember it until all the screaming had stopped and guests had left and the caterers cleaned up.

But when he'd finally pulled the phone from his pocket, out of irresistible curiosity, he'd checked to see what had actually been filmed, and discovered the phone was out of memory. Maybe the guard hadn't captured anything after all. Nathan poked around the phone's menus until he found the evening's video file. He made another discovery. The file was almost an hour long until it abruptly cut off. Hmmm, so that's what depleted the memory. He hit play.

It started with the candidate's remarks, then some yelling as the picture swirled all over the place in the scuffle with the other guards, and finally the screen went black when Sparrow slipped the phone into his pocket. But the sound continued. *Well I'll be,* he thought. *Nobody ever hit the button to stop recording.* He listened on as Grayson cursed him out in the bedroom, right up to the most salient utterance of the night . . .

And now, today, back at Grayson headquarters, right as the staff thought they were about to regain footing, it hit all the TVs at once: "Breaking News."

Every network had it. "*We've just received another leaked tape from the infamous fundraiser in Palm Beach.*"

Another transcript began scrolling up the screen until the unsurmountable "*How am I supposed to tell these assholes what they want to hear and still get elected?*"

In a private office, the campaign director hit the off button on the TV.

"Why'd you do that?" asked Grayson.

"Because I need to start revising my résumé."

"Why? You said we were turning this around."

"Sir, say what you want about the opposition. Heck, even some of our own voters. But when you shit on the donors . . ."

"What are you saying?"

"What aren't you getting? It's game over."

"You fuck!" Another swig of Johnnie Walker. "It's not over until I say it is!"

The director put on his jacket and headed for the door. "Now I'm *glad* this happened."

"You don't walk away from me! Come back here!" Grayson chased him out into the main campaign office. A room full of campaign workers held up phones.

Later that evening, Nathan Sparrow sat alone on a couch watching the massive TV that was used to premiere all those expensive commercials. But now the screen was filled with a drunk Senate candidate stomping through his headquarters, cursing and swinging a bottle of Scotch by the neck.

A network announcer came on. "We have just received a brief press release. Jack Grayson has indefinitely suspended his Senate campaign for health reasons and will be out of the country until further notice."

Sparrow got out his phone and texted his daughter that she could go back to work.

He smiled and went to bed.

Chapter 22

Fort Myers

The 1970 Ford Cobra headed north and was back circling a motel again. Serge finally parked a discreet distance across the street at a gas station with burglar bars. His spider senses zeroed in where they had earlier, on a remote corner of the motel lot with an old Chevy that contained a driver who hadn't moved in an hour.

On the other side of the lot, a happy scene in front of one of the motel rooms. An old man in a red baseball cap sitting in a cheap lawn chair with those crappy plastic straps. A radio was on the game. Smoke rose from a small grill cooking hot dogs. Serge kept watching the Chevy driver, who kept watching the motel guest.

The door of the Cobra opened, and Serge strolled across the street. He reached the motel and inhaled deeply near the barbecue. "Smells fabulous!"

The old man remained in the chair, reaching with a long fork to turn the franks. "Nothing like hot dogs and baseball."

"Why aren't you at the game?" asked Serge.

"Staying down here three weeks, so there's plenty of games." The man reached in his shirt pocket and produced stubs. "Saving my money for the best ones. Got tickets here for the Yankees. I *hate* the Yankees!"

"There's a lot of that going around Sox Nation," said Serge. "My condolences for the Bucky Dent dinger in seventy-eight."

"I'm almost over it. Watched them lose the seventh game of the series in sixty-seven, seventy-five and eighty-six, but they've been turning it around lately."

"My name's Serge." He extended a hand and they shook.

"I'm Cornelius from Marblehead. Retired dock-worker and lifelong Sox fanatic. I hate the Yankees!"

"You already said that."

"I did?" He stood up and grabbed a plate. "My wife says I'm repeating myself more as I get older, but she's not here. Want a dog?"

"I'm good."

Cornelius squeezed mustard into a bun and sat back down. "This is the life! Florida, baseball on the radio, big game tomorrow and a grilled dog!" He took a large, juicy bite.

"Yes, it is the life! Golden droplets!" Serge kept tabs on the Chevy with peripheral vision. "If you don't mind me asking, are you familiar with this area?"

"No, but it's beautiful, palm trees and sun and all," said the fan. "I can't believe how little I'm paying for this place. I almost feel like I'm stealing."

"I know the area, and just to be safe, please follow the tips on the back of the door."

The New Englander laughed. "Are you like some kind of local ambassador?"

"Yes, that's exactly what I am. Enjoy your stay." They shook hands again, and Serge returned to his car across the street. He tuned his own radio to the game . . .

Two innings later, the old man stretched and went into his room. The door of a Chevy opened.

"Shit," Serge said to himself. "It's going down."

The Chevy's driver had a sinewy build, half-inch-long hair, and a ruddy, dark-red complexion. Some people have suntans that look healthy; this was not one of those. He headed straight for a door next to a lawn chair and grill. He knocked hard.

An old man in a red cap answered. "Yes, what can I do—" Before he could finish, he was forced inside at gunpoint.

"W-w-what's going on?"

And before the assailant could answer, the door crashed in behind him. The man spun to see Serge aiming a pistol at him.

"Drop it! I won't ask twice!"

A revolver hit the floor.

"Now lie on your stomach on the bed," said Serge. "And put your hands behind your back."

A shaken Red Sox fan fell against a wall. "Jesus! *Two* robbers!"

"Only one," said Serge, fastening plastic restraints around the would-be thief's wrists. Then he jerked the man to his feet and placed a light jacket over the man's shoulders to conceal the bound hands. "Cornelius, I'm so sorry that you had to see Florida in this light. It's really out of character, so please put it out of your mind and enjoy the rest of your vacation. Go Sox!"

The tourist ran to the window and watched Serge march the robber across the street, arm around his shoulders like they were buddies . . .

The blue-and-white Cobra pulled up to the curb of Fort Myers's mini–Fenway Park just as the game let out. Coleman and Lee were making their way to the car but it was slow going. Fans surrounded the all-star pitcher, getting him to sign baseballs, programs, their hats, anything.

They eventually reached the car, and Lee signed a couple last programs out the window before the Cobra pulled away.

"Serge," said Coleman. "You should have seen it in there. He was mobbed all day, signing like a million autographs. I had no idea that many people read *High Times.*"

"Coleman, that's not why— Forget it. We've got some bitchin' barbecue in our future!"

The Cobra accelerated out of town.

Bam, bam, bam.

Lee turned around. "What's that noise?"

Serge glanced up in the mirror. "I didn't hear anything."

Bam, bam, bam.

"There it is again," said Lee. "It's coming from the trunk."

"Spare tire must have come loose." Serge eased the car onto the shoulder. "I'll just secure it." He reached under the seat.

"You have a gun?" said the ballplayer.

"This? It's just a cigarette lighter. Be back in a flash." Serge popped the trunk lid, and brought the butt of the pistol down hard. *Wham, wham, wham.* He climbed back into the driver's seat. "There, all secure . . ."

The Ford Cobra indeed stayed off the grid, taking remote Highway 80 across the open countryside. Through LaBelle and Clewiston.

Coleman cracked a sweaty can of Pabst and reached toward the back seat. "Want another?"

"I don't know."

"Come on," said Coleman. "You've only had two. *High Times*! Don't let me down."

"Why not? We're going to Tom's." Lee accepted the can and chugged.

"Coleman, you have no idea how jazzed I am!" Serge slapped the steering wheel. "I've gotten to meet one of my favorite baseball players growing up."

"Righteous." Coleman slurped. "When did he stop playing?"

"That's the coolest thing," said Serge. "He never stopped. He's like the modern Satchel Paige, roaming the world with his glove looking for a game, from New Brunswick to Venezuela. One of his jerseys is in the Hall of Fame. But not his Red Sox shirt. The San Rafael Pacifics of the independent North American League. Why, you ask? Because at age sixty-five, he became the oldest player ever to start a professional game. And if that wasn't enough, he pitched the complete game! And won it!"

"I remember that," said Bill. "Had my best junk still working."

Soon music filled the car, and the radio wasn't on.

". . . Me and my Arrow . . ."

All the occupants of the Cobra sang in disharmony. Serge glanced in the rearview. "Thanks for taking requests."

Coleman popped another can. "What song was that?"

"Harry Nilsson," said Lee. "He was the best."

"Why?" said Serge. "Because he also sang the song 'Spaceman'?"

"No, his sixth album was *The Point!*, a fable about Oblio, the only round-headed child in a land where everything must have a point, and he wears a pointed hat, but then he's discovered and banished to the Pointless Forest with his dog Arrow, and, wait. What was my point? . . ." He stared at the headrest in front of him. "Coleman, your head's round. Is your real name Oblio?"

Serge glanced in the mirror again. "Everything okay back there?"

"Not sure," said Lee. "Feeling a little weird." He stared at the can in his hand. "But I'm only halfway through my third beer, so that's not it." Then his gaze shifted out the window at a hardwood hammock on the edge of the scrubland. "There's the Pointless Forest! We must rescue Oblio!"

Serge's head slowly pivoted toward the passenger seat.

"Why are you looking at me like that?" asked Coleman.

"You know." He sighed and faced forward. "What have you gone and done?"

"Okay, okay," said Coleman. "But I only put the tiniest amount of hashish oil in his beer."

"What!"

"It was for his own good," said Coleman. "It's the Spaceman. This could be his big comeback for *High Times.*"

"The engine in this car is vibrating to the key of A minor," said Lee. "The key of my skeleton, in tune with the Dadaist movement of 1920s Paris . . ."

"Coleman," said Serge, "do something before this goes off the rails. You know drugs."

"Got it covered. Where are those supplies for your ancestor corkboards?"

"Under your seat."

Coleman pulled out a shopping bag and discarded a stack of notecards. Safety scissors snipped off a strip of yellow yarn, which Coleman attached to the roof of the back seat with a pushpin.

Serge glanced. "What the hell . . . ?"

"Give me a sec." Coleman attached another piece of yarn to the roof in front of his own seat.

Serge looked around the car as the other two occupants joyfully swatted their respective strings. "What in the name of God? Have you turned into fucking cats?"

Coleman pawed at his yarn. "You don't understand the drug culture. This will chill him out . . ."

Ten minutes later. "I was wrong," said Coleman. "The dose was too concentrated."

Lee was now crawling over Coleman's shoulder, trying to climb out the window of the speeding car.

"Damn it." Serge pulled over. "I'll deal with you later." He ran around the Cobra and grabbed the ballplayer under the arms. "Let me help you the rest of the way out of the window. For future reference the door usually works better. And when the car's stopped."

"Why do I feel so strange?" said the player.

"Sorry about this," said Serge. "Coleman kind of dosed you."

But Lee had already begun wandering into the field. "Even a baseball has a point. Know what I mean? It's unlike any other sport, no clock, the defense controls the ball, Cartesian coordinates from the point at the bottom of home plate, sending ninety-degree foul lines stretching out into infinity across the universe."

"Let me get you back to the car," said Serge, grabbing the player around the waist. "You'll be fine."

Lee was unsteady on his legs but making progress. "And for the record, the Yankees suck."

"I remember that big bench-clearing brawl in seventy-six after Lou Piniella collided with Carlton Fisk at the plate, and Graig Nettles slammed you on your pitching shoulder."

Lee stopped and swayed off-balance as he reached in his back pocket. "Have to show you something." He opened his wallet and pulled out a wrinkled piece of cardboard.

"What's that?" asked Serge.

"Nettles's baseball card . . . So he can smell my *ass*!"

"Wow, after all these years," said Serge. "You really do hate the Yankees."

"Fuck 'em."

Chapter 23

West Palm Beach

The cameras were waiting.

Reinhold looked around the front of the courthouse. "Where's Nathan?"

Nash checked his Rolex. "He's never this late.

"Doesn't he know we're shooting the new commercial this morning?"

"I left five voice messages on his cell phone and called his house and the office," said Reinhold. "Nobody knows where he is."

The director grew impatient. "What's it going to be, guys?"

The pair looked at each other, then the director. "Guess we'll get started without him . . ."

Sixty miles south, knuckles hit wood.

A priest came to the front door of the rectory. "Yes?"

"You don't know me, but my name is Nathan Sparrow. Father Al knew me as Bobby."

"Oh yes, Father Al," said the priest. "He will be remembered well. He touched a lot of lives. Were you at the funeral?"

Nathan nodded.

"How may I help you?"

"Father, I need to ask a favor. I don't know if it's appropriate," said Nathan. "When I was young, I met him a few times here in the main living area, but I never saw his room. Is it . . . ?"

"He only passed a few days ago, so there hasn't been time," said the priest. "It's still just like he left it. I'm guessing you want to see it?"

Nathan nodded again.

"I assumed that, because you're not the first. Follow me."

They arrived, and the priest waited with folded hands outside the open door as Nathan went inside the tiny dark-green room. He moved slowly, gently touching the bed, the bookcase, the modest desk. A Bible was still open to the book of Matthew. Nathan got out the letter and read it again. His lips began to tremble, and the priest politely looked away.

An hour later, the attention of a serving staff swung toward the unexpected sight of a tailored suit that had just come in the door. Nathan removed his jacket as someone approached. "Can I help you?"

"I used to come here as a boy with Father Al."

"Father Al? If you knew him, I'm sure he had an effect on your life."

Nathan answered by tossing his jacket in a corner without regard for wrinkles. He walked around behind a long table for the homeless dinner line. "May I?"

The other person nodded, and Nathan picked up a serving spoon.

Somewhere Else in West Palm Beach

The budget motel on U.S. Highway 1 had a neon sign of a seahorse, and a vending machine with an impenetrable metal grate across the glass.

A baseball player lay still on a bed, staring wide-eyed up at something on the ceiling. "There's a big spider up there!"

Serge sat at a desk in tunnel-vision concentration. "You're still hallucinating."

"No," said Coleman. "There is a spider. I'll get it."

He climbed up on the bed with a shoe and smacked it. "Problem solved."

"This stuff is so much stronger now." Lee had a fistful of bedspread gripped tight on each side of his hips. "How long till it wears off?"

"I'm still ripped, so maybe an hour or two," said Coleman. "Just kick back and dig it."

"For some reason I feel like I'm in Egypt," said Lee. "And my legs are tentacles with suckers."

"That means it's good shit," said Coleman. "If you wouldn't mind mentioning me to *High Times*—"

"Can you guys pipe down?" said Serge. "I'm trying to get something done over here."

Coleman strolled over and took stock of the cluttered work space. There was an awl, a heavy-duty sewing needle, pocketknife, plastic chemical bottle, another smaller container of white powder, superglue, stick of library paste, roll of brown paper towels, red string, a vise, portable drill, plastic bulb syringe, frying pan, and a lighted hobbyist's magnifying glass on a gooseneck clamped to the edge of the desk. On the floor next to Serge's chair sat a gasoline can and shopping bag.

"You doing another science project?" asked Coleman.

"If you leave me alone." Serge sliced string with the knife.

Coleman looked at another part of the desk. An

empty box that used to hold a half-dozen baseballs. Serge stared down through the magnifying glass, continuing to cut the stitches on one of the balls. He removed the cowhide cover and discarded the wool-wound cork core in the wastebasket. He set the cover alongside five other covers that were the result of the same process.

"Why are you taking those baseballs apart?"

"Because I'm making Serge's Extreme baseballs. I need them for Lee's famous Spaceball pitch. Observe."

He reached down in the shopping bag and pulled out a small clear sphere attached to a square of wood.

"What's that?"

"A display case for autographed tennis balls. They have them for baseballs, too, but I needed something with a smaller circumference than a baseball." He snapped the wood base off one of the displays, then twisted apart the two halves of the protective clear plastic sphere where the tennis ball would go. A ribbon of superglue was painstakingly applied around the inside edge of one of the halves, and he twisted them back together again. He grabbed the portable drill with an ultra-small bit and made a hole on the top of the see-through sphere.

"What are you doing now?"

"Adding the prime ingredient." Serge reached beside

his chair, sucking up gasoline with the bulb syringe, then squirting it down through the tiny hole in the sphere. When it was half-full, he grabbed the chemical bottle and sucked up some of its contents with the syringe, filling the rest of the sphere. A blob of superglue gel sealed the hole made by the drill.

"That looks pretty cool," said Coleman. "The liquids aren't mixing. The bottom half is brown, and the top clear, like one of those novelty drinks at a funky bar."

"Oh, it's definitely a novelty." Next, Serge reached for the frying pan. "I had to prepare this earlier because it takes the longest to dry." He removed a brown paper towel spread across the bottom of the pan and applied library paste to one side. The paper was wrapped around the plastic sphere.

"What now?"

"The part I've been dreading," said Serge. "It's excruciatingly tedious, but I can't just phone this in." He fitted the paper-shrouded plastic sphere inside one of the baseball covers. Then his face went over the goosenecked magnifying glass again as he picked up the spool of red string and the thick sewing needle. "There are exactly one hundred and eight double stitches in an official ball." The needle went through a hole. "I don't know how people can do this all day. Luckily I only have six balls ahead of me."

Two hours later, Serge set the third finished ball aside. "Screw it, that's enough—"

Knock, knock, knock.

"Who the fuck's at the door!" said the prostrate ballplayer tightly gripping the bedspread. "Don't answer it!"

"You're just paranoid," said Serge. "And I need backstory."

He enthusiastically opened the door.

Standing outside was a man dressed like the Statue of Liberty.

"Detergent?" asked Serge.

The man nodded.

Serge grabbed a small box off the dresser. "Here you go." He closed the door.

Coleman looked up. "You didn't get backstory."

"Already know it. That encounter was limited to me trying to be like Christ." He sat back down at the desk. "Coleman, what do you think?"

"What am I looking at?"

"I've just made history as the first person to combine the Apollo moon program, Bill 'Spaceman' Lee and Molotov cocktails."

"This is the part again where you need to explain," said Coleman.

"First a little background: The Molotov cocktail is

a glass bottle filled with gasoline or other flammable liquid, with a rag stuck in the opening that's set on fire, and the whole thing is thrown to explode when the glass breaks. Introduced during the Spanish Civil War in 1936, and later named insultingly after Soviet foreign minister Vyacheslav Molotov by the Finns after Russia invaded in 1939. The problem with the cocktail is that it's not entirely reliable. The rag can come loose in flight or the bottle shatters in a way that doesn't ignite. Also, if it's after dark and you're holding a bottle with a flaming wick, you make an easy target for snipers. Some folks decided they needed to go back to the drawing board."

"I'm with you so far."

"This is where the Apollo program comes in." Serge carefully packed the baseballs back in the box. "One of the most dangerous parts of a mission is when it's time to come home and they have to reignite the service module's engine on the dark side of the moon. The first design objective is to reduce the number of things that can fail. So they got rid of the ignition source, which was like eliminating the risk of a bad spark plug."

"How'd they do that?"

"By using hypergolic fuels," said Serge. "Which are two different chemicals that automatically ignite on contact without a 'spark plug.' The same principle was employed when some jokers developed a new and improved Molotov that eliminated the flaming rag."

"Again, how?"

"The same way I 'extremed' my baseballs," said Serge. "I started by filling the tennis ball holders with gasoline and sulfuric acid, which you can get at any hardware store. Then came that white powder, potassium chlorate. You know about it if you were ever in a high school science class, and the teacher wanted to stimulate interest with an experiment called Growling Gummy Bears."

"Except they don't use real gummy bears?"

"No, they do. The teacher pours the chemical into a test tube, sticks the bottom over a Bunsen burner and drops in a gummy bear, which produces a bright flame and screaming sound, because the candy's sugar content is an excellent oxidizer. It's a feel-good experiment, except my baseballs aren't feel-good."

"You can just buy that stuff?"

"Yes and no," said Serge. "It's all over the Internet from chemical supply houses, but the legality is tricky in certain jurisdictions. Like I need more hassles in my life. So I improvised by going to the grocery store and buying (*blank*) and sodium-free salt substitute, because I'm hip to ionic bonds. Then I dissolved them in water and poured the mixture in the frying pan with a stack of paper towels in the bottom and let the whole thing dry before gluing the chemically saturated towels around the spheres."

"Serge," said Coleman, "why did you silently mouth that one ingredient?"

"Because somebody might be listening in the home audience." He gingerly picked up a ball. "I don't want anyone trying this in their garage. I'm a responsible person, after all."

"You always think of others," said Coleman. "But how is that like a Molotov cocktail?"

"Sulfuric acid and potassium chlorate react explosively on contact, like Apollo fuel, so when those plastic spheres break, it puts the acid inside in contact with the chlorate dried into the paper towels on the outside and automatically ignites the gasoline, just like a moon rocket." Serge turned around toward an empty part of the room. "So don't try this at home because there are toxic fumes and a high chance of accidental explosion that could maim or kill you."

"Who are you talking to?" asked Coleman.

"The home audience."

"I don't see anyone."

"The key to life is pretending you have a home audience that's always watching you," said Serge. "It's a morale booster, and an incentive to stay self-aware and not pick your nose."

Coleman pulled a finger from a nostril. "Having a home audience is cool!"

"It's just like *Romper Room*." Serge smiled and waved. "Hello out there! I see Jimmy, and Sally, and Zeke . . ."

Coleman stuck his face next to Serge's and waved. "It's me, Coleman."

A voice from behind: "What's going on?"

"Jesus!" Serge grabbed his heart. "Didn't know you were up. Don't startle me like that."

"That evil stuff finally wore off," said Lee. "What have you got there?"

"Nothing!"

"Yes, you do. Three baseballs and three covers. And chemicals."

"Oh, right. They're just baseballs. Nothing fishy going on." Serge grinned abnormally. "When I said before I just wanted to play catch, I changed my mind. I really do want autographs."

"Be happy to." The player reached for one of the balls.

"No!" Serge's hands flew out to cover them. "I mean, no, *I'll* hold them."

Lee signed the balls with his name, date and location: "Earth."

"That's mighty nice of you," said Serge. "I'll always treasure these. But right now, Coleman and I have to run an errand."

"Okay, I'll get my shoes on."

Serge shook his head. "It's a boring errand, and you need to stay here in case there are any aftereffects. We'll be right back and then go get that outrageous barbecue!"

"If you say so."

"I insist." Serge grabbed the box of balls and headed out the door . . .

A half hour later, a blue-and-white Cobra arrived at a darkened baseball field on the west side of the county. Serge popped the trunk.

"Well, if it isn't my favorite baseball fan!" said Serge. "Have I got a game for you!"

The motel robber squirmed down in the bed of the trunk and tried to yell under the duct tape across his mouth.

"Let me give you a hand."

After getting the hostage out and flopping him to the ground, Serge reached deep inside and grabbed one of those cloth folding chairs that parents bring to soccer games. He set it in the right-handed batter's box next to home plate, and strapped the captive in with nylon rope. "Here's your bat." Serge duct-taped it to his bound hands.

Then he and Coleman went to the middle of the diamond for a strategy conference on the pitcher's mound. "What should I throw him? He's a righty, so I'm thinking a slider low and away."

"I don't know," said Coleman. "Back when you were playing catch with Spaceman, you threw everything over the Indian mound."

"Because I was intimidated by greatness and trying to show off." Serge rotated the ball in his hand. "A common problem among relief pitchers coming into a game is pushing too hard. I'll just dial it back."

"Then I say, 'Batter up!'"

Serge faced the plate. "You're in for a real treat! These balls have been signed by a genuine major league legend!" Serge placed his right foot on the rubber and bore down on the batter with ferocious competitiveness. "Now I'm adjusting my grip on the ball behind my back, so don't even try to guess the pitch."

Serge went into a wildly gyrating windup and let the ball fly. It zoomed through the strike zone and exploded against the backstop in a towering fiery mushroom. The captive thrashed and whined in his chair as he watched the flames flicker against the chain-link fence twenty feet behind him.

"*Steeeee-rike one!*" said Serge.

Another conference with Coleman. "What do you think? He's behind in the count and probably expecting another curve, so I'll go with a four-seam fastball this time."

"He'll never expect it," said Coleman.

Another crazy windup and release. Another stunning explosion at the backstop.

"*Steeeee-rike two!*" said Serge.

The captive whimpered with bobbing shoulders.

"What's the matter?" asked Serge. "You seemed to have all the confidence in the world when you were pointing your gun at that old-timer baseball fan . . . Oh, I get it, you're only cocky while victimizing someone weaker. The young, the handicapped, that retiree. You probably even kick small animals. But facing an equal mound opponent like me is a different ball game, right?"

Just more frantic noises of desperation.

"Coleman, what do you think?" whispered Serge. "He's two strikes in the hole, expecting a ball outside, so I've got him set up perfectly for the knockout pitch."

"Which is what?"

"I'll surprise you, too. Step back . . ."

Serge leaned even farther forward to stare down the batter again. He started his windup, but as his arm came forward, he released slightly early. The captive looked up as the ball traveled in a high, slow arc across the night sky. It fell at a sharp angle, downward through the strike zone.

Home plate exploded in the most violent fireball yet.

"*Steeeee-rike three!*" said Serge. "The Leephus Spaceball pitch gets them every time!"

"Ewww," said Coleman. "What a horrible way to go."

"I considered that. So mercifully, asphyxiation should come fast and end the misery. Because if you can't show mercy, there's something seriously wrong with you."

"You really are dedicated to making others happy."

"As often as possible." Serge led Coleman back toward the car. "I guess there's nothing left to say but 'Go Sox!'"

Headlights streamed down U.S. 1 in Boynton Beach, including two on the front of a 1970 Ford Cobra.

"That barbecue really hit the spot!" Serge sucked hard on a to-go coffee. "Meat practically melting off the ribs. A long wait, but worth it. What did you think, Spaceman?"

The player patted his stomach. "Almost better than I remembered. And after all this time, they still have those same plastic red-and-white-checkered tablecloths."

"I remember the old sign by the jukebox: No dancing during dinnertime."

Coleman blazed another fat one and held it toward the back seat.

Lee's hands went up. "No, no, no, I'm good."

"Tom's Place!" said Serge. "Now, this is what I'm talking about! Florida has lost way too many historic places, but it's like a double bonus when someone cares enough to bring one back to life that you thought was gone forever!" Serge didn't realize it, but he had gotten the gun out from under the seat and was waving it around with zest.

"What's with the gun?" said Lee.

"Did you forget? It's a cigarette lighter that just looks like a gun—"

Bang.

The bullet zinged out the passenger window.

"Serge, watch it!" said Coleman. "You almost got me again!"

"Excuse me," said Lee. "I'd like to get out of the car now, please."

"What are you talking about?" Serge twisted toward the back seat with gun still in hand. "We're having fun!"

"I just remembered I have to go jogging."

"Come on! Hang out a little longer!"

"Please pull over. It would make me happy."

"*Allllllll* right. But only because I've rededicated my life to the Gospels."

The car eased up to a bus stop, and Lee exited as if he were spring-loaded.

Coleman looked out the rear window and watched the ballplayer running away in the opposite direction, frantically looking over his shoulder at the departing car. Coleman turned back around in his seat. "I didn't want to say anything, but your hero was acting really weird the whole time we were around him."

"They don't call him the Spaceman for nothing."

Chapter 24

The Next Day

A few minutes after noon, a white Crown Victoria with blackwall tires drove south on U.S. Highway 1 near Fort Lauderdale. The passenger had a newspaper.

"Here's that story about the guy arrested for jumping on a pelican," said Archie. "They caught him because he put it on Facebook."

Heather pulled up to a red light. "Where did that happen?"

"Key West. He leaped off a dock into the harbor." Archie turned a page. "Talk about your senseless crime."

"It's never boring down here."

Archie pointed out the window. "There's a hooker on crutches."

The light turned green. The sedan drove on.

The next light turned red and the car stopped again.

Archie pointed again. "There's someone dressed like the Statue of Liberty."

"Those sign wavers for accountants are on almost every street corner these days," said Heather. "It's tax season."

"He doesn't have a tax sign. It's a bigger one with a lot of words," said Archie. "'Give me your tired, your poor, your huddled masses yearning to breathe free . . .'"

The light changed, and they sped off as Serge waved at them from under his green spiked hat.

The Crown Vic pulled into a modest neighborhood, and up the driveway of a ranch house with an anti-maintained yard. The law officers stepped over beer cans on the front steps. The door had a dead Christmas wreath. They knocked. It was quiet at first, followed by a violent hacking cough. "*Coming.*" Then the sound of a piece of furniture tipping over. "*Dammit.*" The partners looked at each other.

A man in a stained white T-shirt opened up, eating a hard-boiled egg. "Who are you?"

They displayed gold badges at the same time.

"State agents," said Heather. "Are you Raúl Dixon?"

"Since I was born," said the resident.

"May we come in?" said Archie.

"Am I in some kind of trouble?"

"Oh, no, no, no, nothing like that," said Heather. "Just a routine investigation. You're not a suspect."

"Then suit yourself." He turned unceremoniously back into the house. The agents stepped over a pizza box and took seats on a sofa. Dixon plopped down deep into his own torn La-Z-Boy where the springs had lost their memory. "Now, what's this all about?"

Heather opened a notebook. "Did you send a DNA sample to a company called Ancestors R Us?"

"What a waste of money," said Dixon. "It was three A.M. and I was drunk and an infomercial came on. I have to stop ordering stuff like that. It's how I got the stupid hard-boiled-egg machine."

"But they did send you a report with their results?"

Dixon resumed diligence on a quart bottle of malt liquor. "Apparently I'm part Estonian, part Danish, with a family history of unibrows. I also got worthless hits on distant relatives that I couldn't give two shits about, from Tarpon Springs and Vermont."

"Mr. Dixon, the reason we're here is that we recovered some DNA from a crime scene . . ."

"Not mine."

"Like I said earlier, you're under no suspicion," continued Heather. "We just need your help constructing a family tree to determine whose DNA it is."

"One of my relatives did something wrong?"

"A very distant relative," said Archie, followed by a lie that police are allowed to tell: "And he may not even be involved. His DNA was just found at the scene, but we have to check it out anyway in case he might have witnessed something."

"How distant?"

Heather reviewed her notes. "Potentially third cousin with a six percent margin of error."

"I don't even know what a third cousin is. I don't know my brother anymore," said Dixon. "After that bullshit he tried to pull stealing cable service and blaming me. Is that what you're really here about? Because I can prove it was him."

"Mr. Dixon," said Heather, "I can assure you this is simply about your family tree."

"Then what do you want?"

Heather referred to her notebook again. "We were able to document most of what we needed from public records, but there are still a few gaps. Do you know if your grandmother on your father's side had any siblings?"

"What's that?"

"Brothers or sisters."

"How would I know?"

Heather had the growing sensation of a fool's errand. She looked around the trashed living room and doubted the value of her next question. "Would you perhaps have any kind of family records?"

"No records," said Dixon. "But we did have one of those heavy old Bibles, the fancy kind where you write a bunch of family stuff on some of the front pages. Would that work?"

"Actually, that would be very helpful."

Dixon slowly pushed himself up from the recliner. "Let's see if I can find that thing. Last I saw it was the hall closet."

He disappeared. They heard a door open, followed by a small avalanche of stored junk. "Shit." Then footsteps toward another room and a refrigerator door. Dixon returned with a Bible and another malt liquor. He handed the book to Heather. "Want a beer?"

"We're on duty." She flipped through the front pages and turned to Archie and nodded. Pay dirt. She pulled out a cell phone and snapped photos of the genealogy.

When she was done, she placed the Bible on a coffee table. "One last question. Do you have any relatives that you have a funny feeling about? Where something's not quite right, like they might have a secret life?"

"Yeah." Dixon scoffed. "My shiftless brother."

"Besides the cable thing."

"Not really."

The agents stood up from the couch. "We appreciate your time," said Heather. "You've been of great assistance."

"I don't see how." Dixon swigged from the brown bottle. "But funny thing . . ."

"How's that?" asked Archie.

"I don't usually get many visitors. Actually, none," said Dixon. "Now I've had two in the same week. And the other guy was asking about this ancestor stuff, too."

The agents sat back down. "What other guy? Law enforcement?"

"No, real weirdo. Had this fat clown with him."

"What did he want?"

"To trim my ear hair."

"That's weird."

"Told you." Dixon swigged again. "He said his life was now all about making people happy. And he wanted to know about my family tree."

"Did you recognize him from anywhere?" asked Heather. "Did he say why?"

"Never laid eyes on him before, but he said he had sent in his own DNA, probably the same infomercial.

And it came back with a hit on me as one of his distant cousins."

Heather looked at her partner. "It couldn't be the cousin from Tarpon Springs because that was a woman." Heather went through her phone and pulled up a photo.

"Who's that?" asked Dixon.

"Your cousin from Vermont."

"Not him."

The agents stood again. "You've been more than helpful. Would you mind if we sent over a sketch artist?"

"Only if he brings beer."

"I think we can arrange that," said Heather. "And if you remember anything else, please give me a call. Here's my business card. I'll write my personal number on the back . . ." She set it on top of the Bible.

The agents let themselves out, and a Crown Victoria headed back to the office.

Archie turned in the passenger seat. "What did you make of that odd visitor he got?"

"Something's not kosher," said Heather. "Our investigation might have been compromised. Relatives tipping each other off. We could have touched a nerve."

"But what about the stranger saying he got a hit on Dixon as a distant cousin? It doesn't add up. We only got the three total from Ancestors R Us. If the guy who showed up at his house was telling the truth, then we should have gotten four."

"There are two possible explanations," said Heather. "The DNA company slipped up and didn't provide us with a complete list."

"What's the other?"

"This mystery man sent his DNA in for a family search *after* we received our results . . ."

A vintage Chevelle poured black smoke from the tailpipe as it pulled up to a ranch house. The driver walked up and knocked on a door with a dead Christmas wreath.

Raúl Dixon opened it. He saw someone with an equally stained T-shirt, and a six-pack dangling from his right hand. "Art, come on in. I'll owe for the beer."

"What a shock." The visitor pulled a can off the plastic ring and tossed it underhand to a man in a recliner. "Any pizza left from last night?"

Dixon pointed at the box on the floor.

Art opened it and found the last slice. "Still good." He began munching on the sofa. "What's been going on?"

"Strange week. Remember that whack-job I told you came to the door?"

A cold bite. "That's almost normal for these parts."

"It just got even stranger today," said Dixon. "When you knocked just now, I thought you were the sketch artist they were sending over."

Art stopped eating. "Sketch artist? What are you talking about?"

"For that weirdo who paid me a visit. I guess they're interested in him."

"Forget the weirdo," said Art. "Sketch artist means police."

Dixon nodded as he chugged. "That's right. Two detectives were here earlier asking about my family. Really nosy. The woman detective took photos of my Bible and everything. That's her business card on top of it."

Art leaned all the way forward with elbows on knees. "What did they say it was about?"

"Found some DNA at a crime scene and were trying to trace it."

"But why on earth would they come to ask you?"

"Toss me another one." A second beer can flew, and Dixon popped it. "Remember that stupid ancestor thing I ordered in the middle of the night from that infomercial? What was I thinking?"

"Back to the cops."

"I guess they sent in the crime scene DNA, and it came up with three hits, including me," said Dixon. "I'm supposed to be related to whoever did whatever crime they're looking into. Third cousin or something. They wanted to re-create my family tree."

"Did they give any hint what kind of crime scene?"

Dixon shrugged and chugged. "Probably a stolen car or burglary."

"I seriously doubt it," said Art. "DNA tests, making house visits to research family trees. They only put in that kind of time and money for something really big. I'm thinking a murder case."

"You might be right," said Dixon. "It did seem kind of important."

"Local cops?" asked Art.

Dixon shook his head and pointed again at the business card on the coffee table. "State agents."

Art picked it up. "Florida Department of Law Enforcement? They're the heavy hitters."

"Like I said, strange week."

"Did you say anything about me?"

"No, but they asked."

Art sat up rod straight. "Specifically?"

"No, generally. They asked if I had any relatives that I had bad vibes about that I thought they should look into."

"And what did you say?" asked Art.

"Given all your past shit, I figured you didn't need the aggravation."

"Good thinking."

Dixon tossed an empty can over his shoulder. "Beer."

Another can flew. "So they're coming back with a sketch artist?"

"That's what they told me."

"What if they keep poking around and eventually ask about me?"

Raúl chugged. "I won't bring it up."

"But what if they do?"

"I don't know," said Raúl. "I hear you can get in trouble lying to the police. I mean, you haven't done anything. Not *that* bad. And the statute of limitations has run out on most of it."

Art nodded. "You're right. I don't have anything to worry about. And I wouldn't want you to get in trouble."

Raúl tossed another can over his shoulder. "By the way, while we're talking about family trees, how is it we're related again?"

"Third cousins."

Chapter 25

Ramrod Key

A blue-and-white Ford Cobra sat outside one of the largest tiki bars in Florida.

"Serge, you've returned!"

"You know I can't stay away for more than a few months." He took off a backpack and grabbed a seat at the table.

"So what else have you been up to?" asked Captain Katie.

"Parks, passports," said Serge. "Tracking a serial killer and making people happy."

"In other words, the usual?" said Katie.

"If you get me started you'll regret you asked . . . Okay, you got me started." Serge reached in his backpack for a small personal-effects dry box with a rubber gasket. "Check out the stamps in this book! . . ." Proudly displaying page after page.

She regretted asking, but not much. "You're also hiking?"

"With a magnesium-white flame," said Serge. "I was just walking around out at your Ramrod Beach again."

"Oh yeah, that funky Christmas tree is still up," said Katie. "It's a Keys thing."

"So I told Coleman." He pulled out his phone. "I bought this great new app with all the official Florida hiking trails. I was recently watching little turtles out at Blue Hole, you know, that freshwater depression in the rock in the National Key Deer Refuge on Big Pine?"

"I know."

"Why do turtles always climb on each other? They were like three high. Anyway, I also took both the Watson and Mannillo trails through pine rocklands, buttonwoods and silver palms." Serge held up the phone that had recorded his route. "I'm used to hiking in woods and mangroves with canopies. But down here it's freaky how everything is so low. Plus all the hurricane damage from Irma! Tipped-over trees with exposed roots encrusted in limestone. Imagine the force to pull roots out of rock. And on the way back, that big cross outside the Lord of the Seas church is now at an angle."

"It was a bad one. Let me see that thing." Katie took the phone and scrolled across the screen with a finger. "If you want to hike someplace really neat, go out to No Name Key."

"I didn't know it had a park."

"No park, not even an official trail, but it acts as one." She tapped a spot on the phone. "Right here. There's a locked gate on the south side a little more than halfway to the ferry dock ruins. Looks like there's nothing to see, so only a few locals know about it. You just leave your car outside and walk around the gate. That's where I go when I want to get out in nature and lose myself walking. And there's a surprise you'll never expect."

"I'm there!"

The Ford Cobra rolled across the Bogie Channel Bridge, from Big Pine to No Name Key.

Coleman toked and looked out the window. "Those miniature deer again. They're so cute."

Serge slowed and scanned the side of the road. "Did I already pass it? . . . No, there it is, right where she said." He parked at an anonymous steel gate across an unmarked gravel road.

The pair got out and climbed around the barrier. The trail was straight and wide at first, with patches of white mud, then made a bend to the west and narrowed through sea grapes and slash pines.

"This is cool but creepy." Serge adjusted his bucket hat. "So isolated and unauthorized. The first trail I've been on where I felt like I need a gun." He patted his waistband. "Lucky for me."

Coleman pinched his roach for a last hit. "Wonder what that surprise was she mentioned?"

"I think we're about to find out." Serge outstretched an arm. "That spot in the middle of the trail up there doesn't look normal."

"What do you think it is?"

"Still too far away to tell."

They continued hiking and trying to guess what they were coming upon. Then Serge made out a tiny glimpse of water. "In the middle of No Name?"

They soon found themselves at another gate, this one open, rusted and chain-link. They stopped and stared across an immense body of shimmering water with right angles.

"What the hell?" said Coleman.

"It's an old, water-filled derelict quarry."

The duo looked up at a giant abandoned crane covered with graffiti. Then immense rectangular blocks that were stacked to form a wall along the east side of the man-made lake. It also had been tagged with spray-painted words: *Does anything even matter anymore?*

Serge leaned over the wall. "It's a sheer drop. I can't see the bottom." Just the sound of wind. Not even birds. "As Buzz Aldrin said on the moon: Magnificent desolation."

It almost had them in a trance. Then an unexpected sound from behind made them both jump.

"Hey, Mr. First-In-Last-Out!"

Serge was half expecting to see Katie, but the voice was a notch off. Maybe she had a cold. He turned around.

Not Katie.

"Who are you?" asked Serge.

"A fan."

"Do I know you?"

"Not yet," said the woman. "Sorry about giving you a heart attack."

"I'll live," said Serge. "But seriously, who *are* you?"

"I've been on the dive boat when you've gone out before. Actually, a couple of times," said the woman. "You're pretty impressive in the water. Never seen someone do that many laps around the *Kokomo.* You never stop."

"In my element . . . So you know about this place?"

"Sure, the old quarry. The whole island is fascinating. Remote and harsh."

"Perfect for the CIA to train counterinsurgents for the Bay of Pigs invasion," said Serge.

"But eventually their remnants became of little use, and they were just loitering," said the woman. "In 1963 local law enforcement responded to complaints from residents and raided the island to flush them out."

"I get chills standing in an empty place like this and thinking back about such exciting history." Serge took another slow look around. "War games? Out here? Insane!"

"But history was repeating itself," said the woman. "In 1895 revolutionaries also trained here to invade during the War of Cuban Independence."

Serge's head jerked back momentarily. Then an arm aimed east. "You know about the ferry dock ruins at the edge of the island?"

She nodded. "Ten years before the Overseas Highway was finally complete in 1938, automobiles had to take the ferry over a forty-mile gap from Lower Matecumbe."

The gauntlet was down and the competition was on.

"The upper islands are Key Largo Limestone," said Serge. "But down here—"

"It's Miami Oolite."

"Okay, early pest control was primitive, and they crisscrossed some of these Keys by digging mosquito ditches—"

"And filled them with gambusia fish, which look like guppies and feed on the larvae . . . You up on hydrology?"

"I know porous oolite holds water."

"What about a freshwater lens?"

"Uh, no."

"Freshwater isn't as dense, and down below in some of these islands, up to twenty feet of freshwater floats kind of like a contact lens right on top of the salt water. Back in the day, they could use dynamite to open a drinking hole."

Game, set, match. He stopped and extended a hand. "Name's Serge."

She shook it. "I'm Sandy."

Serge paused to reappraise his new acquaintance. The name didn't match the raven hair flowing out from under her own bucket hat. And freckles? Jade eyes? Some fascinating ancestry. She was wearing a hydration pack with a Florida State Parks passport book sticking out of a pocket, and a Nikon camera hung from her neck. Her calves were like pistons. Black-rimmed glasses. Brains.

"Serge," whispered Coleman. "She has a plaid shirt."

"Shut up." Serge elbowed him in the stomach. "Mr. Blinky already knows."

"First visit to the quarry?" asked Sandy.

"Yeah, what about you?"

"Been here many times."

"What about the reef?" asked Serge.

"Even more times."

"You like to dive *and* hike?"

"And kayak."

"So having been on the dive boat together, and then us bumping into each other today out in the middle of this nothingness is just a coincidence?"

"Not exactly." Sandy didn't realize she was twirling gravel around with the toe of a hiking boot. "I was in the tiki bar and overheard Captain Katie telling you about this place, and I sort of wanted to meet you."

Serge turned. "Coleman?"

"I know, I know." He started walking toward an out-of-sight bend in the trail. "I wish *I* had a girlfriend."

Serge shouted after him. "And stick your fingers in your ears this time!"

They waited until he disappeared. "Well?" said Serge.

Sandy patted a wide slab atop the rock wall overlooking the quarry.

"Won't that hurt your back?" asked Serge.

"Not my back. Yours." She took off her hat and glasses, and gave him a two-handed shove in the shoulders.

Serge gulped . . .

Coleman stood with fingers in his ears, staring at a tree snail. After a while, he figured it was okay to remove them.

"Key Largo Limestone! . . ."

"Miami Oolite! . . ."

Nope, too soon. He stuck them back in.

Finally, the sweaty, disheveled couple rounded the corner, and Coleman dropped his hands. They all hiked back to the road together, where a second car was now parked next to the Cobra.

Sandy unlocked it. "Maybe I'll see you at the tiki bar tonight?"

"Good chance," said Serge. "You like old *National Geographics*?"

"Sure, I'll bring my collection."

Chapter 26

West Palm Beach

The staff at the law firm was more than frantic. It had been five days now.

Two partners hovered expectantly over the reception desk. A secretary hung up the phone and shook her head. "Still no word. Nobody's seen him, and he's not answering anything."

The partners looked at each other with the same thought: *Is it too early to call the morgue?*

A junior lawyer rushed into the office. "I went by his house to check like you asked. The place is empty, but there's a 'For Sale' sign in the yard."

Alarm and relief at the same time. The morgue was

off the table, but not the intrigue. Reinhold turned back to the secretary. "Keep trying."

Before she could, the phone rang. ". . . Mr. Sparrow! Where are you? We've all been worried sick."

The partners spun at the sound of the name, and grabbed the edge of the counter. "Transfer him to the conference room!"

They ran inside and put him on speaker.

"Nathan, thank God!" said Reinhold.

"What's going on?" asked Nash.

"A few things have come up," said the speaker box.

"Hope everything's all right."

"Getting better every day," said Nathan.

"Listen," said Nash, "I'm sorry, but we had to shoot the last commercial without you. We had no choice."

"That's a good start," said Nathan.

"What do you mean?"

"I want you to buy me out."

"Buy you out of what?"

"The firm," said Nathan.

"Are you sure you're okay?" asked Reinhold. "You're a founding partner. *The* founding partner."

"I'll accept whatever you offer," said Sparrow.

"Uh, there's a 'For Sale' sign in your yard," said Nash.

"Can you get someone to handle the closing for me?" said Sparrow.

"No problem," said Reinhold. "Where do you want us to send the check?"

"Make it out to the Salvation Army."

"Nathan, what's going on?"

"I'll get back to you."

Click.

The day was gray as it began. Quiet, except for a few birds and a frog that splashed in a puddle of algae. Nathan Sparrow walked alone in the woods on a dirt path. He had a lot of catching up to do.

His old firm still didn't know what was going on. Just the occasional mysterious phone call out of necessity. They completed the buyout and house sale and other loose ends. They always had questions at the end of calls, and Sparrow always hung up.

Nobody knew where he was, but Sparrow did. Exactly where he wanted to be.

He continued walking through the pines and palmettos. Gone were the suits and five-hundred-dollar shoes. Now, jeans and boots. His pace was slow, deliberate, looking at individual trees. He placed a hand against one of the trunks and examined a leaf. The scenery was overlain with mental images from the inside of his former mansion. In the early years, there had been a young wife and an unplanned pregnancy, followed soon by a divorce without a fight over custody and child support. What did he care back then? He was hardly home anyway. And when he was there, it was all or nothing. Either it was completely empty, or full of party guests, which meant it was still empty. The place was worth a fortune, and it was worthless.

Nathan looked down at his boots. He had just completed his first job interview in decades, since the one after passing the Florida Bar. Given his education and résumé, he easily landed the position. Only a single big question: Why?

"You do understand what this pays?"

"You don't have to pay me," said Nathan.

"Actually, we do. State law, or we get in trouble."

"Then I'll put it to use."

He hiked down a circular path until arriving at a small building.

"You're the new guy, Sparrow, right?"

Nathan was wearing a short-sleeve olive shirt. A uniform shirt. It had an official patch on the shoulder. He extended a hand. "First name's Bobby."

"I heard it was Nathan."

"That was formal, for business."

The other man shook his hand with a slight laugh.

"For business I'm the Duke of York. Call me Carl. Got a tuna sandwich waiting. Thanks for being on time to spell me."

"Who isn't punctual?"

"You'd be surprised." Carl didn't go far, sitting down at a nearby picnic table and opening a small lunch cooler.

Bobby took a seat inside the booth, but not for long. A car full of people pulled up. He stood and walked to the window. "How are you doing today?"

"Great, and yourself?"

"Perfect." He smiled sincerely at the happy family. "That will be six dollars."

The driver displayed a card. "We have an annual pass."

"Then that will be zero." A grin. "Hope you enjoy your day."

The station wagon didn't move. The driver was reaching toward the back seat. Then out the window. "I've got a couple of these for my kids if you don't mind."

Bobby accepted a pair of small green booklets, opened to the appropriate page. The grin extended. He pulled out a drawer and flipped the cover up on an ink pad. The official stamp came out and he pressed it down with careful precision.

He smiled again as he handed the books back with fresh seals: the shape of Florida and the words *Myakka*

River State Park. The father passed them over to the children.

"Wow!"

"You have a beautiful family," the newest park ranger said as the car pulled away. "Take care."

The next car pulled up and the driver paid cash. But no passport book. The uncomplicated pleasure of the ink pad would have to wait.

Carl came back after lunch.

Bobby pointed at the corner of his own mouth. "You got tuna."

The other ranger wiped it. "If you don't mind, it's a tight bunch around here. The others have been asking. Why would you give up that kind of money?"

"I figured they'd be curious."

"I looked you up online and found your TV commercials. You were like a rock star on the other coast."

"It had its purpose in its time."

"That's what I figured," said Carl. "It was just a job, a means to an end. But now you're doing what you enjoy."

"Pretty much," said Bobby. "Just didn't realize it until now."

Carl was roughly the same age, but appeared slightly older from all the sun and elements out in those marshy hardwoods. He looked down at Nathan's soft white hands and manicured nails. "Don't take this wrong, but you're a city boy. Do you really know much about nature?"

"That's why I'm here. To learn."

A pat on the shoulder. "You're at the right place."

Bobby Sparrow came to know the park well, all the hiking trails and campsites, the lakes and river. And the gators, everywhere. He looked forward to his solitary walks deep in rural Sarasota County.

Many of the rangers lived at the park. There was a long old building out in the woods, chopped up into living quarters.

"Here you are," said Carl, opening a weathered wooden door. "Home sweet home. It's unfurnished. And a little tight."

Sparrow stuck his head inside the new residence. "I like tight. Thanks."

He borrowed one of the park's pickup trucks and went into town for some purchases. That evening he unloaded and got to work. He stood on a drop cloth next to a bucket of paint, with a roller in his hand. A couple hours later he was done.

Bobby stopped and looked around and was satisfied. There was just enough room for a modest single bed, a bookshelf and a small table that served as a desk. The walls were dark green, the same shade as back at the rectory. He sat down and opened a Bible to the Gospel of Matthew, where it had been bookmarked with an envelope.

Sparrow unfolded the letter and read it again. He stared at the wall in thought before finally nodding to himself.

He had the next day off and drove back to the east coast. It took a lot of phone calls and knocks on doors, but he finally got an address. He found himself in a quiet room. He approached a bed and took hold of a weak hand. "Hi, Sarah."

Eyes widened. Nasal grunts.

"It's been a long time. I saw you a few times with Father Al."

Her mouth twisted into her version of a smile. She was now an old woman and her parents were gone. The long-term-care facility was on a budget, the cheapest available with what was left from the wills.

He turned toward an attendant standing in the doorway. "Does she get many visitors?"

"You're the first."

"Since when?"

"Since I've been working here."

"How long's that?"

"Been here ten years. Eleven this fall."

Bobby looked around the sparse room. "Where are her pictures?"

"What pictures?"

"The autographed ones."

"Oh, those. They're in a box somewhere," said the attendant. "Some people from the church brought them by when they helped move her in."

"Why aren't they on the walls where she can see them?"

"Regulations prohibit unauthorized material."

He looked at the floor. A head shook. "This won't do . . ."

A private ambulance crossed the state and arrived at the most modern and expensive care facility in Sarasota, not coincidentally a convenient drive from the state park. They wheeled Sarah into her new room. The bubbling cheer of the place extended from the decor to the staff, which was overstaffed. A group of smiling people surrounded her bed and introduced themselves. Bobby opened a cardboard box and pulled out a roll of tape. He placed an autographed photo of an ice skater on a wall.

"What are you doing?" asked a nurse.

"Putting up her photos."

"It's not really allowed."

"She loves them. It gets her through." Bobby pulled out a thick money clip and began peeling off hundreds. "How much?"

The nurse smiled warmly. "Put your money away."

The whole staff became busy with tape until the walls were covered with signed pictures.

A mouth twisted in joy. Bobby held her hand again. “I’ll be back soon.”

His next day off, Bobby Sparrow held a hammer. It drove a nail. He and the other volunteers heaved to erect the stud wall. He was wearing a T-shirt from Habitat for Humanity. So this was happiness? Who knew? He joined crews collecting trash on the beach and handing out relief supplies after storms. He gave blood.

And each evening Sparrow returned to the park and his small green room. The letter was now taped to the wall, just like one of Sarah’s photos:

> Most people have the ability to know what the right things are to do. They just choose not to listen to their inner voice. Follow your heart.
>
> Shalom,
> Father Al

Fingers pressed buttons on a cell phone. Bobby Sparrow put it to his ear. It rang and rang. He left a voice message, just as he did every day, week after week. He hung up.

He dialed another number. This time he got through. He was put on hold. The secretary came back on the line. “He said he doesn’t want to talk to you.”

“I understand.”

A high-mileage Oldsmobile crossed the state again and pulled into the parking lot of a law office in downtown West Palm Beach. Bobby Sparrow entered the lobby. He spoke to the receptionist and pleaded his case. She finally relented and led him to a door and opened it. “Mr. Pickering, he insisted on seeing you.”

The lawyer looked up. “I can’t believe my eyes. You actually have the balls to show up here?”

“I want to apologize,” said Bobby. “The night with the woman in the bar.”

“Go fuck yourself.”

“Apology still stands.”

Bobby left and drove to a private home. Moments later, a woman stood stunned in the doorway, holding a check. “What’s this hundred thousand dollars for?”

“What I cheated you out of,” said Bobby. “The violation of the non-disclosure clause after your settlement. I’m so sorry.”

He parked downtown and entered another law office. Word swept the floor in excitement. The remaining partners came running out of their offices.

"Nathan, for God's sake, we've been trying like hell to get hold of you," said Reinhold.

"Are you okay?" asked Nash.

"Couldn't be better," said Nathan.

They looked at his boots and jeans and finally his face. "You haven't shaved," said Nash. "Are you trying to grow a beard?"

"No, if I don't feel like shaving, I don't."

"Last we spoke, we sold the house," said Reinhold. "But then we couldn't reach you, so we took care of the taxes and put the money in an account in your name. You gave us power of attorney."

"You have the paperwork?"

They sent the clerk for a file and handed it to him, including an unused checkbook. "Have I gotten any calls?"

"A million. Like I said, you were unreachable."

"No, you know what I mean," said Bobby. "A *call*."

The others just silently shook their heads.

He began to leave. "Thanks for handling this for me."

"When will we see you again?"

"I don't know."

The Oldsmobile had more miles to go before dark. It arrived in Miami. Another office building. Bobby was led inside by a man in a starched dress shirt. "Heather, there's someone—"

"Dad, what on earth are you doing here?"

"I've been calling and calling. Leaving voice messages. You never called back."

A firm pause. "And you have no idea why?"

"There's a lot of things I need to say."

"You had plenty of opportunity before," said Heather. "After the divorce, when me and Mom moved out, we never heard from you again. And we were just across town. Heck, even before the divorce you were never home."

"Work."

"I work, too." She pointed up at the seal of the Florida Department of Law Enforcement. "That's no excuse."

"I lost my way."

"And now you've found it?"

"I'm trying." He opened his wallet. He had filled out the check in the parking lot. He placed it on her desk.

She looked at all the zeroes. "You think you can buy me?"

"That's not to buy you," said Nathan. "That's for your security. It's good to have a safety net."

She held it toward him. "I'm not going to cash this."

"Then just keep it."

He left the building.

Chapter 27

The Next Day

The clock struck noon.

The minute hand was six feet long. Up in the tower of another historic old Florida courthouse. This one in DeLand, the seat of Volusia County. The dome was verdigris.

A camera poked out the window of a blue-and-white Cobra. *Click, click, click.* Serge was mildly dejected that he had to drive on to the modern new courthouse nearby.

He entered an office and stood at the counter.

"How may I help you?" asked an assistant clerk.

"I need everything you've got on one Chester Montclair," said Serge. "All the vitals, and don't leave anything out, even if it's embarrassing. I'm researching the best family tree ever!"

"Chester Montclair?" asked the clerk. "I don't have it right now."

Serge was aghast. "You lost it?"

"No, she's got it." The clerk pointed toward a woman Serge hadn't noticed, standing at the other end of the counter in a business suit.

Serge walked over. "What a coincidence!"

The woman looked up. "Excuse me?"

"Imagine two people showing up at the same time in this quaint little hamlet and requesting the same seventy-year-old files. What are the odds?"

"You came here for the Montclair files?"

Serge nodded effervescently with a huge smile.

"What for?"

"Why, just the most incredible family tree anyone's ever attempted!" said Serge. "I got hooked from an infomercial in the middle of the night that targets drunk insomniacs, but I was sober as a judge. And when I pick up a new hobby, stand clear!"

"That's nice," she said curtly, and looked back down at the open files spread in front of her across the counter.

Serge scooted closer. "Heard Chester was a Fuller Brush salesman. The economy is always changing, and people are always shocked. They probably thought selling toilet scrubbers door-to-door would go on forever. I also found another relative who was a big turpentiner in these parts, back in the time when something like that could be big. Today? You're in a bread line. Did you ever read the book *Who Moved My Cheese?* You have to stay nimble in the business world, or you end up holding a bucket of turpentine in the woods and wondering where everybody went."

She smiled professionally and looked back down again.

"You working on your own family tree?" asked Serge. "I can give you some tips. People don't want you to plant grass plugs in their shitty yard."

Without emotion: "Official business."

"Wow!" said Serge. "I'm guessing law enforcement, and by your dress code probably FDLE. That's the bomb! You must have gotten good grades. What's your name?"

A sigh. "Heather."

"Heather, I'm a staunch supporter of the fine men and women who lay it all out on the line every day. And what a thrill getting to watch you doing whatever it is you're doing to protect me. This is so exciting!" He got even closer. "Mind if I look over your shoulder?"

Still looking down. "I'd rather you didn't."

"Right, I'm being annoying again. Have to watch that. I've gotten the feedback." Serge took a step in reverse and clasped his hands in front of himself, staring at her.

After a few moments of silence, she looked sideways. "What are you doing?"

"Not being annoying."

"It isn't working." Then she noticed something else. A plump man slumped in a nearby chair with eyes closed. "Who's that?"

"My trusty sidekick, Coleman."

"Is he drunk?"

A shrug. "Your guess is as good as mine. So what are you really working on? Chester's been dead forever, so it can't be him." Serge suddenly snapped his fingers. "If the FDLE is building a family tree, I'll bet you're tracking the DNA of a serial killer."

She stopped and turned with more attention this time. "What makes you say that?"

Another shrug. "It's what I'd do."

"If you wouldn't mind." Heather looked back down, trying to ignore him and concentrate as best she could. And Serge did his best to remain quiet. It lasted a minute.

Heather flipped a page and began hearing fingers tapping on the counter. Then: "Yep, it must be fascinating being a state agent." More tapping. "I wonder where that Montclair file will lead her in the thirst for justice. Hmm." *Tap, tap, tap.* "Bet it can't top the last file I found, no sirree! Those documents told me I had a great-great-great-grand-uncle, Rafael Cortez, a *lector* in Tampa. Imagine my delight! Those were the guys who sat on tall stands in cigar factories and read out loud the whole day so all the workers sitting shoulder to shoulder rolling tobacco leaves for hours on end wouldn't jump off the roof of the building. They had to sit up high so the whole room could hear, and they read all kinds of stuff: magazines, novels. *The Count of Monte Cristo* was one of their favorites. But what they really loved was newspapers, taking their minds all over the world for the wonders of current events . . ."

Serge began slowly waving his arms back and forth, snake-like, as he stared at the ceiling.

After a few moments of this, Heather dropped her pen. "What on earth are you doing?"

Serge continued moving arms and looking up. "A fade-out."

"Whatever that is, could you please stop?"

"Too late. Already begun." Arms waving faster. "It was more than a hundred and twenty years ago, but seems like only yesterday . . ."

The giant brick factory stood on Seventh Avenue in the section of Tampa called Ybor City, named for Vicente Martinez-Ybor, who helped found the nation's cigar capital in the 1880s.

In 1898, on a crisp afternoon in February, the sixteenth, a tall middle-aged man in a straw hat and suspenders climbed the steps of a small wooden stand overlooking the manufacturing floor. He had a thick, dark mustache, like most of the employees rolling cigars in dutiful silence.

Rafael Cortez took a seat and opened a newspaper. The stories were always entertaining, but this day they were riveting. Cortez informed the cavernous room that there had been an explosion on the USS *Maine*, and the battleship had sunk in the harbor of Havana. Uncharacteristic murmurs rippled through the room. Cortez went on to recount that 260 men had been lost, some of whom would eventually be buried in Key West beneath a statue of a sailor holding an oar.

More murmurs. Cigar-rolling was tedious business, but the workers couldn't wait to get to the factory in the ensuing days for more intrigue. Most were illiterate, and Cortez was one of their only sources of information. The factory owner scratched his head at the unexplained increase in production.

Just over two months later, on April 26, Rafael climbed up onto his stand. Everyone was waiting. The *lector* announced that the United States, citing in part the loss of the *Maine*, had just declared war on Spain. The murmurs in the room gave way to robust banter.

That's when Rafael went off script. He stood up on his stand, dramatically flapping the paper over his head. "This is yellow journalism, I tell you! Just designed to sell papers for William Randolph Hearst! Explosions happen on ships all the time, especially those with lots of gunpowder. Where's the proof? This is a classic colonial expansion propaganda tactic! Don't you believe it for a second! . . ."

The factory's supervisors went outside to summon police walking the beat.

". . . And while I'm at it, I'll tell you what else is bullshit: this whole city! Remember the old days when we rolled cigars in Key West? We had a union back then, *La Liga*, better pay and conditions. And why did they move us all up here? Just to bust the union!" He threw a fist in the air. "Workers unite! Workers unite! Break the shackles of the imperialists! . . ."

The cops came pouring in and climbed the stand.

"Let go of me, you fascists! . . ."

His fingers clung to the railing as they pulled him sideways by upended legs.

"This is supposed to be a democracy, but see what happens when the individual speaks out? . . ."

Four police officers pried his fingers loose and carried him off, still sideways.

"When the workers unite, the power class tries to divide us," yelled Rafael. "Mark my words! In the future, America will be dominated by politicians making us hate each other."

The cops reached the door with their prisoner.

"Have you ever even been to Maine? Who lives there? You'll freeze your balls off! . . ."

Serge gradually stopped waving his arms and dropped them by his side. "Yep, definitely the Serge genes." He looked around. "Where'd she go?"

Chapter 28

Sarasota County

A turkey vulture swooped low over the desolate road slicing through frontier country a dozen miles east of the city. The blue-and-white Cobra slowed and turned through the entrance gate.

Serge was already waving his green book out the window as he eased up to the guard booth.

"Myakka River State Park! My favorite! Here's my annual park pass, so no cash today! Been here a million times, but always before the unfettered joy of the passport book, so get out that ink pad of mutual empowerment and hit this baby!"

The ranger smiled mildly as he stamped the appointed page. "Enjoy your visit."

"Is there even a doubt?" Serge was about to pull through when he stopped and squinted at the ranger. "I know you."

"Don't think so."

"Yes, I'm sure of it, because I never forget a face, especially those that aren't here anymore. Don't read anything into that." He leaned farther out the window. "Why can't I place where I've seen you before?"

"You must be thinking of someone else."

"No, I—" He suddenly clapped his hands. "I remember now! You're that *guy*!"

"That's not very specific."

"You know, those fancy commercials for your law firm," said Serge. "Great production values. All that Norman Rockwell shit and kittens."

Bobby winced at being recognized as the former Nathan. It was the main reason he had chosen a state park on the opposite coast, where the ads didn't run.

"You're probably wondering how I know 'cause the ads don't run over here," said Serge. "But I'm a holistic Florida kind of guy, loving all parts of the state equally without judging. Much."

Another tempered smile from the ranger. "Nice to meet you."

"Seriously, what are you doing in that booth? Why aren't you ripping insurance fat cats new ones?"

"Sort of had a change of careers."

"I get it," said Serge. "Some life-numbing event or two happened, and one day you said, 'What the fuck am I doing with my life? I've lost my way. I need to follow my heart.'"

Bobby was so startled that he uncharacteristically dropped his guard. "How do you know that?"

"Logic. I'm a student of human nature. And the same thing happened to me. Actually it's always happening to me. Most recently I discovered the entire meaning of life. What did you find?"

"At least what makes me happy."

"And what exactly is that?" asked Serge.

"Making others happy."

"Coleman! Holy shit! Did you hear that? We're on the same spiritual journey!" He looked back at the guard booth. "We need to compare notes! I've been trying to make people happy, but judging by the facial expressions I think I'm a peg or two off on the concept. Maybe you can tune me in."

"I'm kind of busy these days with all the new park duties."

Serge pumped his eyebrows. "It would make me happy . . ."

An hour later, lunch break. Bobby met Serge and Coleman at a picnic table. He was actually happy to have normal people to talk to. Well maybe not normal, just different from the Palm Beach social register.

Here was the thing about Serge meeting new people: It was a binary event. Either they hit it off famously, or the encounter immediately crashed and burned with cringing disaster. No middle ground. Laughter or tears. Or worse, screaming and running and flagging down the nearest police car. It was just a question of where Serge currently was in his knitting-ball of intersecting mental swings. Most people quickly figured out that he was unusual. Catch him on the right node, and it would be ascribed to bubbliness, charisma, intelligence, coffee and an overactive imagination. Then it was a random matter of time before the true picture emerged. Could be two weeks, or two minutes.

"You're pretty bubbly," said the ranger.

Serge nodded hard, sipping a Styrofoam cup from 7-Eleven. He tapped his right temple. "Always thinking. Always curious. Like, from the file 'How is this a thing?' Ready? The coconut bra. Your thoughts?"

"Drawing a blank."

"It's not remotely functional, yet it's out there doing its stuff. It's been keeping me up at night for hours."

"Uh, what exactly is your friend doing?" asked the ranger.

Serge turned to the seat next to him at the picnic

table. Coleman glanced around suspiciously, then uncapped a prescription bottle and popped three pills in his mouth.

Serge snatched the plastic container out of his hands—"Gimme that!"—and read the label. "Where'd you get this?"

"Bought it on the street."

"It's docusate sodium."

Coleman nodded. "Guy said it was good."

"But it's a prescription stool softener."

Coleman grabbed the bottle back. "Still a prescription. *Party!*"

"Oh, it will definitely be a party," said Serge. "Remind me to RSVP an enthusiastic no."

The ranger stared with an open mouth.

"Sorry about that," said Serge. "Back to the coconut bra. It's been keeping me up because I have this image stuck in my head. Why do we have it? I was working the problem and I thought possibly if Amelia Earhart somehow survived the plane crash and was able to swim to a remote Pacific island with all her clothes torn off. Then her navigator also survives and swims ashore, and now she's got to see him every day at work. I'm not saying she was a prude, but she did what she had to. And now I have this persistent picture in my head of Amelia Earhart in a coconut bra. At first it was pleasant, but it's become disturbing. If someone says: 'Whatever you do, don't keep thinking about Amelia Earhart in a coconut bra,' what's going to happen? You're fucked!" Serge slapped the side of his head. "Still in there. Can you help me?"

This time it took a whole ten minutes for the picture to emerge. The ranger stood up from the picnic table and tilted his head toward the guard booth. "I kind of need to be getting back."

"You've barely touched your lunch," said Serge. "And it's tuna salad! The *Calvin and Hobbes* treat!"

"I really need to go."

"One more minute, please?" said Serge. "I got off track because of the image, but I seriously wanted to pick your brain. I've been reading the gospel of Matthew."

The ranger paused. "Chapters five to seven?"

"Damn, you're good! How on earth did you know?" said Serge. "I've been doing some self-searching and decided I needed to hit the reset button on my life."

The ranger stood in thought. From his time at the soup kitchen serving the homeless, he realized the country had a serious problem of untreated mental illness out on the streets. This Serge character might have a little or a lot. But given the ranger's new dedication to following in Father Al's footsteps, he couldn't just walk away from a troubled soul. He sat back down.

"Thanks," said Serge. "Anyway, I bore down on those Bible chapters and it completely changed me: the poor in spirit, those who mourn, the meek, the merciful, the peacemakers. I decided to put those teachings in play with a full-court press. I offered to trim a guy's ear hair, watched *Sea Hunt* with an old Greek woman, and gave detergent to the Statue of Liberty. You see my problem?"

"Have you seen a doctor?" asked the ranger.

"Why?" Serge beat his chest like Tarzan. "I have the physical constitution of Bo Jackson."

"I know this free clinic—"

Serge waved him off. "The urgent matter at hand is my awe at the fork in the road you've taken. You had it all! Money, prestige, power, celebrity from the TV ads. Most people would kill for that, but you walked away. You figured it all out and centered yourself. That's where I'm falling short. So tell me, what strategies have you employed to take your life change to the next level?"

"If I understand your question, I volunteer," said Bobby.

"Volunteer?" Serge popped himself in the forehead. "It's so obvious it wasn't obvious." He stood up at attention and saluted. "Reporting for duty, sir."

"What?"

"I'm volunteering."

"Well, I know a number of places," said Bobby. "The homeless shelter, the literacy project—"

"No," said Serge. "Right here and now. Life's too short. Where do I begin?"

Bobby took a deep breath. "Okay, we do have some volunteers at the park who help with maintenance and pick up trash."

"Trash?" said Serge. "But it's a state park."

"What do you mean?"

"The type of people who come here are those who most respect the pristineness of nature," said Serge. "Why would they litter?"

"One thing I've learned is that human behavior will never stop surprising you."

Coleman popped another pill.

"And how," said Serge. "Let's rodeo that litter! . . ."

The next evening Serge and Coleman joined Ranger Bobby at the homeless shelter.

Serge ladled chicken and stars into a bowl, and smiled across the serving table at a man in rags. "In exchange, backstory. Was it heart-wrenching misfortune, or did you never stop screwing up?"

"Serge," said Bobby.

"What?"

"Just serve soup."

Three men walked down a hiking trail east of Sarasota. A candy wrapper went into a garbage bag, then a beer can and an empty Gatorade bottle that had been impaled on a tree branch.

"That's a tricolored heron," said Serge. "Right?"

"Yep," said Bobby.

Serge reached in his pocket for a small weather-resistant Audubon field guide. "Another project I've been working on. I really love these parks, which makes me feel inadequate about my flora and fauna identification skills. I've got most of the wading birds down, but I'm still shaky on some of the trees, particularly the palms, which should be right in my kill box. The royals and Canary Island dates are easy, but some of the low growth looks too similar. Is that a saw palmetto?"

"Yep."

"And a traveler's palm isn't technically a palm at all but a member of another genus?"

"Correct again . . ."

Serge continued on, hiking, collecting garbage and working on nature education, his voice steady, calm and lucid. Almost academic. Ranger Bobby began to reassess his initial take on the visitor. Maybe Serge was on some kind of medication that hadn't kicked in earlier. Maybe it was the coffee. Whatever, he seemed quite normal now, more so than a lot of the oddballs who streamed through the park's entrance.

"I have a question," said the ranger.

"Fire away." Serge studied a photo of a king sago in his guidebook.

"What religion are you?"

"My own."

"You mean non-denominational?"

"Even less structured," said Serge. "Mine is the religion of questions. The big outfits don't dig that."

"Then why were you reading the Bible?"

"Why not?" Serge stepped over a gopher tortoise. "I think a lot of people get turned off on religion, just because some of the followers use love as an excuse to hate. But they're just short-changing themselves on some great teachings. Kurt Vonnegut was a self-described atheist or agnostic, depending on which day you caught him, but the Gospels are a strong thread through his body of work."

"Are you an atheist?"

"Nope," said Serge. "How can you look up at the night sky and not realize that some shit's going down somewhere? I just don't have the remotest clue what. That's why I've decided to work on my people skills."

They moved on to another trail by the upper lake, chatting, growing on each other.

"Now *I* have a question," said Serge. "When we first met, and I mentioned you probably went through some life-altering events, I saw a shock of recognition. What were they?"

Before Bobby realized what was happening, he surprised himself by opening up. ". . . There was the priest, Father Al. Someone had stolen my bicycle . . ." He continued at length, right up to the funeral and the letter the priest had left for him.

"He must have been a truly spiritual guy," said Serge.

"That he was," said Bobby. "And his passing away just happened to come around the time that someone had threatened my daughter."

Serge's feet stopped. "That's terrible, as close to home as it gets. Is she safe?"

"Not a physical threat," said Bobby. "It was political. Her career. But I took care of it."

"Glad to hear."

"But that's my biggest regret."

"Now you've lost me."

"When I was younger, building that law firm was all-consuming in every way," said Bobby. "I got my priorities messed up, and I didn't spend time with my daughter."

"A lot of fathers have to make that sacrifice to put

food on the table," said Serge. "Then they're too hard on themselves, wishing they spent more time."

"You're missing my meaning," said Bobby. "I didn't spend *any* time. All I could think about was money and what it could buy and chasing women. Then we had to go and make those stupid commercials, and my life became overpopulated with friends who were anything but. My life was full. Full of emptiness. My daughter won't talk to me. The only communication we've had in years is a call I got when her job was jeopardized because of me."

"Nothing that can't be fixed," said Serge. "Loved ones reconcile all the time."

"I think this is pretty unfixable."

"Why don't you let me try?" said Serge. "It would be my chance to make a change in someone's life bigger than *Sea Hunt*."

"Please don't take any offense," said Bobby. "When we met at the picnic table, I had big reservations about you. Now I realize it was an inauspicious first impression. But I still don't know you well enough to expose my daughter to you."

"Say no more." Serge tossed a cigarette butt into a litter bag. "I'd be just as cautious."

Chapter 29

The Next Day

A black Lincoln Nautilus pulled up in front of a condominium, and the Uber driver got out to help the passengers because they were ancient.

The old man had a walker with tennis balls on the ends of the legs, but his wife only needed a cane.

It was a low-rise condo with lush landscaping that was the product of a professional service who swarmed with loud, gas-powered equipment every Thursday morning. Azaleas, crotons, fan palms. The stucco walls were bright white, setting off the turquoise doors.

Charlie and Madge Petrocelli, from Kalamazoo.

Someone at the airport had helped them get the Uber ride, because they didn't know how it worked.

Now, at the condo, the driver opened the trunk and began removing an amount of luggage that could sustain a jungle expedition. He courteously carried it all to the door of unit 7.

"You've been so kind," said Madge, snapping open her purse for a generous tip.

The driver left, and Madge looked at her husband. "Didn't that rental agent say there was supposed to be a lockbox on the door with the keys?"

Charlie shrugged. "Try the knob."

She twisted it. "Locked. What are we going to do?"

"Couldn't hurt to ring the doorbell."

She pressed a button and heard chimes inside.

They didn't expect any result, but the door opened. "Yes, how can I help you?"

The confused couple stared at an equally confused retired woman in a bathrobe, who was looking down at a massive pile of suitcases on her porch.

"There wasn't a lockbox on the door," said Madge.

"Why would there be?" asked the woman.

"Because we rented this place," said Madge.

"Paid six months in advance," said Charlie.

"You have the wrong address," said the woman.

Madge opened her purse again, unfolding a document and handing it to the woman at the door. "That's our rental agreement."

The woman read it. "You have the correct address all right, but there must be some kind of mistake. You can't be renting this place because I've already paid until the end of the year."

"How is that possible?" asked Madge.

"I don't know," said the woman. "But I'll call the property manager and get this straightened out. Probably just a paperwork error, and you're in a different unit."

The manager arrived and looked over the document. She got on the phone.

Then the police arrived.

Madge was crying.

The officers tried to explain the situation as gently as possible: The retired couple had rented the condo off of Quirk's List. But there was a big scam in Florida spreading like typhoid. The grifters would find a legitimate rental, then copy all the information and even download beautiful photos of the vacation homes in paradise. Then they'd upload all the fake material anonymously in an Internet café.

"But we paid for six months," said a sobbing Madge.

And the officers were correct when they guessed that the payment was through Western Union.

"These people know what they're doing," said one of the cops. "They're very difficult to trace."

The other officer cleared his throat. "What are your plans?"

"We planned to stay here." Madge blew her nose in a lace handkerchief.

The first officer pursed his lips in heartfelt sympathy. "I'll call and have victims' services come out, and we can get you set up at a motel."

"How much will that cost?" asked Charlie.

"We can get a discount," said the other officer. "The important thing is to get you settled in for the night. Then we'll turn all this information over to the detectives and hope for the best."

Madge stowed her handkerchief. "What are the chances we'll get our money back?"

The officers knew, and they changed the subject. "Let's first work on that motel room."

Sarasota

A blue-and-white Cobra pulled up to the guard booth. Serge gleefully flapped his green passport book out the window.

"Oh, right," said a ranger named Michelle, grabbing her ink pad.

"No, I already have the official stamp," said Serge.

"Just wanted to show you that I'm down with the program. You know what Ranger Bobby is doing?"

"Day off."

"Rats. So he's not here."

"No, he's here. He lives here."

"Really?"

"We got this old building out in the woods that we converted into apartments."

"Great, I'll pay a surprise visit."

"Sorry, that area is authorized personnel only."

"But I'm really tight with Bobby. We're almost family," said Serge. "Could you call him and get us permission? Of course, it will ruin the surprise."

"Give me a minute." The ranger got on the phone briefly and came back to the window. "He says it's fine. Here's the map to get there . . ."

The Cobra rolled through a canopy of oaks until it arrived at the no-frills building nestled in the trees. Bobby was already waiting at the door and invited them in.

"Wow," said Serge. "You really are serious about the life change. You're living like a monk."

"More like Father Al. I arranged it like his room in the rectory. Where's Coleman?"

"So-called 'resting' back at the motel." Serge slapped the side of his head. "Crap, Amelia's back."

Uh-oh, thought Bobby. *Here we go again, meds not kicking in.*

"Hey, you're an attorney," said Serge. "I'll bet I know something about the law that you don't."

Bobby just smiled.

"This is really cool!" said Serge. "There was this one firm that did a lot of product-liability defense for big corporations. Of course, the companies are always selling stuff they shouldn't. I mean, where were the lawyers when they dreamed up lawn darts? On the other hand, there are a lot of dishonest people out there trying to make a fast buck from deep pockets. And from the file named 'I can't believe that's really a job,' the defense firms hire scientists who specialize in analyzing liability evidence, and they made a wacky discovery in one case. The plaintiff was suing a huge soda company because there was a big dead rat inside the can, way larger than the hole from the pop-top. But here's what the scientist found out: The plaintiff had a hobby of building ships inside bottles. He had emptied the soda from the can, and dropped a teeny-tiny baby rat through the hole and kept feeding and growing it inside there until it was a big honkin' rodent, then he opened another can of soda and poured it into the first can, drowning it—that's the downer part of the story—but isn't the rest freaking crazy?"

"I wasn't aware of that," Bobby said evenly. Meds definitely not working.

"Human behavior fascinates me!" said Serge. "The potential daily decisions are equally endless and pointless: A pit bull attacked a family in Tampa when they tried to dress it in a Christmas sweater. That's not really on topic, but the key to life is ignoring the guardrails. I'll calm down. Want to go for a hike?"

"Why not?"

The afternoon proceeded like the day before. Serge indeed mellowed. The unspoiled nature appeared to affect him and the ranger equally. They stopped on the trail simply to look at the geometry of a spiderweb.

"Now this is religion," said Serge.

"Creation," said Bobby. "Amazing."

"You know how people are always talking about a scene?"

"Scene?"

"A spontaneous confluence of people, time and place. Expatriate Paris, fifties Miami Beach, the Tangier Interzone artist movement in Morocco, Haight-Ashbury's Summer of Love, Seattle grunge. Admittedly not all are equal," said Serge. "People are always trying to find the current scene, except you can't just invent them, and when they can't find them, they look in the rearview at scenes through history that only grow more mythical with time. But my entire youth was a scene: old Florida. All the great unspoiled, uncrowded places with distinct architecture and personality. The Dairy Belle near Blue Heron, the Trylon tower, the Everglades Hotel on Biscayne, Jimbo's fish camp, the vaulted Clematis library with the picture windows on Lake Worth, and funky independent drugstores with suntan lotion signs, fortune-telling scales and comic book sections. All of them as dead as three-channel TV that signed off the air each night with the national anthem and a prayer."

"I know what you're talking about," said the ranger. "I once snuck over to the Orange Bowl when I was a little kid, and had to go to confession for that stunt. Years later I saw pictures in the newspaper of a wrecking ball taking down the end zone scoreboard."

"Exactly," said Serge. "I've been driving all over the state for a couple of decades now trying to recapture that. Occasionally I'll find a surviving landmark, but it's always wedged into a wall of sterile new chain stores that identically repeats itself city after city, coast after coast. No scene. Just horrible drivers racing by without any institutional memory of what they're missing."

"We definitely were lucky growing up when we did," said Bobby.

"Then you should clearly remember this iconic childhood memory, as only someone who grew up where and when we did could," said Serge. "The huge blackouts!"

"I don't remember the power going out," said Bobby. "At least not for very long."

Serge threw up his arms. "It might as well have! I'm talking about the Super Bowls in Miami!"

"Oh yeah," said Bobby. "People wouldn't believe it today. I almost still can't. Super Bowl blackouts."

"Allow me to digress, which is my strength."

"Can I stop you?" asked Bobby.

"I just found out a cool story of one of my relatives getting arrested in Miami back in 1968."

"What for?"

"Running onto the field during the Super Bowl, yelling, 'We won! We won!'"

"How many others were arrested?"

"Just him."

"That's odd," said Bobby. "People are always getting onto the field shouting 'We won!' Especially at Super Bowls. They usually let it slide because of the excitement."

"Usually," said Serge. "Except this was *before* the game. He was yelling 'We won!' out of local pride that Miami was hosting its first Super Bowl."

"Okay, I get it now," said Bobby. "But how is that a cool story?"

"Because most people also don't remember that back then it wasn't called the Super Bowl until the third one, when the Jets beat the Colts, also in Miami," said Serge. "The first game in Los Angeles and the second in Miami, when the Packers repeated and beat the Raiders thirty-three to fourteen, were officially dubbed the AFL-NFL World Championship. And before the second one, my uncle's getting hauled off in cuffs, still excited and yelling. 'I feel super! Miami is super! What a super day for the super bowl!' Next year they changed the name."

"I doubt it was because of him."

"I'm going with it anyway," said Serge. "If you don't make up cool shit about your family, nobody else will . . . Allow me to circle back around: Remember the blackout parties in South Florida?"

"Who doesn't?" said Bobby. "Everyone drove north. It was crazy."

"You don't have to convince me," said Serge. "The leagues didn't have their acts together yet, and even though Miami's first Super Bowls—two, three and five—sold out, they never lifted the regular-season television blackouts for the Dolphins viewing area, which extended up through Broward and Palm Beach Counties. I remember having to listen to Dolphins home games all the time on the radio. But Super Bowls? Can you believe that stupidness?"

Bobby smiled. "At least we got to go to the blackout parties."

Serge nodded and smiled back. "Some of my fondest coming-of-age-in-Florida heritage moments. The county line was only ten miles north, and the area's big employers were RCA and Pratt & Whitney. So for each blackout, dozens of the guys got together and drove up U.S. 1 a few minutes over into Martin County, where the blackout wasn't in effect, and rented rooms at the Howard Johnson or Holiday Inn. Just for the TVs."

"I was only a kid," said Bobby. "What eye-opening parties."

"And how," said Serge. "It was like episodes of *Mad Men*, all these old-school guys in short-sleeve dress shirts packing the rooms, smoking Pall Malls and setting up massively stocked wet bars of Canadian Mist and Cutty Sark. Grilling steaks on hibachis in the parking lot. There I am, a little kid looking up at all these professional men shouting with each touchdown and letting me have all the chips and soda my stomach could handle. And by the end, some were falling down, and one needed a butterfly bandage on his forehead."

"It was almost better that there *were* blackouts," said Ranger Bobby. "And digression is indeed your strength. I completely forgot what we were talking about."

"People are always looking in vain for the current scene," said Serge. "But I just had an epiphany: It's been staring me in the face for so long that I feel like an idiot. We *do* have a scene. A thriving one that's never gone away: our natural spaces, state parks and preserves." Serge spread his arms. "This is it."

"I agree totally," said the ranger.

They stopped and stared in tranquil silence out across a prairie between the bridge and upper lake. It was covered with a blanket of yellow.

"I've stood here a million times taking in this vista," said Serge. "But this is the first time I've seen the coreopsis in bloom."

"Tickseed, the official state wildflower," said Bobby.

Serge pointed. "And for decades I've been watching that same lone sabal palm standing out there in the field. What caused it to stray from the herd? Independence? Rejection? . . . Yes, sir, just stopping and getting in tune with this scene makes it all worthwhile."

"I'm with you," said Bobby. "But you do realize that there's a big government movement up in Tallahassee to profit off the parks by designating chunks of land to lease for logging, cattle grazing and, if you can believe it, hunting."

"You're shitting me."

"Soulless politicians who place no value on just existing in the moment in the real Florida like this. Their scene is dollar signs."

"Let me know when they're on the way," said Serge. "I may have to chain myself to something."

"I'll be right next to you."

"Can I ask you a personal question?" said Serge.

"Hasn't stopped you so far."

"Why don't you go see your daughter?"

"There's a non sequitur."

"Seriously."

"I have my reasons."

"I'd be happy to serve as the go-between," said Serge.

"You promised me yesterday you wouldn't."

"That I did."

They ended up back at the ranger's apartment. "So where are you off to now?" asked Bobby.

"To spread the word." Serge reached into the Cobra and showed the ranger a homemade sign.

Bobby just chuckled and waved as he drove off.

Three Hours Later

Serge entered the economy motel room, wearing a shredded green robe and crumpled hat.

Coleman looked up from his bong. “What the hell happened to your Statue of Liberty costume?”

“Got in a fight with two guys.” He tossed a bent piece of cardboard in the wastebasket. “They said my sign was un-American.”

He went over to his corkboard, sitting upright on the dresser, and examined the overflow of notecards. “This is the best! I had a great-uncle who worked on Henry Flagler’s Overseas Railroad at Pigeon Key! Someone else worked with dolphins when the Miami Seaquarium first opened, and another guy operated a backhoe to clear land for Disney World.”

Coleman exhaled a bong hit. “Sounds like you have a cool family.”

“Well, they can’t all be winners. For every scallop farmer in Steinhatchee, there’s three guys living out of their cars.”

“We’ve done that.”

“Because we wanted to,” said Serge. “Did you really have to make a bong out of that?”

“You gave me the idea.” He blew another hit toward the ceiling. “I glued the two halves of a coconut bra together, and poked holes for the stem and carburetor. Plus it’s sexy.”

“Amelia . . .” Serge slapped the side of his head. “You bastard.”

"Uh-oh," said Coleman.

"What is it?"

"The pills again." He sprinted for the bathroom.

Serge went back to his board and tacked up a notecard for a distant aunt from the suffragette movement.

Coleman returned. "Another close one."

"They always say be careful what you buy on the street."

Knock, knock, knock.

Serge threw his arms up in triumph. "Backstory!"

He grabbed a box of detergent and opened the door.

An old woman was crying.

"Whoa! Take it easy!" said Serge. "What's the matter?"

"Can you help with the vending machine?" Sniffles. "My corn chips are stuck on the corkscrew."

"I have a feeling this goes beyond snacks."

"It's been a bad day."

"Why don't you come inside and have a seat." He helped her by the arm like a Boy Scout. "And tell me all about it. What's your name?"

"Madge. Madge Petrocelli."

"What seems to be the problem, Madge?"

She wiped tears. "We rented a condominium down here. Never been to Florida before, but my husband Charlie isn't in good health and doesn't have long."

"What do doctors know?" said Serge.

"It's his pancreas."

Serge winced. That's rarely good.

"Anyway," said Madge. "We decided to use all our savings to enjoy what time he has left down here in the sun."

"What will you live on afterward?"

"I'll figure something out," said the retiree. "The only thing that matters now is spending time with my Charlie."

"That's very noble," said Serge. "Sounds like you're in for some happy days. So why the tears? Is Charlie okay?"

She nodded. "We went to the condo, and it turns out that it was already rented to someone else. The police said it was a scam, something about a cloned website. I don't know what that is."

"I do," said Serge. "And I'm guessing you paid up front by Western Union for several months."

"Six."

Serge winced even harder. "Do you happen to have any of the paperwork?"

She opened her purse and handed over folded documents. "The police were so nice. They got us set up in this motel, but I don't know for how long. We don't know what we're going to do . . ." Sobbing erupted again.

"Easy now," said Serge. "Everything will be just

fine." He read through the documents. "I'll get to work on this for you."

"But the police said these people are very hard to catch."

"For the *police* to catch." Serge set the paperwork on the dresser. "I have more resources."

"More than the police? How can that be?"

"The less you know the better."

"You're such a nice man . . ." Madge pointed. "What's that thing?"

"A glued-together coconut bra. Just spend time with Charlie and put this out of your mind." Serge took her arm again and helped Madge toward the door. "Here, have some detergent. Go with Christ."

The door closed.

"Man," said Coleman. "Life savings. That really sucks."

"Did you have that bong out the whole time?"

"She didn't know what it was." He flicked a Bic lighter over the freshly packed bowl.

Serge shook his head in exasperation.

Coleman exhaled. "So how can you possibly help her?"

"The underground economy of shady favors." He picked up his cell phone and pressed buttons. "Hello, Gypsy? It's me, Serge. I need a favor."

"Again?"

"Hey, didn't I get you to that underground gunshot-wound doctor in time?"

"Right, and you still have my Cobra. When am I getting it back?"

"Forget the car," said Serge. "This is about karma."

"I can't drive karma."

"Then it's about money," said Serge. "You're the best hacker I know, and I need the whole workup on a scam artist—IP address, everything. When I find him, I'll add a surcharge for your trouble."

"Okay, I guess. What are the details?"

"I'll take pictures of the documents and text them to you."

"That car better come back in the same condition—"

"Later." *Click.*

Coleman coughed. "What now?"

Serge headed for the door. "Corn chips."

Chapter 30

FDLE Miami Field Office

A new set of notecards was tacked up on a cork-board, thanks to a family Bible. Heather stretched a piece of red string between two pushpins. "I think we're finally getting somewhere."

Archie cut more string with scissors. "I'm still baffled by that odd visitor Dixon got."

"We'll know more when we hear back from the DNA company about a possible fourth relative. Did you make the call?"

"Yeah, but it was after hours by the time I got through. Left a message."

"What about the sketch artist?" asked Heather. "I thought we would have something by now."

"Told me he keeps calling Dixon, but no answer," said Arch. "Even went to the house. Nobody home."

"That's strange." Heather pinned up another card. "Better put on the coffee."

Archie's cell phone rang. "That's the sketch guy right now . . ."

Twenty minutes later, a Crown Victoria screeched up to the curb in front of a house with a dead Christmas wreath on the door. Ten other official vehicles were already there, along with the TV satellite trucks held back at the end of the block. Detectives swarmed everywhere with gloves and evidence bags.

A lieutenant came over to the car as Heather and Arch got out. "Sketch artist found him. He couldn't reach the guy for days, so he looked in the windows."

They walked briskly inside, where police cameras were still flashing. They had seen a lot in their years, but this sight jarred them. Lying on the floor, surrounded by cans and bottles, was the seriously late Raúl Dixon.

Another detective emerged from the kitchen with an extra-large evidence bag containing a chef's hardwood knife block. All the slots were empty, because the complete set of cutlery was still sticking out of the deceased, standing straight up, including the meat cleaver in the forehead.

"What do you think now?" asked Archie.

"I'd guess we've definitely touched a nerve," said Heather. "Our cold case just got hot."

Then she remembered something and glanced at a family Bible on a coffee table. Her business card was gone.

Sarasota

A small gray cylinder stood on a dresser in a budget motel room. It was plugged into the wall. A blue ring lit up on top.

Two men stared at it in reverence.

"I just bought it off Amazon," said Serge. "I need answers, which is essential for my journey of personal growth."

"How does it work?" asked Coleman.

"Voice activated." Serge leaned closer. "Alexa, what is the meaning of life?"

"The meaning of life depends on the life in question. A good approximation is forty-two."

Serge scratched his head. "She's quoting Douglas Adams? I think it's broken."

"Can I try?" asked Coleman.

"Go for it."

"Alexa," he giggled. "What is smegma?"

"Smegma is a thick, cheese-like—"

"Alexa, stop!" said Serge. The cylinder went silent. He turned to his sidekick. "Can you not?"

"At least you know it isn't broken."

Serge sat down on the end of a bed with a laptop.

"Whatcha doing?"

"Research." Serge's fingers tapped keys. "I need to look someone up."

"Family tree again?"

"Yes, but not mine."

"Then whose?"

"Ranger Bobby." Serge surfed websites. "I want to locate his daughter."

"What for?"

"I'm going to pay her a visit."

"But you promised him you wouldn't."

"Sometimes you just have to do the right thing. You saw what a great guy he is, and he's not going to do this on his own," said Serge. "Alexa, is it ever okay to break a promise?"

"Hmm, I don't know that."

"See? The jury's still out." Serge resumed typing. "Now we're making progress. Three people living in Florida by her name." He hit more keys, pulling up each person's data. "Definitely the second one. The ages of the other two are improbable."

"Wow," said Coleman. "Look what she does for a living. Are you sure it's a good idea to go see her?"

"What can go wrong?" said Serge. "We'd better be getting to bed. Got a long drive ahead of us tomorrow. And I still need to find myself." He turned toward the gray cylinder. "Alexa, who is Serge Storms?"

"Serge A. Storms is the main fictional . . ."

He listened to the rest. "I'm a character in a series of books? That's weird. I didn't realize the name was that common."

"Alexa," said Coleman, "will you marry me?"

"I think that somehow would violate the laws of robotics."

Serge just glared.

"What?" said Coleman. "She sounds hot."

"If it makes you happy." Serge took a seat at a stained desk in the bare-bones motel room with dark paneling from the fifties. He flipped through a little green book. "Which state park to visit next? Pennekamp? Fakahatchee? Bahia Honda? Cayo Costa? The choices are endless! . . ."

A phone rang.

"Hello? . . . Oh, hi, Gypsy."

"I got your address. Have something to write with?"

Serge clicked a pen. "Fire away." He wrote on a matchbook. "What kind of address is that?"

"You asked for an address. I got it. And I want my Cobra back!"

"Still with the car?"

"You said three months."

"Things came up. So I'm a tad late."

"It's been seven. I kept trying to reach you!"

"I'll make it up. Peace, out."

Coleman raised his head from the coconut. "Well?"

Serge checked the writing in the matchbook, then flipped to a specific page in his green book. "Fate has chosen our next park . . ."

A five-hour drive later, Serge stood on a street in Miami surrounded by trendy coffeehouses and martini bars.

"What is this place?" asked Coleman.

"Coconut Grove! One of the oldest and greenest sections of the city! Practically a single giant, lush canopy!" Serge began counting off on his fingers. "You got your banyans, poincianas, champaks, raintrees, African tulips, copperpods, calabash, not to mention all the best palms!"

"But we're in the city," said Coleman. "I thought we were going to a state park."

"And a fine state park it is!" Serge pointed across the street. "The Barnacle! Five acres preserved on some of the most expensive real estate in America! Come on!"

Soon, they were strolling down a long, manicured lawn stretching to the bay. "Cool, another stamp!" Serge stuck the passport book in his back pocket and turned around. "There it is! The oldest house on its original site in the whole county, built in 1891 by yacht designer Ralph Middleton Munroe."

"An old house," said Coleman. "Woo."

"Shut your trap," said Serge. "We're on sacred ground. Back then, you *really* had to want to live down here because there were no railroads or streets yet, just a steaming hot jungle with mosquitoes. Munroe was the consummate frontiersman, fighting all hardships to plant his flag." They walked up back steps, then a staircase. "But the coolest part of his vision is the layout of the house. Check out this towering two-story atrium featuring an octagonal balcony with gingerbread-style trim! Let's go up and run around it!" Serge noticed the smiling park ranger. "Or maybe not . . ."

They concluded the tour and walked back to a parking lot. Serge thumbed the green book as they approached their blue-and-white Cobra. "What stamp of glory next? Oleta River? Homosassa?"

Bam, bam, bam.

The pair stopped and looked at the trunk.

Serge stowed his book. "I'd completely forgotten about him."

One Hour Earlier

Serge stared into Biscayne Bay. Water splashed off the seawall at the downtown Miami marina, across from the historic Freedom Tower and the modern basketball arena. He walked along the dock and stopped at a slip for a luxury sailboat.

It had a brass ship's bell and gold railings.

A bronze man was sunning himself on the rear deck, back to the world. Sipping a mimosa and smoking a cigar. The boat's name was lettered across the stern: WINNING.

"That's quite a vessel," said Serge. "Permission to come aboard, Captain?"

The boat's owner turned around. "Who the fuck are you?"

"If you're Donovan Beck, then I'm interested in one of your vacation rentals."

"Like I said, who the fuck are you?"

"The authorities," said Serge. "Please come with us."

"I'm calling my attorney."

"You can call from the station."

"Let me see some identification."

Serge lifted his tropical shirt to reveal the butt of a .45 tucked in his waistband . . .

Ten minutes later, Serge marched the boat owner back to a Ford Cobra parked in an alley between sidewalk bistros on Flagler. He jammed the pistol's barrel into a spine. "You're not walking fast enough."

"Okay, okay!" The captive picked up the pace. "Could you just tell me what this is about?"

"More than happy to." The gun pressed harder. "The Petrocellis."

"Who?"

"That old couple from Michigan," said Serge. "I can't wrap my brain around exploiting the most vulnerable among us. Life savings. You realize Charlie doesn't have long. Pancreas. Jesus!"

"I swear I didn't know."

"Oh, well then that makes it all swell." Serge stuck a key in the back of the car and popped the lid. "We've arrived at the station. Time to get in."

Donovan tentatively swung a leg over the lip of the trunk. "Really, who are you?"

"I told you, the authorities."

"No, you're not."

Serge coaxed him the rest of the way with the pistol. "People just automatically think you have to be with some official agency, but you're about to experience authority like you've never seen."

The trunk slammed shut.

It was a short drive to one of the ubiquitous and rapacious check-cashing parlors that also sold money orders.

Serge poked his pistol in ribs and whispered over Donovan's shoulder as they stood in line. "Pull any shit and I swear to God I'll drop you right here, and I don't care who sees it."

"Fine, fine," said the nautical man. "Let's just get this over with."

They approached bulletproof glass. Serge told him the amount of the money order he wanted.

"But that's way more than what that couple paid me!"

"I have expenses," said Serge. "You don't know Gypsy, but it's like having an ex-wife."

They got the money order and walked around to the back of the building, where the Cobra was parked behind a dumpster.

"Nice doing business," said Serge, tucking the gun under his arm as he stuck the money order into his wallet.

Donovan used the opportunity to snatch the pistol and step back. He sneered with a malevolent grin. "How does it feel now, tough guy?"

"I'm having a great day."

"And I'll take that money order, if you don't mind."

"Nope, it's not mine to give."

"Don't think I won't shoot!"

"You don't have the stones," said Serge. "Judging from the victims you choose, I'd say they're tiny little peanuts."

"Fuck you!" Donovan pulled the trigger.

Click.

He looked surprised at the gun in his hand and pulled the trigger four more times.

Click, click, click, click.

"Unbelievable," said the scam artist. "This thing was unloaded the whole time?"

"I'm all about gun safety," said Serge. "And I was going to let you off with a stern warning, but you just tipped over the chess board." And Serge punched Donovan as hard as he could in the Adam's apple.

A Ford Cobra barreled its way back across the Everglades toward the west coast. Serge pressed buttons on his phone.

"Who are you calling?" asked Coleman.

"The underground network of shady favors. This time a retired fire chief who attended the state's arson investigation school in Ocala." He put the phone to his head. "Hank, it's me, Serge. I need another favor."

"Last time it took me a year to get my Falcon back."

“And last time I saw your son, he had two black eyes,” said Serge. “Is he still being bullied?”

Sheepishly, “No.”

“Wasn’t he the homecoming king?”

“Yes,” said Hank. “But whenever he walks down the hall at school now, everyone clears out of the way and presses themselves against the lockers, especially the football players.”

“You know my motto,” said Serge. “If in doubt, always over-engineer the project.”

“Okay, all right,” said Hank. “I know I’ll regret this, but what’s the favor?”

“Remember back in the seventies when they had some problems and needed to replace all those underground electrical lines?”

“Yeah, if you were with a fire department, how could you forget? It was a nightmare.”

“And they were supposed to dispose of all the old lines.”

“Supposed to,” said Hank.

“I’m guessing it became too costly and they cut corners.”

“No kidding. Like when they should dig up abandoned gas station tanks and don’t, and now we have to deal with them. They just capped off a bunch of those old electrical lines and left them.”

"Here's the favor," said Serge. "I need a list of a few locations of those remaining lines. Preferably in the Sarasota area. Foreclosed or vacant homes. And they need to have crawl spaces."

"Man, when you ask a favor," said Hank. "What do you want it for?"

"Better you don't know," said Serge.

"That I'm sure of," said Hank. "But how am I supposed to come up with such a list? It was decades ago."

"A-hem," said Serge.

"Dammit! . . . Okay, I'll make some inquiries."

"That's the Hank I know."

"But I haven't forgotten about the Falcon."

"I'll be waiting for your call." *Click.* Serge glanced at Coleman and rolled his eyes. "The cars again."

Chapter 31

Miami

The doughnuts were gone. The clock ticked toward the end of the day.

A last notecard went up on a board, and Heather hoisted a leather attaché case.

"Heading home?" asked Arch.

She shook her head. "Still have to get to a courthouse before they close. Want to come?"

"Sure." Arch grabbed his stuff, and they went outside to the Crown Vic. "Mind if I ask you something? How did you decide on this particular cold case? It doesn't seem like you just randomly grabbed one."

"I didn't," said Heather. "It's personal. I have a

cousin on my mother's side. He was just a boy at the time."

"Oh my God!" said Arch. "Something happen to him?"

"Not like you're thinking," said Heather. "But he did have an experience no kid should at that age. He told me a story . . ."

1997

A white plumbing contractor's van headed down a dirt road. On one side, a drop-off into a deep canal without guardrails. On the other, the snarl of an abandoned orange grove. The day was gray. The magnetic sign on the side of the van displayed the company's motto: WE SHOW UP.

It was the west side of Vero Beach, the country side. Cattle grazed and signs advertised three hundred acres for sale. The driver was rugged, like the Marlboro man, mustache and all. The passenger was a slight eleven-year-old boy named Darryl. For some reason they called him Cubby.

They had just left a convenience store.

"Thanks for the baseball cards, Dad!" Cubby

opened the pack and peeled through them one by one. "Cool, a Cal Ripken. Got that one. Got that one. Already got that." He held a card toward the driver. "A Ken Griffey Jr.!"

"That's nice, son."

The father was on a mission. To man up the boy a bit. The van continued down the remote road, kicking up a dust plume. The father was a firefighter, and his schedule was typical: week on, week off. Everyone at the firehouse had a side gig for the open seven days, hence the plumbing truck. The dirt road led out to a vast spread where they all hunted. The owner didn't hunt. But he was on the city council, and giving all the local first responders recreational access was good for business.

Cubby looked down at the console between their seats. Something he had seen many times before but never asked about.

"Dad, what kind of gun is that?"

"Double-barrel shotgun, twelve-gauge, breech load." And right now the breech was open with nothing inside. For a teachable reason. "Always make sure a gun is unloaded. And even when it's unloaded, always assume that it's loaded. When you're carrying it, never let the aim of the barrel cross anything you'd be sorry for shooting. And whenever you hunt, always eat what you kill."

Cubby recalled many great dinners of venison and wild bird. He picked up one of the scattered shotgun shells rolling around the console's tray. He felt the red, ridged plastic and rubbed the brass end. The hunting land was coming up. It was against the law to bait the field, and it was often baited anyway. But the father's plan wasn't to hunt. He would throw empty beer cans in the air for target practice and get his son used to that mule kick in the shoulder.

"Dad, you're really going to let me shoot it this time?"

"That's right, son . . ." The father became distracted as he let off the gas.

"Dad, what is it?"

There was no answer. He had spotted something down in the canal. What happened next would stay with the boy the rest of his life. It all happened in seconds, through one single fluid motion. In this order: The father hit the brakes, flushing the ducks from the canal, then he threw the van in park, grabbed two shells off the console, slammed them home in the breech of the shotgun, flipped the barrel to snap it shut as he jumped out the door and unloaded both those barrels into the sky.

Cubby's jaw hung open as one of the ducks was hit. He couldn't believe his father had been able to do all that before the birds were able to fly out of range. He was his hero.

But the duck was only winged. It came down like a helicopter in the orange grove. Flying was out of the question. But not running.

"Son, go get him!"

"Run after him?"

"Yes! Hurry! Before he gets into the woods!"

The boy scampered through the field after the injured bird, which began running in circles around the orange trees. Definitely the stuff of a great Florida childhood. The father folded his arms and leaned against the side of the truck and began laughing.

Cubby finally caught the duck by the neck, but didn't know what to do with it. He held it up toward his father, all flapping and feathers. "Dad?"

"Put it out of its misery."

The boy pointed at the duck's head with his free hand, and made it into the shape of a gun. "You got a pistol?"

"No, son." Another big laugh. "Not a coup de grace. Wring its neck."

"How do I do that?" asked Cubby, all manner of calamity flailing in his hand. "Like a washcloth?"

"No, son, just keep gripping it like you are and spin it in a circle. You'll know when you're done."

Cubby extended his arm as far away from him as he could. He cringed and squinted as he began twirling, slowly at first, then getting the hang of it. His T-shirt started collecting a horizontal stripe of red flecks. Finally, the boy grimaced harder as his hand felt the unmistakable sensation of the completed job. He opened his eyes full again.

"What's this?" He reached toward the ground where part of a faux-leather strap was sticking out of the dirt. He grabbed it and pulled, unearthing the rest. Cubby walked back to his father holding the duck in one hand and a filthy purse in the other.

"Cubby, where'd you get that?"

The boy glanced over his shoulder. "It was buried by that tree."

The father took it and looked inside. He opened the wallet, and found the driver's license missing. But there was a library card. He recognized the name. He pulled out his cell phone. "Son, go wait in the truck . . ."

A half hour later, the boy watched out the window as no less than forty police, firefighters, paramedics and even civilians huddled before fanning out. The team had been assembled ahead of time, hoping against hope that they would never have to answer the call.

It started two years ago. Odd reports of garments going missing from clotheslines. Underwear. Women's.

At first all they knew was that they had a pervert on their hands. Then the first body turned up in Sebastian, near the inlet. And another at New Smyrna. Purses found then, too. But no driver's licenses. Someone was keeping souvenirs.

Cubby watched from the truck as the team worked their way through the grove and then woods, walking slowly through the grid at precise intervals so they wouldn't miss anything. Cubby's father ignored the sickness in his stomach. He had been here before, one of the first on the scene to discover partial remains of Adam Walsh, the infamous abduction that launched *America's Most Wanted.* He had seen the strongest men cry.

Another time, a decade back, Cubby's father had discovered another body. It was hidden off a trail, and something nobody needed to see. They didn't announce the location or even the discovery. They just told the search party to go home. Cubby's father had stood by the side of the trail with a police sergeant. And as the volunteers filed by, one of the civilians stopped and peered in the direction of the unseen body. Cubby's dad and the sergeant looked at each other with spine chills. They handcuffed him back at the rallying point and that was that.

But the dark side of humanity always has reinforcements, and now here the father was again on the most reluctant assignment. Some things you just had to block out and do for the greater community.

The commanding officers were waiting back by the cars when three firefighters returned from the trees. Their faces said it all.

The FBI and FDLE were called in. It began to rain, and a large open-sided tent was erected over a shallow grave in the palmettos.

After the first two bodies had been discovered, there were suspicions, but nobody was sure until now. They had gotten DNA from the second victim, and forensics found some here as well.

It was a match.

The state assembled an inter-agency task force, which connected two additional previously found bodies in other parts of Florida. Then a fresh find. This guy wasn't quitting.

The headquarters was in Orlando, and it was noisy. Dozens of phones rang nonstop, thousands of tips catalogued. People in starched shirts moved urgently. They went on TV for the public's help, and put up billboards. The phones rang even more.

"Where did you see this suspicious truck? . . ."

"Why do you think your neighbor did it? . . ."

"No, I didn't watch that episode of Law & Order *. . ."*

With all the calls and new genetic samples, it looked promising. Until it didn't.

A year went by with no further victims. News coverage dried up, and the task force shrank to five investigators, then three, then another year lapsed. It almost never happened this way, but the guy had just stopped, and the command structure had to accept the inevitable.

The investigation was disbanded, and all the documents and evidence were filed accordingly.

A cold case.

Chapter 32

Sarasota

Night fell as Serge and Coleman crawled on their bellies through the dirt. They were wearing coal miners' head lamps.

Coleman bumped his nose on a wooden pier. "Ow! I can't see where I'm going."

"You idiot! You've got that thing on backwards." Serge twisted it around on his pal's head.

"That's much better."

Crawling continued.

Serge raised his head, and his light hit some plumbing coming down through the floor above them. "That's the drain line from the tub. We're under the bathroom." He pulled out a camping trench tool and began digging.

"So your fire chief friend came through?" asked Coleman.

"In a big way." Dirt flew.

"How far down do we have to go?"

"Twenty-four inches was the minimum requirement back then." The spade dug into the ground again.

"How do you know where to dig?"

"Hank said they capped the old electric lines at the meter. He told me to just follow the abandoned junction boxes in the crawl space."

"I still don't understand what this has to do with anything."

Serge sighed and turned. "If you're not going to dig, can you give me a break with the questions while I do the heavy lifting?"

"Ah! Your light's in my eyes. Now I see spots."

"How is that any different?"

"These are green."

Serge thrust with the tool again. "Okay, here's the deal. Years ago they used copper and aluminum for underground electricity lines. It did a decent job, but there was still resistance in the metals, measured in ohms if you're keeping score."

"Now dirt's flying in my face."

"That would be a good clue to move." Serge was a foot down and still going. "Anyway, it used up extra power to push the electricity through those lines, plus those metals aren't cheap. Then someone stumbled onto sodium nitrate."

"What's that?"

"A white powder that conducts electricity surprisingly well. Much cheaper than the other stuff. They saved money on power, the cost of metal, as well as insulation because the lines only needed to be half as thick. It became the best thing since sliced bread, especially in southwest Florida because of the period's construction boom."

"So why'd they have to dig it up?"

"DDT also used to be sliced bread, until the pesticide started working its way up the food chain," said Serge. "All was going smoothly until they noticed a series of unusual house fires."

"The electric lines caused them?"

"No, what happened is the fires started from regular causes: short circuits, faulty toasters, smoking in bed, candles too close to curtains. And when the fire department came out to fight the blazes, there were a number of unexplained explosions. I mean freaking huge blasts as if there was undetonated ordnance under the houses from an old bombing range."

"What caused it?"

"Nobody knew at first, but finally after enough incidents and investigations, they figured it out: If a house burned hot enough during the original fire, it melted the insulation off the nitrate. Then the water from the fire hoses seeped down. Turned out that sodium nitrate doesn't like water."

"Why not?"

"I'll leave it at electron shells and save you a headache."

"Thanks."

"It all probably would have stopped there because the government doesn't give a flip about the physical welfare of working folk. Just ask the lead-poisoned people up in Flint. On the other hand, powerful insurance companies started having to pay out a lot of big claims, and the politicians said that was a tragedy. The lines had to come out."

"I never heard of this."

"Most other people haven't, either," said Serge. "The fire chief told me that for a while the people had a bit of fun with the removed lines, chopping them up into pieces the size of beanie weenies, then throwing them in lakes and ponds and watching the explosions. The fish weren't happy."

Coleman leaned to look into the hole. "How much farther?"

"I think I've arrived . . ." The tool was set aside and Serge excavated with his fingers. "Yep, I got it. Here's the line."

From there, the work became exceedingly tedious. First Serge cleared a long trough around the line. Then he flicked open a pocketknife and began stripping the thick insulation. Inside, more lines, a pair of 110-volts that also needed to be stripped, plus a stream of uninsulated white powder for the grounding circuit.

Finally he was done. "Let's meet our next contestant!"

Coal miner lamps led them out, and they entered the side door of a foreclosed house that didn't have power. Two beams of light swung back and forth as they worked their way through the residence until arriving at the bathroom. The beams hit a man in the face, who squinted as his eyes adjusted. He tried to scream, but there was that pesky duct tape, and he tried to move, but there was, well, rope again.

Serge knelt down and patted him on the head. "Comfy in that tub?"

"Mmmm! Mmmm! Mmmm!"

"Fantastic!" Serge pulled out a portable drill and fired it up.

Even louder: *"Mmmm! Mmmm! Mmmm!"*

"Relax," said Serge. "I'm not going to use this on you. What kind of a sicko do you think I am?"

The bathroom floor was the kind of vintage avocado tile that Serge loved. "I hate to do this, but . . ."

A thick bit drilled down through the tile and the wooden sub-floor under it. Again and again. A half-dozen inch-wide holes in all. Serge flicked the drill off.

"That about does it on my end," he told Donovan. "The rest is up to you. I know how you love vacation homes, and this is yours. Isn't she a peach? And is this going to be the vacation of a lifetime!"

"Bonus round?" asked Coleman.

"Of course," said Serge, swinging his light toward the captive. "Donovan, want to hear your bonus round?"

"Mmmm! Mmmm! Mmmm!"

"Great! I love a contestant with spunk! Always helps the ratings!" Serge plugged up the tub's drain and capped it with waterproof silicone tape. "I poured my imagination into the main attraction, so the bonus round is on the inelegant side. But my loss is your gain! Here's the deal . . ."

Serge explained all the chemistry that he had just told Coleman under the house.

"Mmmm! Mmmm! Mmmm!"

Coleman tugged his pal's cheerful tropical shirt. "What about the neighbors? An explosion is hard to control, and you always take care in your science projects not to hurt innocent civilians."

"As I did this time." Serge reached into the tub to prop the captive into a sitting position. "The exposed wiring is down in the two-foot hole, and the surrounding dirt provides a natural berm like a bunker to absorb the horizontal blast. All that's left is vertical energy thrust upward toward this bathroom in the middle of the house, like a directional charge from an improvised explosive device in the Middle East, which essentially is what this is."

"Mmmm! Mmmm! Mmmm!"

"I know, I know," said Serge. "You're in a serious pickle. So listen up. The bonus round is a Houdini act. I'm going to loosen your ropes a bit. It still won't be easy, but the wiggle room is in the realm of possibility. And to show you what a nice guy I am"—he twisted one of the tub's faucet handles—"I'm turning it on just a trickle to give you an extra-long bonus round. I'm lying. I want it to trickle so you'll have plenty of time to think about the Petrocellis and all the others."

"Serge," said Coleman. "I don't get it. If the house doesn't have electricity, then how does it have water?"

"My curb key from Home Depot. They don't cut

the pipes when they disconnect water. They just turn it off at the sidewalk meter."

"Curb key?" asked Coleman.

Serge grabbed something off the floor. "This long metal pole that looks like rebar, with a precise slot on the end. Another readily available tool of empowerment that people walk right by in the plumbing aisle. You can cut off the water to your entire neighborhood if you want, which would be a prick thing to do, but just knowing you can ratchets up your self-worth. Till now, I've only used it when I want to draw someone out of a house without knocking."

Serge's forehead beam swung back to the scam artist. "If you were paying attention in school, you'll remember Archimedes's principle, about a body displacing water, which, if you contort properly as the water rises, should give you even more time." Serge covered his mouth. "I just remembered, Archimedes also was in a bathtub when he had his 'Eureka' moment. Maybe you'll scream 'Eureka,' too. . . . Come on, Coleman."

Two beams of light headed out the door, leaving the bathroom in total darkness.

The blue-and-white Ford Cobra sat in a parking lot next to a Cuban takeout joint.

Coleman held a newspaper in his lap. "Serge, do I really have to?"

"Do you see what's going on here?" He pointed down at wax paper covering his legs. "You're only drinking beer, but I got paella going on. That's a two-fisted job."

Coleman responded by holding out hands with an open beer in each. "I'm two-fisting, too."

"So put one down. If you haven't noticed, I'm the one who's been bringing in all the money lately." Serge noshed into a messy piece of squid. "The least you can do is read aloud and catch me up on the day's critical watershed moments. I need the tactical advantage over the other guys."

"But reading kills my buzz," Coleman said with a burning roach clenched in his teeth. "Like if I'm really high and have to, you know, work."

Serge snatched one of the beers and held it out the window. "Read or I start pouring!"

"Dear God! Anything but that!" Coleman quickly flipped pages. "Okay, I'll read! Just be careful with that beer."

Serge brought it back inside the car as Coleman found an article in the metro section. "Here's something: 'Woman on meth rides mobility scooter through Walmart, drinking wine and eating chicken . . .'"

"Seen it," said Serge. "Next story."

"'Jacksonville man turns himself in to police for murdering imaginary friend.'"

"Again? Next story."

"'Police discover golf cart chop-shop at the Villages retirement park.'"

"I saw that one coming a mile away. Next."

"'Miami robber with bucket on head as a disguise tries to steal pigeons from pet store.'"

Serge twirled a finger of boredom in the air. "On with it. Next."

"'Twenty-year-old Florida man stabs dad who tried to circumcise him.'"

"And they call that rag a distinguished paper?" said Serge. "That's not even news—"

Boom!

Coleman's head snapped up.

"What was that?"

Serge pointed at a wooden bungalow with flames flickering in the windows. "Real news."

"Did you see him escape?" asked Coleman.

"Nope," said Serge. "Another bonus round reject."

Fire trucks raced down U.S. 41 as the Cobra sped the other way, off into the deepening night.

"Eureka!"

Chapter 33

The Next Day

The main street through the small town was one of those quaint ones. So quaint, in fact, that all the buildings were now antique shops that tourists visited on the weekend. The street T-boned into another rural courthouse with a big clock on top.

Heather smartly entered the clerk's office with an attaché case under her arm. She was about to request a file when she saw one already sitting on the counter in front of her. A murder file. She checked the name on the tab.

"Excuse me?" she asked a clerk. "Did someone from my office call ahead?"

"Which office?"

"FDLE, Miami."

The clerk shook her head. "Why do you ask?"

"Because this file on the counter is the one I came here to see."

"Oh, that," said the clerk. "A guy was just in here who asked to look at it."

"What kind of guy? Another state agent?"

"Seriously doubt it," said the clerk. "A real oddball. Kept talking about all the huge clock towers on the courthouses he had been visiting, and for some reason he couldn't get Flavor Flav out of his head. He kept slapping himself."

"That *is* odd," said Heather. "Anything else?"

"Yeah, he did this . . ." The clerk slowly began waving her arms, snake-like, in front of her.

"What was that about?"

"Said he was doing a fade-out," said the clerk. "Then he told me the strangest story."

Heather closed her eyes and took a full breath. Then she opened them. "Thank you." She began reading the file.

A Half Hour Earlier

A court clerk stared with puzzled eyes. "What exactly are you doing?"

Serge continued waving his arms, serpentine. "A fade-out. Another of my great-grand-uncles. I remember it like it was just yesterday . . ."

A sturdy man with broad shoulders and leathery hands stood in the woods of North Florida. There was a hatchet in one set of his calloused fingers, and in the other a large metal pail. It was 1896. His name was Ezra Snog.

Snog continued hiking off-trail through pine trees. Back then, before radio and TV, people liked to talk and sing to themselves more than today. Snog more than most.

"Going to be a turpentine man, a turpentine man, turpentine man. Hot-diggity-damn, a turpentine man is what I am! . . ."

Turpentine was huge in Florida, at least in the nineteenth century. In Orange County around present-day Orlando, the industry was second only to citrus. But in North Florida, after the great freezes of 1894 and '95 drove the groves south, turpentine was king.

It was rugged work that generally involved chopping a pair of gashes in a pine tree that were variously called chevrons or cat's whiskers. Then a small metal chute was hammered in, and a pail hung to catch the tree's gum or resin.

Through upcoming branches, Ezra spotted a work camp and entered the clearing. "*. . . A turpentine man is what I ammmmm! . . .*"

Nobody else was singing. They all just stared at Snog before resuming solemn work. A single pail hung from each tree beneath a carved woodworking design that was practically artisan from the repetition of toil. Slow, patient, grinding work.

Not Snog. He dropped his pail. Actually five pails nested together as one for convenient transport. And he went to town on his chosen tree in a ferocious blur of endeavor. By the time he was done, all the pails hung from a pine that now looked more like a totem pole. He stood back and beamed with pride as the resin began to drip.

"*. . . A turpentine man is what I am! . . .*"

Another voice: "No singing!"

He turned around. "Why? Who are you?"

"The foreman," said the approaching man. "Now who are *you*?"

An excited smile. "Ezra Snog." He extended a hand.

The foreman just looked down at it with contempt like Snog was insane. "I don't recognize you. Are you with the camp?"

"Nope." Ezra peeked down inside one of his pails of hope.

"Then what are you doing here?"

"I'm going to be the world champion turpentiner!"

The foreman got a funny look. "There isn't such a thing."

Another peek in the bucket. "I'll be the first. I'm taking turpentine big!"

Now the foreman was convinced of Snog's mental faculties. "Where did you come from?"

Ezra pointed west. "Just over on Cedar Key. I worked in a general store selling nails and taffy."

"You had a store job, and you *chose* to be a turpentiner?"

"That's right! Couldn't wait to get started!" said Ezra. "I got the idea last night! On the other side of the haberdashery is a place called the naval store. They have them all up and down the coast because we don't really have a bunch of roads yet, and everyone gets around by boat. Anyway, I was drinking in the old Cedar Saloon with a guy who works in the navy place, and I said, 'Hey, Obadiah, what's with all the metal canisters I see going out of your store at all hours? Some of those customers are carrying like a half-dozen,' and Obadiah says, 'It's turpentine pitch, or tar. Just flies out of the place. We can't keep it in stock.' I asked, 'Why not?' He said all the boat crews now use it to plug holes and seams in their wooden vessels, and to coat riggings so they don't come apart at sea. Then he asks me if I have any connections to get more of the stuff, and he'll pay top dollar, and I told him, 'Enough said!'" Another broad smile. "And here I am!"

"Shut up!" said the foreman. "I don't need your whole life story! If you're going to work here, you need to join the camp. Here's the arrangement: It's a dollar a day and you get paid in trade coins that can only be used in the camp's store or to pay lodging."

"A dollar? Are you kidding?" said Ezra. He looked around the camp. "Obediah didn't mention any of this. No wonder everyone looks so sad. All those people agreed to work for that little?"

"No, half of them are convicts that we lease from the state on the cheap," said the foreman.

"They don't get paid at all?"

"Not a penny," said the foreman. "And the credit at the store I mentioned? If you get behind, you're not allowed to leave the camp until you work it off."

"Or what?" said Ezra.

"The law allows us to bring you back, by force if necessary."

"That's bullshit!"

The foreman got in his face. "What did you say to me?"

"Was I stuttering?" asked Ezra. "I said, that's bullshit! How can you treat people that way?"

Snog had noticed the ax handle in the foreman's fist,

but just figured he had been interrupted in the process of repairing an ax.

Wham!

Ezra felt a stinging pain in the side of a leg. "What the hell? Did you slip?"

Wham!

Now the other leg throbbed. "What are you doing?"

Here was one last detail about the iron-fist power of the turpentine camp owners. The foremen were allowed to beat the workers without repercussion. Just couldn't kill them.

Wham!

Ezra rubbed an elbow. "Okay, I'm now required to inform you that I'm starting to get mad."

Wham! Wham! Wham!

"Have it your way," said Ezra. Despite his husky size, Snog was swifter than the foreman had gauged. Ezra quickly disarmed the supervisor, and now he had the ax handle.

Wham! Wham! Wham!

The whole camp was on its feet now, unable to believe their own eyes.

"Ow! Shit! Stop!" yelled the foreman. "You bastard! You'll go to jail!"

Ezra didn't stop. *Wham! Wham! Wham!* But then he did something else.

The foreman was staggering like a boxer taking a standing count. That's all the time Ezra needed. He dashed over to a nearby worker whose pail had been on the tree since the day before. Ezra looked inside. "Fantastic job." He yanked it off the tree. "I'll pay you back."

Snog returned to the foreman, who was still groggy and swung a punch that missed and left him stumbling. Ezra grabbed the pail and slammed it upside down over the foreman's head. The gummy resin inside was blinding and acted as an effective glue. Then Ezra picked up the ax handle and began banging the pail like a bell.

Clang! Clang! Clang!

The camp was usually completely silent, but now for the first time anyone could remember, there was robust laughter. Ezra chased the foreman in a figure eight.

Clang! Clang! Clang!

Besides working nicely on boats, turpentine also is unpleasant and toxic, but not in that order.

The clanging and laughter continued. Officials later wouldn't be able to determine whether the tree resin or repeated concussions had done the foreman in, but he wouldn't last the night.

Clang! Clang! Clang!

Someone eventually sounded the alarm, and foremen

from other parts of the camp came running. "Hey, you with the ax handle! . . ."

Snog looked up. "Uh-oh."

A final *Clang!* He dropped the wooden shaft and made a dash for the woods. Yelling as he went: "Turpentiners rise up! You have nothing to lose but your pails! Turpentiners rise up! . . ."

The rest of the camp heard his voice trailing off as he disappeared deep into the woods. "Turpentiners rise up! Remember that motto! I think it's catchy . . ."

Serge stopped waving his arms and blinked hard a few times, returning to the real world. "Yep, he definitely had my genes."

Then Serge looked up at a stunned clerk of the court. "I guess my uncle expected that his rallying cry would take off like 'Remember the Alamo,' but it never did . . . I just love history fade-outs! It's fun! You should try it. What do you say? Get those arms moving and give me a big fade-out!"

She just continued staring.

"Not your thing?" Serge sulked. "All right, instead of a fade-out, I guess I'll have to settle for a file. Snog, Ezra . . ."

Chapter 34

Miami

A middle-aged man with three-day stubble stood on a street corner, muttering to himself.

"I could have been a U.S. senator! I'm Jack Grayson, for God's sake! This is so unfair!"

It had indeed been a tough run for Grayson. His wife left him, and she had a good attorney. Then the regulators began looking into irregularities. It was like pulling a tiny thread on a coat and the sleeve falls off. An entire career that was a road map of malfeasance. By the time it was over, wholesale forfeitures and fines to stay out of jail. He wasn't broke. He was in debt. Jack was only able to grab some loose cash from the safe before they changed the locks on his house, and he drove off before his car could be repossessed.

And now he stood at an intersection in South Florida, mumbling grievances about how poor people had done this to him. It had been going on for a week now, and it was approaching full boil.

"Motherfuckers!" Grayson flung a cardboard sign into traffic and began tearing off his green Statue of Liberty costume. He stomped on the pointy felt hat. "Son of a bitch!"

The ex-candidate then stormed up the road and into the nearest bar. The door was propped open to sunlight and cars. He ordered a whiskey sour.

"What happened to you?" asked the bartender. "You look like you've been sleeping in the woods."

"Shut up." He stewed and stared out the door as a blue-and-white Cobra sped by.

The Cobra continued on until it arrived at an official-looking building near the Dolphin Mall.

Inside the office, men in starched white shirts gathered around a box.

"Who took all the jellies again?"

On the other side of the room, a woman stood at a corkboard on the wall. More notecards went up with pushpins.

One of the other agents came over, chewing with glaze on the corner of his mouth. "Someone's here to see you."

"Who?"

"Wouldn't tell me."

"Where is he?" asked Heather.

"Out in the lobby."

"Did he say what it's about?"

"A case."

"What case?"

"Said he would only talk to you about it."

"Okay," said Heather. "Send him in."

The other agent nodded and took another bite on the way to the lobby.

Actually, two people arrived at Heather's desk. The first extended a hand.

"My name's Storms. Serge Storms. And you must be Heather Sparrow—"

A small crash as Coleman stumbled into a chair. "Whoa, a little gravity problem again."

"Is he okay?" asked Heather.

"No." Serge helped his friend into the seat.

"The other agent told me this was about a case," said Heather. "But you wouldn't tell him what."

"That's right," said Serge. "Except I kind of fibbed. It is about a case, just not the kind you're thinking of."

"Wait, I know you from somewhere," said Heather. "But I can't place the face. Have we met?"

"Sure, the courthouse in DeLand," said Serge. He looked up at the ceiling and began slowly waving his arms back and forth. "I remember it like it was just yesterday. You were standing at the counter in the clerk's office when I came in to work on my family tree—"

"No! Stop!" said Heather. "Don't do another fade-out!"

"What? You didn't like the last one?" said Serge. "It had all the elements. Spanish-American War, Ybor City history, rage against the machine—"

Heather sighed. "I don't mean to be curt, but could you get to the point? I've got work."

"It's about your father."

Heather was taken off balance. "What about my father?"

"He's fine. Just want to get that out of the way."

"You know my father?"

"Absolutely. Do you have any idea what he's doing now?"

"No, and I really have a lot of work to do, so if you don't mind—"

"He's a ranger at a state park."

Another off-balance moment. And not that she cared, just curious: "He isn't at the law firm?"

"Quit," said Serge. "And I can vouch that he's a completely different person now from the guy in the slick TV ads. He's rededicated his life to the simple pleasures of the ink pad and stamp."

"Ink pad?"

"Sorry," said Serge. "I tried rehearsing this on the way over, but my mind has a mind of its own. Let that sink in."

"I still don't know why you're here."

"He misses you."

"He should have thought about that a long time ago." She looked down at her desk and began going through a file. "What did he do, send you?"

"It's not like that," said Serge. "He doesn't know I'm here. In fact, he made me promise not to interfere, which obviously I've broken." He pulled out a scrap of paper. "Here's the number for the park."

Heather still looked down at paperwork. "Keep it."

"In case you change your mind." Serge set it on the desk.

"Will that be all?" asked the agent.

"For now. Come on, Coleman . . ." He turned to leave, then stopped. "Wow, a corkboard!"

Heather looked over her shoulder. "You need to leave now."

"You *are* trying to catch a serial killer, just like I guessed at the courthouse."

She looked him in the eyes. "I can't comment on any open investigation."

Serge nodded vigorously. "I have a corkboard just like that. Notecards, pushpins, colored yarn."

"I'm sure you do."

"Yeah, when I was a kid, we mailed in box tops. Now it's spit. Times change. But the anticipation was déjà vu, sitting by the mailbox each day, waiting for my happiness packages. Once it was a kit to join the Monkees fan club, then the Banana Splits fan club, Saturday-morning TV before your time."

"I really must insist that you leave."

"Wait! Wait! Wait! So my new DNA kit arrived with several hits on distant relatives, and I'm building a fascinating family tree, turpentine and sponge divers and everything! I'm having a blast! Plus I'm also tracking a serial killer!"

What a fruitcake, thought Heather. *Watching too many police shows.*

Serge nodded again. "And when I said I had a corkboard like yours, I didn't mean 'like,' I meant 'almost exactly like.' I have some of the same notecards."

"I'm sure it's very nice," said Heather. "And now

I'm going to have to be rude. Leave or I'll have you thrown out."

"My apologies. Please reconsider calling your father." Serge grabbed Coleman by the arm. "Let's go."

Heather shook her head in exasperation as she watched the pair exit through the lobby. Then it was back to work on the cold case.

A notecard went up as another agent came over. "Excuse me for interrupting, but I have a couple of updates. Remember our victim Raúl Dixon with the dead wreath on the front door?"

"Vividly."

"We were able to trace the murder weapons, but it turns out they belong to Dixon himself," said the agent. "Detectives found credit card receipts and listened to a phone call recorded for quality control purposes. He bought the cutlery from an infomercial in the middle of the night while drunk."

"You said a couple of developments."

"Oh, and I just got off the phone with the ancestry company. You were right, someone did send in another sample after we got back our results. A fourth cousin." He handed her a slip of paper. "That's the name."

Heather read it, and her eyes immediately shot toward the door to the lobby. She grabbed her gun and took off running until she was in front of the building on the sidewalk. She looked both ways up and down the street, but nothing in sight.

Arch joined her on the sidewalk. "What is it?"

"I was too busy being annoyed and trying to get rid of him. And angry at my dad," said Heather. "How could I have not made the connection to those courthouse files?"

Chapter 35

Myakka River State Park

A Crown Victoria with blackwall tires rolled up to the guard booth.

Ranger Bobby was waiting at the window with a big smile. "Imagine my surprise getting your call."

"This isn't a social visit," Heather said sharply. "It's official."

Still smiling. "A visit is a visit."

"We need to talk someplace private."

"You were a bit mysterious on the phone," said Bobby. "We can use my apartment."

The other ranger in the booth said he had things covered.

They arrived at a long cabin in the thick woods, and Heather stopped in a doorway. "*This* is where you live now?"

"Everything I need. So what's the visit about?"

The agent pulled up a photo on her cell phone. "Do you know this man?"

"Where'd you get that?"

"Off the surveillance cameras at my office."

"He came to visit you?" said Bobby. "He swore to me he wouldn't."

"So you do know him?" said Heather.

"Sure, he's one of the park's regulars."

"What else do you know about him?"

"Not much," said her father. "Except he did bring us together here today, despite ignoring my wishes."

"I told you this is purely official," said Heather. "I wouldn't be here otherwise."

"Still good to see you," said the ranger. "So is Serge in any kind of trouble? Did he do something?"

"I don't know yet," said the agent, looking at the dark green walls and subconsciously wondering about the paint selection. "It was strange enough getting a visit from him about you. And he's a strange guy."

"No argument here," said Bobby. "And I'm guessing this is about an open investigation that you can't discuss, which would explain why you're being so cagey. Why don't you spell out what you can, and I'll do my best to help."

"It's a cold case, or rather *was* a cold case," said Heather. "Serial killer who stopped years ago, but we might have just had a new related homicide."

"And Serge is somehow relevant just because he visited you about me?"

"No, it's the strangest coincidence," said Heather. "We're trying to solve the case with DNA."

"That was a big breakthrough for law enforcement when the technology evolved."

"And another big breakthrough when culture evolved," said Heather. "There are now all these ancestry sites where nearly a million people have sent in samples."

"I've seen the ads."

"Hadn't heard of it being done before, but the idea just popped into my head," said Heather. "What did we have to lose by sending in a sample from one of the crime scenes under a fictitious name and seeing what ran up the flagpole?"

"You always were smart," said Bobby. "Are you trying to say you got a hit on the killer?"

"Not directly, but three distant cousins. So it's now a challenge of building a family tree back generations, until we reach a common ancestor, then building it back down until we can generate a list of all cousins living today, and check them out one by one. I'm about eighty percent finished."

"I'm missing the part about Serge," said the ranger.

"We were making a round robin of visiting the first three cousins from the ancestry results, and a guy in Broward said someone had been by asking about the same thing. He was building a family tree from the same service and had the same three cousins. But he wasn't one of *our* three. So there had to be a fourth. We put in a call to Ancestors R Us, and waited."

"You mentioned a big coincidence."

"Right after Serge left my office, one of my colleagues got an answer from the company," said Heather. "The fourth cousin is your friend Serge."

"Okay, so he's just another innocent, distant relative like the first three."

"I'm not dismissing him that fast," said Heather. "These DNA companies on TV aren't official forensic laboratories. There are no regulations, and there's a margin of error. It's just fun for the whole family, and if they make a mistake, nobody goes to jail."

"I see where you're going with this, but it still seems like a jump," said Bobby. "Why would you suspect that the company's margin of error could make Serge the hit on your crime scene sample?"

"One thing I didn't mention," said Heather. "Remember I told you about the guy in Broward?"

"Yeah?"

"He's dead."

"What?"

"Yeah, Serge visits him, then a couple days later I visit, and right after that he's murdered. Serious case of overkill," said Heather. "There's a saying in law enforcement: There are no coincidences."

"I thought you just said you had a big coincidence with Serge."

"Semantics, different context. You know what I mean."

"Tell me how I can help."

"We need to take Serge in for official questioning," said Heather. "Fingerprints, and get his DNA looked at by *our* lab."

"You'll need a warrant," said the lawyer.

"That's a little dicey because sending in the DNA under false pretenses raises privacy issues with the company's customers," said Heather. "That creates problems with probable cause to get a judge to sign off. Still working on it."

"Or trick Serge into giving up both by offering him a can of soda during questioning."

"That was my backup plan."

"Okay, I still think you're wrong about Serge, but I'll help if for no other reason than to clear him. I'll talk to Serge next time I see him and do my best to persuade," said Bobby. "But I can't deceive him or force him to do anything or tip you off when he's here. I can't be that person anymore."

"Anything else?"

"Yes, you also can't put the park under surveillance to catch him, or I won't be a part of it," said Bobby. "I need your word."

"Deal." Heather stopped and looked at the open Bible on the chipped desk. She hitched the strap of her leather folio, and firmly: "I have to go."

Bobby stepped forward. "Please . . . just a few more minutes."

Heather stood still a moment without reply.

"I know I don't deserve it," said Bobby. "Far from it. Just . . . stay a little longer, okay?"

Heather inhaled hard. She removed the strap from her shoulder but remained stern. "I have a few minutes. *Only* a few . . ."

Outside the weathered apartment, the weather picked up. Tree branches bent and scratched roof shingles. Brown leaves swirled on the ground. A deer trotted by.

Inside, a father and daughter were having the kind of conversation that nobody else needed to hear. Heather's facade didn't crack and tears didn't come but wanted to. He did most of the talking.

Finally, and no longer stern, "I really have to go now."

"Thanks for staying."

He walked her out the door. No hugs or goodbyes, just a smile on his face . . .

Back down by the lake, in a parking lot at the country store, sat a sunbaked Chevelle. It was empty.

The driver had decided to take a hike, and he decided not to use the trails. He climbed over branches and thickets, and trudged through the fallen late-winter leaves. He saw a beetle on the ground and stomped on it. A few hundred yards deeper into the woods, he caught a glimpse of the first sign of man since leaving his car.

Hiking became creeping. He stopped and positioned himself behind a thick, moss-draped oak. In a crook of the tree, he steadied a zoom lens. In his viewfinder were a man and a woman standing outside a ranger's apartment. The same woman he had been waiting for earlier in the day, parked across the street from her office on the other coast. He had gotten that address from a business card he had lifted off a Bible. And now, here he was, hiding in the trees at Myakka.

He adjusted the focus on his camera.

Click, click, click . . .

Chapter 36

The Next Day

A blue-and-white Ford Cobra pulled up to the guard booth at Myakka River State Park.

"Hey, Serge."

"Hi, Andy." He flapped a green book. "No ink pad needed. I'm solid."

"You told me last time."

"I got a lot going on upstairs," said Serge. "Is Ranger Bobby in?"

"Yes, he's been waiting for you."

Serge chuckled. "You mean 'waiting,' like he knows I can't stay away from this place?"

"No, actually waiting," said the ranger in the window. "Been calling and calling up here to see if we've seen your car in case you went to another part of the park. I think he really needs to talk to you about something. He's in his apartment."

"That's weird," said Serge. "But it must be important, so I'll head right over there . . ."

The Cobra pulled up to the rustic building in the trees, and Serge got out with his coffee mug. "I'm dying to know what this can be about." He knocked on the door, and the ranger answered.

"Serge, Coleman, come in."

"I just found out that frogs can explode!" said Serge. "It's true! Crows have figured out that the tastiest part of a toad is the liver, and they peck them out—"

"Serge . . ."

"No, seriously, once they lose the function of that organ, it triggers a biological chain reaction of irreversible swelling until, bang!"

"Serge . . ."

"Wait! Wait! And then there's Florida's current invasion of poisonous cane toads from Australia—some probably right here in this park—that grow to ten inches and secrete a toxic—"

"Serge!"

"Gee, sorry."

"Didn't mean to yell," said Bobby. "It's just that you

need to calm down and focus. I have something urgent to discuss."

"Then I'm all yours." He sat and closed his mouth and folded his hands. "Go!"

"You visited my daughter."

"Sorry, had to follow my heart."

"That's not the problem," said Bobby. "She's in the middle of a cold case using DNA."

Serge nodded. "Figured that from the corkboard in her office."

"Can you please not interrupt this one time?"

Serge made a zipper motion across his mouth. "The floor's all yours."

Ranger Bobby essentially repeated everything his daughter had explained during her visit. ". . . And she would like you to come in for an interview. Get fingerprinted, and give a saliva sample."

"I'd do just about anything you would ask of me," said Serge. "But that one's not in the cards."

"Serge, I know you aren't involved in this," said the ranger. "This could clear you, so why not?"

"Thanks for the vote of confidence," said Serge. "You're right, I'm not involved, other than trying to crack the case myself." A what-are-you-going-to-do shrug. "You know how I am about hobbies. And I'm sure you also know I've led an unorthodox life. Yes, giving samples would clear me in this matter, but there's some other, let's say, dubious moments that I'd rather leave in the past."

"I figured something like that," said the ranger. "Are you sure there's nothing I can do to change your mind?"

"Afraid not."

"Fair enough," said the ranger. "And I don't mean to rush you off, but I have to take over for Michelle down at the lake."

"Then I'll get out of your hair."

He stood and headed for the door.

"One more thing," Bobby called after him.

Serge turned around. "What's that?"

The ranger's serious, straight line of a mouth curled into a warm grin. "Thanks for getting her to visit."

Serge waved a wrist dismissively. "Don't be getting all mushy on me now, or we'll both start bawling."

They walked out onto the ranger's porch for good-byes. Serge suddenly spun toward the woods.

"What is it?" asked the ranger.

"I don't know. Is somebody out there?" said Serge. "I thought I saw movement."

Bobby laughed. "It's a state park. Birds and animals. Something would be wrong if there *wasn't* movement."

"I guess you're right," said Serge. "My Florida survival radar is cranked to ultra-sensitive. Anyway, great seeing you as always."

They shook hands . . .

Fifty yards south, a zoom lens rested in the crook of an oak tree.

Click, click, click.

Chapter 37

South Florida

A blue-and-white Ford Cobra took a left at the fork, where most people go right.

The fork was outside the Last Chance Saloon, and it led to the high-arching Card Sound Bridge. The road touched down on land again, crossing Saunders Creek, Mosquito Creek, Tubby's Creek and Steamboat Creek.

Almost all the tourists who hit Key Largo head southwest toward the other islands. Card Sound entered the north end, solely the destination of residents. And nature lovers. And historians.

The Cobra sat in a small parking lot next to a public

recycling bin and a trail sign. Coleman was the only occupant, chasing pork rinds with Pabst.

A half mile away, Serge stood in the middle of a gravel path, checking his phone for GPS hiking coordinates.

"Hey, Mr. First-In-Last-Out!"

Serge looked up. "Thanks for meeting on such short notice."

"Wouldn't miss it for the world." Sandy was wearing her bucket hat again and all the trimmings. "Dagny Johnson Key Largo Hammock Botanical State Park." She held up a little green book. "Get your stamp?"

Serge held up his own book. "Stuck the landing."

Sandy knocked him to the ground and undid his pants, and began riding him like a cowboy.

"You don't waste life," said Serge.

Sandy thrust. "The passport books were plenty of foreplay . . ."

They began hearing voices approaching from around the bend. "*Once slated to become condos, this park contains one of the largest tracts of West Indian hardwood hammocks . . .*" Someone leading a tour group. They heard more voices of schoolchildren.

"Better get off the trail," said Serge.

"Good idea."

Fifty yards later, in the leaves, they heard the voices of the tour group go by, and their own voices picked up.

"Oh yes! Oh no! Oh yes! Don't stop! Harder! Faster! Talk dirty to me! . . ."

"Buttonwood! . . ."

"Spanish bayonet! . . ."

"Bulrushes! . . ."

"Weeping banyan! . . ."

They stood up. "Give my regards to Broadway," said Serge.

"You weren't so bad yourself."

The pair began walking down the trail.

"Question," said Sandy. "Why have you been checking your phone so often ever since we got here? And why did you just turn your ringer all the way up? You usually hate people who do that out in state parks."

Serge checked in vain for missed calls or texts. "This is different. I'm worried about a couple of my friends."

"Why?"

"Not sure." Serge pocketed the phone. "Sometimes I just get this strange vibe that something big is about to happen. Can't explain it, but I've been right more than once."

"Anything that triggered it?" asked Sandy.

"Well, I was up at the Myakka park with a ranger friend of mine, and I had that weird feeling we were being watched. I even saw some branches move."

"It's a state park," said Sandy. "Probably a bird or a squirrel."

"Probably, but I want to play it safe. One of the friends is handling a sensitive criminal case."

"And the phone?"

"I have a call in to the dark side." Serge pulled out the cell again, checking the screen. "And that's why I picked this area to meet. I need to be in position in case I have to move quickly. There's a particular law enforcement field office just up in Miami. On the other hand, if I'm wrong, I'm out of position the other way. That's why it's super urgent I get hold of my friend."

"You are an odd one," said Sandy. "That's a good thing."

"Sorry about distracting from the nature experience." He stowed the phone again. "Thank heavens they protected this end of the island. Like that tour guide said, this was about to go condo. And most people wouldn't believe it if you showed them the blueprints, but they also planned to put in an amusement park."

"And not some little roadside gator farm," said

Sandy. "But a big fucking Disney-type thing. Thank God calmer heads prevailed."

"Today, the state preserves the south side of the road . . ."

". . . And on the opposite side, Crocodile Lake National Wildlife Refuge."

"Nothing gets by you," said Serge. He searched her eyes. "What?"

He was slammed down on his back again.

"Senegal date! . . ."

"Strangler fig! . . ."

"Magnolia! . . ."

"Cassia fistula! . . ."

". . . *Also known as the golden shower.*" Sandy propped herself up on her knees and straddled him.

"That wasn't a request," said Serge.

"I have to go anyway," said Sandy. "Why waste a natural resource?"

"Where has love been my whole life? . . ."

They were walking again on the trail, holding hands.

She pointed. "Mahogany mistletoe."

He pointed. "Endangered Key Largo cotton mouse. One of the little guys who stopped the abomination of that planned amusement gulag."

"I love this end of the island," said Sandy. "Ignored and quiet, just before the road ends . . ."

"But the upper Keys don't," said Serge. "And you can canoe across the creeks and tidal flats to islands of aptly named Islandia . . ."

"Old Rhodes Key, Totten Key, Elliott Key . . ."

"And the legend of Black Caesar," said Serge. "I know a lookout point."

"Let's roll," said Sandy.

They dove into the Cobra, causing beer suds that gave Coleman a rare shampoo. "Dang it. You know I usually have a beverage."

"Sorry, Lebowski." Serge sped up the road until they could go no farther at the gates of the exclusive Ocean Reef Club golfing development. He turned to Sandy: "We'll have to go to the shore and hike the rest of the way in the water."

"Done it many times."

They left Coleman behind and trudged through the ankle-deep water, hugging the curling mangrove coastline until they reached the extreme northern tip of Key Largo, overlooking Angelfish Creek. A fish jumped and a blue heron took flight.

"It's up there on the other side of Totten and just southeast of Elliott."

"Caesar's Rock," said Sandy. "Where the black pirate from the early eighteenth century hid out with his gang awaiting passing ships."

"You know about the ring?" asked Serge.

"Of course. That's how they captured those passing ships," said Sandy. "They embedded a large metal ring in the limestone, and ran a thick, braided nautical rope through it. The other end of the rope was tied to the top of the highest mast on their pirate ship."

"Then the whole gang grabbed hold of the rope and pulled it through the ring," said Serge. "Leaning their ship over on its side so passing mariners couldn't see its riggings rising up from the mangroves. But as soon as an unsuspecting schooner came along, they sliced the rope, and their ship immediately popped up for the chase."

"You heard those islands are haunted?" asked Sandy.

Serge nodded. "At its height, it was practically a town. All the pirates, plus captured passengers and even Caesar's harem that numbered in the dozens."

"Jesus, it's between Miami and Key Largo," said Sandy, gazing at egrets across the creek. "Yet scarcely three hundred years ago, a giant freaky outlaw culture ran amok over there."

"Not to mention that the pirate's harem inevitably spawned more than a hundred children," said Serge. "And of course Caesar wasn't the model stay-at-home dad, and most of the kids escaped to the next island, running around naked, eating berries and making up their own language."

Sandy listened to the wind and watched the creek ripple. "People wouldn't believe that's all true . . . Could you put the phone away?"

"Sorry again. That sensation is still there."

More walking.

"This is a little bit awkward for me," said Serge, "but I'd like to ask you out on a date."

"You mean a real formal date-type date? Like a restaurant?"

"Even better!" said Serge. "Let's run around naked, eating berries and making up our own language. What do you say?"

"Almost romantic," said Sandy. "I'll put it on my calendar."

They headed back to the Cobra for one last stop, on the north side of the road, at the crocodile lake refuge.

"Coleman, wait here," said Serge.

Coleman set a six-pack in his lap. "I'm good."

The couple headed off on another nature hike.

"I love ancient ruins," said Serge.

"Me too."

"But in Florida, all the ruins are so new," said Serge.

"Except with the withering elements and thriving overgrowth of subtropical vegetation, it's like *Indiana Jones.*"

They pushed away branches and vines until arriving at a puzzling abandonment, like the Temple of Doom. The name fit, literally. The couple walked through rubble and twisted metal, the remains of radar towers and launch pads.

"Nike Hercules missile battery HM-Forty," said Serge. "Pointed at Cuba when Nikita Khrushchev was being a shmuck. What a place! Pirates, feral children, rockets! Who could ask for more?"

"I can," said Sandy, plucking something from a tree.

"What have you got there?"

She held out her hand with a grin.

Serge looked up in her eyes. "Berries? . . ."

Coleman sat in the car, plowing through the six-pack. He began hearing strange sounds and stared out the window toward the woods.

A hundred yards away, it was another typical Keys thing: A naked couple chased each other through a decommissioned missile site, babbling made-up words, until Sandy tackled Serge near a radar dish and jumped on top . . .

They eventually staggered back to the car, Sandy straightening out her hair and replacing the bucket hat. "Confession: When you first suggested the idea, it sounded stupid. But it was so liberating running around like I was a kid again."

"Me too," said Serge. "Nudity and gibberish are underrated."

They headed back to their cars. "I really do apologize," said Serge, pulling out his phone again. He punched in a number and was put through to voice mail. "Gypsy, you really have to call me as soon as you get this. It's ultra-important." He hung up.

They reached the road. "When will I see you again?" Sandy asked as she opened her driver's door.

"A day? A week?" said Serge. "You caught me in a nutty part of my schedule."

"It would be harder not to." She smiled warmly. "Take care of yourself. And don't change."

Both cars headed back across the Card Sound Bridge. Sandy whipped around him and accelerated away. The Cobra came off the crest of the bridge and touched back down on the mainland. But still miles from civilization. Only one sign of humanity could be seen in all directions.

Coleman bounced in his seat, pointing out the windshield and tugging Serge's sleeve. "Please? I've been waiting in the car all day while you've been doing girlfriend stuff."

"Normally I wouldn't, but it's so historic . . ."

Not just historic, but known far and wide among the natives as one of the best outpost watering holes in all the state.

The Cobra pulled through the parking lot of Alabama Jack's. Coleman practically sprinted into the bar and hopped onto a stool. On the next stool, a man slumped over the counter. He struggled to raise his head with red slits for eyes. "Who the fuck are you?"

"Coleman. Who are you?"

"Jack Grayson, dammit! I could have been senator!"

Chapter 38

The Next Day

The blue-and-white Ford Cobra sped west past a shack with a wooden sign for frog legs.

Coleman held another newspaper in his lap. "But I read yesterday."

"You do realize that you can read more than one day in a row. It's not like being a marathon runner."

"But I'm high again."

"And I'm driving again!" Serge grabbed a travel mug from a cup holder. "I told you I need to keep my edge on the other guys. I'm sure they have helpers who read to them."

Coleman listlessly turned a page and read in an

annoyed monotone. "'Naked driver in car crash discovered with electrical wires attached to his penis.'"

Serge sighed. "Next."

"'Woman tells police the wind blew cocaine into her purse.'"

"Next."

"'Hazmat team evacuates mall after man sprinkles cremated ashes in LensCrafters.'"

"LensCrafters?"

"Says he was going around town to places that had sentimental meaning."

"Next."

"Dude dies after going to girlfriend's house and getting stuck in the cat door."

"Next."

"Florida man murdered with a whole set of kitchen knives bought from a TV commercial."

Serge shook his head. "That's enough data."

"Hold on," said Coleman, pulling the newspaper closer to his face. "There's a photo of the victim."

"So?"

"He looks familiar. I think I've seen him recently."

"You're just ripped again."

"No, seriously. It says here his name was Raúl Dixon—"

The Cobra skidded off the Tamiami Trail, catapulting Coleman into the dashboard. He rubbed a sore spot on his forehead. "Lucky I'm medicated. But my coconut-bra bong's fucked up."

"Let me see that!" Serge snatched the newspaper and read down the article. "This happened several days ago. Why are they just reporting it now?" More reading, and Serge began to nod. "It's a follow-up story. Reporters talked to some neighbors who said detectives visited the house a day or so before the homicide."

"What did they want?" ask Coleman.

"The article says 'No comment,' but a confidential source indicated it might be linked to a serial killer." He tossed the paper over his shoulder and grabbed his cell phone. "Now I definitely have to get hold of Gypsy!"

"What for?"

"Shhhh! I'm dialing!" He put the phone to his ear and listened until he reached voice mail. "Gypsy, call! It's an emergency!" He hung up.

"Serge," said Coleman. "I know less what's going on than normal."

"Don't you see? It's all fitting together now like a puzzle." He retrieved the discarded newspaper from the back seat and slapped it. "This is why I had that creepy feeling I told Sandy about on Key Largo. I'm rarely wrong."

"What's fitting together?"

"I visit Dixon for my family tree, then state agents do the same thing, then he's murdered. Then I had that strange conversation with Ranger Bobby, where I got the sensation we were being watched."

"What's it all mean?"

"That we have to turn around." Serge spun the Cobra's tires in the grassy shoulder and slung the car in a violent U-turn.

"Does this also mean I don't have to read anymore?" asked Coleman.

"Yes. The torture's over." The Cobra sped past the Big Cypress Oasis Visitor Center and continued on through the Glades. Vultures and roadkill and mirages of puddles ahead on the road. Finally, Serge pulled off the road again, much more gently this time.

"Why are you stopping?" asked Coleman.

"We're at a brick wall," said Serge. "Nothing I can do until I hear back from Gypsy. I'll wait for the call here, and then I'll know which way to drive." He opened his door . . .

Soon, they were riding an open-sided tram that looked like a little train. It headed south down a narrow fifteen-mile trail into wildness. Coleman's head hung out the side. "Jesus! I've never seen such huge gators. So *many* gators. And they're in the road. We're having to stop and go around them."

"Shark Valley is renowned for its teeming wildlife." Serge snapped photos of herons and ibis. "Named after the Shark River that flows down into the gulf."

"I thought you'd be more upbeat," said Coleman.

"Part of the *national* park system, so I'm emotionally conflicted that my passport book can't get another state stamp."

"What am I seeing up ahead?" asked Coleman. "Wasn't this supposed to be pure nature?"

"It is, but it's also part of controlled management to balance visitor access and appreciation while preserving impact goals."

As they grew closer, an immense concrete structure rose from the big sky.

The largest part looked like a highway cloverleaf spiraling upward toward a cylindrical panoramic observation tower. The tram arrived and visitors climbed to the top.

"Coleman, are you digging it?" said Serge. *Click, click, click.* "This is what it's all about! . . . Coleman?"

Serge turned. Other visitors were having to walk around where Coleman lay flat on the observation deck. "What are you doing down there? You can't see anything."

"I'm dying."

"Don't be such a drama queen." Serge raised his camera. "Catch your breath and get up here!"

After much effort, Coleman became upright and collapsed against the railing next to Serge. "What am I looking at? It's all flat."

"I know. Isn't it great?" *Click, click, click.* "Possibly nowhere else can you get such an inspirational view of the miracle of the Everglades."

"It's still flat."

"Will you stop?" said Serge. "That incredible expanse of grass dotted with hardwood islands to the horizon is actually a super-wide, shallow, slow-moving river. Right now, we could be looking out there at a wall of shopping centers and gated communities, except Marjory Stoneman Douglas presciently sounded the alarm that there is only one Everglades in the world—"

Serge looked down at his vibrating pocket. He pulled out his phone and checked the display. "I have to take this . . ." He stepped a courteous distance away from the other visitors. "Gypsy! Jesus! And you complain that *I'm* hard to reach!"

"Okay, I kind of owe you an apology," said the voice on the other end. "I got your payment for locating that scam artist at the Miami marina. Lot more money than I expected . . . So what's this emergency you left like ten messages about?"

"I need another favor," said Serge. "A big one."

"I already assumed that."

"I'm trying to solve a murder that's been in the papers. Sure you saw it," said Serge. "One Raúl Dixon."

"Serge, I think you're overestimating my ability," said Gypsy. "I can't solve murders."

"I'm not expecting you to," said Serge. "Just spit out hacked data based on my parameters. I was laboriously working on this with the geometry of genealogy—"

"I don't even know what that means."

"Neither do I, but it sounds impressive. That's how you always must phrase things in life to go big." Serge shifted the phone to his other ear. "Building my required family tree has been slower than I anticipated, but the recent homicide just turbo-charged the process. The murder was overkill-personal, and so full of coincidences that they are no coincidences. My pile of chips is on someone who knew him. I want you to start with Dixon and move outward, compiling a ten-year list of every name that's appeared with his on any public document, and the private ones you have a knack for finding. Then give me the list in descending order of frequency, with any unusual background on the names that appear the most. Meanwhile, I'll e-mail you photos of my corkboard."

"Oh, is that all?" said Gypsy. "You sure you don't

want me to also solve the Amelia Earhart disappearance?"

A horrific scream from Serge's end of the line, then slapping sounds. "You fucker!"

"What did I say?"

"Nothing. Can you just do this simple thing?"

A harrumph. "I'll see what I can find. But I expect to be paid."

"Handsomely," said Serge. "And I promise to fix the windshield."

"You cracked my windshield?" yelled Gypsy.

"Not my fault. Coleman lost control of the coconut bra."

"What?"

"Later."

The Cobra reached the eastern edge of the Everglades next to the Miccosukee casino. It made a right at the Dade Corners truck stop and drove down into the bottom of the state.

Agriculture, farmhands in straw hats, giant sprinklers, barbed wire at the immigration detention center. They reached the end of civilization in the town of Homestead. The Cobra sat at the curb as Serge pointed a camera upward. *Click, click, click.*

"I just love the old Seminole Theatre! Built in 1921

with the period's classic-style marquee extending over the sidewalk. And the name 'Seminole' is spelled out on one of those throwback vertical lighted signs rising up against the side of the building." *Click, click, click.* "Can you imagine such a grand cinema at such a remote edge of humanity?"

"I'm looking at it," said Coleman. "So, yeah."

"It's actually the second Seminole Theatre," said Serge. "The first was built when they took apart the Airdome Theatre in Miami in 1916, and sent the pieces on a train over here . . . Woohoo. I've been waiting for this day forever!" *Click, click, click.* "The joint had been closed for almost forty years, so it became an eyesore unsuitable for proper photographic documentation. Thank God for preservationists! They restored the landmark and now I can have my pictures." *Click, click, click.*

A phone rang, and Serge answered.

"Gypsy, that was fast!"

"Don't get too excited yet," said Gypsy. "But I got an early hit that I thought you'd want to know about right away."

"Somebody with the most documented contacts with Dixon?"

"Actually not," said Gypsy. "I found a dozen people with three to six hits in the records. But it was a dude with only two who caught my eye. In 2013, he bailed Dixon out of jail in Marathon for drunk and disorderly, and three years later, he turned up on a transfer of title."

"Sold a car?"

"No, boat, fourteen-foot skiff," said Gypsy. "Must not have been much of one because it only went for seven hundred."

"So why is the guy with only two hits on your list interesting?" asked Serge.

"Because I traced everything I could find on the dozen above him, and nothing, and then I hit him."

"Leaving me hanging?"

"I hacked into the court systems, sealed juvenile records. Arson and animal cruelty."

Serge nodded. "Two of the markers of a future serial killer."

"That's why I thought you'd want to know."

"Thanks. Anything on the location?"

"The later records show Ramrod Key, but the earlier juvie stuff is from Homestead. I'll keep working on a current address."

"Coincidentally, I'm in Homestead right now. So I guess I'm on my way to Ramrod. Thanks."

"A question," said Gypsy. "Why me? The FDLE is much better with murder investigators."

"Infinitely better," said Serge. "But you can hack

cyberspace like a Nobel laureate, and you're not picky about search warrants. Anything else?"

"Windshield."

Click.

The Cobra drove away from the Seminole Theatre. Farther south. Surrounding neighborhoods depressed, the homes dribbling off as the town gave way to mangrove swamp.

Serge sped past one of the last streets, where a two-bedroom house stood with black stains on the concrete walls. The yard was dirt and the mailbox full of junk flyers. It appeared for all the world to be vacated. The blinds were drawn, and the lights were never on. The only clue was a sunbaked Chevelle in the driveway, which only a few neighbors had witnessed coming and going in the middle of the night. It was one of those houses where the rest of the block thought: Leave well enough alone.

Inside, a light was actually on, but all the windows were taped up with black paper. The light was a naked bulb in the back bedroom. The bureau sat covered with empty beer cans and stacks of unwashed dishes. The toilet in the bathroom remained unflushed. A rat scampered unmolested through crumpled newspapers on the floor.

Then a paradox: a lone shelf on concrete blocks. Full of books. Textbooks. Graduate level. Biology, calculus, theoretical physics and so on. Mensa stuff.

In the corner, a middle-aged man in a white tank-top sat in a lawn chair, transfixed, eating Ramen noodles so slowly as to appear that the resident was coming around after taking a tranquilizer dart. The broth trickled down his chin and onto the shirt. He had been staring for an hour. It was something on the wall.

A corkboard was full of notecards and pushpins and colored yarn, just like Heather's and Serge's. Except this wasn't a family tree. There were pictures and dates and a souvenir collection of driver's licenses. Half of the photos were grainy, long-range zoom shots. The people in them were in shopping malls, strolling through parks, loading groceries, all seemingly unaware. The other half of the photos were the same people. Mostly in the woods. This time they were even less aware, because they weren't breathing anymore.

The resident continued eating soup, staring at the boards, and caressing an unlaundered woman's undergarment in his lap.

Chapter 39

South Florida

Henry Flagler's Overseas Railroad really opened up the Keys.

Christened in 1912, it was converted for automobile traffic in 1938. Today, motorists drive over many of the magnificent original bridges connecting the islands, as well as the new one next to the Long Key Viaduct. Other old spans have also been retired, like the first Seven Mile Bridge over Pigeon Key.

There stands one particular decommissioned bridge, however, that is the runaway favorite among amateur and professional photographers alike.

A blue-and-white Cobra sped across a modern

span near mile marker 37. Serge pointed south out the window.

"There it is! There it is! The old Bahia Honda bridge, still standing after all these years. The most picturesque, postcard-ready sight on this whole highway!" *Click, click, click.*

"It looks rusty," said Coleman.

"Because it's righteously aged." *Click, click, click.* "A fabulous five-thousand-foot monument to camelback truss construction connecting this island to Spanish Harbor Key." *Click, click, click.* "Fun fact: Flagler's trains used to run through the middle of the trusses, which were so frighteningly narrow that upon approaching the bridge, the conductors used to make everyone close all the windows so arms wouldn't get chopped off."

"Arms not getting chopped off." Coleman swilled a Schlitz. "Hooray."

"You sarcastic cretin! Then I shouldn't share with you that when they converted it for cars, the bridge was too narrow for two lanes, so they assembled the concrete highway decks at a harrowing height on *top* of the trusses, and the guardrails weren't much to speak of back then." Serge punched Coleman in the shoulder.

"Ow!"

"I'm imprinting. You're in the presence of glory!"

said Serge. "If there were a list of Florida's Seven Wonders, this would be on it. Even better, it's now a state park."

The Cobra pulled through the entrance and up to the guard shack. Serge flapped a small green book out the window. "Rock that ink pad, dude . . ."

Serge soon stood with Coleman on the shore of the Gulf Stream. "Look at that water! Look at that sand! This place is regularly voted one of the top two beaches in all of Florida, and that's stiff competition, usually neck and neck with Crescent Beach on Siesta Key . . . Coleman, let's go!"

"Where?"

"To climb the bridge!"

"What? . . ."

Moments later, another familiar scene. Serge standing proudly with a chestful of appreciation, enjoying natural magnificence with dozens of other tourists. Coleman on his hands and knees vomiting.

"Coleman, stop fooling around and get up here! You're missing everything."

"Hold on. I got a little more coming." Retching sounds.

"And normally I'd be pissed off, but you're effectively clearing out the other tourists, providing solitude for my experience."

Coleman struggled onto two legs and staggered. “Serge, there’s a gap in the bridge with barricades.”

“That’s right. We’re up on the old concrete highway deck. They had to cut away a small space in the bridge so that jokers and drunks wouldn’t barrel around ‘Do Not Enter’ signs.” Serge slowly pirouetted in an organic buzz. “Dig the view from way up here! Turquoise and emerald water, sailboats, sugar-white sand. Everyone should be taking photos! . . .”

Click, click, click. The sound wasn’t from Serge’s camera, but a zoom lens aimed up at the bridge from behind a coconut palm.

Serge pointed at the corner of Coleman’s mouth. “. . . You got spit-up.” His pocket vibrated. He answered the cell phone.

“Gypsy, word.”

“Serge, I want a grand.”

“I think I can find that lying around . . . someone else’s place. What have you got?”

“An address and name.”

“That’s my Gypsy.” A notebook and pen came from another pocket. “Ready to write.”

“Here it is . . .” He burped out the info. “And I checked it on Google Earth. It’s kind of eerie. You sure you know what you’re doing?”

“What’s it ever looked like?”

“That’s my point. And I want my car.”

Serge lowered his head. “Godspeed.” He hung up and looked at Coleman. “Is it me?”

The 1970 Ford Cobra pulled out of Bahia Honda State Park and headed back to the mainland.

A moment later, a sunbaked Chevelle pulled away from the park onto the same road.

Coleman sucked smoke out of a coconut repaired with duct tape. “What do you want to watch on TV tonight?”

“I want my money’s worth out of my portable DVD player,” said Serge. “So I guess *Sea Hunt*.”

“Again?” said Coleman. “But we’ve watched it every night this week.”

“Because *Sea Hunt* is the best!” said Serge. “It was a magical time. If you watched any television at all in the sixties, you know what I’m talking about, and I give Jacques Cousteau credit. All those educational oceanic specials. And then for some paranormal reason, maybe because scuba diving was still relatively novel, the whole country went gaga. All these TV producers in meetings: ‘We’re stuck on the plot for the next episode of our cops-and-robbers show. Fuck it, make ’em scuba dive.’ If you need any more proof, even James Bond got into the act in 1965 with *Thunderball*. And suddenly all these dramatic network shows began changing their denouements. Instead of gunfire in an alley or a side-swiping car chase, the final confrontations went underwater, and every other TV show ended in scuba diver fights. I've been diving a lot, and not all the divers have sparkling personalities. A lot of broiling rivalry and arguments in the beach bars after dark, and yet I've never seen an underwater fight, not even shoving. But back then on TV, there were always fights, and it was always the *same* fight. A *knife* fight. And you always knew how the fight was going to end: one of the guys would slash the other's air hose."

"I once saw a show where a guy got shot with a speargun," said Coleman.

"The exception that only proves the rule," said Serge. "That scriptwriter was clearly overqualified."

The day drew to a close as a 1970 Cobra crossed the bridge from Key Largo, entering the first spongy mangrove miles of the mainland. Serge glanced down at a scrap of paper in his lap.

"So Gypsy really came through?" asked Coleman.

"We'll soon find out." Serge looked ahead where the road merged with the route from the Card Sound Bridge and Alabama Jack's. "It's right up here."

The Cobra passed the darkened marquee of the historic Seminole Theatre. Serge soon took a left and doubled back south through the badlands of greater Homestead. Headlights reached a fork that led down to the Everglades National Park center on the bottom tip of the state near Cape Sable. Serge took the other spur, into a smattering of concrete homes at the end of the line . . .

A hundred yards back, a sunbaked Chevelle made the same turn. The driver knew the way by heart.

Serge slowed as they approached the address from Gypsy. He stopped at a curb and rechecked the numbers. "I think this is it."

"Looks abandoned," said Coleman. "No lights on, no car, no lawn, grimy walls, junk mail all over the porch."

"That's how all serial killers' homes look." Serge grabbed his door handle. "It's like they have their own *Homes and Gardens* special edition."

"Wait," said Coleman. "You're just going to walk right up to that house?"

"That's the best way to get there unless you have a jet pack."

"No, I mean if he really is a killer, what if he's home? We could get hurt . . ."

Behind them, at the far end of the block, a Chevelle with its lights off slowly rounded the corner and parked ten houses down.

"Coleman, there's no car in the driveway, and this is the kind of remote real estate where you don't exactly walk home." Serge stepped out of the car. "I guarantee it's perfectly safe."

Serge led his pal around the side of the house, looking for the most opportune entry point. "Here we go. An unlatched window."

"That was careless of him."

"Lazy. The latch is broken." Serge raised the window. "Now I'm more confident we're at the right place."

"Why do you say that?"

"Because the glass is completely taped up with black paper. Another decorating tip from that *Homes and Gardens* edition . . . I'll boost you up first because I can climb in on my own. Put your right foot in my hands."

"Okay."

Serge thrust. "And in you go!"

Coleman's drumstick legs disappeared into the house, followed by a violent tumbling noise. "Ow! Shit! Ow!"

Serge deftly followed him in without incident. He felt along the walls for light switches and flicked them, but none worked. "Coleman, here's your coal miner's head lamp. We'll use these until we can find some illumination. Remember, the lamp faces forward."

"Thanks."

A pair of beams crisscrossed the dark stillness as they worked room to room. Coleman's beam kept pointing down. "Look at all the trash. And there's rat poop."

"Stay on mission," said Serge. "We're looking for evidence that this is our guy."

They came up empty, space after space, until there was only one spot left, the back bedroom. Serge's beam hit a lamp with a naked lightbulb. He pulled a chain. The room lit up.

The pair froze. They stared at a wall. "Jesus Christ!"

The corkboard was unsettling. Long-range surveillance photos of future victims, their souvenir driver's licenses and then the gruesome pictures. As their eyes moved, it became increasingly chilling. More zoom photos, but these were recent. Serge's mouth hung open as his gaze slowly moved over them. There were a half-dozen black-and-white shots of Heather walking out of her city office. Then an equal number of grainy pics of Ranger Bobby.

Coleman gasped and pointed. "That's me! And me again! And you! What's going on?"

"They were taken at the park," said Serge. He removed a pushpin and plucked Heather's business card from the corkboard. "Our fellow has been a busy beaver. He somehow got wind that after all these years, the authorities had picked up his trail. Probably from the late Mr. Dixon."

"What are we going to do?" asked Coleman.

"This." Serge stepped back with his cell phone, taking photos of the wall.

"But what if he's nearby?"

"He's very nearby," said Serge. "In a sunbaked Chevelle at the end of the street."

"How do you know that?"

"Because he's been following us ever since Bahia Honda," said Serge.

"You saw him the whole way?"

"No, just when he parked at the end of the block a few minutes ago." *Click, click, click.* "But yesterday I found a magnetic GPS tracking device under my back bumper. I always check every morning. Judging from these photos, I'm guessing he attached it when we were away from the car inside Bobby's apartment at Myakka."

"But how could he have followed us if you threw the tracker away?"

"Because I left it under the bumper." *Click, click, click.*

"What!"

"Relax, I've got him right where I want him." Serge stowed the cell phone and turned off the naked bulb.

Coleman's forehead beam swung wildly around the room in panic. "How can you be so calm?"

"Because I've got a gauge on this guy, and we have a huge organizational advantage." Serge's own beam swung back to the wall. "You've seen my tidy corkboard. Now take a look at how his is put together. That's just embarrassing."

This time, they simply unlocked the front door. Coleman crept behind Serge. "Is he still there?"

Serge looked up the street. The previously occupied spot at the curb was empty. "Damn."

"What's the matter?" asked Coleman.

"He's gone."

"That's a good thing."

"No, very bad," said Serge. "I assumed he was waiting for us to come out and would follow us to our next stop, so he could ambush us in the middle of the night at our motel room. Now it looks like he was just watching to see if we got in the house to know whether he needed to abandon the place. Then he split."

"But how is that bad?"

"He's going somewhere else, and I have a good idea where." Serge pulled out his cell phone as he dashed back to the Cobra.

They sped north and picked up the turnpike in Florida City. Serge kept dialing and dialing.

"Well?" asked Coleman.

"Nobody's answering because it's so late." He continued pressing buttons. "I was able to leave a message on Heather's machine, but Bobby doesn't have one. We have to beat him to the park!"

"How do you know he's going to the park and not after Heather?"

"He'll eventually go after her because she's his main target," said Serge. "These guys like to kill in a particular order. Take out the father first to terrorize her before the finale."

"You sure?"

"Not a hundred percent, but you just have to think like a serial killer." Serge nodded to himself. "Yeah, the park. And he's got a big head start."

Serge hit the gas.

Chapter 40

Myakka River State Park

A nightlight in the shape of a seashell dimly lit the dark-green walls. It also served as a fragrance dispenser. Ranger Bobby lay on his back in the tiny room's single bed. Snoring. The fragrance was pine trees.

The ranger's eyes fluttered open. He got a feeling that something had awoken him, but he didn't know what. Bobby wouldn't have to wait long for the answer.

Knock, knock, knock.

"What time is it?" He looked at the alarm clock. "Four A.M.? The park's closed, so it can only be another ranger, or maybe a camper with a problem."

He yawned as he opened the door, and suddenly became ultra-awake.

Bobby ducked as the fist swung imprecisely where his head had just been.

"You son of a bitch! I'll kill you!"

Another off-target swing from the hand that wasn't holding the bottle. "After all I did for you. Stabbing me in the back with that recording! You destroyed my Senate campaign! My whole life!"

"Take it easy, Jack," said the ranger.

Another attempted punch, this one hitting the door frame. "Fuck!" The former Senate candidate sucked on his bloody knuckles. "You think you could screw me and then just hide over here like a coward? You think I wouldn't find you? Track you down to the ends of the earth?"

"You need to take deep breaths." The ranger extended an arm. "And more importantly, give me that bottle."

"No!" Grayson jerked away the fifth of Scotch and clutched it to his chest. "It's mine!"

"You need to sleep this off," said Bobby. "And you're in no condition to drive. I'll call and make arrangements for a ride and a hotel room. Wait here."

The ranger went inside and reached for the wall phone. The one he always unplugged at night so solicitors wouldn't wake him. By law, solicitors weren't supposed to call so late, but many were now also scam artists who didn't color within the lines. He plugged it back in and began to dial. Through the open door, he saw the ex-candidate weaving away from the cabin, upending the bottle as he staggered.

"Hey, come back here!" yelled the ranger.

"To hell with you! To hell with everyone!" The politician neared the edge of darkness at the tree line. "I'm Jack Grayson!"

"Then I'll call the police!" shouted Bobby.

"Blow me!" And he disappeared.

Bobby closed the door and dialed 911. "Yes, I have an emergency. I'm a ranger at the park, and I need to report someone in danger of driving severely drunk . . ."

The Cobra rolled up to Myakka River State Park in the middle of the night.

Coleman pointed behind them. "You're passing the entrance."

"It's locked at this hour, but I know a back way," said Serge. "An authorized-personnel-only dirt road. It's usually locked, too, with a chain, but nothing bolt cutters can't fix." He climbed out of the car and approached the gate with the long metal tool.

"That's weird. The whole chain's gone. Someone must have gotten careless." He swung the gate open, then drove through on a winding route until he arrived at the cabin in the woods.

Serge almost immediately tripped over something in the darkness. He caught his balance, then held an arm out sideways to block the way. "Coleman, step around . . ."

They got to the door. *Knock, knock, knock.*

From inside: "I've already called the police. Don't go anywhere."

More knocking. "Bobby, it's me, Serge."

The ranger opened up. "What are you doing here? And how'd you get in?"

"This is urgent. You're in massive danger."

"Danger maybe, but I don't know about massive," said Bobby. "He was practically knee-walking drunk."

The park entrance was miles from anything in the isolation of surrounding pasture land, but eventually they heard the distant sirens.

Bobby's head turned in their direction. "Good. The police are almost here. Grayson was in no condition to drive."

"That's an understatement," said Serge.

"What are you talking about?"

"I almost tripped over him on the way in."

The ranger left his apartment and headed for the trees. "Passed out?"

Serge followed. “It’s not something you need to see.”

Bobby stopped, looking at the ground. “Dear mother of God. What happened?”

“Overkill,” said Serge. “I’m guessing an ax.”

“We’ve got a killer out in the woods?”

“This is the danger I was talking about,” said Serge. “If my hunch is right, it has something to do with a case your daughter is investigating.”

“My daughter! Is she safe?”

“For now.” Serge pointed toward the politician’s body. “But I think the serial killer she’s tracking is onto her. He might have come here to target you, just to rattle Heather beforehand. The freshness of this kill at our feet means he’s at least a three-hour drive from reaching your daughter on the other coast. But it’s imperative we contact her as soon as possible.” He pulled Heather’s business card from his wallet. “I’ve left several messages on her office machine . . .” He happened to turn the card over, and popped himself in the forehead. “I’m such an idiot. She wrote her personal cell number on the back.”

“Give me that,” said the ranger, heading inside his apartment and grabbing the phone off the wall. He dialed.

It rang and rang, as could be expected in the dead of night. “Come on! . . . Pick up! . . .”

Around the eighth ring, a sleepy voice answered. "Hello?"

"It's Dad," said Bobby.

"Dad? Why are you calling at this hour? What time is it?"

"Heather, this is extremely important. You're in great danger."

"What on earth are you talking about?"

"Just listen. There's been a murder at the park. Only minutes ago. Serge thinks it has something to do with the case you're working on."

"Serge?" On the other side of the state, Heather sprang up in bed. "He's there?"

"Yes, and he thinks the killer you're tracking is after you," said Bobby. "You have to get yourself someplace safe."

Her feet hit the floor. "I'm coming right over!"

"Honey—"

Click.

Bobby pulled the receiver from his head.

"What happened?" asked Serge.

"She hung up! She said she's driving over! What am I going to do?"

"For now, relax." Serge put a hand on his shoulder. "Heather's a highly trained state agent, and she now has a heads-up. Plus she's mobile and armed. Those are all good things." Serge looked out the apartment's door as the police sirens grew louder. The first flickers of red and blue lights hit branches at the tree line. "And those are bad things. It's not exactly the best time for me to interact with the law." He headed out the door. "Coleman, we need to make ourselves scarce again."

"Serge!" yelled Bobby. "Stop! The cops will probably seal this place off as soon as they see the body, and they'll be scouring the woods. Whatever you're trying to avoid, it will only look worse if they find you hiding in some bushes under these circumstances. Not to mention there's a killer somewhere out there who could get you. Stay here at the apartment."

Serge stopped in thought and began nodding to himself again. "Sage advice. Hide in plain sight."

"I'm a lawyer," said Bobby. "Just stick close to me, and I'll handle anything that might come up by distracting them. And try not to get too chatty."

"Me? . . ."

Fifteen minutes later, at a remote location in Florida known for its quiet, the natural solitude was anything but.

A dozen police cars sat at random angles, some with the lights still going. Every ranger in the park was up and out. Cameras flashed, detectives opened notebooks, and someone with a spool of yellow tape began roping off the body.

It was man-to-man coverage, a detective talking to each ranger.

"I just woke up minutes ago when I heard the sirens . . ."

"I know about as much as you . . ."

"What's going on? . . ."

A lieutenant flipped open another pad. "Are you Bobby? The one who called this in?"

"That's right, but I only reported someone trying to drive drunk," said the ranger. "I didn't expect a response like this."

"That's because we got a second call," said the detective. "Reporting the murder."

"I didn't make that call."

"Have any idea who did?"

Serge whispered sideways to Coleman. "The killer called. Trying to trap and frame us here in the park."

The lieutenant turned. "What did you say?"

Bobby stepped between them. "Nothing."

"Do they work at the park as well?"

"No," said the ranger. "Longtime friends staying with me. They volunteer."

"So let's back up," said the investigator. "You only

called in a potential DUI? So the victim was alive when you last saw him?"

"That's right."

"And why were you seeing him?"

"Didn't want to," said Bobby. "We had a political dispute a few months ago, and he came banging on my door pissed off."

"So you were the last person to see the victim alive, and you argued with him just before he was found brutally murdered just a few feet from your door?"

As a lawyer, Bobby knew where this was going. Then he saw the handcuffs come out. "Look, I called in the DUI thing and went back inside. If I'm guilty, why would I have summoned the law to find that grotesqueness out in the open?"

Other rangers also saw the handcuffs dangling from the detective's fingers and rushed over, including the park manager, vouching up and down for Ranger Bobby.

"All right. For now." The detective stowed the bracelets. "But nobody go anywhere until we complete all the interviews and figure a few things out. We're quarantining the whole park." He wandered off to compare notes with colleagues.

"Man!" Serge whistled. "When you said you'd distract them to protect us, you go all the way!"

"That wasn't precisely my plan," said the ranger. "Let's get you two back inside my apartment to avoid any more unpleasantness . . ."

Hours later, the eastern sky betrayed the first hints of light. A white Crown Vic raced through the woods and up to the cabin.

Heather Sparrow jumped out and showed her badge to the locals. Her status as a state agent carried a lot of water in law enforcement circles, and they showed proper deference.

"Who called the FDLE in on this?"

"My dad!" said Heather. "Is he okay?"

"Your dad?" asked a Sarasota detective.

"Bobby Sparrow. He works as a ranger here," said Heather. "He called me about a case I'm on."

"Oh, we questioned him earlier. I think he's back in his room."

"I know the way." Heather ran down to the last door and knocked hard.

Bobby opened up and got a big, tight hug he wasn't expecting. "Come on inside."

She entered, and the ranger closed the door. That's when she saw his visitors.

Heather immediately unholstered her Glock and aimed it at Serge. "Don't move! Keep your hands where I can see them!"

"Jesus!" said the ranger. "Honey, what are you doing?"

"Stay out of this, Dad." She widened her stance from cadet training. "You don't know who you're dealing with."

"I kind of think I do," said Bobby. "Could you just lower the gun?"

She shook her head. "Back at the field office, I finally completed the family tree I was telling you about."

"Wow!" said Serge. "I'm impressed. I've been busting my ass on that thing and have weeks to go. Good on you!"

"Keep those hands up!" said Heather. "Dad, like I told you, when I finished the family search, he was on a list of cousins."

"Of course I'm on it," said Serge. "I told you at your office I have a corkboard just like yours."

The agent maintained aim and separation as she slowly reached for her own handcuffs.

"Honey, you're wrong," said Bobby. "He came here to warn me. And you. He's been calling your number all night." The ranger held up her business card.

Heather briefly glanced to the side. "Turn it over."

He did.

"Just as I thought," said Heather. "I wrote my

number on the back and gave it to that guy Dixon. You grabbed it off the Bible after killing him."

"No," said Serge. "I plucked it from a corkboard in Homestead. You should see that guy's place. What a loon!"

"Don't make any false moves!"

"Unappreciated moves."

She held the cuffs out with her free hand. "Dad, put these on him."

"I can't do that."

"Dad!" said Heather, taking steps backward and reaching behind for the door handle. "Then I'll get one of the other officers to do it."

Bobby's arms waved emphatically. "Don't! That's a bell you can't un-ring! Just hear me out first!"

Serge wiggled the fingers he had up in the air. "Excuse me? Hello? I can prove it . . . Bobby, grab my cell phone and look at the image gallery. I know it's pretty big because I tend to get carried away with the photos. Ask around. But the most recent images are of the corkboard at the real killer's house in Homestead."

Bobby navigated through the phone until he found them, and held it up toward his daughter. "Serge is right. Here's the corkboard."

Another brief glance to the side. "Dad! That's *his* corkboard."

"Mine?" said Serge. "I'm deeply hurt. That thing is just embarrassing."

Bobby blew up a photo, then another and another. "Hold on a second . . . Heather, there are a bunch of zoom photos on these boards. From outside your office and this park. You, me, even Serge and Coleman. We've *all* been under surveillance. And it would have been impossible for Serge to photograph himself at such a range."

"Don't move!" Heather snapped at Serge. "Dad, hold it closer." She took a series of quick sideways glimpses. Distant blow-ups of her getting in the Crown Vic, then with her father outside the cabin, and more of Serge and Bobby hiking together in the park.

"See?" said the ranger. "These weren't taken at selfie distance. Someone else had to shoot them. And if we don't listen to Serge, we could be ignoring the real danger."

She stood in thought for the longest time, then at Serge: "Take a seat in that corner and don't move and we'll talk about this. Tell me everything you know . . ."

And he did.

Serge's exhaustive detail and accuracy passed the smell test. The side trips into *Sea Hunt* and the Statue of Liberty, not so much. "His name's Artemas Kenilworth Tweel. I have his address and everything. Your people need to check him out."

She finally holstered her service pistol. "Dad, we have to get you into protection."

"You too," said Bobby.

"I can take care of myself."

"Excuse me," said Serge. "Your dad's right. If Tweel could get close enough to shoot photos of you, that's also close enough to *shoot.*"

"Honey, please?" asked the ranger.

She relented and pulled out her cell. "Okay, we'll both get protection. I'll call the office and have us set up in a safe house until this is over."

"May I?" said Serge. "This is my wheelhouse. There's safe and then there's safe. I have a better idea."

"May *I*?" said Heather. "We do this for a living."

"Stop dialing and let me tell you a story," said Serge.

Heather took a hard breath. "Make it a short story."

"No guarantees," said Serge. "Back in the eighties, the cartels were shipping coke in ridiculous amounts, and this state got a little too hot, so they had planes start landing in unsuspecting places like Tennessee, Alabama, Georgia. One Florida pilot landed in Montgomery. His flight plan listed a short hop, but some alert person at the airport noticed an extra-large gas tank and four blades on a propeller that should have had three, meaning a long haul with a heavy load. They found the coke and flipped the pilot to testify for the feds. They put him in protective custody, and sealed all information about him. *He* was supposed to be as safe as it gets."

"Are you saying they got to him anyway?" asked Heather.

Serge shook his head. "Someone pretending to be a defense lawyer called a clerk at the courthouse and was able to trick her into opening a file that she didn't realize was supposed to be confidential, and she gave the address of his mother's house, not too far from your field office, in fact. They sent two guys to knock on her door, and they didn't even wait for her to open it. As soon as they heard 'Who is it?,' they cut loose through the wood with a pair of machine guns. Effectively shutting up the witness for the feds."

"I remember when that happened," said Bobby. "All over the papers on the east coast."

"Before my time," said Heather. "But I've heard the older agents talk about it."

Serge held out his palms. "The human element. Weakest link in any plan. The only truly safe house is one nobody else knows about."

"What are you suggesting?" asked Bobby.

"I know this state like my own face," said Serge. "And when push comes to shove, I've got all the ultimate, tried-and-true fallback positions."

"So what now?" asked Heather.

"Tell your office about Grayson's murder, and your cold case, and that the suspect has had you under surveillance," said Serge. "And that you're making your own arrangements."

"I'll need to go home to get my stuff," said Heather. "I only keep a small overnight bag in the trunk of the Vic."

"Then that will have to be your stuff." Serge stood. "The sooner we get moving, the better."

"But Serge," said Bobby. "The police outside told us nobody can leave the park for a while."

Serge turned knowingly to Heather. "But you can get us out."

"Yes, I can."

"Then let's get moving."

Police were questioning several rangers near the blockaded entrance to Myakka River State Park.

Heather flashed her badge, and a pair of patrol cars backed up to clear exit space.

The Crown Victoria with her dad inside rolled out of the park, followed by Serge and Coleman in a blue-and-white Ford product.

The Cobra soon passed the Vic, leading them through the first light of day on their marathon odyssey of refuge. Shortly after leaving the park, Heather called her people at the field office and relayed the info that Serge had given her. "Right, Artemas Tweel, Homestead. . . . Okay, I'll wait for your call . . ."

The two-car convoy drove down the southwest coast of Florida, then across the Everglades before another turn south, jumping to Key Largo and the Overseas Highway.

Somewhere in the middle of Big Pine Key, Heather's phone rang. ". . . I see, I see, okay . . ." And she listened some more. ". . . Don't worry, I'll stay safe. Bye."

She hung up. Her dad was looking. "Well?"

"Serge was right," said Heather. "Tweel's our guy. A team is at his house at this moment, and it's just like Serge said, the corkboard and souvenir driver's licenses and everything. They worked up a full background check, and he was either living or working near all the crime scenes at the times of the murders. Ocala, New Smyrna, Sebastian, Vero, everywhere."

"I told you Serge could be trusted," said Bobby.

Six hours after they had begun, the two cars pulled into a parking lot lined with natural limestone boulders. They all got out, and the ranger looked up at a red sign with a diagonal white stripe. "The Looe Key Reef Resort?"

"Home away from home," said Serge.

"But I thought you were taking us to some kind of

super-secret remote hideaway," said Heather. "This is the only safe house I've heard of with a tiki bar."

"As safe as they come," said Serge. "I know it seems counterintuitive on the side of a busy highway, but here's the thing about the Keys: Visitors enjoy staying in the upper and middle islands, but once they cross the Seven Mile Bridge, the lure of Key West is too much to resist, and they blaze right through, leaving these lower islands quiet and unruined. About the only people who stop are naturalists into the offshore geology and marine life."

"In other words we're hiding in the obvious?" said Bobby.

"As safe as if we're on an uninhabited island. Follow me . . ." He led them into the combination motel office and dive shop.

"Serge! . . ."

"You're back! . . ."

"Got your favorite room ready! . . ."

Heather turned to Serge. "This seems quite far from low-profile."

"I got this," said Serge, facing the staff behind the counter. "Guys, I have an odd request."

"Nothing will surprise us anymore."

"I'm not here," said Serge.

"Yes, you are. Standing right in front of us."

"No, I mean this trip is classified." He grabbed a postcard of the reef and gave it to Bobby. "If anyone asks, you don't know me and my friends. We're not staying here."

They handed him magnetic room keys. "You know we've got your back."

"Thanks again." Then to Heather and Bobby: "Let's get you settled. You're going to love this place!"

The afternoon dive boat returned. Night fell. The live band played. Suntanned people congregated in the tiki bar to compare notes about the day's adventures.

Serge and the gang sat around a table near the stage. "Check out this *National Geographic*! . . ."

Heather was facing the other way toward the dance floor, watching Coleman's flab jiggle as he twirled his shirt over his head. "Serge, *this* is a plan?"

"Trust me." He smiled and held up a faded magazine. "Loggerhead Key! . . ."

Back up the archipelago in Islamorada, a sunbaked Chevelle raced down the Overseas Highway.

Chapter 41

5:50 A.M.

Pickup trucks full of construction workers clustered in the dark.

A few hundred yards up the road, someone quietly slipped out of a room at the Looe Key Reef Resort. Crushed gravel crunched under a pair of old Velcro sneakers as they walked away from the motel and the convenience store, then in silent solitude along an uninhabited and unlit stretch of the Overseas Highway. The sneakers finally reached the parking lot with all the trucks.

Someone inside the Five Brothers Grocery Two unlocked the door, and the waiting crowd filed inside, followed by the sneakers worn by Serge.

"Excellent, they've got the media noche," Serge said to himself. "It's like a Cuban but not. Different bread with a sweeter taste when you absolutely have to mix it up."

"Excuse me?" asked the woman behind the counter.

"Just talking to myself," said Serge. "I like the company. Anyway, super-thanks for opening a second place up here. I'd been going to the original on Southard in Key West since the eighties. The first time I was in there I got to meet the patriarch, you know, that old white-bearded dude. And I spotted a souvenir baseball cap with *all* five brothers on it that I just had to have, if you know anything about me, which you don't. Yet. And I asked the old guy, how much? And I'll be damned if he didn't just up and hand it to me with a smile. Where does that ever happen in this insane world? Been ultra-loyal to the five bros ever since then."

The woman behind the counter smiled. "That was my father."

Serge gasped. "Imagine my pre-dawn luck! I'm in the presence of ancestral greatness! Pleased to make your acquaintance. Sorry about 'old' and 'dude' . . ." He ordered four Cuban breakfast sandwiches and an equal number of tall café con leches that he needed to have boxed up.

The sneakers headed back along the side of the

highway. It was the best routine, the best place, the best food, the best friends, and an incredible day laid out near that incredible reef. It was great to be alive, and Serge wanted to consume it all at once. He inhaled deeply and happily through his nostrils, taking in the invigorating aroma of the coffee and freshly baked Latin bread, trying to inhale life itself.

Serge got back to the room where Coleman was wedged between a bed and the wall. He sat at the end of a mattress and clicked on the TV. CNN appeared, but Serge switched over to local news for the flavor. The weather came on, and the roll of fortune continued. A grade-A forecast for the day, including a marine report of calm seas and high visibility. Serge smiled. He always loved it when the local weather map on TV was a radar image of the Keys, which meant his existence was keeled. Then the news. A naked Florida man was tased by police after he asked them to. Coleman arose in a fog, and Serge walked over with one of the to-go cups. "Here, drink this. Café con leche is the magic cure for all that ails. Lots of caffeine, sugar and cream. You'll need that if you're not going to ruin our trip."

"Thanks." Coleman ran a hand through a mop of hair and uncapped the cup.

The next hour was the exquisite torture of nuclear anticipation and excitement. Serge checked his watch.

At one minute past seven: "That's polite enough." He grabbed his box and went outside to the next room.

Knock, knock, knock.

Ranger Bobby answered.

"What are you doing?" asked Serge.

"You knocked."

"But you weren't supposed to answer unless I gave the password," said Serge.

"What was the password?"

"I forgot to make one." He grinned and held out the warm box. "Breakfast in bed! Enough in there for Heather, too. I'm knocking on her door next. Tomorrow the password will be Five Brothers. And no hurry, but by the time you finish that, they should be boarding our boat."

"A reef trip? Are you kidding?" asked Bobby. "Given all that's been going on, isn't it better to stay in the room instead of taking a trip out to sea?"

"Absolutely not," said Serge. "You can't think of staying here and not attending that offshore church. Besides, nobody can follow us, and we'll have a three-sixty view for miles in all directions for any shit. What can possibly go wrong?"

"Want me to make a list?"

"Enjoy," said Serge. "I'll be back when they start loading the gear."

Serge returned to his room and inventoried his new diving backpack, then went out to the car for a flex-cooler of Gatorade. He didn't even realize it, but out of subconscious habit, he reflexively felt under the back bumper. He stopped.

"What's this?"

He pulled loose a small magnetic GPS tracker and stared at it in his hand. "But how? . . . I'm always careful . . . I know I checked the last time . . ." And his mind spun through all the places the car had been recently. He closed his eyes and kicked the dirt. "Dammit." He thought back to when he was in Bobby's apartment in the woods at Myakka. After he found the body, and before the police arrived, the Cobra had been sitting alone outside with the killer still lurking who knew where. In their rush to leave the park, he hadn't made his mandatory bug sweep. "I must be losing my edge." Serge looked around. What to do? He dropped the tracker and stomped it to pieces in the gravel. Then he went in the motel office.

"Hey, Serge!" said the manager on duty.

"Has anybody been asking about me?"

"That's what I was just about to tell you. A guy wanted to know if you were here."

Serge grabbed the edge of the counter with white knuckles. "And what did you say?"

"I told him no, just like you asked," said the manager. "But he seemed to be a really good friend, knew all about you. Oh, and he said he was related, a distant cousin or something, so I thought you'd want to know."

"Did he check in here?"

"Not with me."

"Appreciate it." Serge turned to leave.

"You and your friends still going out this morning?"

"Wouldn't miss it." The office door closed.

Serge was in focused motion on a perimeter sweep. First, outward for counter-surveillance and anyone who might have eyes on the motel, then inward, checking the lot and surrounding streets for a Chevelle. He returned with no signs of the car. Now they definitely had to go on that boat trip, for the safety of the open sea until he could figure how to slip them to a more secure location. There was a familiar clanging sound as he stepped out back onto the dock. The crew had started loading the tanks for the scuba contingent.

"Hey, Captain Katie."

"Hey, Mr. First-In-Last-Out." She stowed life preservers. "The visibility is supposed be an incredible hundred feet. You picked the perfect day to bring your friends."

Serge hoisted his backpack over the port railing and onto the boat. "They're going to love it!"

He crossed the dock and knocked on the back door of one of the rooms. "Five Brothers."

Bobby opened again, wearing swim trunks. "You still sure about this?"

"More than ever now. You can board."

Serge walked to the next room. *Knock, knock.* "Five Brothers."

Inside: "What?"

"The new password."

She opened up. "Did we have an old one?"

"That's why it's new—" He stopped. In guilty headlights. Yowza. He'd never imagined her in a tasteful one-piece, and now he tried not to because it was his friend's daughter.

"Something the matter?"

"No! Why? I wasn't checking you out. Shazam! Great visibility! We're boarding!" He trotted off for the dive shop.

"You're back?" The manager glanced in the direction of the dock. "Shouldn't you be on the boat?"

"Last-second thing." He opened his wallet and pointed at a peg board. "I need one of those."

The manager looked at it and turned back around to Serge. "But your certification's lapsed. You're not going to . . ."

"Wouldn't think of it . . . Oh, and one of those, too."

"But you're snorkeling."

"It's a souvenir." Serge grinned impishly. "And they're gadgets."

Fifteen minutes later, the crew did a head count of the thirteen seated passengers. Serge also did a head count. Well, not really a head count. A critical analysis. He searched each face for clues. First, he eliminated all the women, then all the men who were with women. That just left four young divers who didn't fit the age range. Also, Serge had worked up a profile in his head: The guy seemed to not want to get caught, and getting on that boat with them would have left him cornered. So far so good. But Serge couldn't uncoil until they were underway.

Finally, the engine revved up and they pushed off from the dock, and Serge slumped back in relief.

The *Kokomo Cat II* idled down the canal as it had done a thousand times, then throttled up when it hit the channel, spraying water and heading straight out into a perfect sunny day.

Heather and Bobby were smiling for a change. She pointed off the port side at an anchored house boat flying a Jolly Roger and beach chairs in the sand. "What's that?"

"Picnic Island," said Serge. "And up there is Little Palm, where I had my honeymoon."

"I didn't know you were married."

"Neither did I," said Serge. "I mean I took the vows, but Jesus, the strings attached!"

"What happened?"

"Guest towels. I've put it in the rearview."

People on the houseboat waved, and the divers waved back.

"Why is your face all white?" asked Heather.

"Taking one for the planet," said Serge, passing her the pump bottle. "Use this stuff, safe for the coral . . ."

The pontoons slapped the swells as they rounded the last island in Newfound Harbor and it was all ocean from there.

"So beautiful." Heather adjusted the strap on her mask. "I think I'm really going to enjoy this."

"Would be hard not to," said Serge. "Now about the severed ear . . ." And he regaled them with tales of old drama out on those waters.

They arrived at a mooring buoy, and the first mate reached with the hooked pole again.

"It's low tide," Captain Katie announced to the passengers. "So stay away from where those whitecaps are breaking over the reef or you could slam into the coral."

The mate unsnapped the chains on the sides of the boat.

"Okay, everyone," said Katie. "The pool's—"

Serge plunged off the edge.

"—open. No surprise there."

The others jumped in and bobbed in mild waves.

"Heather! Bobby!" said Serge. "Look under the boat! There's a goliath grouper! And circling us the other way is a great barracuda. Don't worry, he's just curious."

"Holy cow!" said Heather. "Where did that swarm of little fish come from?"

"Yellowtails." Serge pointed up to where Coleman was still aboard the boat in an inflated safety vest, heaving over the railing. "He's serving lunch."

And it went on like that, Serge zestfully beckoning them to follow. "I know the best place to see reef sharks!"

"Sharks?" said Heather.

"They've seen a million divers out here and know we're not food. They like to patrol the tops of some coral formations." He held up his GoPro on a wrist strap. "I need footage! Come on! . . ."

It was indeed an ideal day to be out on that reef. And it was almost all theirs. Just a handful of other, widely spaced boats, including one arriving from Bahia Honda State Park.

Back ashore, on one of the Torch Keys, a tourist paid cash for a small rental boat with a Bimini top.

"You sailed before?" asked the cashier.

"Many times."

"This reef?"

"First time."

"Here's a depth chart." He handed over the folded map. "Go slow on your approach and watch the water or you'll lose your propeller deposit."

The customer grabbed the key on a flotation fob and motored off from the dock . . .

Serge checked his waterproof watch. A minute left in the hour at the first dive site. He waited for the last scuba guy to clear the ladder, and climbed back aboard right on deadline.

Katie just smiled and shook her head. "All right, we'll be at the second location in about ten minutes, and then another hour in the water. And remember, if you don't have a watch, when we lower the dive flag to half-mast it's time to get back in."

The *Kokomo* cruised toward a red buoy on the other side of the reef.

Serge was over the moon. Everything he loved. And he had formulated a foolproof plan to get his gang back over to a spot on Sugarloaf Key that nobody would ever find. Nothing to worry about now except how to strangle every second of life from the next hour in the water.

"Uh-oh." Serge stood.

"What is it?" asked Heather.

"Nothing. Just forgot some receipts to expense this on my tax return." But Serge's gaze was unwavering. He'd casually been keeping track of the other dive boats without real concern. Now there was a new arrival, a rental from one of the services he recognized. One person aboard. Which still wouldn't arouse any worry. Except its occupant was the only person out on the reef with binoculars. He was looking at the *Kokomo.*

Serge kept watching, and so did the occupant of the other boat. He was too far for Serge to make out his face, but he was wearing a black wetsuit. Serge saw a scuba tank resting against the stern. What was he up to? It was too far to swim. Did he plan to move the boat?

That's when Serge noticed it. The device was yellow, standing upright in the bow: a small, encased battery-powered propeller with handlebars that divers use to cover distance. So that was his plan. Serge hadn't expected such organization, given the clutter of that bedroom he'd seen in Homestead, but then there was that shelf of textbooks. He nodded to himself. "Okay, two can play at this game."

"What did you say?" asked Heather.

"Nothing."

"You seem distracted."

"Just admiring the view."

The binoculars kept a bead on the *Kokomo.* Serge knew what the guy was waiting for. He wanted them in the water.

Serge glanced around before reaching in his backpack for one of his last-second souvenir purchases from the dive shop, and strapped it to his right calf. Then he grabbed the other purchase—a tiny canister—and stuffed it in a pocket of his swim trunks.

He clapped his hands sharply and smiled at Bobby and Heather. "This location is even better than the other. You're going to have a whale of a time."

Heather grabbed her mask. "I don't know. The last one was pretty exciting, especially the reef sharks."

"Trust me," said Serge. "The excitement has only started."

The crew unsnapped the railing chains again, and Serge plunged over the side. Then the rest of the passengers came in with a series of plops. Serge was usually off in a burst with his huge ocean fins, doing manic laps around the boat, but this time he just bobbed and looked east.

"Serge," said Heather. "We got a giant grouper under the boat again."

"And there's a moray eel in that hole," said Bobby.

"Get ready," said Serge.

"For what?" asked Heather.

A school of yellowtail suddenly swarmed around them. They all looked up at the boat's railing.

"Coleman!"

"I'm good." He waved. "Wait. Nope . . ."

More fish swarmed.

"This way," said Serge. "I think I see a tarpon . . ."

And so on. "There's a parrotfish eating coral," said Heather.

Bobby had a laminated identification guide on his wrist. "Is that a triggerfish?"

"And another barracuda," said Heather.

Serge continued treading water, continued keeping tabs on the rental boat. Finally he witnessed the man pull a tank up on his back and grab the handlebars of the yellow propulsion device. He dove over the side. That was the signal Serge had been waiting for.

"Hey, Bobby, Heather," said Serge. "Why don't you guys get back in the boat?"

"But we just got in," said Heather.

"The sea's about to change." Serge felt down the side of his right leg. "It could get a little rough out here."

"The water looks calm," said Heather.

"I can read the sky," said Serge.

"The sky couldn't be clearer," said Bobby.

"Trust me, this is my turf," said Serge. "Can you just do it as a favor?"

"Something's wrong," said Bobby. "I can tell."

"Oh, no, no, no." Serge felt the contents of his pocket. "It's real nice up on the boat. A lot of divers like to lounge, and they sell snacks and everything."

Bobby gave him a wary eye. "If you say so."

Serge followed the pair as they paddled back to the boat. Once they were up the swim ladder, Serge grabbed the bottom step. "Captain Katie!"

She walked over and looked down. "What's up?"

"You got a weight belt lying around somewhere?"

"Sure, but you're snorkeling, not scuba."

"I'd like to try some free diving down to the bottom," said Serge. "I saw a couple of nurse sharks but too far away for my GoPro. And I'm naturally buoyant in every sense of the word. Just need a few pounds."

"You got it."

She dangled the belt over the side, and Serge strapped it on. "You're the hostess with the mostest!"

Then he turned and flattened out and pumped fins, building velocity.

Soon he was a hundred yards from the *Kokomo*, uncharacteristically ignoring the fabulous spectacle of rays and turtles. He stopped and popped his head up, looking east and west, respectively toward the two boats. Gauging the most direct route between them. He took off again, this time circling wide around submerged debris from the eighteenth century. Serge found the spot he wanted. And waited.

It didn't take long.

Serge had guessed the correct vector and the visibility was ideal. Moments later, slowly appearing out of the deep blue, a form began to take shape. First a blob like a manatee, then human characteristics. It was being pulled through the water by a yellow mini scooter. The small propeller inside wasn't meant for speed, just to cover distance that would otherwise be too physically taxing.

The diver holding the handlebars was intent on his path to the *Kokomo*. He didn't notice Serge treading water off to the side by a ridge of brain coral. When the scooter had passed, Serge flattened again on the surface and took off.

It required tremendous leg strength, but Serge was in a motivation zone. He kept pumping through the cramps, until he was only a few body lengths away.

That's when the other diver stopped to stick his head out of the water and check his bearings. And when he submerged again, he saw Serge coming at him a bit sooner than Serge would have preferred.

The diver pressed a button on his leg and unsheathed a frighteningly large serrated dive knife.

Serge pressed his own leg button, pulling out an equally intimidating blade.

Then, with the other hand, he reached in his swim trunks for his other recent purchase: a tiny pressurized canister with a mouthpiece. Called Xtra Air, often carried by the scuba crowd for an additional ten minutes of breathing in case the unexpected came up.

The other diver released the scooter's handles, and the two raced toward each other.

They clashed near buoy 15, grabbing each other's wrists holding the knives, and the duel was on. They savagely twisted in the water as the tips of the blades swept past their masks. They kneed each other, and clawed and even a head butt to the chest.

Neither was getting anywhere but exhausted. Artemas decided that since Serge was snorkeling, he'd pull him down and let the biology of oxygen give him the advantage. They dropped ten feet, but he hadn't counted on the canister in Serge's mouth. The fight dragged on, each with a vise grip on the other's weapon hand.

Serge chose boldness. And risk. He would only have a split second before he'd be stabbed. He released Tweel's wrist, and the other diver couldn't believe his fortune. His knife went for Serge's heart, but before he could complete the thrust, Serge used his free hand to knock off Art's mask, and salt water flooded his blurring eyes. In panic, Art let go to refit and purge the mask, and that's all the time Serge needed to slice his air hose. He also made a few last slices with the knife for good measure. Then he reached over his opponent's shoulder and yanked a cord to the dump valve, emptying the buoyancy compensator and dropping Art in depth. Serge leisurely swam away.

Bubbles filled the water.

A lot was going on for Artemas. He desperately tried to breathe the air stream straight from the severed hose while simultaneously working on his buoyancy system to get to the surface. Then he remembered his own canister of emergency air in one of his dive vest's pockets. He stuck it in his mouth, which straightened his thinking. Then he unbuckled and dropped his weight belt and calmly fiddled with the compensator. Things appeared to be finally looking up.

Here was the thing: Those final slices from Serge's knife? They had been across Art's legs, cutting through wetsuit rubber and skin. Nothing serious, just a bunch of flesh wounds.

In all the years, the sharks had never bothered the divers at Looe Key. But a sufficient amount of blood in the water tends to shuffle their morning plans. The first to arrive was a lemon shark, nipping his arm. Then a tiger shark, grabbing his ankle. A blacktip joined the party. It was turning into a bad day for Artemas.

The sharks continued thrashing their heads side to side, tearing off chunks. Then one got the inner part of a leg, bursting the femoral artery, and fate was determined. After a half minute of generating a large red underwater cloud, Artemas Kenilworth Tweel gave one last spasm and became still, and what was left of him floated down to the bottom, amid the anchor and cannonballs and other rusted metal from the frigate HMS *Looe*.

Epilogue

Kokomo Cat II

Hands fished through the cooler for cans of beer and soda. Bags of chips ripped open.

The passengers were all abuzz about the sights from the dive, comparing species they encountered. "Hawksbill," "Rock beauty," "Butterflyfish," "Bermuda chub." Some passed around cameras, sharing underwater video on preview screens.

Captain Katie checked her watch. Serge was always the last out, but also never late. She could bet the bank on him being near the foot of the swim ladder when the dive flag was lowered to half-staff. Now she scanned the horizon from behind polarized glasses.

In an unexpected direction and distance, she spotted

him swimming flat-out toward the boat at full speed. He reached the ladder and climbed aboard.

"You had me worried for a minute," said Katie.

"What? Am I late?"

"No, right on time as usual. Almost to the second."

Serge pulled off his fins. "Exactly."

"But you're usually near the boat," said Katie. "Where did you go?"

Serge pointed with his snorkel. "Buoy fifteen."

"But that's a freakin' long swim."

He continued stowing gear in the mesh backpack. "Never seen the wreck of the *Looe*. Figured today's visibility made it as good a time as any."

"Typical Serge," said Katie. "And what's with the knife? Snorkelers don't need one, and I've never seen you with it before."

He pulled a drawstring tight. "I'm a sucker for impulse purchases."

"Okay, but in the future if you ever decide to set out on an expedition like that, can you give me a heads-up?"

"Aye-aye, Captain."

It was a Friday night, and the tiki bar was rocking. The live band plowed through the usual set of Bad Company, Deep Purple, Tom Petty. Couples danced and the Jäger flowed. Patrons famished from a day on the water scarfed up battered shrimp, smoked fish and conch fritters. Coleman's hands dug into a box of Dion's fried chicken.

Serge was holding court as usual at a table covered with his collection of vintage *National Geographics*. As an added attraction, he had a laptop open, playing a DVD from a complete-series box set. The whole gang was there, including the boat crew.

"Don't you just love *Sea Hunt*?" said Serge. "And check out this underwater knife fight. Isn't it ridiculous? Here it comes, here it comes! The air hose just got sliced, every time."

It was gradual at first, unnoticed. Then it was obvious. The normally raucous bar began quieting down until it was hushed. Total attention turned to the flat-screen TVs all around the tiki hut that had been showing a Tampa Bay Lightning hockey game.

". . . *Breaking news at this hour as scuba divers exploring a shipwreck off Ramrod Key made a grisly discovery. The body of another diver has just been recovered by the Coast Guard, and while cause of death has yet to be determined, authorities have identified the victim as a Homestead, Florida, man named Artemas Tweel. More on this as details develop. Now back to the hockey game* . . ."

". . . *A one-timer from Stamkos on the power play. . . . He shoots! He scores!* . . ."

The rest of the bar was back to full volume. Except at Serge's table. Bobby, Heather and Captain Katie were staring at him.

"What?"

The Miami field office of the Florida Department of Law Enforcement was credited with clearing more than a dozen related unsolved homicides stretching back decades. They even received a formal visit from the state commissioner, personally thanking them.

For her role, Heather Sparrow received a commendation and promotion to deputy director of the Miami office. And due in no small part to her input, the demise of one Artemas Kenilworth Tweel was officially ruled death by misadventure.

Bobby Sparrow put in for a transfer. His daughter's career was on the move and required her to work where she was assigned. Bobby was free as a bird.

Each morning, he left a cheap apartment in Miami's MiMo district for a quick drive across the Rickenbacker Causeway. Shortly after reporting to his new ranger position at Bill Baggs State Park, he sat in a lawn chair at the base of the towering Cape Florida Lighthouse, greeting visitors and occasionally offering to take family group photos.

He was in his chair when he saw something in the

distance on the approaching walkway through the corridor of tall old-growth palms. He stood up to greet the visitor.

"Heather, what are you doing here?"

A smile that stretched as far as anatomy would allow. "I want a tour."

Ranger Bobby returned an even bigger smile.

The sun was high and clear as pickup trucks with fishing boats sat at the gas pumps. Customers streamed out of the convenience store with twelve-packs and energy drinks. Others banged bags of ice on the ground before filling coolers. Recreation and partying always went hand in hand in the Keys. As they say, another day in paradise.

A blue-and-white Ford Cobra pulled in, and the doors opened.

"Sandy," Serge said across the front seat. "Thanks again for meeting on such short notice."

A grin. "What other kind of notice is there with you?"

"Beer," said Coleman.

Serge uncapped the gas tank. "You two stay right there. I have to show you something."

Coleman pointed at the store. "Beer."

"You already said that."

"Serge," said Sandy, "why are you jumping up and down like that?"

"Come have a look!" Serge continued bobbing victoriously on the balls of his feet. "I'm not taking this shit anymore from The Man!"

She came around the side of the vehicle. "I don't get it. You're just putting gas in the car."

Serge joyfully wiggled hands in the air. "Notice I'm not holding the handle."

Coleman looked at all the other pumps. "Everyone else is. How'd you do it?"

"Look closer." Serge bent down and pointed. "I used my emergency car tools from the trunk to machine a perfect homemade universal pump handle shim! No more having to wait in agony for pumps with slow numbers. Over the course of my remaining life, this could add up to weeks . . ."

"Where are you going?" asked Coleman.

"Productively using my added life time to buy Gatorade in the store," said Serge. "My body tells me it needs electrolytes. I think the message is potassium."

Sandy followed. "And I need herbal iced tea."

"Beer," said Coleman.

The trio prowled the aisles, loading up on beverages and pretzels. Serge dropped it all on the counter, tapping the side of a glass case. "And I'll take two of your toxic hot dogs that have been turning on those rollers since time immemorial . . ."

They headed back to the Cobra, loaded down with bags. "Yes sir, I feel the beginning of a great day," said Serge. "Micro-victories over The Man are what make it all worthwhile."

Sandy stopped and crinkled her nose. "What's that smell?"

"I don't know, but it's strong," said Serge. "Maintenance is going to have to fix something around here."

"Serge!" said Coleman. "A ton of gasoline is pouring out of the car!"

"Shit, a huge pool's spreading everywhere. It's almost to the street."

"What do we do?"

"Drive away!"

Stunned onlookers stood in silent unison as they watched the blue-and-white Cobra take off down the Overseas Highway just before the fireball.

About the Author

TIM DORSEY was a reporter and editor for the *Tampa Tribune* from 1987 to 1999, and is the author of twenty-three other novels: *Florida Roadkill, Hammerhead Ranch Motel, Orange Crush, Triggerfish Twist, The Stingray Shuffle, Cadillac Beach, Torpedo Juice, The Big Bamboo, Hurricane Punch, Atomic Lobster, Nuclear Jellyfish, Gator A-Go-Go, Electric Barracuda, When Elves Attack, Pineapple Grenade, The Riptide Ultra-Glide, Tiger Shrimp Tango, Shark Skin Suite, Coconut Cowboy, Clownfish Blues, The Pope of Palm Beach, No Sunscreen for the Dead,* and *Naked Came the Florida Man.* He lives in Florida.